THE LACEMAKER

THE
LACEMAKER

Janine Montupet

Translated by Lowell Blair

BALLANTINE BOOKS • NEW YORK

Library of Congress Catalog Card Number: 88-15316

ISBN 0-345-36353-1

This edition published by arrangement with Atheneum, a division of Macmillan Publishing Company.

Manufactured in the United States of America

First Ballantine Books Edition: March 1990

To the memory of Madame La Perrière,
who invented Alençon lace

To Madame Paulette Margueritte,
in religion Sister Mary of the Sacred Heart,
who is bringing it back to life

And to my three granddaughters,
Clémentine, Aurélia, and Pauline

*Art, culture, true civilization—
that, I believe, is what lace is.*

ROBERT SABATIER
MEMBER OF THE GONCOURT ACADEMY

CHARACTERS IN APPROXIMATE ORDER OF APPEARANCE

Julie Perdriel	A young lacemaker
Mathieu Perdriel	Julie's brother, a packman
Thomine Perdriel	Mother of Julie and Mathieu
Gilonne Perdriel	Julie's daughter
Mistress Verlot	Owner of the Moor's Inn
Louis-Guillaume de Ferrières de Pervenchères	Noble knight (chevalier), proprietor of Grand-Coeur
Candelario and Zoltan	Musician-servants to the Chevalier
Lady Bertrade de Ferrières	Mother of Louis-Guillaume
Pompinne	Servant to Lady Bertrade
Contes-Nouvelles	Thomine Perdriel's friends in the poorhouse
Marie	
Chopine	
Coeur-de-Coing	Supervisor of the poorhouse
Ogier (later Count de Beaumesnil)	Falconer to the Chevalier and Lady Bertrade
Mistress Bordier	Gilonne's foster mother
Jérémie	Protestant friend of young Gilonne
Mortimer Morel d'Arthus	Prominent Protestant lace manufacturer of Alençon for whom Mathieu Perdriel often travels
Hélye Morel d'Arthus	Mortimer's son
Mistress Symonne Lescure	Mistress-lacemaker to whom Gilonne is apprenticed at age five

One

SINCE IT WAS HALFWAY BETWEEN THE LACEMAKING SHOP where she worked and the room she rented from the owner of the Golden Cake Bakery, Julie often paused briefly at the Moor's Inn. She would stop under the painted metal sign flanked by two lanterns. The Moor's turbaned head, dark as the night, swung back and forth with a creaking of rusty iron. Now and then his smile, which the artist had painted generously, was lighted by one of the flames flickering in the wind. His white teeth would then gleam while his black face remained invisible in the early morning darkness.

One morning in May 1665, when it was nearly four o'clock and she had been running, Julie stopped under the sign to catch her breath. Her wooden shoes had clattered on the pavement as she approached the inn, and others could be heard clattering in the distance, on their way to the Royal Manufactory and the other lacemaking shops in Alençon. The town itself might have been called an enormous lacemaking shop, ringed by six thousand feet of ramparts, with seventeen towers and five gates, and sometimes shrouded by the milky fog that slowly rose from its two rivers, the Sarthe and the Briante.

Before long the big bell of the Notre-Dame church would strike four, urging on the lacemakers in the streets—"Hurry!

Run!''—and the clatter of wooden soles would become even faster, then stop.

Julie wondered if the meticulous cleanliness of her clothes had suffered on her way to the inn. Had she been spattered by a dog or a rat splashing in the stream of dirty water that flowed along the middle of each street? She worried especially about her stockings. They were *real* stockings, not those cloth tubes that some people wore. They had been knit with the whitest cotton and ended in the exact shape of a foot. They were truly magnificent; none of her friends had any like them. And since they had begun replacing the straw in her wooden shoes only a short time ago, Julie took very good care of them. Her brother, Mathieu, who had brought them to her from the Leipzig fair, said he would give her others when these wore out, but she was determined to make them last for years, knowing the great sacrifice it must have been for him to buy them.

It seemed to her, when she thought about it, that wearing these stockings raised her a little on the social scale. If someday she had leather shoes, or even cloth ones, she, Julie Perdriel, would be almost a bourgeoise. Perched three inches above the ground on painted heels, the tops of their feet tied up with pretty ribbons and bows, like precious packages, the mistress-lacemakers of the town took pride in that obvious proof of their great skill. Yes, someday, maybe . . .

Julie began daydreaming, looking up at the third window on the right on the second floor of the inn. Was her chevalier asleep, or was he still working? If inspiration had struck and put a song into his heart, he might be playing it again and again, ignoring the passing of time. If not, he would have abandoned the spinet and lain down, without undressing, behind the red damask curtains of the finest bed in the house. Maybe he still had his boots on because she hadn't been there to pull them off. Tomorrow it would be a month, a whole month, since the last time he had asked her to spend an evening with him. Who had watched him work the night before, listened to him, and had the happiness of pressing herself against him behind the red curtains? Of all the women who hovered around him and, when they could, clasped him tightly in their arms, hoping to keep him longer, which one had he favored with his presence last night?

Julie knew it wasn't good to think too much about such things. And crying would make her eyes even worse. They were sometimes so irritated that she felt like rubbing them until they came out of their sockets. "We have lace coming out of our eyes," said the women of Alençon.

She suddenly remembered that she had used up all her dried cornflowers. On Sunday she would have to buy some more from the witch in the Perseigne forest. She was a frightening old woman, but her decoctions of flowers eased Julie's suffering. This reminded Julie that she would have to ask Colin, the baker's apprentice, to steal a little bag of bran for her. Her chilblains and chapped skin were about to be cured by the springtime weather, and then she would have to soften her skin with bran water.

Yes, spring was here! Soon she wouldn't need the foot warmer that burned her feet and scorched her stockings without warming her body. She would no longer cry out in pain when the thread of the lace she was making pulled away part of a burst chilblain on one of her fingers. Then she would dare to show her hands to her chevalier. Spring would have no beneficial effect on him, however. No use hoping for such a miracle. An apple tree that was bare and lifeless in winter might suddenly become a young bouquet of lustrous, fragrant blossoms, but who could ever change the look in a man's eyes from distant to loving? Indifferent. That was the word for him. Or, even better, unfeeling. Chevalier Louis-Guillaume de Ferrières was as unfeeling as the Moor smiling so foolishly on his sign that it made her want to throw a rock at him. She thought of how the metal would clang, and how people would open their windows. . . .

The big bell of Notre-Dame struck four. "Hurry! Run!" She ran, toward the eighteen hours of work that awaited her. By the time she finished, she was always exhausted and thought only of resting her aching body on her straw mattress or bathing her eyes in cool water. But if one of the chevalier's servants came to knock on her door and say, "My master is waiting for you," her fatigue would vanish and she would hurry off to the inn. *Dear God,* she prayed, *please make him send for me tonight!*

When the clock struck half-past six in the misty coolness of sunrise, the two turtledoves of Mistress Verlot, owner of the Moor's Inn, flew away, and the chevalier appeared in the doorway. He watched the birds come to rest again after a short flight, apparently satisfied at having exchanged the pink tile roof of the inn for the pink tile roof of the draper's building next door.

His incomparable blue-green eyes sparkled like mingled sapphires and emeralds in the rays of the bright ascending orb. That, at least, was how certain ladies with literary pretensions would have expressed themselves. But if the thin, angular Mistress Verlot had seen his eyes at that moment, she would have kept her thoughts about them strictly to herself. No torture could have made her admit why, on the women's side of the Notre-Dame church, she had chosen—and paid for at the rate of fifteen sous a year—a seat in the third pew where she could gaze enraptured at the blend of blue and green light shining through certain parts of the stained-glass windows.

The chevalier called Candelario and Zoltan, his two servants. When they came out of the stable, he told them it was late; they would have to leave quickly. There was no reproach in his voice, Candelario noticed with relief. He knew he was responsible for the twenty-minute delay, though he could reasonably have put the blame on Mistress Verlot for having disrupted their schedule by not claiming her due until the last moment. In any case, they could easily leave Alençon at daybreak and reach Pervenchères in time for dinner. Unless there was going to be a concert along the way. The chevalier had said nothing on that subject. Candelario pursed his lips; it was hard for him to endure being kept in ignorance of things that, in his judgment, came within his province. Zoltan could have commented at length on his colleague's attitudes, but he had no desire to speak. As for the chevalier, it would have come as a surprise to learn that his servants sometimes had thoughts.

He bowed to Mistress Verlot with the consummate grace that, even though it was only an unthinking reflex, never failed to warm her heart still more than the little glass of apple brandy she drank before going to bed. Born of a dreamy mother from Beauce who, at harvesttime, used to point to the plain and say to her, "Look, darling: God has opened the doors of His palace in Chartres and the gold in it has spilled everywhere," she watched the chevalier's plumed hat sweep through the air in a broad arc and imagined herself in a field where he was bending down to pick a lily for her. For a moment the steady gaze of his famous blue-green eyes held her entranced; then, when she watched him ride away as if she were watching him die, everything turned dark and she was gripped by a chill. She and her spinet would languish together until the next time the handsomest man in the whole Alençon region returned to the inn.

She still regretted not having introduced that spinet to him earlier. He had discovered it long after his first visit to the inn, and without any help from her: Thinking he was going to his room, he had mistakenly stepped into the storeroom where the spinet stood, adorned with painted flowers and birds. "My God!" he had exclaimed. "What a magnificent instrument!" And then he had asked, "Are you a musician, Mistress Verlot?"

Are you a musician? For the joy of having heard these words from his lips, of knowing he had seriously supposed that she might be versed in the mysteries of music, she would gladly have let him stay at her inn a hundred days without paying a sou. Though she ordinarily spoke very little, she now plunged into a long story and continued rapidly without a pause, amazed at her own boldness. She told about a traveler who had been attacked by bandits when he was on his way to Caen for his daughter's wedding, bringing the spinet as a wedding present. The bandits had taken his carriage, horses, money, and clothes, but the spinet had fallen into a ditch and miraculously escaped their notice. He had left it with her at the inn as security, with the understanding that he would retrieve it when he came back to pay her for what he had received there: meals, lodging, a horse, her late husband's best coat, and a small amount of money to continue his journey. That had been three years ago! The poor man had probably been killed by other bandits, or maybe by the same ones waiting farther on. By now the spinet was rightfully hers, wasn't it?

The air was heavy with passion in the little room that held the spinet. Mistress Verlot pressed her trembling hands against her bosom, trying to calm the tumult of a heart that was ecstatic at finding itself beating so close to that of her beloved. And the chevalier's hands also trembled as he amorously caressed the marvelous instrument that, against all reason and justice, belonged to this bony, horse-faced woman, instead of to him. For it was a rare gem of a spinet, one of the first made in Venice, dating from the previous century and signed by the illustrious Spinetti, who had given his name to that kind of instrument. The chevalier blissfully began tuning it, having heard nothing of Mistress Verlot's story. But when she asked him, "It's rightfully mine, isn't it?" for the second or third time, her voice finally penetrated. He became aware of her presence again, wondered why she had asked such a silly question, and, without answering it, offered to buy the treasure from her.

In spite of her strong emotion, she quickly realized that the

lure of the spinet could greatly increase the frequency of his
visits, so she made the agonizing decision to deny herself the
pleasure of gratifying her handsome nobleman. He reacted with
a show of ill humor that upset her painfully, but she still felt her
tactic was sound. She was sure he would soon come back to
play the spinet. And she was right.

Very few inhabitants of Alençon were surprised that morning
when they saw Louis-Guillaume de Ferrières, Lord of Pervenchères and other places, riding through the town with his two
musician-servants, Candelario and Zoltan.

A year earlier, however, there had been considerable astonishment when the three came riding back from war, singing a
tumultuous hymn to the glory of Louis XIV, a song that lavishly
praised the warrior king and loudly evoked the clash of swords,
the shouts of soldiers, and other sounds of battle. Their song
startled its listeners so much that it took a while before they
began paying any attention to the details of the newcomers'
appearance.

First they noticed their horses. Two white mares, trained to
follow the master's black Anglo-Norman without guidance, left
the servants free to play their instruments: a lute or a viol in one
case; a recorder, a trumpet, or a drum in the other. They were
evidently contented animals and even seemed to enjoy the thunderous music that was part of their lives.

The men were disconcerting. Why was this nobleman, with
his proud bearing and fine horse, wearing such ragged clothes?
His worn, scratched, and soiled leather breeches and doublet
showed the effects of encounters with swords, pikes, and all sorts
of harsh weather on battlefields and hostile roads, but his servants' clothes were as new and brightly colored as a rainbow.
One might have wondered who was the master and who the
servants if the shabbily dressed stranger hadn't had the face of
a man accustomed to commanding and not to obeying. And, to
those who knew about such matters, his imposing appearance
in the saddle revealed a heritage of superb horsemanship going
back at least five hundred years. Seen in that light, he made his
servants' clothes and trappings seem all the more ridiculous.
Where did these two rascals come from?

Peddlers who had traveled all over Europe and were regarded
as men of trustworthy judgment examined the tall, thin, dark
servant—whose drooping mustache gave an impression of mel-

ancholy tinged with arrogance—and rightly decided that he was Hungarian, citing his red fur-lined dolman and hat as evidence. To the other servant, shorter and ruddy-faced, they attributed citizenship in the Venetian Republic. His nationality was obvious from his green Genoese velvet tunic with wide yellow sleeves, his flat crimson felt hat of Lombardic origin, and a certain air of bravado. Since Alençon was in conflict with Venice for reasons connected with lacemaking, Hungarian melancholy was preferred to Venetian exuberance.

But this became a matter of only minor interest when the chevalier took off his faded, thinly plumed hat to show his courteous respect for a lady in a passing carriage, and in so doing revealed his hair. Some of the onlookers recalled that such superb naturally blond hair, with glints of both gold and silver, was the mark of a noble family who lived on an estate beyond the Perseigne forest, not far from the source of the Huisne River. And they also remembered having seen, in the streets of Alençon, several of the noblemen from Pervenchères who passed on their spectacular hair from father to son. Standing in his doorway, a lace merchant spoke of Rollo the Viking, King of the Sea, the Scandinavian hero with hair of gold and silver, the first Duke of Normandy. The women watching the chevalier were greatly pleased by the contrast between the darkness of his suntanned complexion and the lightness of his cascading curls. His head was as good as a gold mine, said a water carrier who seemed to know what he was talking about.

When their first surprise had passed, the onlookers wondered why this man from such an illustrious family should ride singing through the streets with two so crude-looking servants.

Thanks to a stroke of luck, the charm of the spinet, and the fact that Mistress Verlot's pear cider was stronger than it seemed, she was the first and probably the only woman in Alençon in whom the chevalier confided. It happened one evening in the room of the inn to which the spinet had been taken, now known as the music room and reserved exclusively for the chevalier. The spinet was polished so lovingly that its painted birds and flowers fairly sparkled. The chevalier came back to it every week, having discovered that he worked almost better here than on his estate. So as not to damage the quality of sound, the furniture in the music room was limited to an armchair and a chest. Mistress Verlot took the liberty of adding only a bottle of her famous Clécy pear cider, which she brought up from the cellar as soon as her noble lord arrived. This sprightly drink was one of the main attractions at the Moor's Inn; it went down smoothly and easily, but it could flatten the hardiest drinker before he knew what was happening to him.

Mistress Verlot couldn't resist the pleasure of walking past the music room again and again when her guest was inside it with the door closed. Her servants noticed, and smiled.

That evening, when she had just finished listening to a new song, the chevalier opened the door, came out holding an empty bottle, and asked to have it refilled. Her constant presence within range of his voice seemed to him no more than what was to be expected of a conscientious innkeeper, so the excuses she stammered whenever she saw him, saying she was there only by chance, or because of some circumstance or other, always surprised him if he paid enough attention to hear what she was saying.

She hurried off to refill the bottle, came back, and nearly fainted when he asked her to come and listen to his music. What a cheerful mood he was in! And his eyes were so green, so green. . . . She sank into the armchair just when her legs were beginning to feel too weak to support her.

"Would you like to hear my latest song, madame? I've entitled it *The Grand Vizier's Turban*. It's about the battle fought near the Saint Gotthard monastery in Hungary. I was there last summer with the French expeditionary force sent by our king to help Hungary's Austrian allies drive out the invading Turks. The cross defeated the crescent—which reminds me, my good hostess, that you ought to make us some of those new crescent-shaped pastries invented to celebrate that victory. My servant Candelario, who dabbles in almost everything, will give you the recipe. He was able to get it in Hungary one day when he wasn't stuffing himself with those pastries to forget how frightened he'd been during the battle."

The chevalier laughed! For her alone!

"So, madame," he went on after taking another sip of the deceptively strong pear cider, "in my song I have the Austrians, the Hungarians, and the French singing more loudly than the cursed Turks. And I depict the act of unwinding the symbolic turban—the turban of the grand vizier, who fought for the Ottoman emperor in that battle—tearing it to shreds, and trampling it underfoot."

But did Mistress Verlot know about descriptive music? Did

she know that three notes arranged in a certain way could only be the song of the nightingale, that three others arranged differently were the sound of cannon fire? One little ritornello represented the French expeditionary force, another the cruel grand vizier's turban. Cruel, yes, but also a valiant fighter and an excellent musician. He drew strange sounds from an equally strange instrument. . . . But this was no time to discuss Turkish music; they could come back to the subject later, however, if Mistress Verlot cared to know more about it.

How lovely that song was! Berthine Verlot loved it, felt like weeping, and wept. It seemed to her that she had lived that battle beside the man of her dreams, who must have been one of the most ardent warriors in it. And, in the simplicity of her humble heart, she made a remark that he found sublime: "Ah, if I were a man, after hearing that song I'd want to go off to war!"

This was exactly what he wanted to hear. He composed his martial music to inspire soldiers, and especially men who weren't yet soldiers, to take the king's banners wherever he wanted them taken. If this lanky, red-handed woman had understood his new song, just think how it would affect noble-hearted young men! Exhilarated, he took still another drink of the pear cider and felt like kissing Mistress Verlot. He didn't kiss her, but he did decide that she deserved to hear about his plan.

"I'm sure you'll agree, madame, that if a great musician, the famous Clément Janequin, hadn't written a song about the Battle of Marignan, no one would still remember the victory of King Francis I."

She agreed. She would have agreed that her inn was on fire and that it didn't matter.

"Our handsome Francis I, twenty-one at the time of Marignan, was a patron of the arts, a warrior king, a king loved by his people. Doesn't he remind you of someone?"

Yes, yes, he *must* remind her of someone, but who . . .

"He reminds us of our Louis XIV, madame! Same heroic temperament, same abilities, same splendor. But while King Francis had songs written to celebrate his reign, his battles and his victories, King Louis likes only ostentatious ballets and pretentious operas at his festive court. That's not the kind of thing that makes men go joyfully off to war. Do you know how far the stories of King Francis's exploits have traveled?" (No, she didn't know, but she waited ecstatically for him to tell her.) "*All the way to Mexico!* Yes, madame, the Hidalgos took the song of Marignan to Mexico. And shall I tell you something else?'' (She no longer even had the strength to nod her head.) ''Wherever that song was sung, men were so carried away with enthusiasm that they leapt to their feet and drew their swords, ready for combat. That's what a real song of war and glory is like. That's what I want to do for my king. And that's why I come here every week on market day to sing of His Majesty's heroic deeds. The story of those deeds will cross mountains and seas, and the whole world will extol them. Then, thanks to your beautiful spinet, madame, you will have served the kingdom.''

At this point the chevalier tried to put his hand into his pocket but inadvertently slipped it into one of the holes in his breeches.

''As you can see,'' he said, ''my clothes have as many holes as my servants' flutes! But we must never forget the Battle of Agincourt, Mistress Verlot, because otherwise I'm afraid that we, His Majesty's cavalry officers, might go back to that time when our ancestors thought only of gleaming armor, fine silk scarves, and lavish gold and silver embroidery. Too many splendid trappings make it hard for a man to fight. What happened at Agincourt? Our nobility, decked out in plumes and richly decorated breastplates, and loaded down with all sorts of showy trinkets, were overcome by agile Englishmen in their shirtsleeves, without helmets and even without shoes. However,'' the chevalier added, looking indecisively at the hole in his breeches, ''it might be a good idea to mend that.''

Mistress Verlot offered to do it. Her face was radiant.

But by the next day, through the normal movement of liquids in the body and the natural dissipation of the alcohol, the Clécy pear cider was eliminated and the chevalier had forgotten singing for his hostess. He had a vague memory of having recently decided that she was a little less foolish than she seemed, but he soon forgot that too.

When he left the Moor's Inn this morning, he found the town seething with excitement. The population had taken to the streets, along with a considerable number of policemen trying to disperse the crowds. People in carts and carriages, or on horseback, had to slow their pace, and, much to his irritation, Louis-Guillaume de Ferrières was unable to move any faster than the others.

Alençon was obviously losing its calm. Feelings had been

running high since the previous August, when the royal edict
regulating the manufacture of lace was first announced. There
was a smell of violence in the air—that springtime air that normally would have carried only the delicate fragrance of apple
blossoms.

All this was annoying to the chevalier. A royal edict was like
an act of God. It *was* an act of God. Trying to argue against it
was irreverent and senseless. Angry shouts would have no more
effect than the cawing of crows, and the shouting fools would
gain nothing but a flogging. For the time being, Alençon was
not a favorable place for artistic or intellectual work; the chevalier would have to leave as quickly as possible and stay away
until the city was no longer in a state of "public unrest," to use
the discreet expression of His Majesty's government. How could
he find the two rhymes he still needed for *The Grand Vizier's
Turban* in the midst of this uproar? Ordinarily he did some of
his best work while he was riding through the town and along
country roads. Before leaving the inn, he had played a sonata in
three movements by his illustrious friend Giovanni Legrenzi,
and it had put him into an excellent mood for creation—but now
it was wasted!

When two beggars gripped his saddle, he made them let go
by flailing at them with his riding crop, thinking how sadly
obvious it was that the irritation rising inside him would be
detrimental to the passage in his *Great Conversation Among
Plato, Ronsard, and the Man for Whom Music Was Only Noise*
that he intended to turn over in his mind as he rode. He realized
he had already forgotten the end of that sentence by Ronsard:
"He who does not honor music is unworthy of seeing gentle
sunlight . . ." what came next? He had to make his way to a
gate, any gate, and get out of this town.

"It looks as if we're not going to have a very pleasant journey," Candelario said to Zoltan.

There had been ominous signs: a certain stiffness in the chevalier's back, and the promptness with which he had wielded his
riding crop. But why hadn't he paid attention this morning when
they tried to warn him that three delegations of lacemakers were
going to inform the Intendant of Alençon of their grievances?

"You know how he is, Zoltan," Candelario went on. "I told
him what was happening and said I thought we should delay
leaving, but he ignored me. Do you want to hear my opinion? I
think there's going to be more and more trouble here. Why?

First, because the minister, Monsieur Colbert, has decided that no one in the main French lacemaking centers can make or sell lace without dealing with the Royal Manufactories. Second, because Colbert feels that Alençon workers aren't skilled enough in making our Venetian lace—the kind most in demand everywhere!—and so he's bringing in workers from my Venetian Republic. That second reason is one too many. It's not good policy to take away people's freedom and hurt their pride at the same time, especially since—I want you to notice how generous I am to say this—especially since the workers here in Alençon are as good at making Venetian lace as the ones brought in from Venice. You can believe me, because I heard it from the Venetian girls themselves.

"They're not to blame for what's happening. They came here as queens who were going to educate their subjects, but did they ask to be put in that position? No. The king said to the people of Alençon, 'From now on, you'll make lace only for me. You'll be paid whatever and whenever I choose. I'll punish any disobedience by deporting women and sending men to the galleys, to row for their king.' And while the people were still choking on that bitter pill, he gave them another one to swallow: He said, 'Since you're not very good at what you do, I've invited some ladies to come from Venice and teach you how to work.' So it's not hard to understand why they're stirred up and desperate. What do you think of all that, my friend?"

"Nothing."

"Nothing? You live here, you eat the same bread and drink the same cider as these people, and you don't sympathize with them?"

"It's not good for a foreigner to pass judgment on the policy of a country that takes him in and lets him share its bread and cider."

"That's the kind of thing we're supposed to say in public. But in private, you must think of something."

"When the Turks occupied my country, do you know what they did to people they suspected of thinking, either in public or in private? They crushed their heads between two stones."

"If everyone were like you, Zoltan, new freedoms would never be won."

"Maybe so, but we'd keep the ones we already have. Especially the freedom to live here."

The three horsemen finally came to the Place du Château,

hoping it would be deserted. Instead, they had the unpleasant surprise of seeing about fifty women workers blocking the path of one Venetian mistress-lacemaker. They were one of the three delegations going to see the Intendant of Alençon; having encountered an enemy on their way, they had decided to prevent her from going into the Royal Manufactory.

The Venetian was in the middle of the square and had almost come to a stop. She was identifiable to the gathering crowd of curious onlookers by the bright colors of her silk clothes. Flattered at having been asked to come and teach French workers, the Venetians had made it a point of honor to arrive in the best clothes they owned. Some of them may even have borrowed ribbons and jewelry from relatives or friends in order to cut a finer figure.

By contrast with the Venetian—in her brightly colored dress and gold-embroidered red leather clogs, with gold and coral decorations in her upswept hair—the drab uniformity of the Alençon women, all in aprons, bonnets, wooden shoes, and linen skirts, made them seem like a flock of hens facing a peacock with its tail outspread. It gave them a feeling of inferiority, and this blow to their vanity was added to the deep wound that had been inflicted by the contempt shown for their knowledge and skill. A poor lacemaker couldn't take revenge on His Majesty's minister, but the Venetians he had brought to Alençon were another matter.

With her heart pounding, Anna-Livia Bardi wondered if she should go forward, retreat, or stand still. She had the dark, fierce beauty that some women of her country displayed proudly, almost defiantly, with their backs straight and their heads held high.

She decided to pretend not to notice the Frenchwomen, but to stop and wait in the middle of the square, looking both serene and provocative. She put all her pride into her eyes and stood with her feet spread slightly apart, to be ready to fight if she was attacked. And she prayed.

The chevalier recognized her.

When Candelario and Zoltan had also identified her, they exchanged first a knowing look, then a look of surprise, and finally a look of concern as they saw a young woman step forward, toward the Venetian, and heard her say loudly, "I'll take care of her!"

The chevalier knew this woman too. Her name was Julie Perdriel. As slender and blond as Anna-Livia Bardi was solid and dark, she continued walking toward her with calculated, impressive slowness. Silence fell over the square.

Those who were seeing Julie for the first time examined her smooth complexion, her sky-blue eyes, and the beauty of her delicate features. She gave them an impression of touching fragility that didn't go with what they had just heard her say. Some of them wondered if it was really this frail, pretty young woman who had spoken.

Her clothes were commonplace; her immaculate little hat was trimmed with lace, but everyone there knew that an Alençon woman would have gone without food to decorate her hat, if only with a piece of *bisette*.*

Someone exclaimed, "She's pregnant!" and the words were repeated all through the crowd.

Everyone saw the bulge that Julie had until then been able to hide by keeping her hands in the pockets of her apron. So the lacemaker who wanted to humble the arrogance of Venice was not only the slenderest one in the group but was also pregnant! And in fact, now that the evidence could be seen more clearly, it seemed that her pregnancy was quite well advanced.

This made a few of the onlookers laugh. Many of them, however, saw the confrontation as symbolic: The town's poorest people had to fight against the formidable royal forces that were behind the Venetians. In the past, when the regiments of the duchy had fought to protect Normandy against the English, they had gone into battle shouting, "Alençon!" And now a voice rose from the crowd, then another, then many others, all shouting encouragement to Julie: "Forward, for Alençon!"

The two women quickly took off their shoes and rushed at each other. For a moment, as they held each other motionless, the onlookers admired the dignity and pride of their condition as women, but then they suddenly fell to the ground and were only a pair of scratching and biting females.

Seeing only the chevalier's back made Candelario nervous. He would have given a great deal to see his master's eyes and judge how he was reacting to this fight between his mistresses. Being able to watch it was enough, all by itself, to make Candelario glad he had left his beloved Venetian Republic. He kept

*A kind of low-quality lace.

glancing at Zoltan, expecting to hear a remark or at least see a gesture, but the Hungarian went on watching with apparent indifference. *It won't end until one of those women is dead,* thought Candelario. He looked at the chevalier's still impassive back. *That man has no soul. I'm a poor Venetian musician living with two soulless men.*

How long had it been since the indifferent chevalier had seen these women? Since the night he had invited them to sing the duet for nightingale and lark that he had just composed? Until that night, they had been only lacemaking competitors. They became enemies when they discovered that they shared the chevalier's favors. Instead of his duet for nightingale and lark, he heard a very different performance. Julie asserted no claims on him and only looked at him with tears in her eyes, but Anna-Livia made enough noise for both of them!

Candelario heard his master talking and quickly rode closer.

"Why were so many Norman slave girls brought to Rome in the time of Emperor Claudius?" the chevalier was saying. "When you look at those two, the answer is clear. It was because their light, delicate coloring formed a delightful contrast with the dark, warm coloring of the daughters of Italy."

"Zoltan," Candelario said when he had returned to his place, "the gentleman we serve has a heart of marble: Those two women are going to die before his eyes, and he talks about history and geography!"

"Wonder at nothing—that's the wise man's motto."

"Well, it's *your* motto, anyway, and what it amounts to is 'Be indifferent.' Isn't there anything that can jolt you out of your unconcern?"

"That blond woman is being jolted a little too much. She's going to have her baby sooner than she expects if someone doesn't stop that fight."

"I'll stop it," said Candelario. "All those dimwits are watching it without knowing what it's about. They think it has something to do with lacemaking, but you and I know it's a fight over love. *Love!* They'll kill each other. . . . Let go of me!"

Zoltan was gripping him by the arm to keep him from getting off his horse.

"We mustn't meddle in our master's affairs," he said.

Just then the chevalier dismounted and walked rapidly toward the two women with his riding crop in his hand.

Anna-Livia and Julie had been fighting ferociously and silently, so the crowd was surprised to hear them shriek as soon as they saw the chevalier. No one understood what they were shouting, but everyone saw them stop fighting and furiously attack the chevalier. He laughed as he dodged the fingernails that tried to lacerate him. His hat fell off, and the two women began trying to pull out his fair hair. He gave them a few sharp taps on the posterior with his riding crop. Then, holding one with his left hand and the other with his right, he picked up his mistresses as easily as if they had been cackling chickens.

"At Saint Gotthard he picked up Turks like that. He's the strongest man I've ever known!" cried Candelario, happily regaining the admiration for his master that he had sadly lost a short time before.

Suddenly a voice shouted, "Here come the police!"

Some of the other lacemakers snatched Julie away from the chevalier with the speed and deftness of sleight-of-hand artists. A few moments later, after being pulled along and almost carried by five or six of her companions, she disappeared.

When the policemen rode into the square, they saw only the chevalier putting on his hat and Zoltan and Candelario leaning over Anna-Livia as she lay moaning on the ground. A wound on one of her hands was bleeding abundantly. A policeman lifted her onto his horse to take her to the nearest apothecary's shop. The chevalier allowed Candelario to go and hear what the apothecary would have to say, but told him to come immediately afterward to the Lancrel Gate, where he and Zoltan would be waiting. They had already lost too much time.

With a sigh of pleasure, Louis-Guillaume de Ferrières finally remembered the end of the quotation from Ronsard. And that brought a smile to his lips.

In the workshop where they had taken Julie, the lacemakers tried to clean her up. The result was unsatisfactory. Even with her face washed and her hair combed, her haggard look would still make her appear suspicious to the police. She didn't seem to care, and kept complaining about having left her shoes in the square. Her friends promised to go and look for them, along with her white hat, which she had also lost.

The women around her now realized that it had been unwise to bring her into the workshop. The police would probably be there before long. They all remembered Mathilde, who, for having taken away a Venetian mistress-lacemaker's needles, thread, and thimbles only as a practical joke, had been sentenced to deportation. What would happen to Julie if the police found her? Women coming into the workshop were asked if she could risk going to a safer hiding place, or if they had seen policemen outside.

Looking at Julie intently without answering this question, two lacemakers who had just come from the apothecary's shop announced that Anna-Livia could never again make lace. Three of the fingers on her right hand would be permanently paralyzed.

"I pounded on her hand with a big stone."

Julie had spoken so quietly that the others could scarcely hear her.

"With a big stone," she repeated, as though talking to herself. "The biggest one I could find. I hit her hand with it, again and again. . . ."

There was silence in the room. It took Julie a certain time to realize it. She was emerging only gradually from the shock of a violent blow to the head sustained during her fight. She listened in surprise to a bee buzzing among the flowers on the altar of the Virgin in one corner of the room, and this finally made her aware of the strange hush around her. She looked at the other women one by one, and what she saw in their faces made her open her eyes wide. No one had spoken, yet she had just understood that although they had to defend their dignity as lacemakers when it was placed in doubt by those despised foreigners, no one had a right to deprive another lacemaker, even a Venetian, of the ability to work. It was contrary to honor.

Because she felt sudden pain, Julie put her hands to her belly. But she quickly withdrew them, fearing she would be suspected of trying to arouse pity. She raised her pretty head, with her hair still muddy from the street, and stood up. She took her cloth bag from the long worktable, made sure her thimble and scissors were there, counted her needles, closed the bag, and then, without saying anything, without even nodding to anyone, she walked out.

They were nearing the Lancrel Gate. Seen between the two towers, the flowering countryside was waiting for them. As he had been used to doing since early childhood, the chevalier said a prayer as he passed the charming little wooden statue of the Virgin that stood in a hollow of the town wall. The faint but cheerful sound of a gentle breeze made a pleasing combination with the delicate fragrance of apple blossoms. With a sense of well-being as delectable as a glass of cool cider, he breathed freely and happily. He felt a need for music. According to custom, he raised his hand to notify Zoltan and Candelario that they were to stop at the next suitable place.

"He's already wrapped up in his songs again," muttered Candelario, "and he hasn't even asked me if poor Anna-Livia is dead or alive!"

"Candelario, my friend," the chevalier said gaily, "play us that pastorale you composed. Look at that field, those apple trees, those sheep and their shepherdess—your flute is all that's missing!"

As he played, Candelario looked back and forth between the two men, from the tall and slender but amazingly strong chevalier to the tall, gaunt Zoltan, each lost in his own reverie. *What would they do without me?* he thought, and his affection was heightened by the feeling that he was absolutely indispensable to them.

It had all begun in Venice, when the chevalier, walking briskly with a distracted look on his face, was about to go into a theater. Waiting at the entrance, Candelario caught him by the sleeve.

"Excuse me, sir, but you seem to have neither a candle nor a libretto."

"That's true."

"You can't follow the opera without a libretto."

"You're quite right."

"And you can't read the libretto without a candle."

"Right again."

"And what about oranges? Would you also like some of them? You can throw them at Thetis and Peleus"—Francesco Cavalli's opera about those two personages was being performed that evening—"if you're not pleased."

During this period of his life, Candelario judged his customers by the number of oranges they bought. He had no direct contact with the great lords who had baskets of oranges brought to their boxes by servants. He did most of his business with the people in the pit, some of whom, though poor, were serious music lovers. But even the poorest of them bought six oranges; many bought twelve, and the most ostentatious bought three times that many without even asking for their change. The chevalier wanted only one!

This was highly unusual; it was, in fact, the first time Candelario had ever known it to happen. No one else in Venice would have dared to make such a meager purchase, if only because no one else would have shown so little concern for his reputation. Always curious about human nature, Candelario took an interest in the chevalier because his behavior was so out of keeping with his aristocratic appearance.

When he had finished his selling, he went to the pit and watched his customer discreetly. Unlike those around him, the chevalier listened without crying out, *"Benissimo!"* or acclaiming the soprano with shouts of "Bless you!" or "Bless the man who fathered you!" But in the light of his candle it could be seen that his eyes were moist. And he had eaten his orange! *He's a great music lover but he's not very demonstrative,* thought Candelario, *and he's very sensitive but he didn't eat enough for dinner.*

Their second meeting made Candelario's life take a new direction. An opera by Cesti was being performed that evening. Candelario noted that the choice was in good taste.

After the performance he went up to the chevalier and ventured to ask, "Did you appreciate the modern manner in the composition of the opera, sir? Did you enjoy the *ritornelli*?"

The chevalier had liked the opera, but this wasn't the first time he had heard it. He knew, in fact, even more than Candelario himself about *buon canto*, the great beauty of Cesti's arias, and the music of other composers—*all* of them! He went not only to Venice but also to Naples, Innsbruck, Vienna! Surprised and delighted, Candelario wanted to make this man tell him everything he knew. He went with him when he left the theater. The chevalier was staying at a mediocre inn on the other side of the city. It was a long walk, but Candelario didn't benefit from it as he had hoped: The chevalier asked questions instead of answering them.

A little breathless from trying to keep up—he had such long legs!—Candelario told the chevalier about himself. His name was Jacopo Cespi; he was called Candelario because of the candles he sold, but he was a musician; his soul was steeped in music! He played the flute, the viol, the trumpet, and even the drum. And he sang. Ah, yes, he had one of the finest voices in Italy! (He sang a few vocal exercises to demonstrate this point.) But, as everyone knew, beautiful voices in Venice were as common as garbage in the Grand Canal. And to make a living and be as close to music as possible, he sold librettos, candles, and oranges, and replaced a sick singer in the chorus whenever God chose to look upon him with kindness.

After listening without comment, the chevalier offered him a position as a musician-servant, in France.

"No, not in Paris. In the Perche district."

Perche? Candelario had never heard of it, but he was willing to go there. Good music could be made anywhere. Would he awaken his master in the morning with a sweet but lively tune? Would he play when guests came to supper? No. The chevalier woke up by himself and never had guests for supper. What he wanted was to have his compositions played whenever and wherever he chose. He would also expect his servant to accompany him when he went off to war. This prospect was less than enchanting, but Candelario, who had delicate tastes, could no longer stand the sickening smell of candles, and oranges were heavy to carry. Furthermore, he had four sisters to whom he owed large sums of money that he couldn't repay. They were ill-tempered women and had begun making life miserable for him. He agreed to go to Perche and formulated a maxim for his future guidance: Do not be put off by a stranger's shabby appearance, for God may have sent him to give you a chance to travel.

They came to the suburb of Lancrel. The unrest in Alençon hadn't spread this far. Everything was calm. They heard only the hammering of carpenters working on what was evidently going to be a handsome building. There were about ten of them. This little assembly gave the chevalier the idea of performing a concert. There was no better encouragement to work than a good song, he thought, and when the time came for these young men to go to war, maybe they would remember how he had let them glimpse the lure of battle one morning in May.

Candelario came up to him to hear what the program would be. First, *The Grand Vizier's Turban*, to get off to a cheerful start; then *The Victory of the Dunes*, to set a more serious tone; and finally *The Great March of Victorious Banners*, to end with an explosion of flamboyant martial ardor. Candelario nodded and tried to say something, but the chevalier was already so deeply absorbed in anticipation of his concert that he didn't listen to him. Candelario shrugged and went back to his place.

"I don't think he realizes what's going on here," he said to Zoltan.

Zoltan went on tuning his viol. He didn't listen either, which prompted Candelario to say, "Sometimes I wonder about you two. . . . You don't live in the world; you live beside it. Yes, beside it," he repeated, pleased with himself because he found the expression accurate.

After the introduction with which the chevalier usually began his songs—"Listen, people of France, while we tell you of our great and most Christian King Louis XIV"—all the carpenters, by order of the man who seemed to be their leader, stopped working, stood in line, took off their hats, and listened in respectful, meditative silence. And when the musicians also took off their hats and bowed to their audience, as was their custom, the workmen returned their bows. The chevalier was surprised by their unusual behavior and decided it was their way of showing an admiration they were too timid to express with enthusiastic shouts of "Bravo!" As he and his servants were riding away, the men's leader ordered the carpenters to resume their work.

"It did me good to see that!" said the chevalier. "We don't often find people who listen so respectfully."

"That's true, sir, and it's just as well we don't," replied Candelario.

"What do you mean?"

"Don't you know what they are, sir?"

The chevalier answered only with a puzzled expression.

"They're Protestants," said Candelario, "who are building a church for themselves in this suburb because their religious services have been forbidden in Alençon. Protestant churches are now being built outside of towns all over France."

"How do you know about that?"

"I now live in Normandy, sir. I look, I listen, I question the Normans around me. In short, I'm *in the world*. And I can tell you that you scared those Protestants half to death. For all they knew, you might belong to the Compagnie du Saint-Sacrement.*

---

*A society of laymen and priests founded in about 1627. It was originally organized for charitable purposes, but its overzealousness (constant investigations and harassment concerning proper religious practices in all social classes) caused it to be officially disbanded in 1665. A few members, however, continued their heretic hunting and religious persecutions, with the approval of the clergy.

If you did, and if you'd seen anything in their behavior that made you think they weren't showing proper respect for the king's courage and glory, you would have turned in a bad report on them, and the building they're working on would have been torn down. So I guarantee you, sir, that you gave them a fright they'll never forget!''

The chevalier's laughter was so loud that the Protestant workmen, who were still within hearing distance, must have been at least perplexed by it, if not alarmed.

When they had come to the edge of the Perseigne forest, the chevalier said to Candelario, ''I remember hearing not long ago that His Majesty had ordered that Protestant children were no longer to be separated from their parents. That's a step in the direction of tolerance, but what you've told me about churches being built outside of towns doesn't seem to go in that same direction.''

''The king is evidently practicing what we call in Venice the coming and going of freedoms: You give one and take away another. It's a game that leaves the people confused. Sometimes they're hopeful, sometimes they're hopeless. Maybe it makes them easier to lead.''

A little later, Candelario rejoined Zoltan and said, ''If you ask me, the master talked about Protestant children because he was thinking of children in general, and he was thinking of children because he believes he's the father of the child that Julie will soon give birth to. What's your opinion?''

''I have none.''

''Don't you ever have an opinion about anything?''

''As seldom as possible.''

''Then you live like an animal?''

''If you like.''

''I don't like or dislike it; I'm just trying to understand you.''

''Why?''

''You ask why? All right, I'll tell you, you pigheaded Hungarian! You saved my life in your country. I never would have thought I'd fight in a battle there—or anywhere else, for that matter. I can still see that Turk's scimitar over my head. And I still have nightmares about it: I dream it's coming at me so fast I can hear it hissing, and the hissing is a whisper telling me I'm about to die. When you punctured that dog of a Turk and kept him from having the honor of beheading the only Venetian in the battle, I said to myself, 'There's a man who likes to fight, and such men are useful, of course.' Then that night in camp I heard you play the viol like a prince and sing like an archangel, and I said to myself, 'There's a prodigious musician.'

"When the slaughter was over, my master took an interest in the Turkish army. He wanted to find out if Montaigne was right when he said that those savages eat dried, powdered meat and drink the blood of their horses. Just between you and me, that's a strange subject to interest a man who never knows what's on his plate or in his glass! I knew someone like that in Venice: He was always working on ways to improve clocks, and never knew what time it was. Anyway, when peace finally came, I saw you doing your civilian work. By then, my master and I were studying Turkish music. I watched you fattening your capons. As far as work goes, it was no better than my old trade of selling candles and oranges. To tell you the truth, I think it was worse. At that point I decided you were the second musician-servant we needed. And I'll tell you why I thought you were exactly the man my master was looking for, assuming you're interested in knowing. It's because the two of you are alike in the sense that it's never possible to guess where you *really* are. There's no danger that your imaginations will ever get rusty.

"You're a Hungarian in Normandy, but right now you're no more at the edge of the Perseigne forest than you were on the bank of the Rába the first time I saw you, when I was really much too close to that Turkish scimitar. Zoltan, my friend," Candelario said imploringly, "please tell me where you are now, in your head, with that diabolical flame laughing at the back of your eyes."

Zoltan's eyes took on a gentler expression. He looked up and down the slopes on either side of the path, and at the primroses and violets that carpeted the ground.

"Those same flowers grow in my country," he said. "In spring, when I was a child, I used to roll in them. My mother would say my hair smelled like the meadows of heaven, and then she'd kiss me. . . . That's where I was: in Hungary, thirty years ago, wallowing in violets like the ones you see here. And if there was a spark of amusement in my eyes, it was because I saw that our master was also in those violets."

The chevalier was no longer among the violets, but he had been there for a few moments. Trying to think of a word to rhyme with *arbalète* [crossbow], he had wondered if *violette* [violet] would suit his purpose. He would decide later.

They rode through the cool shade of the Perseigne forest, with its stands of tall, ancient trees. The horses trampled flowering gorse. And Candelario was thoughtful as he ate one of the buckwheat rolls he especially liked; he kept them warm by carrying them under his clothes, next to his skin.

"Now that I've had time to think it over in the peace and quiet of the forest," he said to Zoltan with his mouth full, "I'm more surprised than ever by Julie's behavior. She was always so gentle and unassuming, until she suddenly turned into the biting, scratching spitfire we saw this morning. Since she had the courage to attack Anna-Livia and then our master, it looks as though she'll never stop."

"She will, because the police will stop her."

"Maybe she'll escape from them."

"I doubt it. France needs young women to send to its colonies in America. And there's something even more serious against her: The state is determined to make an example of her, so there won't be any more attacks against the Venetian lacemakers. She's being hunted down now. The child she's carrying is heavy. The police can move much faster than she can. Poor little Julie, with her angelic voice . . . God help her!"

Candelario would not have been more startled if one of the bees flitting among the flowers had stung him. Zoltan had never talked so much before, or shown so much interest in anyone. Could it be that . . . Candelario decided he would try to find out more.

"Do you remember the first time we saw her, Zoltan? It was on a Thursday, at the market, and she was standing at the front of the little crowd that had gathered to listen to us. She was eating an apple, her eyes were shining. . . . She liked what we were singing, and she sang the refrains with us. She was pretty as a picture, with her white hat and those sky-blue eyes, and she looked so pure and innocent that she seemed to be holding out her hand—the one without an apple in it—to an angel beside her."

Candelario saw that he was wasting his time: Nothing he could say would induce Zoltan to talk about Julie any more. The Hungarian was looking up, ostensibly at the sunlit tops of the big oaks, but what was he really seeing?

He was listening. To the music of Julie's wooden shoes. He had liked her way of beating time with her feet and turning her steps into a kind of dance, and he had noticed that she did it when she was happy. When the chevalier had thought to tell her good-by before he left Alençon, or if he had smiled at her, it was one, two, three, four on one foot, then one, two, three, four on the other, and so on, over and over. The rhythmic clatter of her wooden soles on the pavement could be heard a long time, until it finally faded away in the distance. If the police caught her, they would put chains on her ankles. And when a bird's wings were cut off, it died. . . . Putting his hand on the medal of Saint Stephen that he wore over his heart, Zoltan prayed for the young lacemaker.

But, with Candelario there, it was hard to pray in peace. The Venetian had already begun talking again: "To sum up the situation, I'll say that we're tangled in lace, because I have a strong feeling that if we don't do something for that girl and her unborn baby, no one will." He pointed his chin toward the chevalier's back. "We both know he's the baby's father. I'm sure that if she went with him the first night he invited her to dinner, it was because she was hungry, but afterward—I'd swear to it on the cross—afterward she fell in love with him. She didn't love him like Anna-Livia, always shrieking her highest notes, but sotto voce, and sincerely. Do you happen to have an opinion on that subject?"

"Yes, and it happens to be the same as yours."

"Well, then, what shall we do?"

"Nothing."

"Do you mean to say you think *we shouldn't do anything for her?*"

"It's too late. It's always been too late in that affair. And you and I are only a flute and a viol. Maybe even less, maybe only a few disembodied sounds, without flesh or blood."

To calm his nerves and prove to himself that he had a body made of flesh, blood, and bone, Candelario took another buckwheat roll from under his clothes and vigorously bit into it.

As the three men rode out of the forest they saw the chevalier's ancestral home: Grand-Coeur [Great-Heart], in Pervenchères. Pink in the sunlight, it perched on its hillock like a falcon on a fist.

The fief of Ferrières went back to 1054, when a lord by that name was already in possession of the place and had built a fortress on a man-made hill overlooking the whole countryside. After the Franco-English wars, a manor house was built on the ruins of the fortress, facing a vast horizon of plains and tall trees. It was a rather plain three-story house with a pink tile roof, flanked by an octagonal tower. It had no architectural pretensions; the gardens lacked order and were poorly maintained; the stables were dilapidated. Nothing was really beautiful, yet the overall impression was one of great charm and tranquil harmony.

On the façade of the house, above the main door framed by six windows with chamfered mullions, a stone escutcheon displayed a heraldic heart that the winds had worn down, as they had worn down the tops of the fir trees that bordered the courtyard and hid the outbuildings.

Lady Bertrade, the chevalier's mother, also lived at Grand-Coeur.

When she left her family's castle at the time of her marriage, Lady Bertrade had taken with her—aside from a few chests filled with clothes and linen—only her horse, Picus, her servant, Pompinne, and a big armchair.

She had seen her grandfather, and then her father, meditating by the fire in that enormous, high-backed, majestic chair. It was in memory of them that she brought it to her new home. When she arrived, the servants put it in front of the monumental stone fireplace in the great common room, and that was where it stayed. With his charming but profoundly indifferent courtesy, her young husband, Chevalier Héribert de Ferrières, moved it closer to the fire so she could warm herself better.

It was quite simply one of the most uncomfortable chairs ever made. When you sat on it, it forced you to hold your head erect and keep your back straight as a ramrod. And this seemed symbolic to Lady Bertrade. As she watched her husband constantly walking around her, without ever sitting down or even standing still, and as she heard him describe plans for his life that always required him to be somewhere else, she saw herself spending the rest of her days there, sitting stiffly in that chair, alone and forgotten, but bearing up under her misfortune and waiting for something that would never come: a heart to warm hers, in that house with the motto ''The heart can do anything'' carved above the fireplace.

She had been smitten with her future husband as soon as she was introduced to him, because of his handsome face, his elegant figure, his golden mustache, and the lustrous opulence of his hair, but she had immediately feared the sharp look of his

blue-green eyes, and she had heard the ironic verdict that condemned her: "You're a pretty red apple, gentle lady, prettier
than any that's ever come from my orchards."

In her daydreams, she had tried to imagine herself as slender
and pink; she now had to see herself as buxom and ruddy. One
last shred of those daydreams let her hope that she would be a
delectable fruit, but she soon realized that Héribert de Ferrières
had a taste only for the enticing wildflowers he plucked along
the faithless paths of his life, between the times when he was
gathering laurels on the battlefield.

A vestal watching over a joyless hearth, Lady Bertrade waited
for her fickle warrior's brief, indifferent returns until finally he
died in the Battle of Nördlingen, attacking the Bavarians from
the rear with the great Turenne. Louis-Guillaume picked up the
sword fallen from his father's hand and went off to place it in
the service of his king.

It was a ruinous sword! Anyone who knew Grand-Coeur as
it had once been could enumerate the victories and defeats of
France by noting the farms, fields, and forests that had formerly
belonged to the Ferrières but were now the property of commoners who had made themselves rich. How many young peasants in the region had been paid and equipped by the lords of
Pervenchères to go with them and fight in battles all over Europe? It was better not to count! If only Louis-Guillaume could
be persuaded to stop his expenditures so that no more land would
have to be sold. . . . But it was hard even to broach the subject
with him.

One evening when he was passing through the common room
on his way to the wing of the house where he lived alone in order
to play and compose his music in peace, he saw his mother, a
pensive widow sitting on her thronelike chair, and stopped to
tell her, smiling, that when she had come to Grand-Coeur with
that chair she had, perhaps unknowingly, repeated a practice of
their great ancestors, the Vikings. Did she know that when the
Vikings boarded the ships that would take them to their faraway
conquests, they brought a chair with them as an emblem of
family authority? No, she hadn't known it. And, as a matter of
fact, she had very little interest in it, but she let her son continue
discoursing on the expeditions of the valiant Normans, thinking
that this might put him into a good mood for listening to her
little speech on the condition of Grand-Coeur.

The great feats of those magnificent conquerors, he told her, had been reported only by ignorant monks—the Low Latin they wrote was crude to the point of being sinful—who couldn't distinguish a warrior from a butcher, or a sword from a kitchen knife. By order of the Church, they had written completely false accounts of the Viking invasions, and it was urgent to expose them for what they were. The barbarians were far from having been as barbaric as those fools claimed in their drivel. Louis-Guillaume wanted to correct their distortions as soon as possible, and maybe—this was an old idea that he would be glad to take up again—write about the exploits of the noble Rollo the Viking, who became the first Duke of Normandy. Was she aware that their province was the only Viking conquest in which a dynasty was founded?

Lady Bertrade readily acknowledged this and went on to point out that they, the Ferrières, still owned a little piece of the territory conquered by those heroic Vikings, and that it was in desperate need of care. Did he have a clever idea as to how they could pay for repairs to the rotting roof, from which tiles were dropping one by one, like birds deserting a nest?

Perhaps the chevalier listened only to what he wanted to hear, or perhaps a providential intermittent deafness allowed him to avoid hearing things that might have annoyed him or placed him under a disagreeable obligation. In any case, he ignored what his mother had said and went on to consider an important question. If he sang the praises of Rollo, could he also praise Rollo's son Longsword, whose valor was admirable but whose death posed a problem? Did she know that the second Duke of Normandy was treacherously killed by being struck on the head with an oar? It might not have been dishonorable for the Vikings, the Kings of the Sea, to be killed by a nautical implement, but Longsword had to be regarded as a Frenchman of noble birth, and so it was a supreme disgrace for him to die from what amounted to being beaten with a stick.

When the chevalier had gone back to his violins and flutes, Lady Bertrade—worried about the repairs to the roof that needed to be done immediately, and others that would be needed in the near future—had a moment of self-pity. To cut short that weakness, she left the house, mounted Picus III, and galloped to her forest, which gave her good advice once again, reminding her that, in her way, she was as passionate as her son. She was excessively fond of these long rides among her friends the trees, and, to her, being able to go hunting was worth any sacrifice.

With her unfailingly generous heart she had accepted the idea
that she alone should be responsible for maintaining the estate,
because she had no poetic, musical, or historical works to create. And no wars to fight. What was she good for, except hunting stags and boars? In the gentle rustling of the leaves, she
heard that it was good for things to be as they were.

Actually, however, she was not alone in bearing the burdens
of Grand-Coeur. Pompinne, her servant, whose mother had been
Lady Bertrade's wet nurse, also bore her share. Pompinne was
as solidly built as her mistress, who maintained that as babies
they had both been nourished by the best milk in the county of
Mortagne, and that it had given uncommon strength and health
to the two sturdiest women ever born there.

In the opinion of the boy who worked as a farmhand on the
estate and shared in its family life, Pompinne was as cross as
two sticks, with a temper always ready to flare at the drop of a
hat. Candelario and Zoltan spoke Italian or Latin between themselves and with the chevalier and Lady Bertrade, but they had
no need of an interpreter to realize that Pompinne's good moods
were even rarer than coins in their pockets. Putting up with her
crotchety disposition, however, had its rewards: She had a way
of making buckwheat porridge that turned it into the most delectable dish imaginable, and the two musician-servants would
have walked from Alençon to Paris with cannonballs on their
feet to taste her spiced apple preserves. She wasn't lavish with
these preserves, because the Ferrières' days of living on a grand
scale were over, now that they were less loaded with money
than a frog with feathers. According to her, Héribert de Ferrières had been a good-for-nothing who squandered all his
money and always began bellowing and roaring at the top of his
lungs as soon as he came home from one of his wars. Lady
Bertrade, a poor creature whose kindness showed in her face,
had a life full of sorrow.

By a miracle probably unknown to Chevalier Louis-
Guillaume, Pompinne loved music, and his compositions delighted her. Whenever she heard a new song, she joyfully tapped
her feet in the kitchen and said, "There's another one that's
going to make them jealous for miles around," because she was
convinced that everyone on all the estates in the region envied
the musical talent that flourished at Grand-Coeur. And when
she encountered one of the neighbors' servants she would say,

"We've got a new tune this morning, and it's a good one, take my word for it. You can tell that to everybody at your house."

Everyone knew she had nursed the chevalier when he was a baby and that she boasted of being responsible for his beautiful voice because she had let him cry just enough to make it full and rich, without straining it. And, to please her, one had to believe that she had married one of Chevalier Héribert's servants, a big, gangling fool, so that she could be the wet nurse of Lady Bertrade's children when they were born.

At first she had treated Candelario and Zoltan even worse than she treated the farmhands. The two foreigners hadn't found favor in her eyes until she had heard them play music with her master. She still attributed no human feelings to them, but she fed them decently, to keep them in condition to perform their music properly. To avoid losing face, she said occasionally that one of them smelled of vice and the other of heresy.

Unlike Pompinne, the people on the nearby estates cared little about Chevalier Louis-Guillaume's musical compositions, but they praised Lady Bertrade and her servant, the two granite pillars that held up Grand-Coeur.

When the chevalier arrived, his mother dismounted from her horse and announced in her resounding voice that she had just killed an enormous boar. With her round, ruddy face and her red wool hat, she was still like the apple to which her husband had compared her long ago. She looked at Louis-Guillaume as he took off his big felt hat and bowed to her. His movements gave an impression of both strength and grace, and, as always when she contemplated his virile beauty, she was surprised that such a man could really be her son. As he had been a widower for several years, once again she regretted that he, the heir of the Ferrières, refused to remarry and was evidently going to leave their family without descendants.

And once again those two buffoons who were his servants irritated her. Though she considered that she had no imagination, she easily—and too often for her peace of mind—pictured to herself the spectacle the three men probably made of themselves in the surrounding region. When she had decided to take complete charge of the estate and let her son devote himself to his music, she certainly hadn't thought he would set out to perform it everywhere, traveling with two such ludicrous escorts

THE LACEMAKER 31

and acting as if he were the leader of a wandering theatrical troupe.

She knew that the noble families of the region sternly condemned this infraction of the laws of their caste. Though a few invitations were still sent to Grand-Coeur, it was only because the Ferrières were such good shots that their absence from hunting parties would have seriously reduced the amount of game taken, and because, as she admitted to herself with a half-smile, the local ladies were strongly attracted to her son. If, however, he went on provoking everyone at social gatherings by asserting that he was as proud of his ancestor Raoul de Ferrières, the Norman poet, as of those ancestors who had fought in the Crusades with Godfrey of Bouillon or King Louis IX, Grand-Coeur would no longer be located in Pervenchères, but on an island to which no one of their rank would come.

Seeing his mother unload the bloody carcass of the boar from her horse, the chevalier asked why she didn't have a servant do it for her. And where was that wretched scoundrel of a steward?

Lady Bertrade saw the two musician-servants looking at her, and, although there was nothing disrespectful in their eyes, her face became even redder than usual and her hand quivered when she put it on her horse's head. She would have liked to tell her son that the steward had been dismissed, for the sake of economy, *nearly ten years ago*! And she would have liked to point out to him that, to make it possible for him to take part in the latest Hungarian campaign and outfit his two preposterous servants, they had sold most of the horses they used for breeding, as he might have recalled if he had happened to notice that the stables were almost empty. But instead of saying all that, she didn't open her mouth. Only Picus III, her horse, was aware that her whole body trembled briefly. She drew strength and calm from a deep breath of the fresh air that, on their hilltop, invigorated those who lived at Grand-Coeur.

But as she watched the chevalier's servants leading their horses toward the outbuildings, she had another moment of secret rage at seeing them so richly dressed. "They're two birds with simple souls," her son had said of them, "who are sensitive to appearances and don't feel like singing unless they're covered with fine feathers." How could he think that those two had "simple souls"? Only he could fail to see that Candelario was a perfect mixture of Machiavelli and the Borgias, and a citizen of a republic that had shamefully diverted one of the Crusades for the sake of sordid financial gain. As for the other one, behind his show of stoical wisdom he remained a Hungarian. Although Lady Bertrade didn't really believe what was said about Hungarians—that they drank their enemies' blood on the battlefield—she did recognize that it was almost impossible to say for certain that Zoltan and his Venetian friend weren't bandits. At least they were both Catholics. She had to be thankful for that, since Louis-Guillaume might just as easily have taken a fancy to Turks or Persians.

This thought, followed by another deep breath of pure air, comforted her a little, and later, when she had said a prayer in her chapel, she felt that she again had the strength to cope with her son's appalling eccentricity.

When Lady Bertrade, the chevalier, and the servants were all seated around the kitchen table, in front of the monumental stone fireplace, Candelario became aware, once again, of Lady Bertrade's animosity toward him. It was like a discordant sound, and he loved harmony above all else. As he savored his apple preserves—luckily they were on the menu today—and lovingly spread them over his buckwheat porridge, he decided he would try to eliminate that false note, if for no other reason than that it upset his digestion. After getting away from the scolding, nagging, and complaints of his four greedy, ill-tempered sisters, who had spoiled so many good meals for him, he hadn't come here to endure unjustified reproach, even from someone courteous enough to express it in silence.

What was the reason for that unjustified reproach? Misunderstood people didn't understand others. And before Candelario came to Grand-Coeur, who had understood Lady Bertrade? No one. But he had quickly realized what made her behave as she did. She galloped on her horse, Picus I, II, or III, in an effort to escape her sorrows and worries; she talked to trees— he had heard her!—because she had an unsatisfied need for affection; she hunted furred and feathered game to calm her humors and avoid having to be bled. There was only one remedy for all that: love. Motherly love, in her case. There ought to be children at Grand-Coeur. God would soon send one who, if only by right of birth, would be at home there. It was safe to bet that when Lady Bertrade had an heir to receive her overflowing abundance of love, as well as the family estate, she would no longer see mountains where there were only molehills, and would stop condemning a poor Venetian's healthy appetite or his need for frequent periods of relaxation to rest his eyes from the fatigue of seeing everything.

His eyes now saw, sadly, that no one around that table would ever think of enhancing the subtle savor of their spiced apple preserves by blending it with the creamy warmth of their buckwheat porridge. How dense these Normans were! But he liked them. He had become attached to them all: Pompinne, with her long, suspicious nose; Lady Bertrade, with her round, beaming face, who sometimes tried to look harsh and stern but succeeded only in showing a kind of childish disapproval ready to be wiped away by good-natured laughter; Ogier, the little falconer, such a bright boy that you almost expected him to glow in the dark. And the chevalier, with his splendid talent. And Zoltan, who fought like a demon and played his viol like an angel . . .

What a sweet moment it was for Candelario, sitting with his back to the fire, his belly full and a song in his heart! The famous composer Clément Janequin had grouped his works under the title *Orchard of Music*; Candelario would like to make his life an Orchard of Friendship. He smiled at that pleasant idea.

Lady Bertrade had been watching him for some time now. To her, he looked like a plump monk digesting an overabundant meal and smiling blissfully as he tried to explain to God that the stomach also had its weaknesses. In spite of strict orders to the contrary, Pompinne still overfed these gluttons. But Lady Bertrade felt an agreeable warmth spreading through her whole body, cooled a little by a glass of cider, as a breeze softens a summer day. She forgave. And, to her surprise, she felt like smiling too.

To resist the languor that threatened to take possession of her, she decided to go hunting immediately. Maybe another boar was already waiting for her. Salted with the one she had killed that morning, it would provide meat for Sunday dinners in the coming winter.

As she was putting on her red hat, she spoke to Candelario in the literary Italian she had learned from reading Dante in her adolescence; it always disconcerted him, which secretly delighted her. "We are still eagerly awaiting your sumptuous pasta, but we never see any of it adorn our table."

"I would have made some for you long ago, Noble Lady, if we had any wheat flour here. But we eat only buckwheat, like . . ."

"Like what?"

Lady Bertrade raised her riding crop and stepped toward Candelario, but then she quickly lowered it and strode away.

It was sad to realize how often misunderstanding came between people, reflected Candelario. Was there anyone whose intentions were better than his, and who got less credit for them?

Lady Bertrade had seen Zoltan smile and wondered if she was getting old. Why hadn't she struck that insolent servant with her riding crop? Suddenly overcome with fatigue, she decided to hunt small game—ringdoves or hares—rather than boars. She called Ogier, her falconer, who was in the courtyard feeding a young pigeon hawk that had recently been captured. Absorbed in his work, he didn't hear her. Ordinarily she appreciated his taste for perfection, but she hadn't yet recovered from her recent irritation. She walked toward the boy, slashing the air with her riding crop. Was he going to become as impudent as her son's musician-servants?

He was tearing apart a finch still palpitating with life and was feeding it, as a reward, to the bird he was training. Suddenly he became aware of Lady Bertrade's presence and looked up at her.

"He'll be a proud and brave hunter, Noble Lady," he said. "He doesn't mind being trained. You can put him to work at the new moon, and you'll enjoy hunting with him."

What charming eyes! Lady Bertrade looked at Ogier with the same pleasure she took in contemplating the pure face of the marble statue of the Virgin, by Bernini, that stood in her chapel. Suddenly calmed, as she always was by the beauty of persons and things, she again lowered her riding crop. But this time she didn't wonder if she was getting old. She felt younger, in fact. And her spirits rose at the thought that she was going to hear Ogier's chatter while they hunted. He didn't lack imagination— he had too much of it, said Father Lecoudre, the old priest who was his teacher—and she was sure to laugh her fill as she listened to him. The night before, as she was about to fall asleep, she had smiled at his recollection of the practical applications the priest imposed on his Jansenist convictions. With a smile that made his white teeth flash and his dark eyes sparkle, the boy had said, "Do you know, Noble Lady, how Father Lecoudre has been keeping warm in this long spell of chilly weather? He's still using the Yule log you gave him last

Christmas! But don't think it's been burning in his fireplace for six months, through some kind of witchcraft. It keeps him warm only by its weight—about twenty pounds; I've lifted it. Here's what he's told me. The Solitaires* at Port-Royal resist cold and dampness by climbing stairs, walking around a building or running through the garden, carrying a heavy piece of firewood. They say there's nothing better for fighting off numbness and cold. And Father Lecoudre does the same. Did you know that, Noble Lady?''

No, she hadn't known it, but she found it amusing.

"In my opinion," Ogier had continued, "keeping warm like that is childish. I don't deny that the temperature of the human body can be raised by carrying a heavy object. But why a piece of firewood? That's where the childishness lies. Why not use something that weighs the same but can be carried usefully? Water from a well, for example. I've made a list of ways in which Father Lecoudre could warm himself and do something useful at the same time. Last night he went to give extreme unction to Thomas, your tenant farmer. If he'd run instead of walking, not only would he have warmed himself but he wouldn't have come too late. Poor Thomas died without having received God.

"I must say, Noble Lady, that because Father Lecoudre is so hard on himself he can neither walk nor run very well. Why does he go on wearing only one sock? He insists on protecting only his ulcerated foot, and says the other one doesn't need a sock. But the heel of his sockless foot is always rubbed raw by his shoe. I told him he was wasting money, rather than saving it, because he spends more on ointment than he saves by making a pair of socks last twice as long as usual."

Since learning to read and write in French and Latin, thanks not only to his secretly Jansenist priest, but also to his faultless intelligence and will, Ogier served as the chevalier's librarian when he wasn't training falcons or watching over the sheep. One of his duties was putting away books, since the chevalier never bothered to put one back in its place after taking it out. Ogier had time for a great deal of reading, however, and usually spent part of the night in the big room with shelves that held hundreds of books. In this way he had acquired a hodgepodge of knowledge on a wide variety of topics and had learned to speak and write correctly. Lady Bertrade knew he pilfered candles from

*Jansenists who had retired to the Abbey of Port-Royal-des-Champs.

Pompinne, but she pretended not to notice. Sometimes she even
left a candle out where she knew he would find it.

They mounted their horses and set off for the hunt. Their
gloved right hands each held a hooded falcon. The two birds
wore collars inscribed "To Lady Bertrade de Ferrières" that
had been enriched with a design formed by small sapphires.
The collars had been a gift from her husband at the beginning
of their marriage, the only one he had ever given her. He must
have felt, she had sadly decided later, that it was better to adorn
beautiful birds of prey than pudgy fingers. Monsieur Legrand,
the goldsmith in Alençon, had gracefully engraved the two collars. When the falcons came back wearing them, victorious in
the sunlight, it was as though they were bringing stars wrapped
around their necks.

Lady Bertrade and Ogier rode side by side in the soft, light
air of late morning. Ogier wore an unbleached linen tunic held
at the waist by a rope, with his legs, feet, and head bare. His
dark, gleaming hair fluttered in the wind. She suddenly saw him
as a prince disguised as a peasant, straight out of a fairy tale.
She admired his ungloved left hand. It was long, harmoniously
shaped—perfect, in fact, even though it was suntanned and
scratched. She found herself laughing at the idea that only noble
blood could produce such aristocratic hands. Hearing her laugh,
Ogier laughed too, happy to see her so cheerful. They laughed
together, under the big tree, as if they were singing. It didn't
matter that they weren't singing the same words. Then he began
telling her about what he had been reading the last few nights.

At first she listened only distractedly, wondering how he found
time to carry on amorous affairs with all the shepherdesses over
whom he was said to have such great power, even though he
was scarcely fourteen. But she soon put that subject out of her
mind and listened with amusement to what he was saying, which
came down to this: The aviary at Grand-Coeur, with its two old
falcons, nearly thirty now, and its young one just barely hatched,
was unworthy of Lady Bertrade. Did she know that the barbarian
Tamerlane had employed twenty thousand falconers? Before
him, Genghis Khan must have come close to that number, and
the emperor Charlemagne, the most ostentatious of hunters,
must have far surpassed either of those savage conquerors. It
was hard to know the exact number of falcons kept by French
kings and princes, but there were certain facts that could serve

as indications. The famous Gaston Phoebus, Comte de Foix, for example, who was known to have had fifteen hundred hunting dogs, must have had thousands of birds of prey. And if Tamerlane had twenty thousand falconers, it was easy to calculate the number of his falcons, since each man trained at least three or four birds. . . .

The sun that escorted them was warming their backs. They stopped counting Tamerlane's falcons and, for a time, said nothing. Then Ogier broke the silence.

"Noble Lady, I've read that in the old days, if a knight was captured in battle he was never supposed to give his sword or his hunting bird to ransom himself, because those were sacred things, emblems of his nobility, and it would have been dishonorable for him to give them up. Is that true?"

"Yes, it is."

There was another long silence. Finally he said, "You told me, Noble Lady, that when I'd finished training your young falcon I could capture one and train it for myself, only for myself. Does that mean it will belong to me?"

She nodded, smiling. Though he said nothing more, she could guess the course of his thoughts: He had no right to a sword—not yet!—but he would have a hunting bird, and he already saw himself following in the footsteps of the valiant knights of yore. His ambition amused her, and she encouraged it. She suddenly wondered if she had been right that day when, having discovered him laboriously pronouncing the names of the letters I.N.R.I. (*Iesus Nazarenus Rex Iudaeorum*, Jesus Nazarene King of the Jews) on the crucifix in the church, she had decided to make him Father Lecoudre's pupil. He had been so eager to learn, so ardent in all his studies! By the time he was ten, he could already write better in French and Latin than his teacher, who was astounded by the number of pertinent questions he was always asking.

She would have liked to talk about the boy to Louis-Guillaume, but she could already hear his answer. "You're not complaining that the gold shines too brightly, are you? He's learned quickly and well? So much the better, because he'll be all the more useful to you. For me, he finds the books I need in only a few minutes, whereas I used to waste hours looking for them. We're rewarded for what we've done for him, so all's well."

She sighed. The sun had gone behind a cloud and she shivered, even though she was still warm in her fur-lined coat. Seeing Ogier so lightly dressed, she found it surprising that he had already abandoned the two sheepskins he had skillfully sewn together to wear in cold weather. She concluded that the poor had excellent mental and physical resistance.

"Has the cat got your tongue, Ogier? I've never known you to be quiet this long!"

He looked at her without answering and seemed to be studying her. She asked him what there was about her that justified such interest. Her old coat? Her old hat?

"I'm looking at you, Noble Lady, because not long ago I went to Alençon for the first time. I was taken there by my master, the chevalier, to replace Zoltan, who had a sore throat. I sang there, can you believe it? It's not what I do best! But my master said he would rather have even a mediocre second voice than no second voice at all. While I was there, I went all over the town. I saw noble ladies, and . . . and the noble ladies in Alençon don't dress the way you do. I didn't see any of them wearing a coat like yours, with moths coming out of its old fox fur like bees coming out of a flower!"

Lady Bertrade laughed. The moths flew away. Encouraged, Ogier continued. "If you'd let me trap some weasels or squirrels for you, you could have Pompinne put a new lining in your coat. Genghis Khan had a black sable coat. In Alençon, Candelario took me to the warehouse of Monsieur Léandris, the furrier. I said my master wanted me to ask about the price of a fur coat. Not only did Monsieur Léandris have no sable coats—black, brown, or any other color—but he'd never ever seen one! There's a man who deals in furs, yet he doesn't know all the different kinds of them. In my opinion, Noble Lady, someone who doesn't know his trade isn't worthy of practicing it. Don't you agree?

"Because I wanted to know as much about the town as I could, I asked Candelario where the lords and ladies got the beautiful ostrich feathers I saw on their hats. He showed me Monsieur Fresnel's hat shop, which has a bigger stock, and more customers, than any other hat shop in Alençon. It was the same thing all over again. Monsieur Fresnel had some idea of what an ostrich looks like, but he didn't know its size, so he didn't know that it's the biggest bird in the world and can't fly. I was the one who told him that ostriches are hunted on horseback, by making them run until they collapse, but that sometimes the hunter's horse collapses first. And listen to this, Noble Lady:

He mentioned that the king, his brother, and the lords of his court wear red, yellow, blue, and green ostrich feathers, and I was the one who told him that they didn't have those colors naturally, that undyed ostrich feathers are only white, black, or gray. So there's another craftsman unworthy of practicing his trade.

"Believe me, Noble Lady, if I'd thought those two old men still had a future, I'd have written a report on sables for Monsieur Léandris and one on ostriches for Monsieur Fresnel. But from the way their hands tremble and their backs are bent, I think they must be on the edge of the grave. Maybe they'll spend eternity enriching their minds, though I doubt it when I remember how bewildered they seemed while they were listening to me."

"Why are you looking at me like that?" asked Lady Bertrade.

"Remembering that hatmaker made me think of hats, and that made me wonder, with all due respect, why you let Pompinne sew all those gay feathers on your red hat, which is already ugly enough on its own. They're pretty blue feathers, I won't deny it, but sticking straight up like that, all around your head, they make you look like some sort of strange bird. In Alençon I saw some big felt hats decorated with one or two ostrich feathers. If you only knew how beautiful they were! They're real hunting hats, and one of them would suit you perfectly."

"We're not rich, Ogier."

"Someday I'll go hunting far away and bring back pretty things for you, to thank you for the candles that grow in the library like turnips in a field."

"Don't ever say anything about that to Pompinne. I wouldn't like her to know I'm the one who's been taking those candles."

"So you're afraid of her too."

They hunted for a long time. Their old falcons were perfect murderers, terrifying and killing four hares. Lady Bertrade's soft gray eyes and Ogier's dark ones kept traces of cold cruelty that were gradually dissipated only by fatigue.

They again rode in silence. Finally she decided to goad him a little, to make him more talkative.

"Have you noticed, Ogier, that your illustrious and sublime Roman heroes didn't like to hunt?"

She knew how much he admired the Romans, and how he

kept searching the shelves of the library for accounts of their exploits.

For a few moments he said nothing. Her thrust had struck home. What had made her say a thing like that? But soon a glow of respect came into his eyes: Now that he had thought about it, he realized the old lady was probably right. Why hadn't he discovered that truth for himself?

"Didn't you know," she said, "that the patricians always had their slaves supply them with game?"

The look he now gave her was like a warm caress. Good God! How many years had it been since the last time she had seen such esteem in eyes turned toward her? Maybe the last time had been that long-ago day when she had made an excellent shot during her first boar hunt with her husband.

"As proof of what I'm saying," she went on with a feeling of warmth in her heart, "I'll mention that although the Romans loved to give each other nicknames, they never thought of a single one that had anything to do with hunting."

Ogier's face suddenly darkened with anger. This was too much! Again she had told him something he should have realized for himself.

Lady Bertrade laughed with delight, thought of the shepherdesses again, and wondered if any of them had yet become acquainted with the black fury that could come into their young lover's eyes.

She had decided that, whether circumstances favored it or not, he would someday be her steward, as well as her librarian. He would brighten the old age of those at Grand-Coeur; a wife would be found for him, and he would make the evenings pass happily. In one pocket of her nearly furless fur-lined coat she had brought a lump of spiced apple preserves. She gave half of it to her future steward and bit vigorously into the other.

When Pompinne saw them coming back, laughing and gesturing in a whirlwind of gaiety, her soul was whipped by jealousy. If that little beggar, that son of a thieving, filthy tenant farmer, thought she was going to mend her master's old breeches so *he* could put his ass in them, he'd better think again! He was nothing but a ragged pauper, and always would be.

Julie leaned her back against the door of the Notre-Dame church. She was panting. A policeman had frightened her by staring at her. Had her description already been sent out? While she was giving her pounding heart time to calm down, she tried to make her pause seem normal by looking up to watch a flock of wild geese flying over the town. If only she too had wings! She put her hands on her belly. The baby was moving. She could give it wings, by turning it into an angel. She would only have to wait until it was born, then hold a pillow over its face for a little while. . . .

The geese were still flying over in the sunlight. Julie started when an old beggar woman touched her elbow and said, "I'd much rather have those birds cooking in a pot than flying up there, out of reach!"

Hunger! That was what lay in store for her. Now that the lacemaking shops and poorhouse were closed to her, where could she go for help? No one would give her work, knowing she was wanted by the police. Her eyes still followed the geese as they turned into little black dots in the sky, but she no longer saw them. She felt sudden panic and told herself that she had to be calm, pull herself together, think only of finding a hiding place. Exhausted from all the running she had just done, she let herself slide down the door until she was sitting on the ground. With her arms clasping her legs, she leaned her head down over her belly, closed her eyes and saw only the blackness of despair. For a moment she imagined, as she had done as a child, that with her eyes closed no one could see her.

Where could she hide? The police must already have gone to question the baker who rented her a room. She wouldn't miss that airless little cubicle. She would miss only the roll that Colin, the baker's apprentice, had stolen for her every morning. She had eaten it as she walked to her workshop with light, dancing steps. After having made the most beautiful lace in Alençon, and therefore the most beautiful in the world, here she was, sitting on the ground like a beggar, listening to the rapid beating of her heart and feeling the pulsating life of the poor little baby in her belly.

Where could she go? She had to think calmly. Who would help her? Her twin brother, Mathieu. But where was he? She prayed that he wasn't in Russia, then realized it was too early in the year for him to have gone there. Russian roads were probably still impassable. What had he told her about that? She should have listened to him better. But in this fine spring weather the ladies of the French court would be expecting deliveries of lace. Mathieu must not have gone any farther than Paris! She could go to his room and wait for him. The police and their shrewd captain—she had seen him in action at the workshop after a keg of thread had disappeared—would think of looking for her there, but Mathieu had a secret closet where he hid his lace, and the police captain would never find it, no matter how shrewd he was. She would hide in it whenever there was a danger of hostile visitors. She again put her hands on her belly, and this reminded her of her condition. Could she even get into that closet, big as she was now? She clenched her fists to fight off the panic. If she had to crush the baby to squeeze into the closet, she would crush it.

She stood up, and there was fierce determination in her eyes. She had regained her strength. She now knew where she should go and what she might have to do there. Getting to Mathieu's room would be risky. She would have to slip past the tannery, go into the courtyard, cross it and climb the stairs, all without being seen. She wasn't worried about old Monsieur Dérouet, who owned the building, but she would have to be careful of his two young apprentices.

It was a relief when she reached Mathieu's room unnoticed. She smiled at the little wooden angel that adorned the top of the door and could be made to turn if you knew how to go about it. The statue was hollow and held the key that Mathieu the packman had hidden in it, following the principle laid down by his father, who had also been a packman: "Never carry any useless weight, even if it's less than an ounce."

She stroked the angel's wings. They had been worn smooth by the hands of members of her family who had loved her on earth and were perhaps looking down on her from heaven, glad to know she was safe. She would stay here a few days without making any noise, lighting a fire, or showing herself at the window. And at the slightest danger she would hide in the secret closet.

Mathieu had foresightedly made preparations in case he came back at night: There was bread in the breadbox and water in the pitcher, and Julie saw apples lined up on the mantelpiece, in order of size. Her twin brother was the most orderly person she knew. She smiled affectionately at the thought. Then she sat down, almost happy, on the old straw-bottomed chair, facing the empty fireplace in which no trace of ashes could be seen. A clean fireplace, an oiled lock, a polished floor, fresh straw in the mattress—that was how Mathieu kept his room, without help from any woman.

Julie drank from the chipped pitcher she remembered from her childhood. She was putting it down with a sigh of pleasure when a stabbing pain struck her and made her tremble so much that she spilled water on the table. She couldn't be about to give birth: That wasn't supposed to happen for another month yet. The pain must be from her fight with Anna-Livia, and she must be feeling it more strongly now because she was relaxed and safe from the police. It was already dying down. And she was hungry!

She took an apple from the mantelpiece, so high that she could barely reach it. Was she still growing, now that she was almost seventeen? Mathieu claimed he could feel his legs getting longer from all the walking he did. But she had spent most of her time sitting.

The apple was a little shriveled, and for a few moments she caressed its wrinkles. Nothing was better than to smell, touch, and hold something good to eat. She liked fruit, whether it was dried out, green, or ripe. The same apple could have so many tastes, and give off so many smells, during its life. It was the same with bread. It could give you the feeling that you were eating a dozen different things as it changed from tender freshness to hard dryness. In their childhood, Mathieu had liked bread better when it was stale and hard; he would cut it into little cubes and she would put them into the cloth bags that hung from their belts. He felt that eating bread fresh was less enjoyable because it made you eat too fast. She disagreed: The pleasure was shorter, but so much better.

She savored her apple very slowly. She had always liked to let food melt in her mouth. In 1662, a year of famine, she had repeated a prayer of her own invention each time she ate: "Thank you, Virgin Mary, for every crumb, thank you for every drop, thank you for today, and thank you for tomorrow. By the blood of Our Lord I beg you, Holy Virgin, not to forget tomorrow." During that famine she and Mathieu had learned never to eat all of any portion they were given, but to put aside at least a quarter of it for later. Not only did they have to be satisfied with little but they had to do what they could to provide for the next day. Eating was good, their mother used to tell them, and knowing you would eat again was even better. There had been times when it wasn't easy to stop short of finishing off their meager rations, but they had always managed to do it. It was the best way, their father told them, to get ready for the next famine.

Once again, Julie left a quarter of her apple uneaten, and put it under an upside-down bowl. One night when the chevalier had taken her to dinner at the Moor's Inn, she had told him about her habit of saving food and asked if she could take a slice of bread with her. At the thought of him, she suddenly began weeping. Big tears fell on her hands as she sat in front of the empty fireplace.

When the pain came back, she was still weeping. She finally wiped her eyes and decided to eat the rest of her apple. But for the first time in her life she wasn't hungry! She went over to the bed. It was the bed her parents had slept in, and Mathieu now rested his long, tired legs in it when he came back from his journeys. The mattress smelled of fresh straw and, for some reason, this made her weep again.

It was time for her to begin praying to Saint Margaret, who had asked Jesus to make women suffer less. When her mother had helped a woman in childbirth, she had always chanted, "You who love us, Saint Margaret, help me. You who pity us, Saint Margaret, pray for me." And what else had her mother done when she helped a neighbor woman to give birth? First there had been water. A full pot of it, heating over the fire. Then a big supply of cloths. And the knife. Julie couldn't go down to the well or light a fire without letting the tanner know she was there, but at least she wouldn't have to do without a knife, because Mathieu had two of them. She stood up and went to get the sharper of the two. Cold, trembling, and in pain, she prepared to give birth alone.

Knowing that she mustn't cry out gave her strength. She was less afraid of pain than of the police. A thought that was like an image of heaven came into her mind: Soon she would be on the road, free, holding Mathieu's hand, walking toward another lacemaking shop where she would be warmly welcomed because of her skill.

To be sure that no one would hear her scream, she made a gag for herself by wrapping the piece of apple she had saved in coarse muslin. Then she stood facing the fireplace with her skirt pulled up. She had always seen women give birth that way, in front of the fire, supported by two other women. She had no fire, and no one to help her, but she had to do what was needed anyway.

When she finally pushed out the baby, the piece of apple had been chewed to a pulp and she was smiling with tears in her eyes.

She had just finished cutting the umbilical cord when someone scratched on the door. Panting, she kept the bloody knife in her hand. Then she heard a soft voice: "It's me, Julie, it's me."

Thank God! It was only her mother, Thomine Perdriel, a small, agile woman whose tousled hair, now gray, had once been red.

Julie's relief at seeing her caused a pleasant sensation to spread all through her body. A moment later she thought she was dying, happily, lying in a barn that had just been stocked with hay. When she came back to her senses, she was again on Mathieu's bed.

The baby was a girl. Thomine had gagged her lightly so no one would hear her crying and was giving her the customary vigorous rubdown with apple brandy. As soon as she sensed that Julie had regained consciousness, she asked, without interrupting her rubbing, "You're wondering how I knew, aren't you?"

And she explained. All the old women in the poorhouse where she lived had been told about the fight between Julie and Anna-Livia by their friend Conte-Nouvelles [News-Teller], who had learned of it as quickly as if the king's fastest courier had been sent to her less than half an hour after it happened. Conte-Nouvelles had also known that the police were looking for Julie and that there was a good chance her pregnancy was about to end.

"She told me you were probably going to have your baby very soon, because of the way that Venetian girl hit and kicked you," said Thomine. "I was sure you'd come here, because of the secret closet."

"How were you able to get out of the poorhouse?"

"If you give the gatekeeper or his wife a piece of cheap lace, they'll do anything you want."

Thomine also said the tanners had seen her passing by, but that she had taken the precaution of telling them she had come to get some clothes she had left in Mathieu's room, and would spend the night there.

She set about making a fire. Soon the room was lighted by high flames, water was singing in the pot, and the baby, wrapped in a blanket, was lying in front of the fire. It was soothing for Julie to watch her mother bustling around the small room where she had once lived, and to drink tea made from a little bag of herbs she had taken from under her skirt. Thomine was sorry she couldn't make some of the chicken broth that was so good for bringing back the strength of a woman who had just given birth.

There was a silence, broken by Julie: "A baby girl . . . Another one who will work with a needle all her life and starve anyway. We'll take her to the orphanage tomorrow."

"Children die like flies in the orphanage of the poorhouse, from consumption. And the ones who don't die have scabies."

"We'll take her there anyway."

"She was born with a caul: When I washed her, she still had her skin hood over her head. A child born with a caul shouldn't be put in an orphanage. God is against it."

"Then will you bring her up in the poorhouse? Or will Mathieu bring her up on the road? Or will I bring her up in prison, or take her with me if I'm deported?"

"They haven't got you yet!"

"Remember when Mathilde ran away and went out into the country? Besides the police from Alençon, she also had all kinds of other policemen after her, like a big pack of hunting dogs."

"No one in our family has ever left a child in an orphanage," Thomine said harshly, with a stubborn frown.

"Then tomorrow morning it's going to happen for the first time. If you won't take the baby there, I'll take her myself and run the risk of being arrested. You can understand why I can't keep her. I couldn't even pay for a wet nurse."

Thomine didn't answer. She picked up the baby, holding the needle she had taken from her pocket a short time earlier. After making sure the gag was still firmly in place, she waited, listening. The clock of the Notre-Dame church began striking midnight. With the needle she pricked the baby's thumb at the first stroke, her middle finger at the second, her forefinger at the third, and so on to the tenth. At the eleventh, she put the baby's right hand, with its five little drops of blood, over her right eye, and at the twelfth, her left hand over her left eye, murmuring, "Lord, give her great skill and keen sight. Amen."

The baby's face had turned red from stifled crying. Thomine rocked her in her arms and softly sang her a lullaby. Then, when she was calm, she put her down next to Julie on the big bed and said, "She has a lot of hair!" Now that it's clean and dry, what do you think of it?"

Julie raised herself on one elbow.

"It's exactly like *his* hair," she said. "I'm sure there's no need for me to tell you who the father is. Conte-Nouvelles must know that too."

Thomine poked the fire without replying.

"You know I earn only six sous a day," Julie went on, "and you know it's not enough to keep me from being hungry. Did you think I was going to be given capons and good wine for nothing? And do you want this baby to be like me, begging for a bowl of broth and a slice of bacon?"

She looked intently at her baby, whose wrinkled face was made even more touching by the white cloth gag; then she took the pillow and pressed it down hard over the little head. But only for a few seconds, because Thomine Perdriel shoved her daughter aside, lifted the pillow, and picked up the baby.

How had she known? Had she guessed it? Sensed it? Julie was frightened by the almost supernatural power of this woman with sightless eyes. It was because of her blindness that Thomine had been admitted into the poorhouse. The register described her as "Thomine Perdriel, age 45, lacemaker. Blind. Can still spin, and should be put to work at a spinning wheel."

Holding the baby, she said to Julie, who was hiding her face in her hands, "Give her a chance. She was born with a caul and that's supposed to be a sign of good luck, so who knows . . . And I promise you that tomorrow I'll take her to the poorhouse."

"Do you swear it by the Virgin?"

"Yes, by the Virgin."

The two women fell silent, both with the same thought. Death had come into that room and then left, but its presence hadn't been wiped away. They knew that its shadow still lingered as proof of its anger at having been called for nothing.

As she prayed, Thomine caressed the baby's face, traced the outline of her eyes and nose with her thin fingers, or smoothed her hair.

Twice during the night, when Julie had finally fallen asleep, Thomine took the gag from the baby's mouth and gave her a little water mixed with cider. Then she held her tightly against her chest until dawn. When the bell of Notre-Dame rang matins, she left without waking Julie, carrying the baby wrapped in a piece of cloth she had cut from Mathieu's blanket. And so the tanner and his apprentices saw that she really was taking the bundle of clothes she had forgotten when she went to the poorhouse a few months earlier.

As she was passing the Saint-Blaise church, where she herself had been christened, she decided to name Julie's daughter Gilonne, after her own mother, who had been the best embroideress in Alençon. She had died at the age of twenty, during the great famine of 1634, after starving herself so that her share of food would go to her children. But this new Gilonne had been born with a caul: She would survive famine and hardship. Thomine was sure of it, and her certainty gave her the confidence she needed for what she intended to do.

At the poorhouse, the best beds in the "old women's room" were numbers 15 and 16, on either side of the big stone fireplace. They were the warmest during the three winter months when a fire was kept burning from five in the morning until noon. And when the poorhouse stopped supplying wood, it was permissible to burn wood bought from the gatekeeper.

Those two beds were the recognized, respected, and envied property of four lacemakers, three of whom were blind.

Thomine shared number 15 with her childhood friend Chopine (the Bottle), who had never been known to turn down a glass of cider. Number 16 belonged to Conte-Nouvelles (the News Teller), who always knew everything and a little more, and Marie (often called Marie the Nap), who had been noted ever since her apprenticeship for her readiness to take a nap at any time of day. The older they became, the more Conte-Nouvelles chattered and the more Marie slept. To the other women's amazement, Marie sometimes snored loudly while Conte-Nouvelles talked on and on to her.

Marie was the only one who still had good eyes, and that was a shame, said the three others, because she kept them closed most of the time. But when she was awake, she was entitled to great respect because she was the only one in the old women's room who lived there as a paying guest. She had a contract with the poorhouse guaranteeing that she would be provided with food, clothing, and shelter in exchange for forty livres a year, which she paid from the small nest egg she had amassed by selling lace. She could have had a private room, but she dreaded being alone, knowing she was a prey to the evil spirits that made her sleep as much in the daytime as at night. Those spirits were tough as well as evil, because two exorcisms had failed to rid her of them. She gave Conte-Nouvelles two sous a day to watch over her and recite prayers to ward off any sorcery that might make her condition even worse. A candle burned beside her bed at the beginning of each night; she never discovered that Chopine blew it out soon after it was lighted and, in the morning, took it to the poorhouse baker and traded it for a big chunk of fresh buckwheat bread. Marie always had her share of it, blissfully unaware that she was eating her candle of the night before. She sometimes said that as soon as she was feeling a little livelier she would go and thank the baker for being so kind to old women.

Thomine's plan was to keep Gilonne in the old women's room, rather than putting her among the orphans. (And she wasn't breaking her promise to Julie, because she had said only that she would take the baby to the poorhouse.) This plan depended on Marie's generosity: Only she had the money needed to buy milk from the miserly gatekeeper, who kept four goats in one of the little meadows that belonged to the poorhouse. And, in case of danger, she could pay to silence anyone who might talk.

It was obvious that Gilonne's presence would quickly become known, but nearly all the women would keep it secret because of their hatred for the poorhouse's supervisor, known as Coeur-de-Coing [Quince-Heart] because the quince was considered to be hard and tough, compared with the apple. The possibility of treachery couldn't be ruled out, however. Two or three beds were suspect. Mularde, in number 8, was always sullen and usually kept her mouth shut, but now and then she opened it to say things that shouldn't have been said to someone who wasn't supposed to hear them. In number 12, Baboline, so stupid that she hardly knew whether she was coming or going, was less dangerous for the moment, though she might become a threat at any time, precisely because of her stupidity. Thomine was mainly concerned about Courapied,* the twelve-year-old orphan girl who swept the room, helped the old women to change the straw in their mattresses, performed other little services when she felt like it, and saw everything. Courapied would have to be won over from the start. She wasn't malicious, but she tried to reduce the misery of her own life as much as she could by taking advantage of the misery in the lives of others.

*A nickname given to young servants who did all sorts of work.

Supported by Chopine, Marie sat up straight and listened to her friends persuade her that the little angel who was going to live under bed number 15 for a while could only be beneficial to everyone in the old women's room. And since she, Marie, was the one most in need of added protection, she ought to give two sous a day to buy a pint of milk. She remembered that she already spent three sous a day on firewood for a good eight months of the year, because of the constant dampness in the poorhouse. She also had to count the money it took to buy candles and reward Conte-Nouvelles for praying all night and watching over her while she slept. She didn't regret these expenses, but there were limits to what she could afford. Wide awake for once, she said firmly that she would give only one sou a day for milk. Thomine and Chopine turned their blind eyes toward Conte-Nouvelles. Did she really need so much money for praying? After all, prayers were one of the few things in the world that didn't cost anything.

Conte-Nouvelles frowned, and her pockmarked face took on a thoughtful expression. Then she conceded that she would have to do something for the illegitimate child, since she had been one herself. But she had to point out that babies could be kept from getting impetigo by giving them goat's milk or cow's milk—she favored goat's milk because it made a child more agile—mixed half and half with water. Wasn't that true? The others acknowledged that it was, and Conte-Nouvelles drew her conclusion: One sou a day for milk would be enough.

Now that this had been settled, she went on to a more disquieting matter: Courapied (Run-on-Foot), who was always turning up where you didn't want her to be. And had the others "seen" her inquisitive eyes? It was terrifying to feel them following you everywhere, spying on you. Conte-Nouvelles didn't hesitate to say, almost in a whisper, that there was something diabolical about those eyes. To ward off that danger, she was willing to make a great sacrifice: She would give Courapied ten sous to go and do her spying somewhere else. And if it took twenty, she would give twenty!

It took fifteen, but once the bribe had been paid to her, Courapied proved to be a resourceful conspirator. With a piece of fine cloth she turned a wine bottle into a feeding bottle for the baby, and for that she was rewarded with a spoonful of the honey Marie used for sweetening her herb tea.

Coeur-de-Coing, the supervisor, soon became aware that

something was going on. She sensed a certain excitement that seemed strongest at the far end of the room, near the fireplace, and weakest at the other end, near the door. She had the impression that the old women's speech and gestures were now livelier. She listened to silences and sounds and made surprise visits, but was unable to discover anything out of the ordinary, and finally she decided that her frequent headaches must be to blame for her vague feeling that something had changed. Even so, she questioned Courapied, who opened her innocent eyes wide as if she were trying hard to understand what the supervisor was talking about. Something unusual happening in the old women's room? Oh, she never paid any attention to *them*! They were always rambling on and on, without making any sense.

After Courapied's warning—''Be careful. Coeur-de-Coing is getting suspicious!''—Thomine and her friends took the gag from Gilonne's mouth only when she was asleep, and several times they woke up Marie when the supervisor came in, so she could say she needed the milk she was buying from the gate-keeper because it was helping her to regain her strength. But it was urgent for Mathieu to come back. Even the simple task of burning the oat chaff the baby had soiled during the night was becoming complicated and risky because of Coeur-de-Coing's untimely intrusions. And Baboline had begun talking so loudly in her sleep about her anxiety over hiding the baby—''We'll all be thrown out!''—that they had decided to take turns staying awake by her bed all night, ready to quiet her.

On Sundays, when none of the women worked at the spinning wheels or in the lacemaking shop and Coeur-de-Coing was away visiting her family, Gilonne was the center of attention. Courapied came in to finish off the milk left by the baby, who didn't have a big appetite, or lick the honey that remained on Marie's spoon after she had sweetened her tea.

''Courapied, tell us what she looks like,'' one of the women would say.

''I've told you a hundred times! She's little and pink.''

''What about her eyes?''

''They're blue.''

''Last time you said they were green.''

''That's because the sun was brighter then than it is now.''

''Courapied, would you like to earn a sou?''

''What would I have to do for it?''

"Maybe even a sou and two spoonfuls of honey."

"Tell me what I'd have to do and we'll see."

"Marie will give you a piece of ribbon too. A yard of blue ribbon, a sou, and two spoonfuls of honey."

"All right, but you still haven't told me what you want me to do!"

After a long discussion interrupted now and then by heated exclamations, agreement was reached, with one added condition: Courapied would receive a third spoonful of honey if Coeur-de-Coing hit her with the washing paddle.

The plan was as follows: When Good and Noble Lady de Courteille came to hand out her pieces of cake (stale as always) on Easter Sunday, Courapied would create a little disturbance of some sort and take advantage of it to tear the hem of one of the visitor's petticoats.

"I'll never manage to do it by myself!"

"We'll help you."

"*You'll* help me? You're blind as bats. You couldn't even see a bull charging straight at you!"

The reason for all this had to be explained. Noble Lady de Courteille always wore three or four petticoats under her skirt. Once Courapied had torn one of them, the women would offer to repair it. As they were helping her to take off the damaged petticoat, they would also take off a second one, without letting her know. When the damage had been repaired, only one petticoat would be given back to her. The purpose of the operation was to get cloth to make into diapers for a baby who couldn't go on spending all her time with her bottom bare.

When it had been successfully carried out and a fine white linen petticoat was hidden at the bottom of the baby's basket, Courapied escaped punishment. Coeur-de-Coing suspected her of having been up to something but had no proof of what it might have been. Then that evening Courapied sang as she helped to serve supper, and it was for this slight infraction of the rules that she was punished. A little later, during the victory celebration in front of a fire fed by three sous' worth of Marie's wood, Courapied ate honey, fulminated against the supervisor, and rubbed her ribs, which Coeur-de-Coing had caressed with the washing paddle. Marie was so excited by the exploit that she couldn't sleep, and she gave its heroine her old pink ribbon.

* * *

When Mathieu finally came back and took Gilonne away, the four friends learned from him that there were bruises all over her body. Courapied must have been taking revenge on the gagged baby for the attention and affection given to her by everyone in the room. After all, this was the same Courapied who had been known to trip blind women as they passed! Mathieu made the old women control their indignation: Punishing Courapied would be a mistake, because she would immediately go and denounce them for having Gilonne in the poorhouse. They swallowed their anger. But two months later, when Courapied died of cholera, Thomine, Chopine, Conte-Nouvelles, and Marie knew their prayers had been answered.

Mathieu placed Gilonne in the care of Mistress Bordier, the widow of a packman who had been his friend. Known for her integrity and cleanliness, she had a small farm in the suburb of Montsort, where the air was pure. She raised turkeys and sometimes took in babies to nurse.

To pay her, Mathieu would have to make one or two extra selling trips a year. He was sure he would have the strength to do it. His money problems would have been solved if he had been willing to smuggle lace, but he had seen packmen sent to the galleys for violating royal edicts and he now had too much family responsibility to take such a risk. Julie was counting on him to get her out of France. The police were still looking for her. The state was meting out exemplary punishments to make insubordinate lacemakers realize they had to obey Minister Colbert's orders. Lace would be made and sold as the minister wanted, or not at all.

Mistress Bordier cried out as shrilly as her turkeys when she saw the baby's bruised body. And why that redness around her mouth? Mathieu explained about the gag. Mistress Bordier wept for the misery of the world and rubbed the baby's skin with a salve made of turkey grease perfumed with rose petals from her garden. Compresses of hawthorn-blossom water would relieve the soreness of the poor little mouth that had been gagged so long.

"Oh, Mathieu, you've brought me a lovely flower! You can count on me to take good care of her."

Before bringing Gilonne to Montsort, Mathieu had obeyed her four protectors by taking her to the parish priest of Saint-Blaise, an understanding man who never refused to christen an illegitimate child. He had done it at night and without ringing the bells, of course, but what mattered was that he had done it. It had been harder for Mathieu to obey the second order from the foursome: to take advantage of his visit to the presbytery to bury the baby's umbilical cord, which had just fallen off. It couldn't be either thrown away or kept, but had to be buried at the foot of a pink rosebush to ensure that Gilonne would have a pretty complexion, and the finest roses in Alençon grew in the garden of the presbytery. Mathieu didn't know whether the good priest was aware of such furtive burials or not. Maybe he was resigned to having his garden turned into a cemetery for the umbilical cords of girls born in his parish.

A month later, Julie was able to go to Germany with Mathieu. Her plan was to find work in a shop near Leipzig where they made a kind of needlepoint lace that resembled the lace made in Alençon.

It took them a month to walk there, Mathieu usually did it in two weeks when he was alone, but Julie still hadn't fully recovered from childbirth. Bright sunlight, a meadow glittering with dewdrops, the welcome shade of a tree—these things no longer moved her as they had done before. She looked dully at sights that, in the past, had delighted her whenever she ventured outside the town in which she was used to living. After spending a night in a barn, which would once have made her laugh with happiness, she awoke sobbing and wondering if people in hell were hungry and thirsty. Once she wept all morning as she remembered the terrible day during the famine when she had pounded a fish bone into powder, then pressed it into a ball and sucked on it for hours. And many times during the trip she told Mathieu it was good that their mother had been admitted to the poorhouse, since it meant that in case of famine she would at least have a little something to eat. Mathieu wasn't sure that was true, but he kept his doubts to himself because Julie seemed so weak.

Candelario had come to Alençon to say good-by to Anna-Livia Bardi. With her hand bandaged, her eyes sunken, and her face pale, she was suffering. The alarming news from Venice made her feel even worse. The doge, regarding his lacemakers' stay in France as a crime against the state, had ordered them to return. If they refused, their children and parents would be imprisoned, and they themselves would be hunted down and put to death by his emissaries. Three sons, a husband, and a mother were waiting for Anna-Livia in Venice, and she and her companions were going to leave on the next stagecoach.

Her heart was filled with rage and despair. Her fortune-teller had warned her that things wouldn't go well for her in France. She should have listened to her. Who would support her family, now that she had only one good hand? Certainly not her lazy vegetable-peddler husband! Oh, how she hoped that whore Julie would be caught and deported! She told Candelario to write to her in Venice as soon as it happened. Looking forward to getting that news from him would make her unhappiness a little easier to bear. He promised. And he told her, with just the right amount of sadness in his voice, that he couldn't give her even a little money for her trip, as he would have liked to do, because his master hadn't yet remembered to pay him his wages.

"It's revenge I want, little musician, not your money."

How arrogant she could be when she put her mind to it! Some people had a real talent for being offensive. Candelario knew he would never have given the woman a sou, but he couldn't bear to hear her reject his hypothetical generosity with such contempt in her voice and eyes. If she thought he was going to do anything to help the police catch Julie, she was in for a big surprise!

With sugary solicitude, he asked if he should also give her news of the chevalier in his letter.

"He was the biggest weakness of my life," she murmured. "When I go back to Venice, I'll leave a piece of my heart here."

But Candelario would be glad when the rest of her was gone. She had a good voice but no manners. During the time when she had sporadically shared his master's bed, she had spoken to him only to order him around: "Come here. Do this. Do that." With Julie, it was completely different. She never asked anything of him, and once she had said to him, "Signor Candelario, when you play the flute I feel like running, or singing, or rolling in a meadow, or picking flowers." He remembered the time he had whispered to her, "I just passed by Mistress Verlot's kitchen. There are sublime roasted capons for this evening, heavenly capons, the kind that Saint Peter must eat"; she had laughed, clapped her hands, and said, "Oh, that's wonderful, Signor Candelario! Thank you for telling me!"

If the chevalier had ever really looked at her, he would have been captivated by her charm and discretion. But what did he ever see? Did he at least see women when they were in his bed?

Maybe not, because in spite of the talents that God had given him, he had only a partial view of the world. When he was sitting at the table in the warm kitchen of Grand-Coeur, with its good smells that would have made a dying man get up from his deathbed, he didn't know what he was eating and couldn't tell the difference between a turnip and an egg.

The delightful memory of that table brought Candelario back to a plan he perversely enjoyed thinking about in front of Anna-Livia: to take Julie's baby to Grand-Coeur, where it could have a full belly and bask in the vigorous warmth of the big fireplace. The old lady could hide the baby under her coat and take it with her when she went riding. Her laughter would mingle with the joyful whinnying of Picus III, who loved hunting and the forest as much as his mistress did. Then there would be three of them frolicking under the big trees. Candelario smiled inwardly at this image and said to Anna-Livia gravely, "I give you my word, *bellissima signora*, that you'll know all about that girl's punishment."

A short time later, when he was going all over town in search of Julie, Candelario was more firmly convinced than ever that he had been sent there on a mission and was planting the first seeds of his Orchard of Friendship. Saving little Julie would be the finest tree in that orchard. She must have waited in despair for her handsome chevalier to notice that she was bearing the fruit of their love, asking only for an affectionate smile. And nothing would happen until he, Candelario, arrived!

But where was Julie Perdriel hiding?

Julie died in Saxony before she and Mathieu could reach Leipzig, in a hamlet where he usually stopped to stay with his friends Johann and Anna Hassler, who had once been peddlers but had now given up their wandering life and settled down in a cottage with a thatched roof. Mathieu was exhausted by the time he arrived, because he had been carrying his sister for several hours.

It was cold; summer was late in coming to Germany that year. In spite of warm bricks and hot broth, Julie had shivered for two days and nights. It broke Mathieu's heart to hear her teeth chattering and see her body shaken by the icy shudders of death. When he wasn't rubbing her with straw or hot milk, he held her tightly in his arms. She died there, without even a sigh, just before dawn on the third day, at the hour when she used to go into her lacemaking shop.

They were only a few weeks away from their seventeenth birthday, and Mathieu had planned to give his twin sister the most beautiful loaf of bread she had ever seen, one of the ring-shaped loaves that were made in that part of Germany, fine white bread so fragrant she would have pressed her face against it and smelled it with a kind of piety before eating it.

Since the snow had melted only a few days before, Mathieu looked in vain for a flower to put in Julie's coffin. Instead, he went to town and came back with a loaf of the kind he had intended to give her on her birthday. He crossed her hardworking little hands over it, sure that she was happy.

Only after leaving the humble cemetery in the Saxon countryside where Julie had been laid to rest was Mathieu finally able to weep. For as long as he could remember, he had never allowed himself to shed a single tear while she was alive. He had been convinced from early childhood that she needed to believe he was always strong, so she could draw her own strength from that belief.

Two

$\mathscr{A}$ CONSTANT FLURRY OF FEATHERS, BEAKS, SPURS, CLAWS, and blood-red wattles—such was the frightening world in which Gilonne took her first steps, the world of Mistress Bordier's beloved turkeys. The gabbling flock could pride itself on being descended from the first turkeys ever seen in France: the six pairs given to the Queen of Navarre, Duchess of Angoulême and Alençon, in the previous century. Mistress Bordier's great-grandmother, a childhood friend of the queen's steward, had obtained from him four eggs of those monstrous birds and had them hatched by her hens. Since then, the women of the family had always had their flock of turkeys.

In that world of encircling danger, Gilonne found safety by gripping Mistress Bordier's big, rough hand and hiding her head in the folds of the woman's green fustian skirt. She was then at the center of a terrifying whirlwind, experiencing peril and rescue, fear and joy. Sometimes, in a rash moment, she felt capable of confronting that maelstrom of feathers alone. At such times she would again be saved by Mistress Bordier, shouting and gesticulating, and using her stick not only to drive away the turkeys but also to hit Gilonne on the legs with the strength born of her fright.

"Are you trying to get yourself blinded, you little fool? I've told you a hundred times that they attack children in the face! They have a grudge against us for putting out their eyes when we start to fatten them.''

Except for Thursday, market day in Alençon, Mistress Bordier nearly always stayed at home. Since the great famine of 1662, when a starving mob had battered and bruised her and eaten her flock nearly raw, she had been reluctant to leave her farm.

The world came to her. No one in Montsort was more respected than the buxom Méline Bordier. Her customers appreciated her honesty as well as the quality of her turkeys. Mistress Verlot would sometimes say to her apprentice cook at the Moor's Inn, ''I want you to roast four Bordiers today.'' And during a blissful digestion the Intendant of Alençon had once remarked that if King Henry IV had known Mistress Bordier he would have ennobled her and given her a coat of arms bearing the image of a turkey.*

Being at the pinnacle of glory didn't make Mistress Bordier's round head swell beneath her white hat, nor did it slow her nimble fingers. ''A minute saved here and another one put to good use there,'' she would sometimes say, ''and before the year is over you'll have a yard of lace.'' And in fact she usually had a needle in her hand whenever she wasn't in the middle of her flock.

Because she was lively and a good storyteller, every evening there were people who came to do needlework with her in her big kitchen. The first two were Céronne, the priest's servant, and Jérémie, the young assistant churchwarden. Jérémie had been born into a Protestant family. When his parents were sentenced to deportation, he was taken away from them and put in an orphanage, and then, at the age of twelve, he was placed in the care of the parish priest of Montsort. Since he had a weak constitution, he had been taught to make lace in the orphanage, and now, as soon as he had finished his day's work at the church, he took his needle and thread and joined Céronne. She liked him, and to build up his strength she gave him hot spiced cider sweetened with honey and enriched with brandy. She also for-

*An illusion to an Alençon legend that when the king stayed overnight in the town, a commoner supplied a plump turkey for his supper, then asked to be rewarded by ennoblement and the right to have a turkey in his coat of arms.

tified herself with it, and as a result they were both in a buoyant
mood by the time they came to Mistress Bordier's kitchen.

Three or four other neighbors also came often, perhaps to
save on firewood and candles, but more for the pleasure of conversation. A former public writer, whose eyes had become so
bad that he could no longer write or make lace, did his spinning
and commented on the almanac, the *Almanach du Grand Com-
post des Bergers*.* which he had been able to read earlier, in
bright sunlight. Or rather he had misread it, said Mistress Bordier, who contradicted him because it amused her to see his
anger.

To keep their tongues from overheating, the company cooled
themselves in summer with milk flavored with honey and cinnamon, and in winter with red-currant syrup diluted in water.
But that didn't prevent conflict. The greatest battle was fought
over the interpretation of Gilonne's horoscope as revealed by the
almanac. Would Gilonne foment a revolution in Alençon, or
would she be the victim of one? Would hearts fall as she passed,
like apple-blossom petals in the wind, or would her own heart
be wounded by the treachery and callousness of men? Only one
thing was sure: Her life would be completely out of the ordinary.

Jérémie, who spoke little in public because his persecuted
childhood had left him with a fear of words, ventured to remark
that you didn't need a horoscope to know that this pretty little
bud would blossom into a young woman with a bright future.

In that universe of feathers, needles, and thread, Gilonne was
happy. She had been welcomed into it as a gift from God and,
to her, everything in it was sweet as honey and tender as a
roasted turkey breast. Until she realized that the delicate meat
she savored two Sundays a month was the flesh of the birds that
had become her friends. Then, as a kind of silent protest, she
refused to eat any meat. Mama Bordier craftily hid what she
called the supreme food in Gilonne's porridge or vegetables.
Gilonne was first taken in by the deception, then discovered and
accepted it.

When Mistress Bordier told the public writer, he sighed and
said philosophically, "The girl is really entering into life now:
She's bowed her head." Mistress Bordier didn't like to think of
her little Gilonne as being already vanquished by life. She called

---

*A kind of yearly newspaper that was sold in the French countryside by
peddlers.

her neighbor a wretched fool, and that Sunday she didn't send him the turkey giblets with which he liked to make an invigorating soup.

The Bordier house was next to the presbytery, home of little Father Dutilleux, who, while he had a stick for punishing lazy pupils, also had a cookie in his pocket for rewarding good ones. The cookie was seldom eaten in its original form because more often than not he inadvertently sat on it and crushed it, but the rewarded pupil could put the crumbs in the palm of his hand and lap them up. In the presbytery also lived Jérémie, who told Gilonne stories that he warned she mustn't repeat to anyone if she didn't want to be burned at the stake; and old Céronne, who wove flowers from the garden into collars and crowns and would give her one in exchange for threading needles and winding thread into skeins; and Martagon, the dog, who liked to lie down in the lilies and who became so torpid from their fragrance that he had to be revived by having cold water thrown on him.

The garden was haunted by the ghost of an old priest who hadn't been what he should have been during his lifetime. He was paid to say masses but didn't say them, and that was no way for a priest to act. Father Dutilleux would never have done such a thing.

"Don't look out the window," Mama Bordier told Gilonne when they heard the sound of weeping in the garden. "You mustn't let your eyes meet a ghost's: You'll make his punishment last longer, and it's bad for you too. You know Guillemette, the baker's daughter on the Rue du Jeudi. She's been cross-eyed ever since she saw Marie Anson.* That poor ghost out there needs to say masses to redeem himself, and he's been looking for the key to the church for years and years. Father Dutilleux keeps it hanging on a nail in the kitchen—like the other priests before him—and of course the ghost can't go there. That's why he weeps and moans. As a priest, he was closer to God than most of us are, so he was a real fool for not living in a way that would have let him spend eternity doing something better than wandering around a garden!"

Gilonne was nearly four when, in April, she was given the responsibility of watching over the setting turkey hens, to keep them from starving on the sacred throne of their eggs. Austere

*A ghost in the castle of the Dukes of Alençon.

queens with cold, stern eyes, they yielded to neither temptations nor entreaties. Every year the oldest one was in danger of dying of hunger. Her beauty and her heroic behavior during the famine of 1662 had made her the favorite of that kingdom. She was so majestic, and such a credit to the benefactress of her ancestors from America, that she had been named Marguerite in memory of the Duchess of Alençon. But Mistress Bordier preferred not to have that widely known. It was unwise to praise Marguerite of Navarre and Alençon in that time of religious intolerance. Everyone knew she had not only encouraged turkey breeding but had also protected the Protestants.

Marguerite, with her beautiful reddish-brown plumage, was the empress of some two hundred turkeys, and she was the hardest to move from her nest while she was setting. She refused to lower her beak toward even the most delectable food. If she was picked up and carried away from her nest, she ran back to it without so much as a glance at the food to which she had been taken.

Mistress Bordier was convinced that there were mysterious bonds between children and animals. "See if you can make her eat," she said to Gilonne. "The poor old bird is already so thin that you can pick her up by yourself."

It was then that Gilonne created her first song; she sang in her pure voice: "Eat, eat and drink, Marguerite, because it's good to eat and drink. God will be so pleased if you eat!"

And the intractable turkey began eating the grain Gilonne held out to her in her cupped hands.

"If you could only have heard her!" Mama Bordier said to Mathieu when he came to visit a few days later. "It made tears come to my eyes!"

From then on, Gilonne and Marguerite were close friends. The king's naturalists would have been interested to know that as soon as she saw Gilonne coming, Marguerite—whose eyes were so sharp she was always the first to see a hawk soaring above her chicks—would run to her and leap into her outstretched arms. After Marguerite's eggs had hatched and her weight had returned to normal, Gilonne would fall to the ground laughing when she met her charge.

Gilonne was then assigned to watch over the flock in the field. She knew she had to be on her guard against poisonous foxglove, whose tubular purple flowers were so tempting to turkeys, but Marguerite managed to eat one before Gilonne could stop her.

For several days Marguerite staggered as much as old Céronne did after drinking too much spiced cider laced with brandy, then she sank into a torpor and wasted away until she was nothing but feathers. One morning she was found dead.

Gilonne clung to her body in such despair that Mama Bordier, not wanting to separate her from her friend too soon, decided to put off the burial until the next day. In a corner of the kitchen where Marguerite had been allowed to warm her frozen carcass during her illness, Gilonne spent the night lying beside her. No remonstrance or plea from Mama Bordier could make her go to their bedroom.

In the morning, Mama Bordier found Gilonne sleeping on the floor while Marguerite pecked briskly at crumbs that had fallen around the table.

"I knew she couldn't die," Gilonne said when she awoke.

"Do you realize she was dead for a day and a night?" said Mama Bordier. "And now she's come back from heaven! Maybe she saw God. Yes, I'm sure of it. *She saw God!*"

Marguerite had already survived a famine, and now she had been to heaven and come back. After that, who would dare to choose her for the big slaughter in March, or the one in December? Maybe she would never die!

A steady stream of visitors began coming to Mistress Bordier's house to hear about the resurrection.

"You can take my word for it," she told them. "The poor turkey was really dead, cold and stiff, like a frozen piece of wood."

What had happened could only have been the result of prayer. Which prayers had Gilonne said? Old Céronne reported that she had heard her appeal to the Virgin Mary, and Jérémie confirmed this. Gilonne remembered only that she had fallen asleep, but she said nothing; it would have been hard for her to make herself heard when everyone was talking so much.

Mistress Bordier told her visitors mainly about the turkey's brave attitude during the famine. Jérémie, still wary and cautious, had advised her not to say very much about Marguerite's visit to God: Members of the Compagnie du Saint-Sacrement always kept their eyes and ears open, and they wouldn't appreciate that story. Or maybe they wouldn't be able to recognize its beauty, he added when he saw the incensed look she gave him. But once she had thought it over, Mistress Bordier agreed with him.

"Remember how intelligent that turkey was during the famine," she said to her visitors. "She understood that she had to stay hidden in my bedroom, without making a sound, so that the poor people who were roaming all over the countryside, shouting and weeping from hunger, wouldn't find her."

And, only to those she trusted, she added, "I wonder if she didn't see God as a reward for all that."

Eating a foxglove flower—was that all it took to see God? Gilonne ate one. Or rather half of one, since it tasted so bad. She didn't see how Marguerite could like that taste. Did God live farther away than Germany and Russia, those countries where Uncle Mathieu sometimes went? And what if, on her way up to heaven, she were to be attacked by those hawks that tried to eat little turkeys?

The skill of the doctor brought by Mathieu; the knowledge of medicinal herbs possessed by Thomine, Marie, Chopine, and Conte-Nouvelles; Father Dutilleux's prayers—nothing seemed to have any effect. Little Gilonne would indeed see God, but she would stay with Him.

When Mathieu told his employer, Monsieur Mortimer Morel d'Arthus, that he couldn't leave to deliver his lace because his niece was dying, the lace manufacturer recommended giving her coffee, which was said to cure some cases of poisoning. Mathieu had heard of coffee, but where could he find it in Alençon? Monsieur Morel d'Arthus immediately gave him a little bag of it that had been brought to him from Rouen the day before.

No one could ever say for sure whether that black liquid was effective, but it seemed to have been, since Gilonne survived. Mistress Bordier killed her second most beautiful turkey and had it taken to the Morel d'Arthus mansion on the Rue du Château.

As for Jérémie, he knew what had saved his little friend: It was the sacrifice of his Protestant Bible. He had dug it up from its hiding place under the lilies in Father Dutilleux's garden and secretly burned it during a moonless night. He felt guilty for having told her beautiful stories from the Bible to entertain her, because he was sure they had given her the foolish idea of going to see God. He had nothing more precious to sacrifice than that book. It had come to him from his great-grandfather and had cost his family blood and tears. He offered his treasure to save Gilonne's young life.

When the public writer said he was going to put the edifying story of Gilonne's resurrection into an article and send it to the almanac, Mistress Bordier nearly deprived him again of the turkey giblets he liked so much. She accused him of wanting to make himself interesting by using joys and sorrows that didn't belong to him.

Having heard the news from her apprentice cook, Mistress Verlot sent a few bottles of her famous pear cider to Mistress Bordier for her little convalescent, whose family origin would have stirred up strong emotion if she had known it.

Gilonne was sick for a long time. And sad at not having seen God. Only Marguerite had the prestige of having been to heaven and back. Someday she would tell what she had seen. Gilonne knew that all animals talked on Christmas night. She would just have to wait until then.

One morning Mistress Bordier with great seriousness placed a needle in Gilonne's hand. In a year she would have to begin her apprenticeship in Alençon—Mama Bordier's heart bled at this thought—and there was no time to lose.

On Sundays when Mathieu took his niece to the poorhouse to see her grandmother, the chorus of old women, including Marie, who had the others wake her up so she could enjoy the child's visit, kept asking, "How's she doing with her needle?" She was doing very well. She had a talent for needlework. Thomine remembered having seen to that during the twelve strokes of the first midnight after her birth. And Mathieu said that Mistress Bordier had asked him to tell them that Gilonne already knew how to do the buttonhole stitch.

"I knew it too, at her age."

"You knew the buttonhole stitch, Marie? No, when you weren't sleeping, you *sold* lace, you didn't *make* it, Marie the Rich!"

"Maybe so, but I still knew the buttonhole stitch! And I wish you'd all stop complaining, day after day, about me selling lace while you were making it. Some people have to make it and others have to sell it."

"But the ones who sell it get rich!"

"I don't hear any complaints when I give you some of my money!"

Marie liked Mathieu, because sooner or later he always intervened and put an end to these quarrels.

"Mathieu," she said to him one day, "I'm going to leave

everything to you: my little house on the Rue aux Sieurs, and my clothes, and my cross, and—"

"Don't be too hopeful, my boy. She's already given her fortune to each one of us at least a dozen times!"

"Help me, Mathieu! They're trying to take everything I've got!"

The others shouted angrily, but Mathieu silenced them by saying they were frightening Gilonne and she wouldn't want to come back any more if they didn't stop.

Gilonne, however, liked these visits to the poorhouse. The old women told her about her life there when she was a baby, and how the odious Courapied had mistreated her. With a mixture of horror and delight, she heard that her feet and hands had been twisted, that her hair had been pulled out, that she had been pricked with big needles all over her body. Her heart pounded as she waited for the story of her tormentor's punishment. "Then God punished her, Gilonne, without mercy. God always punishes. Don't forget that." She was shown bed number 15, under which she had been hidden. Once, knowing it would make them laugh, she said, "I remember. And it smelled of cider, because Chopine used to sleep with a bottle too."

But always the conversation came back to needles and thread. Did she really like learning to make lace? It was Thomine who asked the question, taking Gilonne's hands, which were already marked by needle pricks.

"What difference does it make whether she likes it or not?" Conte-Nouvelles said irritably. "Did *you* like it?"

Yes, Thomine had liked making lace all through the lifetime of her eyes. Her mother had liked it too, and had died with a needle in her hand. Thomine's only regret was that she couldn't die that way too.

"Then you like what took away your eyes?"

"You get too upset over your eyes," said Marie. "Everybody closes them to go to sleep, and since sleep is the best part of life . . ."

They laughed. But Thomine was worried. Had Gilonne recovered enough from her sickness to begin her apprenticeship? "Marie, since you're lucky enough to still have your eyes, even though you don't do much with them, open them wide for once and tell me if Gilonne has any color in her cheeks, or if she's still as pale as last time."

"I swear her cheeks are red as apples. Come here, Gilonne, and let me give you a spoonful of honey. It's good for you."

"If she looks the way you say she does, she doesn't need your honey."

Gilonne would have been glad to do without that customary treat. Being used to Mama Bordier's cleanliness, she was disgusted by the sticky wooden spoon that Marie cleaned only by licking it. But she didn't dare to refuse, and she thanked Marie with a smile that the old woman said was like divine balm to her.

"Oh, if the rest of you could only see it!"

Gilonne resented Marie's saying that to her three blind friends. And her heart was heavy when, after kissing her, her grandmother held her head between her hands—hands so thin they made her think of a turkey's feet—and asked, "You'll come back won't you? When?"

"Very soon," replied Gilonne.

At that moment she wished she could be alone with Thomine. She would sit on her lap and sing the song she had made up for her one day in Father Dutilleux's garden. She would tell her that when a cornflower was near the end of its life it turned the color of her eyes, and that it was pretty. She was sure this would please her grandmother, who loved flowers so much.

One day, after leaving the poorhouse, Gilonne asked, "Uncle Mathieu, why doesn't my grandmother live with me in Mama Bordier's house?"

"What? Talk louder. What did you say?"

"Nothing."

Mathieu had already noticed that she would almost never repeat a question she had asked, especially if it concerned something that meant a great deal to her.

On Sundays after they visited the poorhouse, Mathieu didn't take her directly back to Montsort. Since her sickness, walking there had been too tiring for her, so she spent the night in Mathieu's room in the tanner's house. He had put a little straw mattress in one corner for her and hung a curtain from the ceiling to the floor to cut off the candlelight when he stayed up late to work. She liked being there and hearing him tell about his travels, about the roads and paths, the cold air and the warm sunshine, the mysterious cities, and all the beautiful things he saw. She didn't often question him, but he knew when she wanted him to talk about his journeys. It was when she was lying quietly on her mattress—he had never known her to misbehave—behind the curtain, eating the apple that was her supper. He sat at his table with his candle in front of him, carving a walking staff or resoling his shoes. Sensing that she was waiting for one of his stories, he would ask, "Do you want me to tell you about my last trip to Russia?"

She had recently begun answering this kind of question with "Yes, Marguerite would like that."

He had realized that he intimidated her and that she reassured herself by hiding behind her friend the turkey. If he talked for a long time without hearing anything from the other side of the curtain, he would ask, "Are you listening?"

"Yes, we're listening. Marguerite is interested."

This game had begun when he told her that, to avoid losing time while he was on the road, he ate his bread and apple, or his bread and cheese, as he walked, without ever stopping except to drink water from a spring or a bowl of milk in a cow shed. She had made no comment, but the following Sunday she had said, "Marguerite and I tried eating while we walked. Marguerite doesn't like it."

Marguerite wanted Mathieu to explain the "big Justine" and the "little Justine" she had heard about. He told Gilonne that his father, Juste Perdriel, also a lace carrier, had made two garments—with the help of his wife, Thomine—designed to let him hide his merchandise instead of carrying it in a bundle on his back. With this invention he had complete freedom of movement, could use his staff more effectively, and was harder to recognize as a packman when he was on the road. The "big Justine," worn in winter, was long and thick and had sleeves. The "little Justine," worn in summer, was short, light, and sleeveless. They had both proved their worth, and Mathieu never traveled without one of them. The strong points of his father's invention were its clever arrangement of secret pockets and its use of German waxed cloth, ventilated with holes in just the right places, to protect the lace he carried from sweat and rain. Marguerite would have been surprised to see Mathieu leaving on one of his expeditions with his back straight, not bent beneath a pack, with his staff in one hand and his other hand free. Free to take out a discreet but cruel little dagger.

"And be sure to tell your Marguerite that all this has to be kept secret. She mustn't talk about it to anyone, not even her best turkey friend. There are many bad people who would like to know the secrets of Juste and Mathieu, and if they knew them, they'd wait for me at night, at a bend in the road. If you and Marguerite behave yourselves, one of these days I'll tell you about the blessed nail from Santiago de Compostela that my father left to me. It was in one of Saint James's sandals. I never go off on a trip without it. And if you both learn to make lace well—I'm sure Marguerite will learn as much from your apprenticeship as you do—I'll tell you about the 'clever shoes' I invented.''

Mathieu also had other wonders to reveal, but first he had to make sure that Marguerite could keep a secret. He couldn't go on talking to her through Gilonne without knowing if he could count on her discretion. As soon as he was sure he could trust her, he would tell the two of them about the most mysterious strokes that could be used in fighting with a staff: the ''dog-fooler,'' the ''false upright,'' and the terrible ''bracelet'' that had already saved his life several times.

Mama Bordier told Gilonne that her uncle Mathieu was the most famous packman in the region, and maybe even in France. He was the only one who could go from Alençon to Paris in less than forty-eight hours, and from Alençon to Leipzig in two weeks. And no one else had ever walked to Moscow in two months, as he had done. But there were wicked people in the world, and if it hadn't been for the secret strokes of his staff, he would never have come back in one piece from so far away.

Mathieu had a whole collection of staffs. He was always taking care of them: smoothing them, carving them, changing their studs. He rubbed them with beeswax, milk, and a certain herb whose properties were known only to him. He rubbed and rubbed them, so long that Gilonne sometimes fell asleep watching him. She was annoyed with herself when she did that. She wanted to see everything. How many staffs did he have? Maybe as many as the fingers on both her hands. He kept them hidden in his secret closet. They were made of ash, oak, applewood, and other, unknown woods. He said that the King of Beggars, the Great Coesre, had a staff like his, made of applewood, with a good little dagger in one end. But daggers were seldom used; secret strokes with a staff were preferable. He promised that one day she, Gilonne Perdriel, would know how to fight with a staff, like the famous Mathieu Perdriel. Why shouldn't women be able to defend themselves against bandits on the roads? She already had a little ash staff, made to her size, and she briskly tapped the road with it when they walked together from Montsort to Alençon.

Marguerite also knew why Gilonne tried not to go to sleep too early when she spent the night in the tanner's house. It was because the best part came after Uncle Mathieu had finished rubbing and polishing his weapons and tried them out. Then, on the curtain, she saw the big shadow of the most famous packman in France practicing strokes with his staff. It was more wonderful than Saint Michael and his dragon in the church. It was immense and terrible, and it killed all the bad people in the world. On Christmas night, when Marguerite could really talk, Gilonne would have to ask her if Uncle Mathieu was partly an angel. Marguerite had seen angels, so she would know. Mama Bordier had said that with his blond, curly hair and his gentle blue eyes he looked like an angel. And if Gilonne half closed her eyes while he was whirling his staff above his head, she saw him with big wings on his back.

Before going to sleep himself, Mathieu always pushed back the curtain to look at the sleeping child. He saw nothing in her that reminded him of his twin sister, and yet, when he talked to her, he was sometimes surprised to find himself feeling that he was talking to the little Julie of his childhood. Gilonne looked like her father: the same long blue-green eyes fringed with dark lashes that so strongly contrasted with the mingled gold and silver in the shimmering cascades of her hair.

Mathieu knew everything about Julie's sad adventure but didn't judge her. He only wondered what would become of her child, and sometimes, as he walked along a road in solitude, hearing nothing but the sound of his hobnailed shoes, he worried about the future.

Where would Gilonne serve her apprenticeship, since it had been decided she would learn the trade of her mother, grandmother, and great-grandmother?

Mathieu went to discuss the question with Thomine and her three friends. He had to describe the situation to them in all its details because they didn't know much about what had happened in the five years since they had begun living at the king's expense. The walls of the poorhouse, which plunged into the Sarthe, let a great deal of humidity come through, but kept out most news of the town. Conte-Nouvelles reported what she heard from newcomers, in the men's section as well as the women's, but there were far too many personal interpretations in what she said.

The situation that Mathieu tried to describe was as follows. Since 1665, whether they liked it or not, the edicts of the king and his minister Colbert—posted at crossroads, announced in the streets and public squares, read in the churches—had taken away nearly all freedom to work on the kind of lace they knew how to make. They knew that, didn't they? Yes, they knew it, but they thought that if you were clever enough, you could still . . . No. The police were ever vigilant. They kept coming to ask questions, look at everything, and stick their noses everywhere, and a bad report from them meant punishment by being fined, imprisoned, deported, or sent to the galleys.

Mathieu was moved by the three pairs of sightless eyes turned toward him. He asked Marie, who still had her sight, if she realized that even if she could stay awake long enough to make the kind of lace she had made in the past, she wouldn't be allowed to make it now. As for *point de France*, the beautiful but difficult new lace imposed by the king, she had hardly learned the first of its nine elements.

"She never even knew how to make *bisette*,* Mathieu. She sold lace, that's all."

"What do you mean, I didn't know how to make *bisette*? What about my Alençon lace? Let's hear you dare to say I didn't know how to make Alençon lace!"

Mathieu calmed and reconciled them, as he was used to doing. He waited awhile, then suggested that they all have a drink from the jug of cider he had brought.

When their throats and minds had been cooled, he went on. "Listen to me and be sensible. We have to see things as they are." He leaned toward them and lowered his voice. "For example, you'll never change your Coeur-de-Coing into a kind and gentle woman. It's the same with the king's edicts: Nothing can change them. And they're terrible. They're . . . they're like angry, ferocious animals that stand watching you with their fangs bared. If you make one false move, they'll jump at you and tear you to pieces. That's how things are in Alençon. You don't want us to throw Gilonne to those animals, do you?"

Frightened, the four old women began mumbling prayers. Then Thomine asked quietly, "Well, son, what shall we do?"

*The cheapest kind of lace at the time.

Mathieu answered that they had to take the only road that would lead them safely past the ferocious animals: the road of legality. (He was proud of this figure of speech.) And what was legality in Alençon, now that the terrible edicts had been in effect for the last five years? It was Monsieur Colbert's Royal Manufactory and the few lacemaking shops run by the contractors he had chosen.

"Are you saying, Mathieu," asked Thomine, "that you want to send little Gilonne to those wolves who don't let poor people work? Are you trying to tell us that doing what we've always done, only doing it in secret now, is worse than smuggling Venetian lace into France? I know smuggling is a crime, but I can't believe it's also a crime to make our lace! Why should they want to stop lacemakers who still have their eyes from doing the kind of work they've done all their lives?"

Mathieu stood up, leaned against the big fireplace, and said slowly, stressing each word, "Neither you nor Gilonne can make the lace that used to be made here. No other lace but *point de France* is now allowed to be sold or worn in France. Since very few people knew how to make it at the time the edicts took effect, the king and Monsieur Colbert created the Royal Manufactories, where the lace is made and lacemakers are trained. His Majesty knows you may want to decorate your clothes with a little lace, so he's graciously decided to let you make *point de Paris* for your own personal use, provided you don't sell any of it. You know better than I do what kind of lace that is."

"I can tell you what it's not. It's not fine lace."

"You said it, Mother, I didn't. One thing is so sure that there's no use trying to argue about it: Lacemakers aren't free to work as they please now. They have to do what the king wants, or do nothing."

"Then they must be as miserable as a fish in a bird's nest," said Chopine, after downing the last drop of cider from the jug.

"Mathieu, don't you think the sheep are going to dance faster than the shepherd?" asked Conte-Nouvelles.

"Maybe some of them will, but if they do, they'll end up being deported."

"Poor people like us used to be able to earn a few sous making the old Alençon lace," said Thomine. "Are you saying that because of the new law, that edict from the king, they can't do it anymore?"

"That's exactly what I'm saying, Mother. But you must know what's happening here, in the workroom of the poorhouse."

"Here, they have the young ones mending and the old ones spinning. There's talk about setting up a lacemaking shop, but it seems there still aren't enough mistress-lacemakers in town to send one of them here. In the sickrooms—we're hardly ever allowed to go there—women who are only partly disabled make lace in their beds, and a *leveuse** comes by to pick it up. Maybe it's the new kind of lace you were talking about. I'll try to find out about it from the new Courapied. But this one doesn't do much talking. We've got the bad luck to have a Courapied who's not interested in anything except sweeping and praying. Her parents were Protestants. She was converted by force, and she's still watched so closely that she's afraid even to say hello to anyone."

"Let's come back to Gilonne."

"Don't be impatient. I've got some old friends who still have their eyes, and I'd like to know how they're doing. There used to be people in the country who made lace for money to pay their taxes, and people in towns who made it for money to buy food. Is it true that nobody can do that anymore?"

"It's been true a long time—for people who haven't learned to make the new lace."

"Then for the first time I'm glad I'm blind, so I don't have to see that!"

The others thought Marie had fallen asleep, but at this point she surprised them by sitting up on her bed and saying, "Hasn't anybody been brave enough to go on making the same kind of lace as before, since so many people still want to buy it?"

"Ah! The lace seller is waking up because she just realized she wouldn't have anything to sell now!"

Mathieu quieted the outcry that followed, then answered Marie. "Many people are still doing what they did before, workers because they have to make a living, manufacturers and merchants because they don't want to go bankrupt. But they're taking a big risk."

Baboline, in bed number 12, had been listening. Although she was thought to be abysmally stupid, she was the only one

---

*An intermediary who bought lace from individual workers and sold it to merchants.

who thought to ask Mathieu, "Since you're still a packman, what do you carry now?"

"That's something I won't tell you."

It was time to end the discussion and decide where Gilonne would serve her apprenticeship. But the old women couldn't help him. They understood nothing about the new town of Alençon, so different from the one they had left when they entered the poorhouse. Conte-Nouvelles sighed and turned toward the fireplace to warm her belly. Marie went back to sleep. Thomine said quietly, "Do whatever you like, son. We don't know enough anymore to help you decide."

"Don't worry, Mother. I'll do what's best," said Mathieu.

He took her thin hands to communicate some of his young, warm, and confident vigor to her.

As he was leaving the poorhouse, he wasn't surprised to find Conte-Nouvelles waiting for him at the front door. She sometimes joined him there when she wanted to talk to him in private.

"Don't think I didn't know how things are nowadays, Mathieu."

He smiled. The old woman was worried about her reputation for being the first to report all the news, good or bad.

"You can be sure I've been keeping up with what's happening as far as lace is concerned!" she went on. "But I didn't want to tell the others too much about it. Their memories keep them warmer than Marie's firewood does. Your mother thinks I don't know, but I feel it every time she takes out the old piece of Alençon lace that she's kept. She runs her hand over it and 'sees' each stitch with her fingertips."

Mathieu handed Conte-Nouvelles the few sous he could spare and asked her to give it to Courapied to buy the next almanac and read it to them. Learning about life on the outside was one of the pleasures his mother still had left.

Mistress Bordier advised Mathieu against having Gilonne serve her apprenticeship at the Royal Manufactory in Alençon. The Benedictine nuns who were her neighbors were also her friends. Every Christmas she brought them a beautiful plucked and trussed turkey laid on a white cloth in one of the bark baskets woven by the wives of the wooden-shoe makers in the Perseigne forest. Gifts like that, given wholeheartedly, weren't intended to make people indebted to you, of course, but there was no denying that they counted in your favor when you needed help.

Wasn't that true? Mathieu agreed that it was, and smiled as he went on listening.

"The nuns have told me, not just once but at least a dozen times, that they'd take Gilonne into their workrooms whenever I wanted . . . I mean whenever *you* wanted. And believe me, nobody will lose anything by teaching her, because she already has gold in her fingers."

Mathieu sighed; again he would have to explain. He told Mistress Bordier that the Benedictine nuns weren't approved by the Royal Manufactory. They secretly, and illegally, made the old Alençon lace that the king had forbidden. Gilonne had to learn to make *point de France*, in safety.

"Listen, Mathieu," Mistress Bordier said with her hands on her hips, "that isn't even the worst part of it. The worst part is that she's only five years old. Yes, I know, that's the age when all girls start to work, and I started then too, but she . . . How can I tell you? She's not like us, she's . . . an angel. And who would she be working with at the Royal Manufactory? Loose women, whores! It's not the best women in Alençon who are willing to obey the king! The recruiters took what they could get, and sometimes it wasn't very pretty. How do you know the women there wouldn't mistreat Gilonne, or teach her devilish things? Are you listening to me or are you daydreaming?"

Mathieu wasn't daydreaming. He was thinking of the warm trust he felt in Gilonne's little hand when they walked together from Montsort to Alençon or along the streets of the town. The trust of a child who believed he knew everything and would always make the best decision. . . .

"Are you trying to tell me," Mistress Bordier continued, "that the king, the eldest son of our Church, will attack servants of God like my friends the Benedictine nuns? They belong more to heaven than to earth. Who would ever dare to go into their convent to find out what's happening there?"

Mathieu granted that no policeman had ever searched a convent. But he still didn't like the thought of placing Gilonne in such a situation. People in Alençon and its environs, and probably all over France, were working illegally so that they could go on earning a living, and he was doing the same when he transported the lace they made. They had to take risks, because otherwise they couldn't survive. They were at war and had to defend themselves. But he didn't want Gilonne to live in the midst of lying and cheating. Even so, he was shaken by Mistress Bordier's arguments.

"Nuns must not be the best teachers of how to make lace," he said, "because, to them, wearing it is sinful vanity and self-indulgence."

"You know the Church accepts lacemaking! Father Dutilleux is a shrewd man, and he says, 'If making lace is the only way you can keep from starving, make it and let the people who wear it bear the weight of their sins and the need to repent of them.' "

The next day the old public writer, temporarily restored to Mistress Bordier's good graces, played a part in deciding the course of Gilonne's life. Following instructions from Mistress Bordier, he told Mathieu that he had received shocking information about the state of morality in the Royal Manufactories. There had been revealing articles on the subject in the almanac. He gave details and offered to lend Mathieu a pile of almanacs— greasy and torn because he rented them out at the price of one sou per week—that would confirm what he said.

With a little bitterness in his voice, Mathieu told Mistress Bordier that she had won. Gilonne would spend a year with the Benedictine nuns in the Montsort convent. Then, having almost reached the age of reason, she would go to the Royal Manufactory in Alençon.

Mistress Bordier wept for joy—but in secret, after Mathieu had left. She was especially generous in feeding her turkeys that day.

Gilonne would need new clothes for her stay with the nuns. Mistress Bordier told her circle of regular visitors about it and put them to work. After all the money she had spent warming them in winter and cooling them in summer, it was only fair that they should help to make clothes for Gilonne! They were perfectly willing—even flattered to be asked. Mathieu brought some cloth back from a trip to Germany, and Jérémie, the young ex-Protestant, offered to decorate some of the clothes with *point de Paris*. In this way he was able to show not only that he obeyed his Catholic king but also that it was false to accuse Protestants of being so straitlaced that they didn't like any kind of frills.

An old lacemaker who belonged to the little group and was a skilled seamstress made a dress of green fustian bunched up over a red woolen petticoat. Its hem and bodice were decorated with pink Genoese velvet that was a gift from Céronne, Father

Dutilleux's servant, who had saved pieces of it left over from re-
covering the two ceremonial prayer stools, donated by the lord
of the parish, that were used for weddings. It was quite attractive, and so was the white apron that kept it clean and could also
be bunched up, like the skirt, but on the opposite side. Before
work on the headdress began, Mathieu was asked if the edicts
allowed the use of old lace that was among a family's heirlooms.
He answered that the king, in his clemency, did allow it, provided the use was not excessive and none of the lace was sold.
So Gilonne's batiste bonnet was trimmed with Valenciennes lace
that Mistress Bordier's husband had given her in the days when
he was a peddler.

The little girl's cheeks turned pink with joy when she saw the
pair of German wooden shoes her uncle brought her from Leipzig one day. They were made no better than the ones that were
carved in the Perseigne forest, but their maker in faraway Germany had had the idea of painting them red, bordering them
with cheerful white festoons, and putting two cornflowers, with
green stems and leaves, on their insteps. No one in Montsort,
and surely not in Alençon either, had shoes like that. Gilonne
hid them under her pillow and slept with them next to her, smiling happily.

Since Mathieu was responsible for her and she hadn't yet
reached the age of reason, they were both made to swear on the
altar of the Virgin that they would never tell anyone what took
place in the workrooms of the convent. The mother superior, a
beautiful lady who smelled good, held Gilonne's hand in her
own, which were as warm and soft as a kitten's belly. The look
in her eyes went through you like a long needle, maybe to kill
whatever was bad in you, but Gilonne's mind was at ease; she
hadn't done anything wrong lately, and she gave her promise
without reserve.

Mathieu had explained the situation to her: The charitable
nuns of Montsort were still helping women in the suburb and
the surrounding countryside to make and sell the old Alençon
lace, and they also taught little girls to make it, since they felt
that the new lace was too hard for most children. And so—

At this point, Gilonne interrupted him. "Uncle Mathieu, the
king wants us to make very beautiful lace, the kind that French
lords and ladies aren't allowed to buy in Venice. Marguerite
thinks that if we work hard, we can learn to make that new
lace."

Mathieu laughed, then said, ''For now, you'll do as you're told. Later, we'll see. . . . As far as your Marguerite is concerned, I advise you to leave her here tomorrow when we go to the convent. The nuns are used to eating turkeys at Christmas, not hearing them talk about lace.''

In later years, when Gilonne recalled the time she had spent with the Benedictine nuns, she thought first of the great, mysterious silence that had enveloped her as soon as she went into the convent, pressing in on her so powerfully that she felt as if she were smothering. It was in the shade of the halls and rooms, in the sunlight of the gardens and courtyards. Then she gradually began to hear the buzzing of bees among the fragrant carnations, the creaking of the gardening sister's wheelbarrow, and the murmur of the fountain, so soft it might have been the sound of nuns praying in the chapel. And still later the joyous noise of the recreation sister's wooden clapper drove away all the mystery and silence, as the musket shots fired by Léonard, Mama Bordier's neighbor, drove away the cloud of hail that threatened his lettuce.

For Gilonne, life at the convent was like a celebration. She dipped her bread in vegetable soup as smooth as the voice of the reading sister telling Bible stories while the others ate. And the water . . . Did she only dream that it smelled as good as the flowers blooming beside the spring? And the bell that rang for this and that! She heard it laugh as it announced each part of the day, seeming to enjoy repeating how much God loved the Benedictine nuns, since He had given them so much pleasure to dispense.

But when the king's spy suddenly arrived one day, the joyous bell wasn't able to do anything about it, not even to whisper, ''Look out! Look out!''

Of all the places in France that enjoyed the privileges of the Church and knew they were inviolable, none was less prepared for a visit of this kind than the Benedictine convent of Montsort, because the nuns were absorbed in making candied apricots to be sent to their benefactress, the Marquise de Nonant.

When she opened the door for old Françoise, one of the lacemakers accustomed to bringing their work to the convent, which helped to sell it for them in spite of the king's prohibition, the portress had no qualms about also letting in the man Françoise introduced as her cousin, a draper from Paris who wanted to buy some lace from the nuns.

Deciding whether visitors of this kind could be trusted to keep the transaction secret was ordinarily the responsibility of Sister Saint-Ambroise, who was known for her shrewd judgment. But she also had the distinction of being the best maker of jam and candied fruit in the community—''and maybe in the whole district,'' the bishop had once added with a greedy expression. When Françoise's cousin arrived, Sister Saint-Ambroise was standing in the glow of her fire, waiting to make sure that just when her sugar syrup began to bead, it would receive the avalanche of apricots already generously flavored with cinnamon and cloves. Unfortunately, the lay sister given the task of pitting the apricots had thrown away the kernels, not knowing that some of them were to be sliced thin and added just before the last boiling of the fruit.

The four kitchen helpers were frenziedly looking through the poplar-bark baskets used for refuse, trying to find the sixty kernels needed to make the candied apricots come out right when Sister Vincent hurried in to announce breathlessly that two policemen had arrested old Françoise as soon as she left the convent. Her cousin had been seen mounting his horse and serenely trotting away, having done his ignoble work.

Accompanied by the smell of apricots gently simmering in their syrup, panic spread through the convent. Sister Saint-Ambroise wiped her hands, restored calm, and pointed out reasons for hope. First, God would never permit charitable work done for starving people to be censured by ignorant policemen. No one had ever dared to challenge the inviolability of their sanctuary, and it would remain sacred. Like all others of its kind, the bill of sale given to the spy would be useless to a judge, because it listed only innocent merchandise: various cloths of hemp and wool. There would be only a commoner—Sister Saint-Ambroise was from a noble family!—claiming to have bought lace at the convent. Who would believe him without proof?

There was still the great question: What would Françoise answer when she was questioned by the king's intendant? That was where the danger lay. Would she have the wit and strength to say nothing? It was better to assume that she would talk, and be prepared for the consequences, though they wouldn't be serious. Françoise would admit that there was a trade in lace forbidden

by the king. The mother superior would say the opposite, with
God's help, and that would be the end of the matter.

Sister Bathilde, who had been the one who sold the lace to
the spy, now revealed that *he had seen the little girls*. In spite
of the bright color given to her cheeks by the heat of the kitchen,
Sister Saint-Ambroise turned pale. Then she summoned up the
courage that the men of her family had always shown on the
battlefield.

"How many of them did he see?"

"All of them!"

"Did he talk to any of them?"

Sister Bernard, who was in charge of teaching the children
lacemaking and the catechism, went off to ask them about this.
And since they would soon leave the inviolability of the convent
walls and encounter policemen who would then be entitled to
question them, it was urgent to make sure they knew how they
were to answer. Sister Bernard pushed her little flock—like Gilonne driving her turkeys—into a safe, isolated room, far from
the policemen waiting in ominous silence at the gatehouse while
their horses impatiently pawed the ground.

The eight little girls seemed bewildered as they listened to
Sister Bernard.

"God, the bishop, and our mother superior order you to answer like this if anyone asks you what you're doing here: 'We're
learning to make *point de Paris*.' It's safe to say that; people
who can't make *point de France* are allowed to make *point de
Paris*. Then you must say, 'The lace is only for us and our
families. We'll never sell any of it, because we respect His Majesty's orders.' "

Sister Bernard questioned them and corrected their wrong
answers. Nearly all their answers were wrong. She began losing
her temper. The girls cried. Some of them even wet their pants
and called for their mothers. Dark powers had come into that
holy place! Old Françoise and her vile cousin were manifestations of the devil! Sister Bernard knelt, clasped her hands and
told the girls to join her in prayer.

When they had prayed and become calmer, she asked if "that
man" had spoken to any of them. He had spoken to several of
them, she was told, but only Gilonne had answered him.

"What did he ask you?

"What my name was and what I was doing here."

"And what did you say?"

"I said my name was Marguerite d'Indes* and I was learning to make jam."

With joy in her heart, Sister Bernard crossed herself and thanked God for having inspired the child so well. Then a belated thought came to her and she asked, "Why Marguerite d'Indes?"

"That's my friend's name. She's a turkey who went to heaven and came back, and she told me to use her name."

Sister Bernard crossed herself again and had the girls resume their prayers. No doubt about it, the devil had come into the convent! She would have to tell the mother superior without delay.

Meanwhile the portress was keeping watch. The policemen still hadn't left. They knew the little girls were there, and they intended to turn them into witnesses against the nuns as soon as they came out.

The mother superior decided to keep the girls in the convent. A lay sister who knew the countryside like the back of her hand furtively left by way of a secret door and went to notify their families, taking roundabout routes.

Just to be sure, the children were kept in hiding for three days and three nights. They spent delightful hours in an atmosphere of mystery and danger, believing in it just enough to quiver with laughter.

The Intendant of Alençon ordered the police to look for little Marguerite d'Indes, or Dinde, or Linde. She was never found. Rather than having to defend herself, the mother superior was able to accuse her enemies of treachery. The Marquise de Nonant, pleased with her candied apricots, had no difficulty in putting an end to an investigation that she considered totally unjustified.

Mama Bordier, however, wasn't at all pleased. Gilonne had saved the nuns from God only knew what punishment, yet the mother superior had decreed that, in confession, the child must accuse herself of lying! Choking with anger, Mama Bordier confided in the old public writer, who was always there to listen when embittered hearts poured out their secrets in spite of themselves. He swore to say nothing. But a few bits and pieces of the

*This name has the same pronunciation as the French word *dinde*, "turkey"—translator's note

episode reached the big ears of a few religious zealots. It was noted that Gilonne Perdriel, age five, was suspected of practicing witchcraft and having conversations with an animal, believed to be a turkey, that was no doubt a servant of Satan.

The authorities released old Françoise, as they must have promised her cousin they would do. But the Benedictine nuns had been frightened. For a time they stopped helping lacemakers to sell their work and teaching little girls to make lace. Since the community's resources were meager, it was decided to have Sister Saint-Ambroise increase production of her candied fruit, which soon gained a certain renown in Alençon and its environs. Mistress Verlot put it on her menu.

The Intendant of Alençon had to accept reality: He couldn't stop the making of the forbidden, inferior lace that threatened the future by hindering the struggle against Venice. He sadly wrote his conclusions in a letter to Colbert.

Sister Bernard remained convinced that the devil had had a hand in the whole affair. How else could you explain why nuns were persecuted for helping poor people earn enough money to pay their taxes and buy buckwheat? Now and then she dreamed of turkeys. As time passed, she could no longer understand why they pursued her in her sleep.

Mathieu was sorry he had let Mistress Bordier influence his decision. He now did what he wished he had thought of doing sooner: He went to ask the advice of Monsieur Mortimer Morel d'Arthus, the man for whom he transported lace, as his father had done before him.

Monsieur Morel d'Arthus told him regretfully that his lacemaking shops had been forced to stop taking in apprentices since the promulgation of the royal edicts forbidding Protestants to train children. A few Catholic mistress-lacemakers in Alençon had, however, opened shops for apprentices under the supervision of the state. He recommended the one directed by Mistress Lescure who had been trained by Madame La Perrière herself.* After Gilonne had spent two or three years with Mistress Lescure, a further apprenticeship in the Royal Manufactory would be advisable, if not obligatory. Later, when she had become a good lacemaker, with God's help, she could come to work in the Morel d'Arthus shops if she wanted to.

* * *

*A famous lacemaker regarded as the creator of Alençon lace.

"Those people are Protestants!" Mama Bordier said when
Mathieu told her about his conversation with Monsieur Morel
d'Arthus. "Are you going to start taking advice from heretics?
If you listen to *them*, I don't want anything to do with the consequences!"

She knew she was lost. From Alençon, Gilonne wouldn't come
back to her house every evening, as she had done when she spent
her days with the nuns in Montsort. She would be housed and fed
by the mistress-lacemaker. And everyone knew how those skinflints starved their apprentices to fill their money bags.

It was Mama Bordier's sorrow, sometimes loudly expressed,
sometimes silent and all the more poignant, that led Gilonne to
think about the old priest's wandering ghost. Without her, Mama
Bordier would lie in bed alone and terrified on nights when the
ghost was in the garden. The poor woman would no longer be
able to say, "With you, my little angel, I feel better." And with
all the work her turkeys made for her, she needed restful sleep
at night. Jérémie said he would help Mama Bordier, but Gilonne
knew how he was: He didn't always do what he promised. When
he had cleaned the whole church, even in its darkest nooks and
crannies—where Jesus had never thought to set His bare,
wounded feet—he was too tired to do anything else and went to
lie down in the flowers with Martagon, the dog, in summer, or
in front of the fire in winter. And he drank too much spiced
cider. "Because I'm afraid," he said. Afraid of what? The
priest's ghost? He claimed he never heard or saw it. Was he
afraid of dragoons pursuing Protestants and running them
through with their lances? Yes, probably. He said that every
night he heard the clang of cruel cavalrymen's weapons and the
hoofbeats of their horses, even though he had been promised
that those nocturnal terrors would end if he became a Catholic.

One day in the kitchen, Gilonne was still trying to think of
how she could help Mama Bordier as she watched her take down
the big knife that hung on the wall, to cut a slice of bread for
her afternoon snack. This reminded her that the key to the church
hung in the kitchen of the presbytery, and it occurred to her that
she could take that key, use it to open the church to the priest's
ghost, and throw it out into a field where no one would ever find
it. The priest would then have time to say all the masses he had
failed to say during his lifetime. He would be forgiven and sent
to heaven, and he would stay there, leaving people on earth to
sleep in peace. Gilonne smiled to herself because she was proud

of her idea. Mama Bordier saw her smile and wiped away a tear, reflecting on the cruel indifference that all children, even the best of them, sometimes showed.

On the day before she was to leave, Gilonne put the turkeys into their dark house one last time and said good-by to them. Marguerite realized that they weren't really going to be separated, since their hearts would still be united.

Gilonne had no difficulty going to the presbytery next door and doing what needed to be done. Jérémie and old Céronne had once again drunk a little too much spiced cider, probably to console themselves for knowing she was going to leave them, as they had been saying for the past week. They were dozing on their chairs in front of the cold fireplace, stiff and dignified, like two hens asleep on their perch, with half-open eyes that saw nothing.

Gilonne's memories of her expedition were dominated by the coolness of the stone floor on her bare feet and the good smell of spiced cider—cinnamon, cloves, nutmeg—in the air of the room, more vividly present than the two sleepers. For a long time she associated coolness and good smells with having been brave. Yes, she *had* been brave: Just think what would have happened if the two guardians of the key had waked up!

It was poor Jérémie who paid for Gilonne's effort to help the ghost. He was upbraided vigorously by Father Dutilleux and old Céronne for having lost the key to the church, a serious matter in a time when stealing from churches was common. Disgusted by the unfairness of their accusation, Jérémie went into the garden to swear angrily and weep with his face against Martagon's fur. After a time, he was certain he could hear a voice coming from the flower bed under which he had buried his Protestant Bible, a voice telling him that he wasn't made to be a Catholic and an assistant churchwarden and ought to join his parents in Switzerland. A forgotten name suddenly came back into his mind, there, near the place where he had hidden his Bible: It was the name of a man who took people out of the country in secret. This, too, was a sign.

During his years in purgatory he had been saving money, one sou at a time, to pay for his journey to another country. If it turned out that he didn't yet have enough, he would rather beg along the roads than stay here any longer. He couldn't bear to go on making lace the rest of his life, when he liked only mathematics. And the lace he was making was forbidden by the king! He could accept the idea of being sent to the galleys for refusing to renounce his faith, but not the idea of being sent there for having pulled a needle in the wrong direction.

Losing Gilonne was the real reason for his decision to leave. He didn't admit it to himself, though he did recognize how much she had kept his heart warm during those five years. He felt that he was the one who had been most concerned with her. For one thing, he taught her the poetry of the Bible, which Catholics hardly appreciated at all. (This idea was deeply rooted in him.)

He abandoned the Montsort church, Father Dutilleux, old Céronne and her spiced cider, Martagon, and the flowers of the garden. He trampled on his two steel needles and his iron thimble, then he slipped away at night, holding his shoes in his hands. After thinking it over, he had decided he would be less afraid walking along the roads than waiting in Montsort for one of the Catholic zealots' spies to come and tell him he wasn't a wholehearted convert and was going to be punished for it.

It was Mistress Lescure herself who came to open the door when Mathieu and Gilonne arrived at her house, but she allowed only Gilonne to come in. Parents and guardians, she said with a stern expression, were not permitted to be present during the examination. Mathieu could come back in an hour. She would then tell him whether or not she was willing to sign an apprenticeship contract.

Gilonne let him leave without saying anything, but he felt her little hand cling to his a few seconds before letting go of it. He tried to console himself with the thought that it was time for her to leave the overprotective Mama Bordier, the affectionate turkeys, and the half-dozen senile old people who lived nearby. He didn't believe all that for one second, but he pretended to think it was true.

He went to wait in the Moor's Inn, with a half a jugful of pear cider to keep him company. Chevalier Louis-Guillaume de Ferrières, whom he knew from having seen him give concerts in the marketplace on Thursdays, came in soon afterward and strode across the room as if he were making his way through a flock of sheep in one of his meadows. Mistress Verlot greeted him by bobbing up and down in a long series of bows, her face so flushed with emotion that it matched her red skirt. Mathieu might have smiled at their extravagant behavior if he hadn't been absorbed in the thought that Gilonne's father and uncle were now under the same roof. He wondered what questions she was being asked, and how she was supposed to answer them. Then, since the pear cider was already beginning to produce its heartening effect, he told himself that, assuming Mistress Lescure had even a little sense of humor, she wouldn't be bored talking with Gilonne if Marguerite the turkey also joined in the conversation.

Suddenly cheered up, Mathieu treated himself to another half-jugful of pear cider. As his euphoria increased, he was amused by the thought that Gilonne and her father not only resembled each other physically but also were equally eccentric. Then he wondered—the idea had never come into his mind before—if he should take pride in the fact that his niece was an aristocrat on her father's side. The drowsiness that was coming over him left the question unanswered.

When Mistress Verlot walked past him without paying any more attention than if he had been a chair, he had an urge to speak up in his loudest voice and proclaim the family tie that existed between him, a common packman and the handsome nobleman who was being served with such obsequious respect. Luckily, however, he fell asleep instead, and so avoided the great regret that would have overwhelmed him if after emerging from the vapors of the pear cider he had realized that his tongue had betrayed him.

Gilonne looked at Mistress Lescure and saw a certain resemblance between her and the old public writer. She wore the same kind of spectacles and had the same thin, miserly lips. But she was cleaner. She wore a big white apron that went all the way around her and covered her from the head down; she was like one of the plucked Christmas turkeys Mama Bordier wrapped in a white cloth to make a good impression, believing that money spent on showy frills wasn't wasted.

And Mistress Lescure looked at the little girl in the big, heavy dress that would have to be changed because it would interfere with her work. Those ridiculously painted wooden shoes would also have to be changed: They would attract the other girls' attention and make them waste time. They were so stupid, these families who got their children all dolled up before sending them to her! She almost preferred the girls who came in filthy rags that had to be burned as soon as possible. They, at least, didn't howl in despair when they had to put on different clothes. And now here was another one who probably thought she was as elegant as the Grande Pandore!* There was going to be trouble when she heard she would have to give up that dress.

Behind their spectacles, the mistress-lacemaker's eyes seemed cold and hard. Marguerite thought so too. Gilonne looked out the window and saw a garden with only one tree in it, an ancient apple tree that held a chirping bird at the end of one branch.

"Let me see your hands."

Gilonne held them out. They had been baked by the sun and scratched by her taste for the berries that grew along the roads of Montsort, and one forefinger was honorably decorated with needle holes. But her palms were smooth as satin, because Mama Bordier had always made her prepare food for the turkeys by mixing bran and whey, using all her fingers: it was good for them, and therefore good for lacemaking. "Lace likes us to caress it with soft hands," she had said. "It won't make itself beautiful unless it's treated gently." The old public writer sometimes remarked that in Mistress Bordier's house even the different parts of a piece of lace were spoken of as if they were persons. He had once heard, for example, "It's getting dark now, and if you work on bars when there isn't enough light, they'll play you the dirty trick of not looking like each other."

"Have you ever been sick?" Mistress Lescure asked.

Sick? Trying to go to heaven, just for a visit—was that being sick? Gilonne decided it wasn't.

"What do you eat every day?"

A bowl of soup. No use mentioning the pieces of turkey breast they ate on Sundays. "The less the tax collectors know about what's in your bowl, the better it is for your taxes." Mama Bordier had said that not once but a hundred times. Gilonne looked Mistress Lescure straight in the eyes and saw an even stronger resemblance between her and the old public writer, who was always trying to steal your secrets.

Her heart began beating faster. She knew so many secrets that no one else must ever know! Uncle Mathieu's secrets, which could put him in danger from bad people on the roads during his travels. Jérémie's secrets about his first religion, which could

*A mannequin, used for displaying Paris fashions, that was sent all over France and to foreign countries.

send him to the king's galleys. And her own secrets too. She had several important ones, but there were two she had to be especially careful about, because terrible things would happen if she told them. The one about the blood of Christ was so heavy to bear that it sometimes woke her up at night. She didn't know if she had been right to watch the work of mending Jesus' nailed feet, which rats had gnawed up to the ankles during the great famine of 1662, on the beautiful picture in the church. The artist's servant had been told to make preparations while his master had a drink at the inn. He was gluing a piece of canvas over the hole when Gilonne came into the sacristy.

He told her that he and his master hadn't been able to come any sooner because of the great number of paintings chewed by animals during famines. And when a piece of Our Lord had to be re-created, the difficulty was in finding some of His blood to put on the wounds made by the nails that held Him on the cross. Ordinary paints—green, yellow, blue—presented no problem. Blood was a different matter. *Real* blood was needed, some of the blood that had flowed from Christ's body while He was alive! There was still some of it left in one of the faraway Eastern lands where so many brave men had gone to fight in the Crusades. He, a lowly servant who prepared an artist's paints, had gone there and been lucky enough to find one of the last bottles of it. It was alive, here, under his doublet, in the warmth over his heart. Every painter in the world would like to have it. If they knew about it, other painters' servants might kill him to get it for their masters. And it was a magic bottle. It was now saying to him, "Give this nice little girl a drop of the blood in me, to bring her good luck." On a little piece of the canvas that he had used to prepare Christ's feet the young man carefully poured a single drop of God's life and whispered, "Make sure no one ever sees it. If you tell anyone, Our Lord will punish you and take back His blood, and heaven's blessing will leave you."

Gilonne had never said one word about this to Uncle Mathieu, or Jérémie, or even Marguerite. Mama Bordier had a holy relic: thirteen blue wool threads from the Virgin's veil, which a lame peddler had given her in exchange for a dozen eggs. Gilonne would have liked to tell her that her own relic had cost less, because the generous servant had asked her only for a small jug of cool cider. And the wool threads had turned almost gray, while the blood was still as bright red as a poppy in the sun! But a promise was a promise. She would never say anything about her relic, and especially not to this mistress-lacemaker who didn't seem at all likeable.

No one else but Jérémie knew her second secret. She had told it to him one day when he was weeping, downhearted at not knowing where his parents and two sisters were. He moaned that no one in this sad world could understand his unhappiness, not even Gilonne, in spite of her love for him. She told him he was mistaken, that there was sympathy all around him. First, the roses in the garden: They wept all through the night for the great sorrows of the Protestants, and were still wet from it in the morning. Didn't he see the tears on their petals and in their hearts, when he went to get water from the well at dawn? Of course he did. And he was glad to know why the roses shed so many tears, many more than lilies did. Lilies were the king's flowers; they shed only little tears in imitation of the roses, without knowing what sorrows they were mourning. There were people like that too, who laughed or cried just because they saw others doing it.

No, she wouldn't open her heart to that lady sitting there so stiffly, with eyes as hard as stones. She pressed her lips together tightly. She had to remember that words could pop out of your mouth just to spite you, and afterward you couldn't make them come back. She remembered Jérémie exclaiming one day in the garden, "Dear God, I should never have said that! If some religious fanatic had heard me, I'd be lost!" And Mama Bordier had once said, after clapping her hand over her mouth, too late, "I let my tongue wag too much again today, in the market. Ah, Saint Shutmouth, where were you, instead of being there to watch over me? Nowadays, when people know more than they tell and are always doing things on the sly, you never know what to say or who to say it to. You can't even be sure your prayers are really going to the Lord. We live in a time when everything is turned upside down!"

"Show me your back," ordered the mistress-lacemaker.

Mistress Lescure knew that the woods were full of little girls whose parents wanted to have them turned into lacemakers, and she had learned from costly experience that she had to choose carefully from among that multitude. A girl who seemed to have unquestionable ability could ruin everything through a defect in her character or constitution

Gilonne's back was sound. Furthermore, she hadn't laughed like a fool when she felt each vertebra being examined.

"All right. Since you want to learn to make lace, let's find out how well you can see it. Look at these two pieces of lace. Are they exactly the same, like twins, or are there differences between them?"

The lady's eyes were like those of some people Jérémie had once pointed out to Gilonne, saying, "Look at them staring at me over there. They want to know what color I pissed this morning. If it wasn't a beautiful Catholic yellow, if it was an ugly Protestant yellow, they'll say, 'Send him to the galleys!' " Well, if the lady wanted to know about these two pieces of lace, it was easy to tell her. At first sight, the patterns seemed almost identical, but the connecting bars were of slightly different sizes and the petals of the flowers weren't shaped exactly alike. And also . . . Gilonne closed her eyes, took one of the two samples in each hand and caressed it between her thumb and forefinger.

"The threads are different," she said. "The thread in this one is just a little bit thinner."

It was true. Both threads were supposedly of the same size, but they came from different places: one from Flanders, the other from Germany.

"Who's blind in your family?"

"My grandmother, Thomine Perdriel, in the poorhouse."

Mistress Lescure was pleased to note that the child had benefited from her blind grandmother's teaching. In a town where so many women tapped a stick in front of them when they walked, hardly anyone thought of trying to learn their highly developed sense of touch.

"Was she the one who taught you?"

Taught? No, they had only talked together, sitting on Thomine's bed in the old women's room of the poorhouse. Gilonne would keep her eyes closed to be closer to her grandmother in her darkness. Often they felt pieces of lace that Thomine had made when she could see, and she told about them. The most beautiful one was a flowered pattern that was a sample for the dauphin's christening cloth.

"Who's your mother?"

Her mother's name was Julie Perdriel, and she also made lace, in heaven. Could people go blind in heaven too? She wondered about it, but didn't dare to ask.

Mistress Lescure knew her lacemaking aristocracy. She remembered Julie. Skilled hands but a wandering mind! She also

remembered hearing that old Thomine had worn out her eyes
making fine lace.

"And who's your father?"

Her father. This was the first time anyone had ever even mentioned him to her. No, she didn't know who he was. Did that
mean she wouldn't be allowed to become a lacemaker? Probably
not, since the lady now wanted her to blow in her face, so she
could tell what her breath was like. Bad breath turned lace yellow. Gilonne knew hers was good. Mama Bordier said it was
purer than a cherub's.

"Show me what you already know."

Mistress Lescure pointed to several samples on a table and
told Gilonne to see if there were any she knew how to make.

Gilonne reached for the one most familiar to her, a piece of
parchment on which a bar ground had been begun. Just as she
was about to touch it, a stick struck her violently on the back of
the hand and left a broad red mark on it. Tears of pain came into
her eyes.

"Never—do you hear me?—*never* touch a piece of lace without wiping your hands first. That's what the cloth is for. Didn't
you see it?"

Gilonne hadn't seen it. She felt like telling the lady that only
a little while ago she had given her two pieces of lace without
saying anything about wiping her hands, but, not wanting to
seem argumentative, she kept her thoughts to herself.

"Didn't they teach you cleanliness at home?"

At home? In Mama Bordier's house? How she wished she
could go back there right now! She could never like this woman.
It was like her grandmother and her friends with their Coeur-
de-Coing in the poorhouse, or Jérémie with his Catholic fanatics. . . . *Drop of Jesus' blood over my heart, please let me go
home. Very soon.*

Having little aptitude for amusement, Symonne Lescure was
now amusing herself as well as she could. She enjoyed making
prospective apprentices undergo this kind of inquisition, known
in Alençon as "putting them on the rack." She liked to foresee
and calculate everything. That was her pleasure, and her supe-
riority over other mistress-lacemakers. Teaching girls to make
the most beautiful lace and keep it immaculately white was no
laughing matter. They had to realize that from the start.

Mistress Lescure had once had an unforgettable adventure.
Marie Colbert, sister of the king's minister, was a nun who

directed the Royal Manufactory in Reims. When she became ill, she asked Mistress Lescure, whose reputation was already well established, to replace her for a time. Flattered, Mistress Lescure went to Reims. There she had the shock of her life when she discovered that *the lace made in Reims was whiter than the lace made in Alençon!* She looked again and again. It was beyond question: The white there was a whole shade lighter.

She spent endless hours comparing the qualities and origins of different kinds of thread, studying the Reims lacemakers' methods of preserving cleanness, investigating their breath. She ordered a keg of the finest, most skillfully bleached Flemish thread, kept half of it in Reims, sent the other half to Alençon, and had lace made from it in both places by workers of equal ability, using the same pattern and following the same procedures. Comparison of the two samples of lace only confirmed that the Reims white was whiter than the Alençon white. Her obsession reached the point where it made her feel ill. She made a minute search of the workshops she would still be directing for a few more months. An evil influence, or at least a mysterious one, had to be the cause of that difference.

When the Intendant of Reims said to her with a smug smile, "There's nothing you can do about it: It's in the air here, air that will always make our lace whiter than yours," her suppressed rage built up such pressure inside her that she irreverently turned her back on him. And then that fat, doddering old fool added venomously, "Whether you like it or not, Reims is the city of whiteness. Take our champagne, for example. Until recently it was red, but now it's become white, even though it's still made from the same dark grapes!" He laughed. "And now it sparkles too and makes the cork pop out of the bottle."

She made no reply, but at that moment it would have given her great pleasure to see him frying in hell. Those combined images of dazzlingly white lace and frothy champagne were unbearable to her. Alençon was the queen of lacemaking centers and therefore ought to have the whitest lace. Reims must be under some sort of special protection. Who, or what, made everything whiter there? She had thought and thought about it, to no avail. What saint, or holy relic, or blessed object, had that power? Who was keeping watch there? Was it Saint Remi, Bishop of Reims, Apostle of the Franks and baptizer of Clovis? His relics were kept in the abbey that bore his name, and three big portraits of him were displayed in the Royal Manufactory.

There was also a picture of Joan of Arc, shown attending the king's coronation, in the cathedral. Was she the one who watched over each workshop? And what about Marshal Duplessis de Praslin, who had delivered Reims from the Spanish invaders?

She badgered the workers, nuns, and lay sisters with questions. Was one of those three protectors invoked more often than the others? Was some sort of secret rite performed in the seclusion of a basement or a cave? She constantly spied and questioned. Time passed, and Reims lace was still whiter than Alençon lace.

Marie Colbert came back. And in despair she wrote to her brother, the king's minister, "There has been an affliction in the house of the Reims Manufactory for the last three or four months. Several of our girls have been attacked by an illness unknown to the doctors. The vicar general and the parish priests have told me that it is sorcery. And after all imaginable things have been done to restore them to health, three or four of our lacemakers are still in very bad condition."* But the nun, so close to the God of Mercy, didn't dare to tell her brother, so close to the king who dispensed justice, that she believed Mistress Lescure to be guilty of having tortured those under her authority.

She assured Mistress Lescure of her sorrow at having to part with her and even offered to let her take a piece of lace with her as a remembrance. A piece of Reims lace? No, never! Symonne Lescure asked to be allowed to take, instead, two paintings she had discovered in the attic during her patient searches: one of Saint Remi and one of Joan of Arc. They were in a wretched state, having suffered violence at the hands of Protestants, in the course of one of their revolts in the previous century. Remi had lost an eye, and Joan had been stabbed in the heart. When the paintings were given to her, Mistress Lescure said she would have them restored. Marie Colbert was moved by her piety and realized that she had been right not to denounce her to the police. She did penance, accusing herself of having had bad thoughts.

Saint Remi and Saint Joan of Arc were now on a wall of Mistress Lescure's workshop. And it seemed to her—yes, she was almost certain of it—that the lace made there was coming closer and closer to being as white as the lace made in Reims.

From the next room came the sound of a hymn sung by sev-

*From an actual letter

eral voices, one of which was exceptionally beautiful. Gilonne had been looking down at her shoes, she now raised her head and listened.

"Can you sing?" asked Mistress Lescure.

Gilonne nodded. In Mama Bordier's house, the old public writer and his friends had said that singing too much caused fatigue and took away a little strength from the hands. Grandmother Thomine said it wasn't true, and the sweet songs Gilonne sang were almost enough to make you cry. The old woman wasn't sad from being blind, though. She had known that making lace might take away her sight, but she had made it anyway, because she had to, she said, because she couldn't do anything else. Would the same thing happen to Gilonne someday?

"Mistress, I don't want to go blind," she said softly.

The singing was still coming from the next room, and Symonne Lescure didn't hear her.

When Mathieu came back, the contract was ready for signing. It said, "On April 3, 1670, Demoiselle Symonne Lescure declares to Mathieu Perdriel, a packman, that she will teach his niece, Gilonne Perdriel, five years of age, to make *point de France* for a period of four years. The child will be given food and heated lodgings, her clothes will be washed, and she will be taught reading and writing. She will be permitted and required to practice the Catholic religion, go to mass each Sunday, and read and listen to the Holy Scriptures. Mathieu Perdriel agrees to pay twenty livres a year for his niece's living expenses and education."

That sum was originally twenty-two livres, but the promise of a monthly basket from Mistress Bordier, containing a turkey and a dozen eggs, had brought it down to twenty.

On Mistress Lescure's crucifix, taken down from the wall above her bed, Mathieu and Gilonne swore not to reveal anything about the work they saw done in her establishment, and not to show anyone patterns and designs that were her personal property.

Gilonne also swore not to be disobedient or argumentative. She acknowledged that laziness was the meanest of sins, and she promised not to waste thread or food.

She and Mathieu then left and began walking back to the tanner's house, hand in hand.

"Now we'll go and buy two big slices of bread," he said. "I'm hungry. What about you?"

But he quickly forgot his hunger because he was thinking about the twenty livres he would have to ask Monsieur Morel d'Arthus to lend him that evening, and he bought only one slice of bread. Gilonne stopped in the street, in front of the Saint-Blaise church, and broke the slice into two equal parts. They resumed walking, and greeted the blacksmith, whom they knew well. Gilonne didn't eat her share of the bread.

As they were approaching the tanner's house she said, "Uncle Mathieu . . . I don't want to go blind."

Again she spoke very softly. He didn't hear her either.

In the afternoon, Mathieu took her to the poorhouse to say her farewells. From now on she wouldn't be able to spend Sundays there, except perhaps on important holidays. Thomine and her old friends wanted to shower their fortunes on her. They squabbled over which of them would give Gilonne her embroidered cloth case containing lacemaking implements. Eventually, Mathieu had to intervene by limiting their gifts. Whoever gave her a thimble wouldn't give her scissors. They would draw straws.

The blind women and even Marie the Nap, who was now awake, would have argued for hours, each one praising her own tools, and denigrating the others', if something extraordinary hadn't happened. Coeur-de-Coing took from under her skirts a red damask purse embroidered with fine beads, an object of great splendor, and gave it to Gilonne, saying with a smile less forced than usual, "I hope this will bring you good luck in your workshop."

The old women were astounded. Coeur-de-Coing had given a gift! They remained silent and only Gilonne's polite "Thank you very much" was heard. Those who couldn't see imagined her curtsy.

When Coeur-de-Coing had left, Marie, who fortunately hadn't gone back to sleep, was the center of attention.

"You saw her eyes, Marie. Did they say she knew we kept Gilonne here when she was a baby?"

"Did they say, 'You thought you put one over on me, but I've always known, and this is how I'm getting even by giving the child a present'?"

"Did they say, 'You fooled me, you old hags, but this purse has a curse on it and brings bad luck to anyone who owns it'?"

Overwhelmed by the importance of these questions, Marie collapsed into uncertainty. No, Coeur-de-Coing's eyes didn't really say that . . . Or that either . . .

"Not really, but a little?"

"Maybe, maybe . . ."

Mathieu, who had also seen, tried to give his opinion. For that kind of thing, the old women didn't have too much confidence in men. They listened to him, however, when he agreed that the purse was probably dangerous and they shouldn't take any chances with it. They decided to throw it into the Sarthe. It was a pity they couldn't sell such a valuable present, but they knew that money obtained by selling a cursed object was as strongly cursed as the object itself. The purse had to be a thing of the devil, because otherwise that evil, miserly creature who persecuted poor women would have sold it herself. It began to seem so alarming that they changed their minds about throwing it into the Sarthe, whose water touched the walls of the poorhouse. They preferred the Briante because it was farther away. Mathieu would go there after dark and throw in the purse, weighted with a stone. That way there would be no danger of its being washed up on the riverbank where Coeur-de-Coing often took a walk during her hours of leisure.

Were the water nymphs of the Briante, familiar to the town's poets, surprised that those land-dwellers hadn't realized they were seeing the first sign of warm feeling in a heart that was much less hard than they thought? But perhaps the water nymphs didn't know how much land-dwellers feared what they didn't understand.

At supper that evening in the tanner's house, Gilonne wasn't hungry. Neither her bowl of milk nor her apple seemed tempting.

"I wish I could go back to Mama Bordier," she murmured.

Mathieu was upset. Then he had what he later called his inspiration. He wouldn't leave Gilonne alone in the room while he went to borrow twenty livres from Monsieur Mortimer Morel d'Arthus. He would take her with him and ask to have her shown some beautiful lace. Until then it hadn't occurred to anyone that she was about to begin learning a trade without knowing what splendors it could produce!

"Would you like to see what I'll soon take to Russia in my two-legged wagon?"

To his great satisfaction, she laughed. He had guessed what she wanted. He didn't do so badly with children! Gilonne had probably been wanting for a long time to admire some of the fine lace made in Alençon.

"Are you laughing because of what we're going to do this evening?" he asked.

"Yes . . . but mostly because I like to hear you say 'my two-legged wagon.' "

So that was what had made her forget her sorrow. The day before, Florianne, a pretty young woman with a smile and a bosom he greatly admired, had asked him if his two-legged wagon was beginning to wear out a little from being used too much. He would have enjoyed getting to know her better. He sensed that she was dying to find out what he transported, and for whom. But he knew the Morel d'Arthus family wouldn't approve of his having an affair with a talkative girl. He had sworn on the Bible, as they demanded, that he would say nothing about their collaboration. Mama Bordier maintained that an oath sworn to a Protestant had no value. And the parish priest of Saint-Blaise, who had taught him to read and write, once said to him resentfully, "If I'd known you were going to be a heretic's henchman, I wouldn't have gone to so much trouble to educate you. Your father is also guilty, because he showed you the wrong path and led you to those rich, unscrupulous Protestants." Rich, yes, but why unscrupulous? They paid promptly and well. And this evening he was going to ask them to lend him twenty livres. Since Gilonne was such an adorable, irresistible child, taking her with him to ask for the loan was a clever idea. He smiled. For some reason Mama Bordier thought he had a kind of angelic innocence, but he considered himself rather Machiavellian.

"Are we going there after dark, Uncle Mathieu?"

"Yes. Are you afraid?"

No, she wasn't afraid. But even so, she decided to arm herself with her little staff. She began polishing it with great seriousness and asked, frowning, "How long will it take you to go to Russia?"

He told himself she was worried about his travels, now that she was no longer under Mama Bordier's wing.

"Two short months," he answered, forcing himself to laugh, "but to get there that soon I guarantee you I won't be plodding along like a plowman, or stopping to sing with the larks and the nightingales! Then two even shorter months to come back, trying to go as fast as the swallows. And between those two little strolls I'll rest for three days and three nights in some nice, soft straw. I won't have to stop up my ears to keep the birds from waking me. . . . Do you know what I think? I think that somewhere in Russia, in a wooden house covered with snow, someone may be carving a pretty pair of wooden shoes for me to bring back to a certain little girl I know."

He was pleased to hear Gilonne laugh.

When they reached the Place du Château, the night was dark and the clock of Notre-Dame was striking ten. They saw no one but a group of drunken revelers returning from a tavern, walking along the gutter, kicking the filthy water in it, loudly proclaiming that they were His Majesty's proud ships on their way to America and waving their plumed hats, no doubt meant to represent sails. While they waited in the shadows for the wine-soaked fleet to pass, Mathieu whispered to Gilonne, "You're not afraid?" She didn't answer, but she held up her little staff, to indicate that she was ready to defend herself if they were attacked.

But there was no need for self-defense. They encountered no one else, and no one saw them arrive at the carved wooden door of the Morel d'Arthus house.

This house was even more beautiful than the intendant's, where Mama Bordier had taken Gilonne one day when she delivered some turkeys. When Uncle Mathieu told her that the Morel d'Arthus were Protestants, she had associated them in her mind with Jérémie, and so she wasn't prepared for such magnificence. When she expressed her surprise, Mathieu pointed out that this was the house of the largest lace manufacturer in Alençon.

"They also have a branch office in Amsterdam, Holland, where I often make deliveries, and a bank in Geneva, Switzerland, where I go now and then."

When she had counted six lighted windows—and how many unlighted ones were there?—Gilonne had a better idea of the Morel d'Arthus' fortune than Mathieu could give with all his talk of branch offices and banks, which meant nothing to her. The parquet floors, made of different kinds of wood that gleamed

more brightly than if they had been rubbed with the secret polish
her uncle used for his staffs, seemed worthy of her painted shoes.

"Do your curtsy."

She bowed to a very old gentleman dressed in black, with
hair as white as the collar and cuffs of his coat.

"So this is the little foxglove eater who's going to be a lacemaker!"

"God willing, sir. She'll do her very best to learn. She's not
mischievous, she knows how to listen, and she does as she's
told."

Hanging on the wall just above the old man's head was the
portrait of a beautiful lady wearing a blue silk dress and working
on a piece of lace. The portrait was framed in gold and glittered
in the light of eight, or ten, or maybe even twelve candles.

"I see you're looking at the portrait of my late wife," Monsieur Morel d'Arthus said to Gilonne. "She was an excellent
lacemaker. It was a Dutch painter who put her on canvas like
that, forever, in sunlight and the glow of her youth. He called
the picture *Needlepoint*." He smiled a little and added, "My
son Hélye, who likes to match colors, has decided that here,
where we show our lace to our customers in front of his mother
dressed in blue, we'll always present our merchandise on silk of
the same color, rather than on red, as is customary in Alençon."

Mathieu nodded. This was already known in the town.
"Those Morel d'Arthus," he had heard one day, "are just trying to be different, and it won't do them any good, because
nothing is more beautiful than our lace on a red background."
And a fanatically religious woman had said, "Changing from
red to blue won't save those Protestants from getting what's
coming to them when God and the king have finally had enough
of their arrogance."

If the old gentleman had heard this kind of talk, it apparently
didn't worry him. He looked at the portrait and said, "Isn't it
beautiful, that light on her face? The painter's name is Rem-
brandt Van Rijn. Some people like him, others don't. My son
Hélye says you could spend hours daydreaming in front of his
pictures if you had the time—and the weakness!" He sighed.
"What would you like me to show this child, Mathieu?"

"Whatever you please, sir."

Gilonne was perched on a stool in front of a long table made
of smooth wood that looked soft. She reached out to stroke it,
but quickly drew back her hand: the red mark left by Mistress

Lescure's stick was too conspicuous. She hadn't told her uncle about that painful incident.

The old gentleman spread out a piece of silk that was almost exactly the same shade of blue as his wife's dress in the portrait. Then he began taking lace from big drawers and laying it on the cloth. There were flounces, collars, lappets, bonnets, scarves, shawls . . .

"They're lovely, aren't they?" he asked Gilonne. "Doesn't it seem to you that only angels could make such things?"

Yes, it did. The table, blue now, was a miniature sky in which the angels—she saw them!—playfully threw flowers, garlands, and ribbons at each other, fluttering their white wings in the candlelight.

"Look at those wonders, Gilonne. Look at them carefully," Mathieu said proudly.

Now that her eyes were used to the darkness around the table, she also saw wooden lace on the walls: the same flowers and garlands. And there was iron lace beside the stairs that led up to the second floor.

Finally, Monsieur Morel d'Arthus said, "Come, Mathieu, let's settle our business," and they left her to wait for them in a vast gallery, on a red velvet chair so wide it could have served as her bed. A door was partly open. By leaning to the right without leaving her seat, she could see what was in the next room. A forest! Trees, green plants, more trees. She knew, of course, that they were in a tapestry. Mama Bordier had shown her one like it at the town hall last Christmas Eve, when they had gone there to see the intendant because he wanted to compliment her on the richness of her poultry yard. (Mama Bordier had been far from delighted to hear the word "richness" spoken in a room full of inquisitive people waiting their turn to speak to the intendant. How could she be sure there wasn't a tax collector among them?) "That's called a tapestry," she had said to Gilonne. "Rich people like them."

Here, the forest was inhabited. In the midst of all that greenery, there was a desk and behind the desk, a gentleman. A handsome young gentleman, the real master of this house. It had seemed to her that the old gentleman in black didn't fit in with the magnificence around her. But this young one was a prince. He sat writing in the dazzling light of silver candlesticks with many branches. His clothes were chestnut-brown velvet; his eyes, perhaps gray, were sad. Yes, she could swear that when he looked at her there was as much sadness in his eyes as she had seen in Jérémie's one day when he was in despair at not knowing what had become of his two little sisters. Did he, too, think that no one could understand the Protestants' sorrow?

Without having really decided to do it, Gilonne stood up and walked toward the forest and its melancholy prince. She stopped, leaned forward, and put her head between the two halves of the door. Her skirts, white stockings, and red shoes remained in the gallery.

"Sir," she said in a scarcely audible little voice, "would you like to know the secret of the roses?"

The prince of lace put down his pen and seemed interested in hearing that revelation.

Jérémie had been right to say that when secrets knew they should be told for a good purpose, they came from your lips all by themselves.

"The roses feel very sorry for the Protestants," Gilonne said to the handsome prince. "They cry so much for them every night that in the morning there are still tears on their petals and in their hearts. If you go out to the garden and look at them, sir, before the sun has drunk their tears, you'll know how much sympathy they have for you."

Hélye Morel d'Arthus smiled with joy at learning this. As a reward for sharing such a beautiful secret with him, he told Gilonne, he was going to share a secret of his own with her. He stood up—how tall he was when he unbent!—held out one hand to her, took a candlestick with the other, and led her toward the mysteries of the house. On the way, they talked about Jérémie and agreed with him that lilies, belonging to the king, shed tears only to imitate roses, or maybe to make themselves more attractive, because they also agreed that those pearls on flowers were very beautiful. And finally they agreed on the immense danger that would threaten the roses of France if the king became angry with them and sent his dragoons to cut off their heads.

They went into a little room that could be reached only through a secret door at the back of a closet. Two masked ladies lived there, wearing lace dresses whose long trains were spread over the floor.

"The marquise, here, is entitled to a train two ells long. The duchess has the right to wear one three ells long. If Her Majesty the Queen of France did me the honor of being one of my customers, I'd have to make a train eleven ells long for her! As for the hats, the ladies themselves decide on their height.''

Gilonne looked up to examine the two ladies' hats and the elaborate structures on top of them. She had quickly realized that they were wickerwork ladies and that their masks hid only cloth faces. No need to bow to them, as she had almost done. The young gentleman would have laughed.

''These marvels are the finest work we've done this year. Hardly anyone has seen them. Each of the women who worked on them made only one small part, and doesn't know what the others did. The parts were put together by an old cousin of mine who lives in the attic of this house and who is so devoted to lace that she never goes out. When those two dresses are folded, they'll take up so little space that your uncle will be able to hide them under his clothes when he goes to deliver them to the ladies in Paris who have been waiting long years for them. Sometimes ladies place an order with us but die before the work is finished.''

Did the prince of lace mean that God punished them for wanting to own such beautiful things?

''Put your hand in mine,'' he went on, ''and repeat after me: 'I will never tell anyone what I have seen here.' And I'll swear never to reveal the secret of the roses.''

They both took an oath of secrecy.

Mathieu and Gilonne walked back to the tanner's house in darkness.

''The old gentleman and his son are rich,'' she said, ''but they don't wear lace collars or cuffs. Why?''

''That's how Protestants are, Gilonne.''

In Mathieu's pocket was the heavy purse containing the twenty livres that were a gift, not a loan, from Monsieur Mortimer Morel d'Arthus. He felt the weight of that gift not only in his pocket but also in his soul. He was used to struggling and fighting like a wolf on the roads; having obtained such a sum of money so quickly and easily had left him a little disoriented.

Before going to sleep, Gilonne asked more questions. Mathieu answered them distractedly. Yes, it was Monsieur Hélye himself who designed his lace. No, Mathieu wasn't the only carrier employed by the Morel d'Arthus. Not all of their lace was delivered by men on foot: some of it was sent by post. But the most valuable lace, secretly ordered and made without the authorization of the Royal Manufactory, was entrusted to him.

"Then you're the one they like best?"

He acknowledged that he was. And wasn't that why they had given him the twenty livres? He went to sleep with his mind at peace.

He awoke long before dawn. When he went to tell Gilonne it was time to get up, he found her lying on her straw mattress with her eyes closed. But she had been awake a long time, gripped by sorrow and fear.

"Are you hungry?"

No, she wasn't hungry. Her little face was pale and her eyelids were reddened. She wanted to go back to Mama Bordier. He wished he could carry her to the river, the wooden bridge, Montsort, and her beloved foster mother. She was still so young, so fragile.

"I'm afraid," she said, and the way she spoke reminded him of her mother.

He sighed, but quickly forced himself to laugh. No one, he said, had ever been as scared as he was in his childhood. Had he ever told her about his terror when his father sent him off with his friend Joseph, a packman who knew every shortcut between Alençon and Paris?

"The first thing Joseph tried to teach me was how to be alone. 'Learning to be alone without being afraid,' he used to say, 'is half of becoming a packman.' The other half was learning shortcuts. There was also a third half: learning how to fight with a staff. And a fourth one: breathing right and keeping your legs in good condition. If anyone told him he had too many halves, he answered that you could never have too many. Learning to be alone wasn't easy, believe me! I was scared to death because Joseph's way of teaching me was to make me walk half a league behind him, all by myself. I trembled like a leaf in the wind. I was even more afraid during the day than at night. For some reason I'd taken it into my six-year-old head that a kind of red monster, all covered with blood, was following me. At night I was afraid he'd grab me, but in daylight I was even more afraid I'd see him coming out of a ditch or a clump of trees. I was sure that if I ever actually laid eyes on him, I'd drop dead on the road."

He had succeeded in making Gilonne eat a quarter of an apple while he told his story.

They left the house. The big bell of Notre-Dame struck four just as they reached the Rue aux Sieurs, on their way to the Rue du Marché aux Porcs, where she would live from now on.

"Do you know what that bell says to lacemakers? 'Hurry! Run!' You'll hear it every morning, as if you were already a real lacemaker."

They had to stop when Gilonne had a moment of nausea. The day before had been a day of slaughter in the town, and the gutters of the streets still ran with blood and offal from the animals killed by the butchers. The sweetish smell, mingled with the stench of the tanneries, made her feel sick.

In front of Mistress Lescure's house, two more little girls who were also going to begin their apprenticeship that day were already waiting for the door to open. Mistress Lescure appeared, thin and white in the dark morning.

Mathieu kissed his niece and slipped a few sous into her hand—that little hand of which so much was going to be required. Then he hurried away without trying to see if she was crying. When he came back from Russia, he would go and have a look at the Ferrières estate in Pervenchères. Maybe he hadn't done his duty; maybe he should have asked about the Ferrières family and tried to let them know about Gilonne. Someone, if only a servant, would have listened to him and talked to them later, and then who could say what would have happened? Yes, he would go there; he swore he would.

That morning Marguerite discreetly tiptoed out of Gilonne's heart so she could give it entirely to Louise-Marie, known as Michanteau [Half-Chunk], when she saw her for the first time, tied to her chair in front of the big table in the workshop.

A cloth strap went around Michanteau's waist and the back of her chair. And since the apprentices' chairs were attached to a plank fastened to the floor, girls who were punished in this way couldn't escape until the strap was untied by Mistress Lescure, when she decided that the punishment had lasted long enough.

"She tied me to my chair because I always feel like dancing, and this isn't the place for it!" Michanteau said to Gilonne, laughing.

She had red lips, little teeth as white as lilies of the valley, and black hair beneath a white hat.

"Don't cry," she went on, bowing her head so the others

would be less able to hear her. "It doesn't do any good, and you can't spend four years moaning and groaning! I've been here eight months. I'll help you. . . . Stop staring at that strap— I don't even feel it."

Gilonne's admiration of her new friend increased when she learned that she was nicknamed Michanteau because at the age of four—she was now six—she had stolen half a chunk of bread from the baker on the Rue Saint-Blaise.

"Are you going to ask me why I didn't take the other half? And if I tell you it was because one half was all I needed that day, will you ask me why I didn't think of the next day? If you're the first one who doesn't ask me those silly questions, it will show you're different from everybody else!"

Gilonne hadn't thought of asking any questions at all. Stealing seemed to her such an enormous thing in itself that nothing more needed to be said about it. And she was absorbed in wondering if she would have had the courage to do it, even if she was starving. But she had quickly understood why Michanteau had stolen only what she needed for one day, without thinking of the days to come, when taking a whole loaf of bread would have been no harder than taking only a piece of it. Michanteau, so small that she had to have a chair higher than the others, had an optimism all out of proportion to her size. Solidly anchored in her heart was the hope that anything in her life might change for the better at any moment. So, why should she worry about tomorrow? Who could say that her guardian angel wouldn't come to help her? If he wasn't there in the morning, he might be there by evening! For example, once when she was hungry again, without a single sou to buy food, she had been seen by Mistress Verlot, who happened to be carrying a basket of hot cookies and gave her enough of them to last her for several days.

She always looked on the bright side and saw reasons for cheerfulness all around her. Maybe things would have been better in another place, but she had to be somewhere to learn the trade of lacemaking so it might as well be in Mistress Lescure's house rather than with some other teacher who would beat her more often. She now had enough to eat, so there was no more stealing and no more running away from the police. Even when she was complaining about how much she wished she could again be free in the fields where she had kept a flock of sheep, she managed to laugh. During rest periods she would run around and around Mistress Lescure's apple tree, and whenever she could do it without being seen she would climb to the top of it and cry out, ''I see the steeple of the church! Hello, Blessed Virgin! Please make the old lady break a leg so she'll know what it's like to spend hours and hours without moving.''

Gilonne and Michanteau decided they would be friends the rest of their lives.

Strangely, Marguerite the turkey died that day. Of old age. But Mama Bordier always claimed the poor animal had died of sorrow, knowing that Gilonne was unhappy on a dark, foul-smelling street in Alençon, held prisoner in a house where there was probably never any fresh air or wholesome food.

Unlike Mama Bordier, the townspeople considered Mistress Lescure's house to be exceptionally pleasant and comfortable, and felt that the children she took in as boarders were lucky to be there. The women who went there to make lace were envied. They carried lanterns to light their way when they arrived at four o'clock in the morning in summer, five o'clock in winter, and they again carried lanterns when they left, eighteen hours later.

It was a house with a half-timbered façade. On the first floor was a big room with a stone fireplace; it served as a kitchen and dining hall on one side and as Mistress Lescure's bedroom on the other. The second floor was divided into a large and a small workshop. Under the wooden stairs was a narrow room, scarcely larger than a closet, where Mistress Lescure's father, a retired soldier who had been a pikeman in the army of the late King Louis XIII, slept and kept his clothes. In the attic, under the thatched mansard roof, was the apprentices' dormitory, with their straw mattresses lined up in a row. It could be reached only by climbing an outside ladder, and its only source of heat was the kitchen fireplace, which barely kept the air in the upstairs rooms above the freezing point in winter. Near the apple tree was the well, from which the girls took turns drawing water.

Juniper was a constant occupant of the house. All year round, juniper twigs were burned, berries were roasted, and leaves were boiled. Mistress Lescure's mother and grandmother had always used it as a disinfectant during epidemics. There had been no plague or cholera in the town for a long time, but purifying the air of the house could only be favorable to the whiteness of the lace made there. For years, Gilonne's terrors of the first months of her apprenticeship were associated in her mind with the rather harsh smell of juniper leaves simmering all day long in the fireplace.

The obsessive thought of having to sit still for hours, and her fear of not being able to do it, made her tremble from head to toe as soon as she sat down at the big table in the workshop. Neither Uncle Mathieu nor Mama Bordier had told her she was going to be a prisoner. Why had they hidden it from her? And how long was it going to last? Tomorrow, or the day after, would she again be strapped to her chair as she had been today, until Mistress Lescure rang the bell of deliverance? And even then, would she again have to wait for Mistress Lescure to come slowly, so slowly, to unfasten the strap while the other girls were already running in the garden? Michanteau said she didn't feel the strap. That was a lie: The strap was as painful to wear as Jesus' crown of thorns. Was old Martagon, Father Dutilleux's dog, made that miserable by his collar and rope?

"You mustn't cry," Michanteau told her. "Afterward, your eyes hurt and you can't see to do your work right."

How could she keep from crying when she and Martagon were going to be prisoners day after day, month after month, year after year? And it wasn't true that when her wooden shoes had fallen on the floor they had made a noise that bothered the other girls, or that they were ridiculous, painted red and decorated with cornflowers. She had been given ugly cloth slippers and a gray fustian skirt that she had to wash in the river on Sundays, then wait, in her petticoat, for it to dry.

The first night, Michanteau said to Gilonne, "Listen to the new girls sniffling instead of sleeping. I cried all night too, for several nights. And what good did it do me? I was strapped to my chair for a whole week, and I had to do all kinds of extra work. You don't die from being unhappy. And unhappiness gets tired and goes away, like everything else. You'd better go to sleep as soon as you can. The leper may come out tonight. He often shows up on nights when there's a full moon, and if you see him, you can forget about sleeping!"

Who was the leper? Banban, an older girl, a cripple with a lively tongue, bright eyes, and cheeks the color of ripe cherries, explained to Gilonne: "A charming young man, a draper's son, used to live in that dark old house between the midwife's and the fishmonger's. He was so handsome that someone ugly and spiteful must have cast a spell on him, because he got leprosy. The intendant had him sent to the leper-house in Rouen. He died there, but they say his ghost was brought back here by Saint Roch, who watches over lepers. Sometimes he walks back and forth in his house at night and you can see him through his windows. Saint Roch sends his dog to him, to bring him food. The dog has been seen too: He's huge and reddish, and he carries a basket by holding its handle between his teeth. One of the lacemakers in the workshop says she's seen him three times this year, when she was working late. Mistress Lescure is sure she's heard him and says he doesn't bark like other dogs.

"When there's something white moving in the windows of that house, don't look. It's the leper's ghost, with the hood he wears to hide his face because it's all covered with sores. Don't listen when he yells that he's hungry and the dog hasn't come. That big dog must come from far away to bring him his supper. One thing is sure: It's not good for anyone to look at a leper. If you see him, close your eyes, say a prayer for him and another one for yourself, and put Sister Adelaide by the window to protect you."

And who was Sister Adelaide?

Michanteau and Banban introduced her. She was the protector of the attic dormitory, a doll with a wooden head and a body stuffed with bran, wearing the habit of the Clarist nuns: brown robe and cape, white collar, black veil, long rope belt. There was so much to say about her powers that it would have to be spread over several nights. Banban, who had a lot of words piled up inside her because talking wasn't allowed in the workshop, would tell Gilonne what she needed to know. For now, she would say only that she should take Sister Adelaide to bed with her at night when she was sick. Banban often had a fever and got over it with the doll's help. Mistress Lescure thought her herb teas cured the girls' sicknesses, but they knew Sister Adelaide did it, when they held her tightly against themselves at night.

That first night the leper didn't appear. Gilonne had just fallen asleep, relieved, when Michanteau shook her awake.

"You don't pee in bed, do you? She can't stand that, and she won't keep girls who do it. She says she doesn't want any rotting mattresses or girls who stink and spoil the lace thread with their smell. All she ever thinks about is keeping her lace white! You've seen her father, the old man with a beard. She won't let him smoke his pipe in the house. You now what he says about her? He says she's like Saint Catherine: If you cut off her head, milk would come out instead of blood. The old man is very nice, you'll see. He used to be a pikeman in the king's army. One day he gave us some sugar he'd won playing cards with Fulgence, the grocer. Fulgence's wife won't give him any money to play cards with, and Mistress Lescure won't give her father any either, so he catches eels in the Briante and Fulgence steals things from the shop, and that's what they gamble with. Fulgence is almost always the one who wins. They say our old pikeman doesn't have any luck. They also say the eels end up in Mistress Verlot's inn. Banban asked him why he didn't just take them straight to the inn and sell them. He said he'd rather gamble with them because they give him more enjoyment that way. One day he won some herrings that the grocer had stolen from his wife, and he brought them here, along with his own eels. The eels weren't fresh anymore and the herrings stank. Mistress Lescure yelled at him so loud you could hear her at the end of the street. He bowed his head like a little boy—and he'd killed Turks when he was in the army! Do you want to go back to sleep?''

No, Gilonne didn't want to go back to sleep. She had some stories to tell too. And the mattress filled with fresh straw reminded her of the one in Uncle Mathieu's room. She talked about the famous packman without telling any of his secrets. Michanteau was interested to hear about the two-legged wagon and glad to know that maybe she too would be given a staff when Uncle Mathieu came back and learned that she was Gilonne's friend. The two girls fell asleep holding hands.

When Gilonne awoke, her terror returned.

"I don't want to be tied to my chair today," she murmured to Michanteau.

But Michanteau didn't hear her. She was busy putting Sister Adelaide deep into the straw of a mattress.

"There, that's a good hiding place for her. The straw is fresh, it's changed often—that's another one of Mistress Lescure's ideas about keeping her lace white! They bring bundles of straw up here and the smell makes us think we're back in the country. Banban sneezes and coughs, but she wouldn't trade places with the king, would you, Banban?''

Banban didn't answer. She was trying to comfort two newcomers, two little peasant girls who had begun crying again when they herd Michanteau talk about being back in the country. They huddled at the back of the attic with their arms around each other and refused to move. They were saying, in their way, that learning to make fine lace was not at all the same thing as making *bisette* while they watched over a flock of sheep. They

wanted to go back home, right now. If they did, Banban told
them, they would be beaten, and it would be worse than what
they would have to put up with if they stayed here. Did they
know how much their parents had received from the intendant
and "on behalf of the king," in remission of taxes, for having
their children serve an apprenticeship with a lacemaker? No?
Then all they knew was how to cry and complain! And Banban,
who was eight years old and knew life, advised silence and
resignation. Seeing their bewildered faces, however, she doubted
that they had understood her. Too bad, she thought, her experience could have served as an example. She could have told
about the time she went back home. Yes, she had been foolish
enough to do that, three years ago. She had limped to her house
in the suburb of Courteille. Her mother had immediately brought
her back, after a beating with a knotted rope that made her limp
still more. No parents, unless they suddenly lost their minds,
would give back the money they had been paid for apprenticing
their children to lacemakers.

The two new girls didn't seem to be reassured by listening to
Banban, whom they scarcely knew. One of them tried to stop
sobbing long enough to explain what frightened them, and the
other girls finally understood that they were in constant dread
of "the lady's" punishments because they struck as quickly and
unexpectedly as lightning. Gilonne felt the same way.

"All right, I'll break my word one more time," said Michanteau, "and tell you how to keep from being punished. I'll
make up for it by spending more time in confession this Sunday!"

But Banban persuaded her not to do it. Mistress Lescure had
said, "Next time, Michanteau, I'll send you away for good,"
and she had meant it. Banban couldn't break her oath either.
Maybe Hélisende could tell the new girls what to expect, since
she was given special treatment.

"Her father sends fresh straw for our mattresses every other
month, and that's important to Mistress Lescure, so it won't be
as sinful for her to break her oath as it would be for the rest of
us."

The oath in question was taken by all the apprentices on the
evening before Saint Remi's Day, the day when new girls came
each year: "I swear by the cross not to say anything about the
rules of the workshop to the girls who will arrive tomorrow."
These rules consisted of the prohibitions that Mistress Lescure

intended to impress on the newcomers in her own way. Knowing that a list of rules would only partially penetrate children's brains if it were simply recited to them, even several times, she made it her policy to wait until they did something wrong, then punish them for it instantly, severely, and by surprise. Experience had shown the effectiveness of this method. The difficulty was in getting cooperative silence from the other girls. She dealt harshly with those who betrayed her.

Two apprentices had been sent to Madame Maillon almost as soon as they arrived, because they were covered with lice. Madame Maillon lived nearby and was a delouser as well as a midwife.

Having finished their treatment, the two girls had returned, and all nine apprentices, five of them newcomers, were now seated around the table after saying their prayers standing up, with their hands joined.

Mistress Lescure inspected them all for cleanliness before distributing the needles and thread. She was always ready to pounce on any girl who hadn't cleaned her fingernails with a pointed stick, or who had a lock of hair sticking out from under her hat, because she would later soil her fingers when she pushed it back. Since their clothes had to be free of any wisps of straw from their mattresses, the girls made it a habit, and a brief diversion, to search each other for straw every morning.

They liked that time before the day's work began because they didn't yet have to sit completely still. They could look around, be amused by the strange picture of a bishop with one eye open and the other closed—a portrait of Saint Remi, according to Michanteau—or admire the picture of Joan of Arc on horseback. Was it an apprentice who had made that hole in Saint Joan's body? If so, she must have had to spend at least three nights in the cellar!

The long table was even longer than Mama Bordier's, on which thirty-five plucked turkeys, wrapped in white cloths, could be laid side by side at Christmas. How those white cloths of Mama Bordier's would have pleased Mistress Lescure! Michanteau said that in the houses of many other mistress-lacemakers the apprentices' straw mattresses were laid on the floor under the tables at night. But, Mistress Lescure was afraid that the sleeping girls' breath would warm the air and turn the lace yellow, so they slept in the attic. Gilonne wondered if she wouldn't have preferred sleeping on the floor of the workshop, rather than having to climb up to the attic every night on a ladder in the garden, between the apple tree and the clothesline. She didn't like to think of what might happen in winter, when the rungs of the ladder would become slippery with ice. Banban said you always had to watch what you were doing if you didn't want to go down a lot faster than was good for you and that it was also a good idea to pray to Jacob for help.

That morning, as she waited to be given her piece of parchment, Gilonne looked at the other girls. Banban, so pale when she slept, now had red cheeks and eyes that were too bright. Mama Bordier didn't like eyes like that, she said they were the traveling companions of fever. The four other new girls had eyes as round as peas. Gilonne wondered if she looked as stupid as they did.

Perrine, who had been there two years, had a winsome face, with her turned-up nose. She was deaf, but Michanteau said it wasn't sad because she didn't hear the leper's dog or the sound of clanging metal from the nearby blacksmith's shop. Colombe and Ermeline, the butcher's daughters, were not particularly attractive. Banban said that on Sundays, when they were allowed to go home—a special favor that was granted, according to Michanteau, because Mistress Lescure believed in always being on good terms with her butcher—they ate so much meat that when they came back they looked like two pâtés.

And then there was Hélisende. She was older than any of the others, at least ten, and intimidated them. They didn't dare to look at her very much, even though she smiled at them when they did. Hélisende was tactful, purehearted, and gentle, and she had marvelous violet eyes. Jérémie, who always gave his opinion on the girls of Montsort, would have said she had all the feminine graces. Her father, Monsieur de Rochefilde, had decided that she would enter a convent. The family estate would go to his older son, the younger one would serve in the king's army, and, so that she could worthily become a Clarist nun, his daughter would earn her dowry by making lace. Hélisende was the only apprentice who didn't live in Mistress Lescure's house. One of her aunts had a big house in Alençon, and she went there every evening, when the nurse who had brought her in the morning came to take her back.

It was this same nurse who had dressed Hélisende's doll as a Clarist nun and had it blessed one day when there was a religious procession. One winter when Banban was coughing more than usual and had a fever that made her delirious, Hélisende had brought Sister Adelaide, hiding her under her skirts, and said, "Give her to Banban and she'll get well." Sister Adelaide proved to be effective against sickness and was very helpful on nights when the leper appeared. After Banban's recovery, the girls in the attic asked to keep her a little longer. Months went by, and Hélisende still didn't take back her doll. Michanteau thought she had already taken her vows in her heart, that she was living more in her convent than out of it, and that she had little interest in dolls. Gilonne didn't entirely agree. "Maybe she's already living with the nuns," she said, "but that's not why she lets us keep Sister Adelaide. She does it because she loves us."

And it was good to feel that Hélisende loved you, comforting to listen to her beautiful violet eyes. They said, "Cheer up: In a little while Mistress Lescure's bell will ring for the beginning of the rest period, and the morning will be over." Then, with a happy little sigh, Gilonne would go on making evenly spaced needle holes along the inked lines that formed the lace pattern on parchment. This was pricking, the first operation in making *point de France*.

The bell rang. She felt such joy in stretching that she had to thank God for it. But why should she cry again? Was she going to be crying all the time? Hélisende's hand came down on her shoulder, like a warm, affectionate bird that murmured, "Don't be sad."

Lunch—a piece of bread and a bowl of soup—was taken under the apple tree in good weather. Now, in spring, it was a warm day, and sparrows came to feed on the crumbs that were thrown to them. If Gilonne didn't think of Mama Bordier, or Uncle Mathieu, or Grandmother Thomine, she hardly had a lump in her throat at all, and for the first time since coming there she was able to swallow some food.

"Eat it all," said Hélisende. "It's good. Mistress Lescure's father is the one who does the cooking, and since he loves to eat he does it well."

After lunch Hélisende took Gilonne to the back of the little garden, near the pigsty. The pig was kept not to be eaten but to rid the Lescure house of peelings and other edible garbage. In six months or so, when he became fat, he would be sold and replaced with a thin pig. Girls who hadn't seen the exchange were sometimes surprised when they came out in the morning and saw only a shadow of the huge animal that had been there the day before. Each successive pig was given the same name: Torchette.

"Listen carefully, because we don't have much time," Hélisende said to Gilonne. "I'll tell you about Mistress Lescure's rules, and tonight in the attic you can tell the other girls. Don't talk while you're working, or laugh, cry, shout or make signals. Don't move your legs, scratch yourself, touch your hair, keep any food in your pockets, or spit. If you blow your nose, be sure to wipe your hands afterward. Have you seen the rag we're supposed to use for that? When you wash your clothes on Sunday, don't get wet, because we're punished if we catch a cold. In church, if someone asks you who you are, answer, 'I have the good luck to be one of Mistress Lescure's apprentices.' She likes us to say that. And whatever you do, make sure you never lose a needle or spoil the slightest bit of thread. . . . Wait, there's more."

But, led by Michanteau, the other girls had started a round dance, and when Perrine passed close to Gilonne she took her by the arm and pulled her away. Was there sadness in Hélisende's eyes? Gilonne thought so, and it spoiled the pleasure she would have taken in dancing.

That night the other new girls were informed of the rules to be obeyed in the workshop.

The next day one of the butcher's daughters set off a disaster by asking "Where's the rag?" after blowing her nose. The newcomers weren't supposed to know about that ritual, since no one had performed it since their arrival. Mistress Lescure glared accusingly at Banban and Michanteau.

"I'm the one who told," Hélisende said in her gentle voice.

Mistress Lescure seemed to hesitate, then she sent her favorite to stay in the cellar until the sandglass had emptied five times.

"She'd have given *me* twenty!" Michanteau said under her breath.

When Hélisende came back to her place, she was even paler than usual. She reported that she had been bitten by a rat, though only slightly. She had killed the revolting animal by throwing a stone at it, and she seemed glad of what she had done. It was disconcerting to see her guileless face and kindly eyes showing jubilation over that death. "I killed him, I killed him," she murmured several times, with her hands trembling.

A smile from Hélisende or a wink from Michanteau or Banban was enough to make Gilonne hope that things would go better, but not enough to make it happen. The torments of hell couldn't be much worse than having to sit still so long. Sometimes she felt as if bugs were crawling on her legs and she couldn't help kicking the air under the table, at the risk of being punished. At other times the lower part of her body seemed so numb that she wondered if she could still walk. She dreamed of running wildly in the fields with her turkeys, and nearly wept from despair and fatigue. But she managed to keep sitting up straight on her chair and pricking her parchment.

In the evening, Michanteau congratulated her on having held out through another day and let her take Sister Adelaide in her arms even though the leper hadn't appeared and no one was sick. Banban was a little Conte-Nouvelles who knew all about the town and its gossip. Her stories worked as well as lullabies in helping Gilonne to fall asleep without thinking too much about the next day. How did Banban gather all her information? Did she get it from the grown-up lacemakers in the big workshop, who were allowed to talk when they weren't singing hymns? But apprentices weren't allowed to go and see them. . . .

Gilonne had little interest in Alençon gossip. To her, Banban's stories were less a satisfaction of her curiosity than a soporific that made her gradually sink into sleep. What she liked about the town was its everyday life. She enjoyed picking up traces of it from Hélisende, who came in every morning smelling of fog and smoke, and the cream sold by the milkwoman she had stopped to greet, admiring the ease with which she carried her two heavy earthenware jugs, and the powder swept out of the wigmaker's shop by his little apprentice, and the fresh bread that the baker had just made. Someday Hélisende would meet Uncle Mathieu, or Chopine. . . . In the meantime, Gilonne asked her if people were getting ready for the market and if the old water carrier was already shouting loudly enough to wake the dead.

Every evening, when darkness began to fall, each girl lit her candle and put it in just the right place behind the water-filled glass bowl that would increase its light. They had to be careful not to make any abrupt movements that might disrupt that delicate arrangement. Later, when it was time to stop working, Gilonne was disheartened by the thought that only Hélisende would make her way through the mystery of the streets. Never again would she walk in the moonlight with Uncle Mathieu and go to see the prince of lace.

The day always began with what the lacemakers in the big shop called "the old soldier's last war."

The Intendant of Alençon had decreed that each inhabitant of the town must pile up the rubbish in front of his door so that it could be more conveniently loaded and taken away by the driver of the collection cart. Mistress Lescure had ordered her father to go to work with his shovel every morning at dawn. As soon as he came out of his little room under the stairs, with his old-fashioned goatee and turned-up mustache still tousled from the night, Gérasime Lescure put on his wooden shoes and took his shovel, just as, in the days when he was one of His Majesty's proud pikemen, he had put on his boots and helmet and taken his pike to go off and face the enemy. Two adversaries pressed in on him, from the left and the right, when he stepped into the battlefield, which was still shrouded in morning mist. This state of war had been going on for years, ever since the Lescures, father and daughter, were accused of shifting part of their rubbish to their neighbors' piles. Everyone on the street knew the lacemaker's hatred of any kind of dirt, and it was commonly believed that every night she diminished her own refuse heap to the detriment of others, to make it less disturbing to her during the ten to fifteen days that the irregular town cart took to come and remove it. The old soldier's battles were therefore defensive, rather than offensive. He stood guard, shovel in hand, to protect his pile from the neighbors who tried to augment it with things that, according to them, had been added to their own piles during the night. The apprentices, who liked him, always hoped he would be victorious in these daily combats, and it saddened them to see him struggle until he was out of breath. They dreamed of routing his enemies.

It occurred to Gilonne that since the leper's ghost walked at night he probably saw what happened and might be helpful in exposing the real culprits. She mentioned this idea to Gérasime Lescure one day. He was interested, but said that his determined, spiteful adversaries wouldn't accept the testimony of a leper, especially one who had died a hundred years ago. So he would have to go on fighting against the good-for-nothing on the left and the lunatic on the right.

Gilonne thought it over that night, lying on her straw mattress, and the next day, as she was putting away the books after a reading lesson from Gérasime (who also served as the apprentices' teacher), she suggested to him that maybe the big reddish dog had something to do with moving the rubbish at night. She used to have a dog friend named Martagon who played pranks like that. It was worth considering, said Gérasime; some night he would stand guard with his big pike and kill that beast if he proved to be guilty. This threw Gilonne into a panic. No! He mustn't do that! The leper needed the dog to bring him food. All she wanted was to find out if it was the dog that had been moving the rubbish. Animals sometimes did annoying things without meaning any harm.

Deeply touched, Gérasime tried to reassure her. She mustn't cry over such a small matter. He gave her an apple and asked her who had taught her to read and write so well that she was better at it than any of the others except Banban. She told him about Father Dutilleux, Jérémie, and Uncle Mathieu. From then on she talked about them with her new friend every Sunday, while he watched her and the other girls playing knucklebones in either the garden or the kitchen, depending on the weather.

This game was Gérasime's idea. He had convinced his daughter that it would develop the girls' dexterity and keep them out of mischief. He knew she was opposed to the advice of her confessor, a Jesuit who recommended games involving physical exercise because he considered them necessary to children's health and the good quality of their work, and praised the excellent results that the schools of his order had obtained by following this principle. Mistress Lescure had calculated that half an hour a day of these diversions, multiplied by the number of apprentices and the number of working days, represented seven hundred hours of lost work. She might as well throw two inches of lace onto the rubbish heap and take a loss of two hundred livres! Besides, washing clothes in the river was good exercise and didn't cost anything. She was resentful of her Jesuit for always bringing up the question between confessions. But after thinking it over, she had decided in favor of her father's suggestion. Just to be sure, however, since the word "game" was a kind of blasphemy as far as she was concerned, she consulted the Jesuit about it.

"It's an innocent game," he told her, "and it's been known since ancient times. Roman soldiers used to play it."

Gérasime supplied the five sheep bones that each child

needed. He got them from the butcher and boiled them in several pots of soup to make sure they were totally free of any trace of flesh. When he gave them to the apprentices he laughed and said that, in a way, he was giving them his emblem, because he was known as the Lord of Boiled Meat and his motto was "Everything in the pot!"

He explained: To avoid the danger of having burned fat or anything else in the air that might dull the whiteness of her lace, Mistress Lescure refused to allow any food to be fried, roasted, or fricasseed in her house. What was there left for a poor cook in such unfortunate circumstances? Boiling. He could cook only by boiling things in his pot. Gérasime dreamed of roasts, omelets, and fricasseed eels, but he had to boil everything, even the splendid turkeys that came from Mistress Bordier every month. When they had eggs, each girl broke one in her bowl and he poured hot soup onto it. Michanteau said he looked so sad at those times that she felt like kissing him to cheer him up, and she might have done it if his goatee and mustache hadn't had such sharp points.

Lean, emaciated, thin as the bleached thread she bought from Haarlem, Mistress Lescure had no interest in food. She would take a little bouillon, dip a piece of bread in it—white or black, it made no difference to her—and then stand up from the table almost as soon as she had sat down. Her father said that if he didn't remind her when it was time to eat, she would forget to do it altogether, and crumble into dust before she was buried. He was comfortably plump and was suspected of eating lunch and supper at least twice a day: once when he kept tasting the food as he cooked it, and again when he sat down at the table "with his women," as he said with a good-natured laugh. That his daughter disapproved of his lightheartedness didn't surprise him, since he associated a gaunt body with a grim disposition.

The rule that the apprentices and lacemakers had to wash their hands after meals was obeyed with mockery in the big workshop, where it was said that when Mistress Lescure went to heaven she would insist not only on washing her own hands but also on having the Lord and all the saints and angels wash theirs. But, whether they admitted it or not, the lacemakers were all proud to be working in a shop renowned for its cleanliness, its order, and the exquisite, immaculately white lace it produced. Even Thiphaine, a beautiful red-haired young woman who had worked in Mistress Lescure's house since childhood, felt the same pride as the others. The apprentices looked at her with admiration and apprehension, thinking of what was said about her: that if she ever had a carriage she wouldn't need horses for it, because plenty of men would be glad to pull it in exchange for a smile. It was also said that her wantonness would take her straight to hell and that she was already expected there.

Mistress Lescure was often in despair over Thiphaine, but she couldn't give up her skilled hands and golden voice. Sometimes one of the "carriage pullers" would stand outside the house and wait for Thiphaine to come out. Mistress Lescure's fingers would then become tense as she worked, and woe to any apprentice who made the slightest mistake!

When Thiphaine left the house after her eighteen hours of work—sometimes nineteen or twenty—she laughed so infectiously that people in the street turned to look at her, wishing they could go wherever she was going and laugh with her. She went to the arcades of the Place du Palais, where the lights were bright and you could watch a theatrical performance, eat hot apple fritters, and drink spiced cider. And it was there that a man presented an amazing spectacle: a troupe of ducks dressed as noblemen, with swords hanging at their sides and plumed hats on their heads. Michanteau and Banban had heard of it, and said they would gladly spend the time of twenty sandglasses in the cellar, with the rats, for a chance to see that show.

Unable to see it themselves, they thought of asking Hélisende to go and then describe it to them in detail. But they decided against it because they didn't think Hélisende was capable of describing such a thing in a way that would be worth hearing. If only Banban could see it! She would describe it in a way that would make them feel they had seen it with their own eyes.

It wasn't the troupe of ducks that Banban saw and told about, but a much more astonishing exhibition, something that the people of Alençon had to look at twice to make sure they weren't imagining it.

Mistress Lescure seldom needed anyone to run errands for her in town, but when she did, she sent Banban. Everyone, including Banban herself, wondered why she made this choice. Did she want to give Banban a chance to exercise her bad leg, the one that was shorter than the other? Did she feel that an occasional diversion would make it easier for her to bear her sadness at being crippled? Whatever the reason, it was Banban who went to deliver a pound of Flemish thread to Madame La

Perrière, the greatest maker of Alençon lace and Mistress Lescure's revered teacher. She walked past the Royal Manufactory, and what did she see there?

"Oh, mistress," she said when she came back, "in front of the door there was a pillory, and in it was a beautiful flounce made of Alençon lace! A flounce in a pillory! Like old Célestin the cutpurse, or that bandit who robbed the Rouen stagecoach. They were real criminals, but . . . a flounce? There was a sign on it giving the name of the lacemaking shop that worked without permission from the Royal Manufactory. It was Antoine Lantier's. The names of his lacemakers were on the sign too: Jaquine, the daughter of the fishmonger on the Rue du Bercail, and big Toinette. They were there for a while, crying, but some of their friends took them away so the police wouldn't notice them. Antoine Lantier has been fined a thousand livres. They say it's going to ruin him, and his shop will soon be for sale. All the people who saw that lace being spoiled by the wind and rain, and knew the hours and months and years of work it took to make it, said it was a shame to do such a thing, and some of them were crying, like Bérangère and Toinette."

Mistress Lescure heated the inside of her wooden shoes, put on her warmest clothes, and went off to see the outrage Banban had reported. It would be hard, she said, for the women of Alençon to forgive the people in Paris who had ordered it to be done. It reminded her of the time when the Venetian lacemakers had stirred up a rebellion in the town. A piece of lace in a pillory! Who could ever have imagined that anyone would do something so despicable?

Gérasime, who watched over the apprentices while his daughter was away, sighed. The good old days were really gone; such monstrous things would never have been done in the reign of his beloved sovereign, Louis XIII. When the girls finished singing one of their hymns, he suggested that they sing a more cheerful song, hoping it would make them forget their troubles.

One day when the apprentices had been pricking for thirteen hours, sitting around their table, and it was still two hours before the time when Mistress Lescure's bell would announce the end of the day's work, Colombe threw down her stiletto and began shrieking something that no one could understand because she was sobbing at the same time. Her sister trembled at seeing her like that, then she too began shrieking. The other girls seemed to be wondering if they could stop working. A look from Mistress Lescure removed all doubt on the subject: work continued. The two sisters smothered their screams in the wet cloths that were pressed against their faces.

"Even a butcher's daughters can lose their self-control," murmured Michanteau.

A short time later, when darkness was falling and the branches of the apple tree could no longer be seen through the window, Perrine collapsed. Without saying anything, she put down her work and sighed, then her head wavered and fell onto the table as if it had been cut off. She had fainted. Her hat, which fitted loosely over her stiff hair, flew through the air and came down on Michanteau's hand. Bérangère, a girl who worked badly and was in danger of being sent away by Mistress Lescure, later said she had seen a black angel with red eyes hit Perrine on the head and playfully toss her hat in the air. The girls were frightened. That night in the attic they moved their straw mattresses closer together. This was the second time Bérangère had seen the black angel: The first time she had seen him lifting the lid of Gérasime's pot. The others hoped the evil intruder would leave the house at the same time as the incompetent apprentice.

One night Aveline, one of the two peasant girls, awoke with a scream, sat up on her mattress, and shouted, "No! I won't!" She had been tied to her chair all day for having cut her thread with her teeth, a crime against whiteness. The others went back to sleep after giving her Sister Adelaide. They knew that being tied to a chair for fourteen hours always gave a girl nightmares.

Gilonne had given up counting her days and nights of imprisonment, so she didn't know how many times she had cried with her face against her mattress. But when Mistress Lescure confiscated her knucklebones to punish her for having broken her glass bowl—five Sundays without playing the game she liked so much!—she decided it was time for her to stop crying. Her heart could go on crying sometimes, but would have to do it in silence, because she would soon be six years old.

Banban was still coughing. Much too much. It was very cold now and the girls had painful chilblains on their hands. Gérasime filled their clay foot warmers with glowing embers so that they had hot feet and numb legs, but the rest of their bodies remained icy cold.

At night they heard wolves that came to the ramparts and, it was said, clawed at the gates in their rage at not being able to come into the town. In the attic the girls huddled up against each other and asked Sister Adelaide to protect them. But did she also have the power to drive away ferocious animals and strengthen the gates of Alençon?

On one bitterly cold morning, when even the hot milk that Gérasime gave the girls was not enough to warm them and it seemed to them that their heads were full of fog, Banban began coughing almost as soon as she sat down at the table, and continued a long time. Suddenly, on a piece of lace in front of her, the other apprentices saw a spot of blood, then another, and another. . . . Maybe it was the cold that paralyzed them and kept them from standing up and screaming.

They looked at Banban. Her cheeks had been bright red when she got up, but now she was white as a sheet and her frightened eyes seemed to be calling out for help. The others couldn't help looking at those horrible spots again and again. They knew that bloodstained lace could never be really white again. They had heard of beautiful pieces that would never be sold because one drop of blood had fallen on them from a lacemaker's pricked finger. What was Mistress Lescure going to say? They turned to her and saw that she was pale too. Was it from anger? She said nothing. She took Banban by the hand and led her toward the kitchen. Hélisende had tears in her eyes. Soon they were all weeping.

Banban drank some hot bouillon and was put to bed in Mistress Lescure's alcove. The curtains were drawn when the others went to lunch. They talked quietly so as not to disturb her.

Banban stayed in the alcove for the rest of the day and all that night. The next morning it was Gilonne's turn to draw water from the well. She looked through the half-open door and saw Mistress Lescure sitting beside Banban. She motioned Gilonne not to come any closer, but said softly, "She's been asking for Sister Adelaide. Who is that?"

"She's our doll, in the attic. She makes you well if you keep her with you."

"Go and get her."

The second night, Gérasime wrapped Banban in a blanket and took her to the hospice. She was so frail, so thin, that big tears of despair trickled down to his mustache. He knew why his daughter had told him to take Banban away: She didn't want the others to see her die. He sobbed and had to stop and sit down for a moment on the steps of the Saint-Léonard church. Banban had another fit of coughing. He felt blood flowing onto his hands and worried that the bleeding might frighten her. He was trembling—he, the old soldier who had killed Turks with his pike. But Banban would never be frightened again. She was delirious. "Saint Roch's dog," she was saying, "the one that brings food to the leper . . . I know how he comes. He doesn't come through the Sagory Gate or the Lancrel Gate—he comes through the gates of heaven!"

By the time Gérasime came within sight of the hospice, Banban was dead. When he heard someone calling his name he thought he must be imagining it, but he turned around anyway and saw that Gilonne and Michanteau had followed him.

"Sister Adelaide!" cried Gilonne, short of breath from running. "You forgot Sister Adelaide!"

Gérasime didn't understand what she meant, but he took the doll she handed him and had the presence of mind to say, "I'm in a hurry to get into the hospice because it's cold out here."

A moment later he had disappeared into the building. Gilonne and Michanteau sighed with relief. Everything would be all right: Sister Adelaide had never let anyone die.

On their way back, the darkness made them uneasy but they were able to laugh at the thought of what they would tell Banban about their escapade when she came out of the hospice. They encountered the Moor on the sign of the Mistress Verlot's inn, were startled by the white gleam of his smile in the darkness, and decided to tell Banban they had been attacked by the Moor.

The girls all waited for Banban's return. Whenever they asked Gérasime about her, he answered, "They're taking good care of her at the hospice, but she's still not well enough to work without getting too tired, so they're going to keep her a while longer." Once they were surprised to hear him say, "Before she left here, she told me, 'I like the egg and hot soup you give me. It's smooth as velvet and it keeps me from coughing.' Yes, she told me that."

Mama Bordier arranged to bring her monthly basket to Mistress Lescure's house on Thursday, after leaving the market. She couldn't talk to Gilonne, however, because family visits were not allowed. There was already enough time wasted, with all the religious holidays required by the Church! Mama Bordier and Gilonne waved to each other from a distance, but that was worse than not seeing each other at all, because they showed falsely smiling faces that didn't deceive either of them.

Chopine and Conte-Nouvelles were more devious: They never set foot in Mistress Lescure's house but, having spotted Hélisende's daily trips to and from it, they gave her messages to deliver to Gilonne. Grandmother Thomine was doing well. Marie was still sleeping most of the time. Coeur-de-Coing hadn't improved, but the new Courapied was a godsend. She knew how to read, and every month she stole an almanac from the gatekeeper, so deftly that he was at his wit's end trying to discover who the thief was—and it served him right for being so stingy! The best part of it was that he told his troubles to Courapied because he trusted her completely, though only the devil knew why. This added a little spice to the affair of the stolen almanacs and gave the old women another reason to laugh until they nearly split their sides.

For Gilonne's sixth birthday, Chopine, Conte-Nouvelles, and Thomine came to serenade her outside Mistress Lescure's house, singing a Christmas carol with its words altered to show clearly who was singing it, and to whom.

Now that she was six, it was time for Gilonne to learn outlining, the second operation in making *point de France*. Over the pattern of little holes she had made so evenly, she had to form an outline of thread. It wasn't easy—she had to use two needles, one working above the parchment, the other below it—but learning something new made sitting still seem more bearable to her.

All of Gilonne's apprenticeship with Mistress Lescure took place during the affair of the dress-fronts of the king's sister-in-law, which lasted four years and became the darkest memory in Symonne Lescure's life.

It was a long story that had begun with a visit to the shop by a very elegant lady in a dark red silk dress adorned with gold braid and bows. The lustrous pearls that encircled her round, smooth neck were beautiful enough to captivate even Mistress Lescure. Smiling in all her finery and cooing like a dove, the lady sat down and explained her visit. She had just left the Royal Manufactory in Alençon, where an overload of orders had thrown everyone into a frenzy. Unable to accept the order she had come to place, the director had suggested that she go to the Royal Manufactory in Sedan. This was a laughable suggestion, she said, but she wasn't amused by it: Having already suffered through a three-day journey from Paris, she wouldn't have the strength to go back and then make an even longer journey in the opposite direction. As an alternative, the director had advised her to see Mistress Lescure, who worked with the Royal Manufactory, sheltered beneath its majestic wings, so to speak.

The lady was the owner of Les Dentelles d'Or [The Golden Laces], a Paris shop that supplied lace to the royal court. What she wanted was to have two lace-fronts made for the Duchess of Orléans, the king's sister-in-law, one of her faithful customers. From a large purse made of the same silk as her dress and decorated with the same gold braid, she took drawings by Monsieur Le Brun, the king's painter, who, with His Majesty's authorization, had designed the dress-fronts to be made for the duchess.

Mistress Lescure was dazzled. These were lace designs of a kind she had never before held in her hands. She tried not to tremble when she took them. She knew she was going to have some hard bargaining to do and she didn't want to give her adversary any kind of advantage beforehand. She had to avoid showing too much admiration, but she also had to avoid giving the impression that she was a peasant who couldn't appreciate what she was seeing.

From the firm set of their mouths, the two women had shrewdly sized each other up as implacable negotiators. The graceful curves of the Parisian's neck and cheeks concealed as much hardness as there was behind Mistress Lescure's sharp angles. With ruses and concessions on both sides, accompanied by false shows of generosity and renunciation, they finally reached an agreement. Mistress Lescure would put her workshop into a state of siege. Six lacemakers, all unmarried and without family obligations, would be assigned to the project, and would be expected to work nineteen to twenty hours a day for a year and a half. During that period they would live in Mistress Lescure's house, sleeping on mattresses in their workroom and eating with the apprentices.

Before a notary, Mistress Lescure acknowledged that she had in her possession the valuable designs created by Monsieur Le Brun, the king's painter, and she agreed to have her lacemakers swear to reveal nothing about them to anyone. She also agreed to deliver the finished work for a price of eight thousand livres, minus advance payment, within eighteen months. And to balance what she had received—the designs and the advance payment—she would leave on deposit at Les Dentelles d'Or, as security, twelve lappets and six pairs of cuffs, to be returned to her when the dress-fronts for the duchess had been delivered, along with the original designs.

On June 29, when Mistress Lescure and her lacemakers had been working on the order for more than a year, Henrietta Anne, Duchess of Orléans, suddenly fell ill, and that night she died. The news didn't reach Alençon until a few days later. Conte-Nouvelles learned of it in the poorhouse, when she heard the director mention it. She told it to Hélisende's nurse, and Hélisende reported it when she came to the workshop.

After a few moments of panic, Mistress Lescure became calmer. The wonders she was making wouldn't go to waste: Les Dentelles d'Or would sell them to some other great lady, or else they would be bought by the king's brother or the king himself. She waited, with a confidence that was occasionally shaken by twinges of anxiety, for a letter or a visit from the owner of Les Dentelles d'Or. Finally a letter announced a visit. The lady came, more elegant than ever in a moss-green silk dress with plum-colored flounces.

With a sigh of satisfaction she said that everything had first been lost, then saved, and she explained herself. She had sent an emissary to the Duke of Orléans, the king's brother, soon after his wife's death. He had refused to hear anything about the dress-fronts that had been ordered. (At this point, a knowing smile. It was easy to understand why the duke had no interest in dress-fronts, since he liked making love only in the Italian manner!) Les Dentelles d'Or couldn't sell them to anyone else because they had been made from designs belonging to the royal family. And it wasn't clear who would inherit those designs: As soon as Mistress Lescure returned them to Les Dentelles d'Or, they were to be turned over to the lawyers of the duchess's heirs. But just when things seemed hopeless, a miracle happened: The duke was going to remarry! Yes, so soon! The king had been trying to arrange a marriage for his brother that would be advantageous to the kingdom, and, after long negotiations, an agreement had just been concluded with the elector palatine: he was going to give his daughter, Elisabeth Charlotte, to France! As soon as this became known, Les Dentelles d'Or had again sent an emissary to the duke, to ask if he would like to give the dress-fronts to his future wife. He had said yes!

He had just bought the dress-fronts, and everything was saved!

Mistress Lescure greeted this news with the first radiant smile of her life. The sight of it encouraged the lady in the silk dress to add that the sale of the dress-fronts involved one little detail: They would have to be slightly altered to make them fit the new duchess. There would be no payment for the alterations, however, because the duke had stubbornly insisted on paying the original price and nothing more. Mistress Lescure graciously said that since Les Dentelles d'Or had approached the duke and negotiated with him, she would absorb the whole cost of the alterations. A new contract was drawn up and signed.

Ten days later the measurements of Elisabeth Charlotte of Bavaria arrived and were compared with those of Henrietta Anne of England. The first duchess, who had drunk only chicory water and eaten hardly anything at all, had been exactly half the size of the second one, who consumed great quantities of beer and sausage! "Slightly altering" the dress-fronts would require a complete reconstruction that would take at least fourteen thousand extra hours of work.

This catastrophe not only swallowed up all of Mistress Lescure's profit, it also cost her fifty livres from her own pocket. She felt she had been deliberately swindled, because she was sure the owner of Les Dentelles d'Or had been well acquainted with Princess Elisabeth Charlotte's shape and size. When she returned the designs, which she couldn't look at without having a strong urge to burn them, she swore that nothing would ever make her work for the royal family again. She would be satisfied, as she had always been before, to make lace without knowing where it would go. Thank God there were plenty of drapers in Alençon who would buy everything she produced.

Princess Elisabeth Charlotte of Bavaria never knew that for several nights her abundant bosom and awesomely large waist had made a mistress-lacemaker weep behind the curtains of her alcove in an ordinary-looking house in the town of Alençon. It would have saddened her if she had known, because she had a kind heart and was unhappy herself.

Gilonne learned of Mistress Lescure's worries and sorrows from Gérasime. He signed as he stirred his pots, and on the day when the dismaying measurements of the future duchess became known, he broke an egg into each plate of soup, hoping it would help to comfort his little troupe.

It was during this time that Gilonne began learning the third operation in producing *point de France*: making the ground, a kind of net composed of looped bars. She was now doing the same kind of work as Michanteau. This made her so proud that her days seemed shorter. She knew that only a few apprentices, considered capable of learning everything and becoming mistress-lacemakers someday, were taught all the operations of lacemaking. Some girls would never do more than one or two of those operations. The two peasants, for example, would do outlining all their lives. But they weren't at all unhappy about it. It was just what they wanted, in fact: They would go back to their village of Pré-en-Pail, which specialized in that single operation, and they would earn a decent living. Gilonne and Michanteau were surprised that anyone could be satisfied with so little.

A short time later, one of the lacemakers in the big workshop was reprimanded by Mistress Lescure for taking snuff in spite of the rule against it. She shrugged and said she wasn't going to give up her snuff. She needed it to help her hold up under the strain of working twenty hours a day. If she had to make lace without it, she would rather go back to working in the fields. She wouldn't be making lace much longer anyway: Her eyes were going bad, and soon she wouldn't be good for anything but begging. And why shouldn't she use snuff, since it was good for the lungs and would keep her from dying like Banban?

Seeing that the apprentices were listening, Gérasime tried in vain to convince them that the lacemaker didn't really mean that Banban had died. He knew how hard it was to put anything over on Michanteau and Gilonne. Unable to face the mixture of accusation and despair he saw in their eyes, he went off to heat water for linden-blossom tea. To calm the sobbing he heard, he dropped in a handful of petals from what were called "sleep flowers," gathered the previous summer in the Perseigne forest at dawn, in accordance with the rule.

Time passed. The apple tree gave its blossoms and fruit; the succession of pigs named Torchette continued; the icy water of the Briante, which burned the girls' skin when they washed their clothes, was transformed into a cool, soothing balm; chilblains came and went; but Banban's memory didn't fade. The girls couldn't help crying sometimes. Their backs often ached and the last hours of the day were so hard to bear that it was all they could do to keep from screaming in despair. They missed Sister Adelaide. Gérasime had told them—and sworn it was true—that he had put her in Banban's coffin. It was comforting to know that the two of them had gone up to heaven together. But here below, on earth, the girls weren't sure how much longer they could go on.

The following year, Gilonne learned the fourth operation: making *remplis*, which completed the ground with a broadening of the mesh obtained by skillfully looping the thread. That year her painted wooden shoes, which she had been keeping hidden under her mattress, became too small for her. But they fit Michanteau, who was growing more slowly and who said that Gilonne was now the leader of the apprentices, since Hélisende, gentle and calm as ever, continued to be mostly somewhere else as she steadily plied her needle.

Gilonne's days were darkened by a great anxiety: She hadn't heard from Uncle Mathieu for over a year.

In July 1671, Mathieu had gone to Grand-Coeur, as he had made up his mind to do. Feeling uneasy about his arrival, he made the trip there last longer by stopping to watch a thatcher roofing a house. When Mathieu expressed admiration for his work, the thatcher came down and told him it was a work of life because the new thatch would be covered with irises and crocuses in spring, from seeds sown by the birds who acted as his helpers. He would come back next year, he said, to see what he called one of his ''roof gardens.''

Mathieu also met a shepherdess driving her sheep before her. Unfortunately, she was shy and hurried away from him. He had begun to think of marrying, and in an effort to overcome his timidity with women, he forced himself to talk to them whenever he could. Someday, when his breath began to run short, he would have to give up his wandering occupation, and a wife would be able to help him carry on a trade in lace at the fairs of the region. Furthermore, it was becoming dangerous to remain unmarried: The king's recruiting sergeants were everywhere, always on the lookout for bachelors to put into the army.

At Grand-Coeur, a dog rushed toward him as he walked along the drive that led to the house. He had a great deal of experience with dogs and knew all the breeds in Europe. It was his conviction that people and dogs resembled each other all over the world: They were all afraid, and that was what made them bark. The woman who stood watching him approach was obviously feeling the same wariness as her dog. She was tall and strongly built, with a long nose and small eyes.

He told her he was a packman. She asked him where his pack was. He didn't have one, he said, but he had a load of merchandise anyway. She looked at him mistrustfully with her hands on her hips, and her nose seemed to grow even longer. He was all smiles. He finally disarmed her to the point where, with his white teeth, blue eyes, and blond hair, and his remarkable neatness and cleanliness, he seemed to her an archangel who had just come down from heaven. In her emotion, she clutched her apron, which was dotted with red stains left by the currants she had been pulling from their clusters.

"Then you must sell butterfly wings, my boy, since your merchandise takes up so little room."

He laughed. She wasn't so far wrong! But he had no desire to talk about lace. It was a risky subject: Many people were being arrested these days for violating the royal edicts. He said that what he had in his pockets was worth being shown. Could he come in? She offered him a bowl of buckwheat porridge.

In the big, attractive kitchen, two people were seated at one end of a cherrywood table: a strange, imposing lady and a little servant.

"Will you allow this packman to eat here, madame?"

Lady Bertrade nodded her consent and continued eating spoonfuls of buckwheat porridge with slow, regular movements.

Where had he come from? Where was he going? What countries did he know?

It was Pompinne who asked the questions. Lady Bertrade listened without saying anything. Mathieu mentioned one country after another. When she heard the name Sweden, Lady Bertrade put down her spoon, looked at him, and said that her son, a soldier, had once told her that the Swedish army was the best and most modern in the world. Was it true that Swedish soldiers used cartridges in their muskets? From what she had heard about that recent invention, it was an amazing improvement.

Yes, it was true. Mathieu had seen cartridges, and in fact he owned two of them. Lady Bertrade put her hand on her curious red wool hat as if she were afraid it might fly away, which was highly unlikely. He soon saw that this was one of her habits, and that her hand trembled.

Did he *really* own two cartridges? she asked.

He said he did. She became agitated and even tried to stand up. Pompinne prevented her from doing so by putting a firm hand on her shoulder and said she would bring her cane, but later. She then explained to Mathieu that, a year ago last Saint John's Day, Lady Bertrade had had an accident that had left her with a wooden leg. Pompinne seemed to want him to entertain her mistress.

"Tell her about those things, I forget what they're called. . . . You know, the things she likes," she said, as if Lady Bertrade were deaf.

He talked about Sweden, since that was evidently what interested her.

"When will you bring them to me?" Lady Bertrade asked.

"The cartridges?"

"Yes. When will you come back with them?"

He promised to return the following week. She told Pompinne to bring her cane, used it to help herself stand up, and announced that she was going to bed. When she was about to leave the room, she stopped in the doorway and asked, "Next week, without fail?"

"Without fail."

Pompinne sighed.

Gilonne's family on her father's side had a beautiful house, thought Mathieu, but it wasn't a happy place. He even wondered if the child wasn't better off where she was.

Pompinne told him he could sleep in either the kitchen or the barn. He chose a place beside the kitchen fireplace, not because he was cold, but because staying there would give him a chance to gather more information.

He gathered an abundant harvest. Pompinne sat down by the fire, set to work on a piece of lace, and talked. Everything was going from bad to worse here. The lord of the estate, Chevalier Louis-Guillaume de Ferrières, had gone off with his two musician-servants to fight in the war against the Dutch. Before leaving he had sold the little he still had left to sell. Lady Bertrade hardly had any sheets for her bed. If only she were willing to make lace, the two of them could earn a fair amount of money in spite of the *leveuses*. Those devilish, bloodsucking *leveuses* lived off lacemakers like fleas on a dog, but you had to deal with them if you wanted to sell your work. Arguing with them wouldn't do you any good: They would just buy lace from someone else, because there was plenty of it for sale. But Lady Bertrade didn't like to do any kind of needlework. She lived only for hunting, especially since her accident.

Mathieu waited patiently for an account of the accident. He made it a rule never to question people who talked to him that way, of their own accord, because they might stop short if they felt they were being pressed. Eventually, he learned what he wanted to know. The year before, when Lady Bertrade had such bad rheumatism in her left leg that she couldn't help groaning from the pain and was unable to ride a horse, she had gone to Bagnoles-de-l'Orne, about twenty leagues away, and the waters there had cured her. She felt so good that she stayed too long and didn't come back until winter. Wolves were prowling the forest when she went into it. She could have passed through without stopping, but, unluckily for her, she couldn't resist the chance to hunt wolves. The hunt turned into a fight and a wolf bit a piece out of her leg—the left one, the one that had just been cured by the waters at Bagnoles-de-l'Orne. It had to be just *that* one! The way Pompinne said "just *that* one" made Mathieu feel like laughing, but he restrained himself.

Herb plasters would have had their usual effect, she went on, but that wolf must have had a poisonous bite, because the wound kept getting worse. Finally Lady Bertrade's leg had to be amputated. Since then she had been suffering even more, because her stump hurt and her rheumatism had come back. Nearly every day she would have herself lifted onto her horse and gallop off to hunt wolves. Killing those devilish animals was all she ever thought about. The infection in her leg had gone into her head! She saw wolves everywhere, in all seasons, and kept after them relentlessly. It was a great pity.

Mathieu also learned that Lady Bertrade was sad at having lost her little falconer, who had gone to join his uncle and cousins in New France, where there were said to be savages, but also great wealth. He would surely have to fight with the Indians to take their property away from them, and if he got himself killed, the ungrateful boy, it would be divine justice. Lady Bertrade loved him like a son, and the stories he told her had always cheered her up. He should never have left her, the little ingrate! But a falconer was still only a falconer, even if he had learned to speak Latin.

There was a thumping sound overhead.

"She's calling me," said Pompinne. "She bangs on the floor with her cane."

She went to her mistress's bedroom, came back a short time later, and said, "She still wants to talk. Go up and see her."

Now that Lady Bertrade wasn't wearing her hat, Mathieu saw that her hair was white. She was sitting up in a big canopied bed, leaning back against her cushions, stiff, imposing, intimidating. Yet for a moment he felt sorry for her. He thought the time had come to tell her about the little girl who could replace the boy whose absence saddened her. But she launched into such a long, rambling discourse on cartridges that he began to have doubts about the clarity of her mind and wondered how she would take the news about Gilonne if he gave it to her. He said nothing. It would be better to wait and maybe talk to the woman downstairs, though her mind seemed a little cloudy too.

When he had explained to her how, in his opinion, cartridges were made, she asked him to go back downstairs. As he walked toward the door, he was sure she had decided to make her own cartridges.

He spent the night in the kitchen, had a bowl of porridge when he woke up, and left. He had to think. Would these people be of any use to Gilonne?

It was a joyous sunrise. The plain sparkled with a festive coating of dew. Mathieu decided to go through the village of Pervenchères and talk with the parish priest, thinking it might not be a bad idea to find out more about the chevalier. It was an unfortunate decision. He was approaching the outskirts of the village when two recruiting sergeants came running out of a thicket, grabbed him, tied him up, and threw him into a hay-filled cart that seemed to have been specially prepared for him. He hadn't had time to use his finely polished staff, and the sergeants didn't bother to pick it up from where it had fallen on the road.

Lying in the soft hay, calm but humiliated, Mathieu watched the clouds drift above while the cart carried him off to war.

What war? He hadn't kept abreast of such things. He guessed he would be fighting against the Dutch, and sighed. He, the best lace carrier in Alençon—Gilonne and her turkey Marguerite had called him "the greatest of all"—had cut a sorry figure this time! In spite of all his experience, he had let himself be caught as if he were only a beginner. His father and his old friend Joseph must be laughing so hard they were about to fall out of heaven! "That'll teach you!" he could hear them saying.

They were right to laugh. They had both told him again and again never to relax his attention. "Even if you're not carrying merchandise,'' his father had said, ''even if you're only gathering dandelions for the rabbits, don't forget that someone who wants to harm you may be hiding behind any tree or bush.''

''Go and see what war is like from close up—that'll teach you too!'' Joseph had said.

Mathieu didn't feel like laughing. His lips stretched a little, but maybe it was only a faint smile meant for the robin that had perched on the cart to ride a little way with him. He had always liked the example set for human beings by the smallest and most fragile of God's creatures. When winter came, this robin would die of cold without a cry or a moan.

When the second dress-front had been finished and delivered at the beginning of 1674, four years after the first order had been placed, and when she had learned that, by divine grace, the Duchess of Orléans hadn't gained any more weight, Mistress Lescure felt great weariness. Her father attributed it, not without reason, to the loss of fifty livres combined with the sudden deterioration of her eyesight. He tried to make her eat more, to no avail. She appeared to have given up, to have lost the vigor she needed for the task of directing her establishment, which now seemed to her an overwhelming burden.

Thiphaine's conduct had become unbearably irritating. With three of her admirers, the beautiful redhead stood outside the house one day and shouted invectives with a vehemence that frightened the children. Gérasime took his pike and went out to drive away the unwelcome visitors, but everyone in the street laughed at the poor old soldier whose rusty weapon frightened no one. Gilonne felt for him the same sad and worried affection she felt for Grandmother Thomine. And Mistress Lescure, whose hands she saw trembling as she cut a sheet of parchment, suddenly seemed very old to her.

Some time later, on a Sunday morning when she had just come back from attending mass at Notre-Dame with her apprentices, Mistress Lescure announced that she was going to close the little workshop and keep only the big one with four lacemakers.

The butcher's daughters had finished their contract. Now that they knew how to do pricking, outlining, and grounds, they could work in the back of their father's shop, or in the workroom of a convent, to earn their dowries. The two peasant girls, who were still doing outlining, would be glad to go back to their village and join the other specialists. Having learned four of the operations, Perrine, Michanteau, and Gilonne would go to work in the Royal Manufactory, where they would be taught what they still needed to learn. They would take part in the prestigious work of making lace for the French court, using the finest designs created by the king's painters. Hélisende, who was now fourteen, would be paid for the lace she had made in the big workshop, where she had been since the previous winter. She had earned nearly a hundred and fifty livres, which would be quite a respectable contribution for her to make when she entered the Clarist convent. Mistress Lescure was going to tell the girls' parents all this, and then on Saint Remi's Day, instead of taking in a new contingent as she had always done before, she would close the apprentices' workshop.

Since Mathieu still hadn't come back, it was Mama Bordier who went to talk with Mistress Lescure. Was she getting old too? Gilonne was worried to hear her accepting Mistress Lescure's decisions without even discussing them. She didn't notice that Mama Bordier looked at her with a certain perplexity, surprised to see what a big girl she had become, and also relieved not to have to take any responsibility for what was going to happen.

Michanteau had no family, except for an older sister who lived in Perche and showed little concern for her, so she made up her mind on her own: She would go to the Royal Manufactory with Gilonne.

Perrine, the deaf girl with the little turned-up nose, surprised everyone. Instead of continuing her apprenticeship at the Royal Manufactory, she wanted to go back and work for her aunt, who owned an inn on the road to Montsort. At first Mistress Lescure was dumbfounded at this decision, then she opposed it, but finally she gave in.

"You may be right," she said with a sigh. "Lacemaking is a hard, thankless trade."

And one bright autumn morning when a light wind was already bringing the fragrance of new cider and the first pressed apples, Mistress Lescure took the girls she had called her most talented apprentices—without ever telling them so—to the director of the Royal Manufactory.

She was astounded by the size of the buildings and the swarm of people talking loudly and moving busily in all directions. Could she, in good conscience, abandon two defenseless little girls to that Babylon? She reasoned with herself. This was no doubt the future of lacemaking, unfortunately, and she had to resign herself to letting the girls have a chance to succeed in that temple of haste, disorder, and waste. On the floor she saw pieces of good thread and candle stubs that were still usable, and she glimpsed a room—a whole room!—filled with rows and rows of the glass bowls used to brighten candlelight. How many must be broken in a year's time, to need such a supply in reserve! And what about cleanliness? She doubted it was taught here as it ought to be. She was sure any lace that didn't come out perfectly white was treated with white lead, a poisonous powder she had always avoided.

She kissed Gilonne and Michanteau—for the first time, except at Christmas. Associating that kiss with the smell of the oranges that Mistress Lescure had always given her as a present, Gilonne cried. She had loved the Christmas Eve celebrations in Mistress Lescure's house. They had all thrown orange peels into the fire, which heightened their fragrance; Gérasime had opened a jar of jam to savor with hot buckwheat porridge, and they had sung Christmas carols.

Gilonne had controlled herself when she said good-by to Gérasime, but she had shed abundant tears, wetting his beard and mustache and making his cheeks as shiny as his eels were when he pulled them out of the Briante or the Sarthe.

Mistress Lescure began giving her apprentices some final injunctions—"And remember: don't do anything in a hurry, don't make any abrupt movements, or . . ."—but she was unable to go on because she became caught up in the whirlwind of the courtyard: waves of horsemen coming and going, carts bringing kegs of thread, coaches taking customers and suppliers in and out. Feeling more and more distraught, she finally had to leave the two girls convinced that she was abandoning them on the threshold of hell and that God would hold her accountable someday.

Gilonne and Michanteau were assigned to a workshop where the mistress-lacemaker welcomed them as if they were a blessing from heaven. Madame de Montespan, the royal favorite, had ordered an ornamental covering for a dressing table, and it was to be sent to court within a week. The men who would take it there were already waiting in the courtyard with their horses.

"They must have been promised a reward for every minute they gain," said one of the lacemakers.

"Or maybe they've been promised one lash for every minute they lose!" said another.

The women and girls talked loudly and joked with each other. Some of them stood up to kiss the two newcomers and pat their cheeks. Others at the back of the room were singing. But not a hymn! It must have been something amusing, because they laughed a great deal. Gilonne and Michanteau were placed at a table with girls and women of all ages.

They were told that Madame de Montespan had made one of the king's painters get up in the middle of the night and design a hat to match the dressing-table cover now being made in the workshop. A courier had brought the pattern as fast as his horse would carry him, and now the lacemakers had to work around the clock to make sure they finished the hat in time for it to be delivered with the rest of the order.

Did they know how to do pricking and outlining? the girls were asked. Could they make grounds and *remplis*? Yes? Thank God! They would go to work immediately on that damned hat, and do the best they could. The illustrious painter's pattern was tossed to them, without due respect for its noble origin. They took it and began working, so proud that they forgot everything except the piece of paper showing a half-overturned basket from which a profusion of flowers spilled onto the ground of the hat. The flounce that would frame the face simulated a gracefully gathered and tied ribbon. They were filled with wonder, but their hands were steady as they thrust their thin stilettos into the parchment and pricked rapidly. The pattern had been divided into eight pieces so that eight lacemakers could work on it during the day and eight others at night. They would have to do a total of about sixteen hundred hours' work in the coming week, and pray it would be enough.

"By the time we're through, our needles will be red-hot and we'll be bled white, and all for a whore," said one of them. The others sang:

> Mon pere m'a donné un mari,
> Quatorze et pis quat' font dix-huit!
> La première nuit qu'avec lui j'couchis,

Remua la paille et s'endormit.
*J'prins une aiguille et je l'piquis. . . .**

   Gilonne and Michanteau joined in enthusiastically, as if they
had been singing such songs all their lives.
   "We should have come here long ago!" exclaimed Michanteau.
   The apprentices in the dormitory had horsehair mattresses,
which proved to be a deceptive luxury because each of them
was occupied by an army of bedbugs. Gilonne and Michanteau
missed the fresh straw provided by Hélisende's father, but they
laughed at the thought of how horrified Mistress Lescure would
be if she knew they spent part of each night hunting bedbugs.
Gilonne told her friend that Jérémie had dreamed of finding a
way to exterminate those vermin forever. If he succeeded, the
king—whose bed was said to be as heavily populated with them
as Versailles was with courtiers—would reward him by granting
him the right to be a Protestant. Jérémie would promise not to
tell anyone else about his secret extermination method, so that
the noblemen at court would go on scratching themselves and
His Majesty would be amused every morning when he saw poor
bitten and bleeding courtiers come into his bedchamber to hand
him his shirt and breeches. In his good humor, he would then
allow the Protestants in his kingdom to rebuild their churches.
After that, said Jérémie, Protestants would sing a hymn of gratitude to bedbugs every Sunday. But Jérémie had gone away, God
only knew where, before he could discover how to wipe out the
vermin.
   And what about Uncle Mathieu? Where was he?
   Every night, just before going to sleep, Gilonne prayed that
he would come back soon. Hoping to make her less worried,
Michanteau told her about the nobleman for whom her mother
had once worked as a washerwoman. He was away from his
estate for more than three years, and during that time he was
thought to have died on a battlefield. He hadn't. He had only
broken his leg, in Germany or someplace like that, and waited
patiently until it was completely healed. It was said that a pretty

*My father gave me a husband,
Fourteen and then four make eighteen!
The first night I went to bed with him,
He rustled the straw and fell asleep.
I took a needle and pricked him. . . .

woman had helped him to pass the time. Gilonne's uncle was probably sick and being taken care of by a pretty woman of his own who listened in amazement to the stories of his adventures that he told her while she held his hand and stroked his forehead. That was how things always happened: Handsome young men who fought with swords or staffs were always wounded sooner or later, and then a pretty woman was always there to dress their wounds or soothe their fever. Such was love, not only in books— Michanteau had read two of them—but also in real life. Gilonne talked about that possibility so much with Michanteau that she came to regard it as a certainty and sometimes said dreamily, "I wish I could know Uncle Mathieu's sweetheart."

At the Royal Manufactory, the words "love," "lover," and "passion" were constantly used in conversation and songs. Gilonne and Michanteau quickly added them to their vocabulary. The joys and sorrows of love were the favorite topic of the lacemakers as they talked among themselves without ever taking their eyes off their work.

Except for one who was old, ugly, and ill groomed, who chewed tobacco all day long and always had charcoal dust on his hands, the painters attached to the establishment were young and attractive. They appreciatively eyed the women, who in turn vied for their attention. Fights often erupted when one lacemaker attacked another who had taken her place in a painter's good graces.

One of the artists, a handsome young man with a blond mustache, came up to Gilonne and Michanteau one day and offered to paint their portrait. It would mean immortality for them, he said. They would see themselves in a painting ordered by a nobleman of the region. Since they had by then lost some of their shyness, they composedly answered that they would think it over.

Gilonne later met the artist when she was alone, and he told her he would like to paint her as a pretty young lady holding her pet monkey by the hand. She went off to try to put her thoughts in order, feeling flattered, sad, and worried all at the same time. She had to admit that she liked being called a pretty young lady—it was good to know she wasn't ugly—but she was sad to realize that Michanteau *was* ugly, and worried that she might discover it. The pleasure she took in knowing she was pretty made her aware that being ugly might drive her to despair. A few days later, however, she was reassured when she heard

Michanteau say, ''I know I'm not much to look at, but I also
know that beauty isn't the only thing you can use to make your
fortune.''

When the shareholders of the Royal Manufactory sent word
from Paris that they were about to make their annual visit, the
director of the establishment inspected the girls and chose Gilonne as the one who would present the customary piece of lace
to the visitors. It was an honor that for the last few years had
gone to a girl who bore the name of Angeline, even though there
was nothing angelic about her. She waited for a chance, then
tripped her rival and made her take a violent fall. At the sight
of Gilonne sprawled on the floor with her nose bleeding, Angeline and her followers shouted for joy. Pale with rage, Michanteau charged them with her fists clenched. The chaplain
happened to be passing by at that moment. He seized the shrieking, disheveled girls, took them to the chapel, lectured them
sternly and told them that lacemaking and prayer were all that
was allowed in His Majesty's Manufactory. Our Lord, he said,
wanted the humble people of this world to serve Him, as well
as the king, the elder son of His Church, with work and prayer,
and anyone who failed to respect that wish would be in a grave
state of sin.

Gilonne and Michanteau were no longer working on Madame
de Montespan's hat because they had finished everything they
knew how to do. Wishing they could go farther in making the
hat, they became aware of their ambitions and eager to learn
what they didn't yet know. One of the older workers smiled at
their impatience and said to them, ''Since God took seven days
to make the world, you shouldn't mind taking seven years to
become lacemakers!''

Now that they belonged to the big troupe of the Royal Manufactory, they had Sunday off. Every other Sunday they would
get up at dawn, while many of the others were taking advantage
of their chance to sleep, and hurry off toward Montsort and
Mama Bordier. It was impossible for them to walk: they had to
run. They would never run fast enough, they thought.

They arrived at the Sarthe Gate before the drawbridge had
been lowered and talked awhile with the gatekeeper, a retired
soldier who lived in one of the towers with his wife. The old
couple spun flax that their son grew on the other side of the
ramparts, and for recreation they watched people coming and
going through the gate. In their younger days they had made

lace, but their eyes, they said, were no longer good enough for
the complicated *point de France*. Gilonne and Michanteau nodded, proud of their knowledge and skill. When the gate was
finally opened, they sped through it like a pair of bullets. The
gatekeeper and his wife laughed as they watched the girls disappear into the slowly rising mist.

Along the road, the last apples of the year were being knocked
off their trees with long poles. The two girls picked up a few
almost without stopping, and by the time they had each eaten
one, they had arrived at the kingdom of turkeys. There, when
they had exchanged kisses with Mama Bordier and spent a little
time watching the heavy gait and ponderous flight of those
"gravel eaters," as Michanteau called them, they couldn't stand
still any longer and so began running again. "They're possessed!" Mama Bordier said to herself, and she didn't see them
again until it was time for lunch.

The turkeys had finished molting without getting sick and
were fattening up well, which meant that Mama Bordier could
expect a good sale at the end of the year, so she bought clothes
to replace the threadbare ones in which the girls had arrived.
There was too much washing at Mistress Lescure's house: It
wore things out! The red fustian dresses were simple and there
was no lace on the aprons and bonnets because, without Mathieu's help, frills were out of the question. But Gilonne and
Michanteau were delighted with their new clothes just as they
were. And the old public writer said that when he looked at the
two charming girls he felt as lively as the new cider.

On alternate Sundays, when they didn't go to Montsort, they
went to visit Thomine and her friends in the poorhouse. But on
those days they still had to eat, and the Royal Manufactory fed
them only when they were working. Michanteau thought of a
solution: They earned their food by working in the kitchen of
Mistress Verlot's inn as poultry pluckers. "We're with poultry
every Sunday, only sometimes it's alive and sometimes it's
dead," she said, laughing.

In exchange for lunch and a piece of bread and a slice of
bacon for supper, they worked seven hours, coughing because
of the wisps of down in the air, from dawn until the first stroke
of the bell at the end of high mass; by the time the second stroke
came, they were gone.

The bread and bacon the cook gave them were deliciously
fragrant and made the old women's nostrils quiver, so the girls

always gave it to them, laughing with pleasure. Afterward they talked about lacemaking and often about the beautiful patterns designed by the king's painters. A description of a flounce designed by Charles Le Brun, intended to be a gift from His Majesty to the Spanish court, required several hours of explanation. The old women always wanted to hear more and enjoyed learning the new lacemaking vocabulary concerning the composition of decorations. They were enchanted by royal symbols and emblems: the sun of Louis XIV; the fleur-de-lis of the Bourbons; canopies, domes, urns, palm branches, and other military trophies. Gilonne gave the impression that she had worked with those motifs for years, whereas in fact she often talked about them only a day or two after seeing them for the first time.

The new Courapied—the one who stole almanacs—often came to listen. She was a pleasant girl who seemed to like the old women, made them laugh by calling them "ladies from the old days," and curtsied to them every morning and evening in a way that won praise from Marie.

One afternoon Gilonne and Michanteau took out their last reserves, the apples they had put into their pockets, and gave them to Courapied. Then they quickly left, to give themselves a little time before nightfall, which came early now that it was October. They went to the Place du Palais, happy at the thought of seeing all the things they had dreamed of during their years with Mistress Lescure. They weren't disappointed by the spectacle of the ducks dressed as ladies in fancy clothes and gentlemen with swords and plumed hats, and they often watched it.

This time, however, the usual performance didn't take place. Instead, each duck came onto the little stage, made of two trestles and a board, with a sign hanging from its neck: "I am a bad actor. My master is so dissatisfied with me that he is going to cut off my head." At first Gilonne and Michanteau couldn't believe their eyes; then they were deeply pained. How could anyone kill that charming gentleman-duck who dragged his sword on the ground behind him so amusingly, or that pretty lady-duck in a dress with a lace collar and a long train?

The showman appeared and said, "Before I slaughter these stupid animals who keep forgetting their parts and tearing their clothes, I'll give you ladies and gentlemen a chance to buy them if you'd like to have one for your own amusement."

Several ducks were sold. The two girls waited anxiously between sales and sighed with relief each time a duck was taken away. Finally three remained unsold.

"All right, I'll spare those three," said the showman.

The girls applauded him for his magnanimity and, happy and hungry, enviously sniffed the good smell of apple fritters from a nearby street stall. Someday, they promised themselves, they would buy half a dozen of them, all at once!

They were on their way back to their dormitory at the Royal Manufactory when they passed by the showman's booth again and saw him putting *all* his actors into cages! What had he sold to the charitable spectators who thought they were saving those trained ducks from death? It didn't take the girls long to realize what the bandit had done: He had only pretended he was going to kill his performers, so that he could sell common barnyard ducks to people willing to pay high prices in the belief that they were serving the cause of art. They were both outraged, but then Michanteau laughed, admired the man's cleverness and even justified it: Maybe it was the only way he could afford to keep his actors and have them go on giving people enjoyment with their performances. Gilonne still said it was dishonest. For the first time she had the feeling that she and her friend were not in complete agreement.

Though the girls had more freedom at the Royal Manufactory than they had had with Mistress Lescure, their work was no less exhausting. Their meals were scanty and unappetizing. How they missed Gérasime's creamy soups and buckwheat porridge! And they had to be constantly on their guard in the dining room. If you relaxed your attention for just one moment, your piece of bread would disappear. Some girls would even take it out of your hand with a spiteful laugh and threaten to disfigure you with a stiletto if you complained about it to anyone in authority.

There were several little ones, five or six years old, who were exploited and terrorized in this way by a band of girls two or three times their age. Michanteau said that something would have to be done, but it was Gilonne who had the idea of asking for help from the charming painter with the blond mustache. How he solved the problem she never found out, but the older girls stopped taking bread from the younger ones without even seeming to have been frightened by the painter. Afterward, in fact, the leader of the group made obvious efforts to charm him.

When Gilonne politely thanked him, he said with a smile, "What will you give me as a reward?" And he didn't wait for her answer to caress her round, soft neck with his lips and mustache. Then, no longer smiling, he murmured, "Before long, I'd like to see you again, my pretty little pet."

She hurried away, her heart pounding, and told Michanteau what had happened. Philosophical as usual, her friend said that if you asked someone for a favor you always had to pay for it when it was done, but if you were clever enough you could sometimes get away with paying very little.

At the Royal Manufactory they learned the fifth operation, which consisted of making perfectly regular hexagonal bars decorated with picots that looked like little teeth. And it seemed to them that with this increased knowledge of lacemaking they also acquired a greater understanding of life. For example, they now realized that Gérasime, whom they often saw on Sundays, sitting on his chair in front of the door and smoking his pipe, was bored. They were in the habit of taking the old women outside on sunny days, and after thinking it over they decided to bring them to see Gérasime. Talking with Grandmother Thomine and her friends would surely put him in a more cheerful mood. They began "mixing up their old people," as Michanteau put it, once or twice a month. They always brought a bench out of the Lescure house, on which the old women perched like swallows.

Marie was usually too sleepy to join her friends on these outings, but she asked them to take her potted wild thyme plant and give it some sunlight and fresh air. Chopine grumbled that it was just like Marie: always wanting people to do things for her, and making a nuisance of herself. They already had enough to do, holding their canes and avoiding the stones, holes, and mud in the streets, without having to carry a pot!

But Conte-Nouvelles, who always wanted to stay on the good side of her benefactress, carried the plant by tying it to her waist with a cord. Gérasime would carefully untie it, find a good place for it on the bench or the ground, and evaluate its slow growth. Then he would give news of the war. The illustrious Condé had had three horses killed under him in some far-off battle, he didn't know exactly where. He had heard about it from the nobleman who sang every Thursday in the marketplace. The flags captured from the enemy in that battle numbered in the hundreds. The title of the song, in fact, was *And We Will Harvest Flags*, or something like that. But he, Gérasime, the old soldier, knew what that kind of glory meant. It meant butchery. That, of course, was something the nobleman didn't sing about. All those wars . . . When would they end? He sighed.

Conte-Nouvelles talked about Versailles and its marvelous festivities, which were reported to her through channels unknown to her friends. Boat rides on the Grand Canal (she had no idea what it was), fireworks that were like flowers of flame bursting in the sky, and especially meals: lunches, suppers, and lighter meals in between. Descriptions of all that food and drink never failed to make Chopine thirsty. Gérasime would then serve cider to his guests.

Michanteau felt she now had a family. She would almost have been surprised if anyone had told her that Thomine wasn't actually her grandmother. Gilonne was glad, for her old women's sake, that she and Michanteau were such good friends with Mistress Verlot's cook. He had begun augmenting their bread and bacon with a piece of cake or preserved goose meat, or a slice of ham, or even a quarter of a chicken. Michanteau had her own way of stimulating his generosity, and she worked alone. She would say to Gilonne, "Wait here. I'm going to tell him some story or other and ask him for something extra." She always came back with the something extra, and it always delighted the old women.

But one Sunday she came back with nothing, not even the bread and bacon, and her eyes were red.

"He caught me," she said. "God help us, because I don't think we'll get much here from now on!"

A moment later her gloom vanished and she laughed. Then she told Gilonne everything. Actually, the stingy old cook had never given them anything. Not even the bread and bacon. She had taken it on her own, from the start. During the time she had supposedly been seeing the cook, she had slipped into the pantry and helped herself, but with moderation. She had really taken only what was owed to them, because they deserved a little extra food after their long hours of work.

"It's still stealing!" Gilonne objected.

"Well, what of it? When God sees our old women sick because the soup in the poorhouse is sour, what do you suppose He thinks? He thinks I'm right to do what I do because He doesn't have time to do it Himself. Besides, I confess every Sunday. You don't agree? Believe me, I'd be glad if I could open my purse, take out a handful of money, give it to that rotten old cook and say, 'Here, take this and let me have a nice roasted capon for some blind ladies who are friends of mine.' Don't you think I'd like that better than trembling when I steal?''

"You tremble?''

Michanteau hesitated, then admitted, "No, I don't. The truth is that I like to steal. But I swear I confess everything: what I do, and the fact that I like doing it.''

When her surprise and anxiety had passed, Gilonne suddenly remembered something Jérémie had said to her one day: "You Catholics go to confession, accuse yourselves of this or that, recite the Lord's Prayer and the Hail Mary, and you're brand-new again, as if you'd never done anything wrong. That doesn't make sense to me. It's unfair. And it's too easy. We Protestants have to keep our bad acts; they gnaw at us inside, in our heart and soul, and won't leave us in peace even when we're asleep. That's what I call punishment.''

She would have to keep an eye on Michanteau, thought Gilonne, and not let her risk being taken to the police, which was what would happen if she were caught stealing again and the cook or Mistress Verlot herself got really angry with her. But was it possible to keep watch on Michanteau when she was as agile and wily as the conjurer's monkey in the gallery of the Place du Palais, who played a drum and leapt onto spectators' shoulders to pull feathers from their hats? Gilonne felt that from now on she was going to dread those Sunday mornings spent in the Moor's Inn.

For the next few days she worked badly, was reprimanded, and found it harder than usual to sit still on her chair. There were times when the delicate lace felt heavy as lead to her.

Suddenly a royal pronouncement drove everything else from her mind: The edicts regulating lacemaking were revoked. The people of Alençon were so astonished that they scarcely knew what to do with the freedoms they had just regained. Over the last ten years they had developed habits that now had to be given up. Some of them had become adept at deception, learned to live with it, and found it profitable; and finally they had even come to enjoy taking great risks in order to succeed. Then there was the disappointment of those who had long since abandoned the forbidden forms of lacemaking and now discovered, when they went back to them, that they had lost their old skill.

There was less rejoicing than might have been expected after all those years of recrimination and complaints. There was no dancing in the streets. People calmly told themselves that they would have now to take on new habits. The old ones.

On a market day, Mistress Bordier went to the Morel d'Arthus lacemaking establishment to try to find out what had become of Mathieu Perdriel. Only at the cost of a painful effort did she go to see heretics for the first time in her life. She wasn't sure she should believe anything they might tell her, but she felt it was her duty to Gilonne to try to get the information.

It was Mortimer Morel d'Arthus who spoke with her. In spite of her bias, he didn't make a bad impression, and his anxiety and sorrow seemed genuine. He was afraid, not that Mathieu had been attacked while he was transporting lace—he had been taking a three-day vacation between trips when he disappeared—but that he had been ambushed by recruiting sergeants. After long thought, Monsieur Morel d'Arthus and his son had reached what seemed to them the only plausible conclusion: Mathieu was fighting in the war. There was no way of knowing when anyone would hear from him. Maybe he wasn't even allowed to send letters.

The old public writer had come to the same conclusion. The worst bandits on all the roads of the kingdom, he said, were those vicious recruiting sergeants. They must have been overjoyed to make a prize catch like Mathieu! And the king let them do as they pleased! He closed his eyes to the way his ministers kept a stream of new recruits flowing into his army, and his ministers closed theirs to the methods used by their suppliers of cannon fodder. Mathieu was on one battlefield or another—if he was lucky enough to be still alive. God grant that he would come back someday!

Conte-Nouvelles hadn't needed to make any visits to learn that many young men in the region were being seized and put into the army. She had been told about it by several beggars who came to the poorhouse for a meal. They had heard heartrending cries and moans. Conte-Nouvelles was annoyed at not knowing one thing: why Mathieu had gone out into the country just before his disappearance. She sometimes thought of an amorous escapade, but that seemed unlikely to her. It wasn't the kind of thing she could imagine him doing. Instead, she imagined him coming into the old women's room at the poorhouse someday, holding a pretty girl by the hand and saying, "We're engaged."

* * *

Mistress Lescure was consumed with remorse. In her dreams she kept seeing Gilonne and Michanteau exposed to all the depravity that surely flourished in the Royal Manufactory, and Banban appeared in these nightmares to reproach her for having abandoned her two friends. Since Banban had been Mistress Lescure's favorite in her heart, her nocturnal appearances were a sign that ordered her to act. When she learned that the royal edicts had been rescinded, she was sure the result would be even more disorder and license in the royal establishments, and so she went to ask that Gilonne and Michanteau be sent back to her.

They returned from their Babylon one windy morning in November. She opened the door in response to their knock and saw them standing with their bundles of belongings. They seemed a little bewildered and asked a few questions about their future, but they weren't at all sad about having left the Royal Manufactory. A new band of predatory lacemakers had begun exploiting the youngest and weakest girls. Threatening them with their stilettos, they forced their victims to work in the dormitories part of each night, using stolen thread to make lace that their oppressors sold for their own profit. And it soon became obvious that the blond painter's charms would have no power over these bandits.

Gérasime gave Gilonne and Michanteau a heartfelt welcome, then went back to work in his kitchen while Mistress Lescure told them what she had in mind for them to do. She couldn't increase the number of her lacemakers because she did only a limited amount of work now, but even if she had been able to take back her two former apprentices, it wouldn't be in their best interest. They needed to go to someone who could teach them more and even better. Although she was ordinarily stingy with praise—she regarded it as an encouragement to arrogance—she acknowledged that they were too gifted not to deserve the best teaching in Alençon.

This compliment gladdened their hearts. But what were they going to do?

Mistress Lescure was proud of what she had obtained for them: nothing less than permission to stay in the house of the great, the incomparable Madame La Perrière, the creator of Alençon lace!

"But isn't she . . . almost dead?" ventured Michanteau.

"She's old and ill, it's true. If she weren't, you'd have no chance of even setting foot in her house. She's a Protestant, and according to the latest decrees she's forbidden to train apprentices.''

"Then why should we go and stay with her?'' asked Michanteau.

"It so happens that Esther, her old servant, broke her leg three days ago.'' Mistress Lescure spoke slowly, savoring in advance what she was going to say. ''She can't walk, and Madame La Perrière is confined to her bed. They both need help. I told them you'd come today and serve them. What do you say to that?''

They didn't know what to say to it. It was too confusing. Mistress Lescure was an ardent Catholic, yet she was sending them to live with a heretic. And turning them into servants. Maybe there was something they didn't understand. . . .

Irritated by their lack of enthusiasm, Mistress Lescure felt they didn't understand anything at all.

"There aren't two women in the whole world who can give you perfect teaching in the art of lacemaking. *There's only one!* I'm sending you to her, and all you do is stare at me like a pair of half-wits!''

"Maybe we'll learn more about sweeping floors than about making lace,'' remarked Michanteau.

Her contact with several headstrong girls at the Royal Manufactory had give her a certain brashness. Mistress Lescure deplored it with a sigh and turned to Gilonne for comfort.

"How do *you* feel about it? Are you happy?''

"What shall I tell Mama Bordier if I'm living in a Protestant's house?''

"Tell her the truth: that I'm sending you there with the finest mission a human being can accomplish. I'm sending you there to save a soul. Maybe two, since the servant is as old as her mistress, and as close to the grave.''

Symonne Lescure explained herself. She wanted to make her two girls the best lacemakers in Alençon, and at first she had thought only of that. But she soon realized that God had taken this means of having her send an angel to save a soul that had gone astray.

She didn't say ''two angels.'' This made Michanteau laugh heartily.

"Gilonne will pray and I'll sweep,'' she said.

"You'll both make lace,'' said Mistress Lescure. ''Although

Madame La Perrière has to stay in bed, she can use her hands as well as ever. But when the time comes for her to pass on, you'll be there to call in the people who can save her from damnation by making her recant her errors. They can also save her servant, if God wills it so.''

She added that, as a precaution against the possibility of a denunciation that would lead to an investigation by the religious authorities, Gilonne and Michanteau were now to be Madame La Perrière's nieces, two dyed-in-the-wool Catholics who had come to help her in a difficult time. The bishop and his staff would consider it beneficial to have them staying with a Protestant. The whole arrangement had been made in agreement with the Jesuit who was Mistress Lescure's confessor and advisor, and he would smooth out any complications that might arise.

Not knowing whether they should be pleased with this new turn of events, the two girls picked up their bundles and went off toward the Lancrel crossroads, where Madame La Perrière lived.

Darkness was falling, and so was a fine drizzle. The house seemed gloomy to them. But they liked the cat purring in front of the kitchen fireplace. They also liked the kitchen itself, after they had considered it for a few moments.

The servant, sitting in her armchair, was very old and very decrepit. "You've come just in time to take Madame's supper to her," she said almost amiably. "I can't go upstairs and she can't come down. Be careful not to spill the soup."

They climbed a staircase whose old wood had the same soft luster as Mathieu's staffs.

The door of the room was open. Madame La Perrière, as white as her sheets, was asleep. And she too was very old. The girls looked at each other, wondering what this poor woman could teach them. In the meantime, what were they to do with the soup if she didn't wake up? They waited patiently, standing near the door. They examined the plain little bed, the dark wooden table with a candlestick on it, the glass light bowl, the basket containing an unfinished piece of lace, the armchair beside the window, and the white curtains. There was nothing else in the room, not even a rug.

"We have to do something," whispered Michanteau, "because the lady downstairs won't like it if we stay here until the soup gets cold and then bring it back to her.''

Gilonne waited a little longer, and said softly, ''If you want to eat your soup while it's hot, madame, you'd better wake up soon.''

Madame La Perrière raised her pale eyelids and smiled at the two children.

She was sitting up in bed to eat her supper, leaning back against her pillows, with a girl on either side of the bed. She ate little and spoke quietly. Was Mistress Lescure still in search of perfect whiteness for her lace? Was Gérasime still catching eels? The three of them were on familiar ground.

''Go and have something to eat, girls,'' she said, ''then come back and see me.''

All things considered, they were better off here than at the Royal Manufactory. But they were still skeptical about what they were going to learn. Madame La Perrière seemed terribly weak. . . .

She was, but it turned out she had hours when she felt fairly well. And then they saw how right Madame Lescure had been. It was amazing to see those pale, slender hands working with such calm speed and rigorous precision, and also, Gilonne thought confusedly, with a kind of music. Those hands sang! She was going to tell Michanteau what she was thinking but, before she could say anything, her friend expressed the same idea. Gilonne was glad, because there had been a shadow between them the night before. After helping Esther to lie down on her straw mattress in one corner of the kitchen, and after promising to draw water from the well and light the fire at five o'clock and then help her to get up, Michanteau had stuffed her pockets full of nuts just before leaving the room.

''You shouldn't do that here,'' Gilonne had said.

Michanteau hadn't answered, or even laughed. They had told each other good night without saying anything more. But this morning they had gaily braided Madame La Perrière's fine white hair and tied ribbons in it, and helped her to put on a freshly ironed bed jacket and hat. And now, as they watched her work, they understood each other without speaking. Lace would always bring them together. It was a long thread that bound them to each other.

So many people knew that little house at the Lancrel cross-

roads! This morning two notaries came to ask for Madame La
Perrière's expert evaluation of some lace that was about to be
distributed among the heirs of its dead owner. Before examining
a piece of lace, she always laid it on a big red silk cloth spread
on her bed in front of her, because the red background brought
out the beauty of the lace, as well as its flaws. She would then
render her judgment: "Good design, but faulty execution and
insufficient size for satisfactory use. The white has turned a little
gray and there's a rust spot, there, lower right. Sixty livres. And
you owe me twenty sous." Or: "Now here's a really valuable
piece of lace! Who left this fine legacy?" She never took payment for her appraisal if the lace in question came from a Protestant family.

She was also visited by great painters passing through the
town or on their way to the Royal Manufactory. They showed
her their designs for lace and discussed the difficulties of exe-
cuting them. One of them gave her his most beautiful pattern,
saying he would be delighted if she would do him the honor of
making lace from it for her own use. She thanked him a little
sadly and said she didn't think God would be generous to her
much longer. She had been sick for twenty years; the Lord must
be getting tired of keeping her alive.

But she quickly regained her good spirits, pointed to Gilonne,
who was bringing the bottle of rosolio that Esther had told her
to serve to the distinguished visitors, and said, "This young lady
will finish making the lace from your pattern if I can't. Look at
her carefully: she'll be an excellent lacemaker because she has
not only great skill but also a poetic turn of mind. . . . Pour
some for yourself too, Gilonne. A little rosolio from time to
time is good for encouraging girls who still have a long road to
travel."

Sitting day after day on either side of Madame La Perrière's
bed, Gilonne and Michanteau learned the marvelous sixth operation: embroidering on the lace, which gave it life by making
its contours and decorations stand out in relief. What they liked,
what left them silent, attentive, and determined to do well, was
what Madame La Perrière said to underscore the things she
taught. They must never forget that the whole beauty of lace
rested on the embroidery. If it was badly done, the piece was
lost. But firm, intelligent stitches would bring it to fulfillment;
there would then be sunlight on the flowers and a light breeze
in the foliage, and the ribbons would flutter. Did they see that?

Of course they did. They realized how important it was to keep trying to make lace more beautiful, always more beautiful. Yes, they now knew that nothing was really achieved, that they had to go on seeking, and sometimes finding.

Often when she was tired, Madame La Perrière would stop, rest her head on the pillow, and ask quietly, "Will you remember all this after I'm gone?" And in the silence of the little white room it seemed to Gilonne that she was gathering, one by one, the falling petals of a rose. How could she ever forget?

In the evening she and Michanteau brought supper to Madame La Perrière. Then, after tidying up the house to suit Esther—made irritable by her infirmity, she pounded the floor with her cane or called them cursed papists when she felt they weren't prompt and diligent enough—they went back upstairs. They slept in a room next to Madame La Perrière's so they could go to her quickly if she should call for them. They took off their hats, braided their hair, put on the coarse linen nightgowns Mistress Bordier had given them, waited to hear Madame La Perrière's gentle, rather faint voice say, "Come and tell me good night, girls," and then hurried into her room.

This was the best part of the day, when they didn't make lace but heard about its history. Before, they had naïvely assumed that Madame La Perrière had simply sat down one morning and invented Alençon lace all at once. Now they listened with surprise and admiration as she described her years of slow, trial-and-error efforts. What a long way she had come! Had she taken Venetian lace as her starting point? Not really. Had she invented her lace just when Venetian lace was being invented? Maybe she and a lacemaker in Venice had both been inspired at the same time. Who would ever know? She had learned cutwork* from her mother and grandmother, and from that she had developed what came to be known as Alençon lace. Others would develop it still further.

But there was one thing she was sure she had thought of before anyone else: dividing up the work of lacemaking. She said this without vanity because she believed that she had been only an instrument, that God had created through her. The idea had come one day like a light that suddenly dazzled her: Lacemaking should be divided into several operations, each assigned to a lacemaker who would always do the same one. Constant

---

*An early form of openwork embroidery.

repetition would teach her to do her single operation rapidly and well, whereas doing it only rarely would make her hesitant and cause her to waste time. The girls had seen for themselves that someone who did nothing but make bars, for example, could make them better and much more quickly than someone who made them only occasionally. That was the whole point. It now seemed so obvious to her that she was surprised no one had thought of it before her. It also seemed to her that the same principle could be applied to other kinds of work; sooner or later it would surely be done.

"Isn't it true," asked Michanteau, "that the new lace—*point de France*, since that's what the king wants it to be called—is really only your Alençon lace with a few little changes?"

"With the changes and embellishments that others have made in it, it's becoming everyone's lace."

"It's being stolen from you."

The man who invented the plow and made the first furrow did it for everyone," said Madame La Perrière.

But Michanteau still looked perplexed.

The two girls learned to cut a piece of lace away from the parchment, and to repair the parts of it damaged in the process of cutting it away. Then they learned the last of the long series of operations: joining the sections of lace with invisible seams.

Madame La Perrière wanted to have a little celebration for her young lacemakers. She had to make an effort to appear to be feeling well, because she had in fact become even weaker in the last few months. Esther, now able to walk again, hid behind a door and wept into her apron. The three others shared a cake and drank a little rosolio, but Madame La Perrière wasn't really in the mood for celebrating.

They were so cozy in the little house, and so absorbed in their work, that they hadn't heard the news that the king's cousin, Her Royal Highness the Dowager Duchess of Guise and Alençon, had come to her town with the intention of living there for six months each year. During one of the girls' Sunday visits to the poorhouse, Conte-Nouvelles told them about it, and added that the duchess was devoted to the king. They concluded that since she was also an ardent Catholic, from what they had heard, she would do nothing to improve the lot of Protestants like Madame La Perrière.

The children were increasingly concerned about Madame La

Perrière. When Mistress Lescure came to visit, she never failed to urge them to act quickly if they saw that Madame La Perrière was about to die. They were greatly upset by something that had just happened in Alençon: Rather than being given a religious burial, the body of a Protestant woman who had refused the Catholic rites on her deathbed had been thrown into the garbage dump. The whole town was talking about it. What were the girls to do? Should they let Madame La Perrière be buried without saying anything, or call in a priest to try to save her soul?

Esther spared them that choice. On the cold night of January 12, when they were sound asleep under their quilts, she didn't tell them that Madame La Perrière was dying. Instead, she hurried off, limping and sobbing, to notify the members of her church, who would do what needed to be done.

Unhappier than they had ever been before, Gilonne and Michanteau found themselves carrying their belongings in an icy wind, on their way to Montsort and Mama Bordier. That morning, Esther had given each of them a little package from Madame La Perrière containing a collar of Alençon lace and several very valuable patterns.

They showed none of this to Mistress Bordier who, they felt, would spoil their treasures by belittling them. They loved her and were deeply religious Catholics, but they also loved Madame La Perrière.

Mathieu had often reminded Gilonne of something Mortimer Morel d'Arthus had once said to him: "When your niece has become a lacemaker, we'll take her to work for us." Since then, however, new edicts had forbidden Protestants to have workers younger than fourteen, so Gilonne and Michanteau could have no thought of going to work for the Morel d'Arthus family. But several Catholic lacemaking shops were willing to take them in immediately. Mistress Lescure had recommended the one belonging to Monsieur Taunay, on the Rue de l'Ecusson.

They were walking toward it, leaning into a wind that lashed their faces and took their breath away, when Michanteau slipped and fell. An oncoming carriage was unable to avoid her. Her small size saved her: Seeing the horses rushing toward her, she curled up on the ground and escaped being injured by either hooves or wheels. The mishap left her only with a fright that made her teeth chatter for hours.

Inside the carriage were a man and woman who had the appearance of merchants. They hurried to Michanteau as soon as the driver had stopped the horses. Their concern was unusual for the passengers of vehicles involved in such accidents. Michanteau found them likable. So did Gilonne, who was so relieved at seeing her friend still alive that she would have had friendly feelings for anyone, even a hangman. Since they were only a few steps away from the Moor's Inn, they all went in for something to calm their nerves.

The girls were lacemakers? And knew all the elements of *point de France*, at their age? Surely there was no one else in Alençon who had acquired so much skill at such an early age! And what were they doing now? They had been on their way to ask for work? It was Providence that had made one of them slip on the ice, because they, Marie and Blaise Lemareur, had come to Alençon to have lace made from patterns they had bought in Paris from excellent artists. They had just found lodgings on the Rue du Château and were looking for lacemakers to hire. If the girls would show what they were capable of—not that there was any doubt about their ability!—the Lamareurs would show them their marvelous patterns. Then they would talk business and sign a contract with their parents, before a notary, as was right and proper. They had no parents, only a foster mother? Then the contract would be signed with the foster mother.

Mama Bordier was overwhelmed. These good people were going to promise in writing, signed in front of a notary, to give each of the girls a hundred livres for two years' work when they were only twelve and thirteen years old! A hundred livres plus food and lodging!

The contract was signed without notifying Mistress Lescure, who would have insisted on sending her pupils to spend a year in the Taunay shop, where the mistress-lacemaker was an artist. But weren't they now artists themselves?

They served their two years. They couldn't have done otherwise, since Mama Bordier had signed for them and would have had to pay a hundred-livre penalty if they had run away, as they so often felt like doing.

The Lemareurs proved to be completely ignorant of lacemaking—not even knowing, said Gilonne, that it was done with a needle and thread. And, afraid of being duped, they were more demanding than other employers.

They asked the girls what they had to complain about, when

they had such easy work. Always sitting down—who wouldn't like that? When they, the Lemareurs, had been in the grocery business in Paris, they had been on their feet from dawn to dusk.

Marie Lemareur, a gaunt, dark-haired woman with piercing eyes and precise movements who was always neatly dressed, came to wake them before four o'clock each morning, winter and summer. After giving them time to wash, dress, and eat a quick breakfast, she took them to the worktable and kept them there until lunch. She sat facing them, with her knitting and mending, and left only to prepare meals. Her husband then took her place, holding a newspaper that he sometimes read and sometimes didn't, depending on his mood. Being plump, he seemed more jovial than his wife, though he was occasionally taciturn, probably when he wasn't satisfied with his accounts, to which he devoted a great deal of time. He carefully noted each purchase of thread, needles, candles, and bread. With brief pauses for lunch and supper, the girls worked until ten o'clock in winter, eleven in summer.

They were decently fed and kept comfortably warm in the winter. On Sundays they were allowed to go to church and walk for an hour afterward, accompanied by their employers. Once a month they could visit Mama Bordier or Grandmother Thomine and her friends, but the Lemareurs still went with them. "They're afraid we'll fly away!" said Michanteau. It was specified in the contract that they would work on all religious holidays except Christmas and Easter. The Lemareurs had agreed to obtain the indulgences needed to save the girls from being in a state of sin.

Gilonne and Michanteau felt they were caught in a trap and realized with horror that it wouldn't open until two long years had passed. Sometimes they were seized with panic. One day when they walked past the Guise palace, where the Duchess of Alençon lived with her court, and saw servants carrying orange trees in tubs out of the greenhouse and putting them in front of the palace, Gilonne remarked that she and Michanteau were like those orange trees: From time to time they were taken out into the fresh air, then quickly brought back inside.

Although they were allowed to talk while they worked, they hardly ever felt like saying anything because either Madame Lemareur or her husband was constantly there. They always intended to catch up on their talking in the evening, when they were finally alone in their room with the door closed, but they were usually so exhausted that they fell asleep as soon as they lay down. Sometimes, however, when their nerves were tense because the pattern of the lace they were making was especially complicated, or because they had made a mistake that took great concentration to correct, they were unable to sleep. Then they would lie in the stillness of the night and make plans for the future. Once they were out of this prison with their two hundred livres, they would be free to buy patterns, thread, and needles, rent a room, make lace, and sell it themselves, instead of letting a pair of Paris grocers take the profit from it.

But although the night sometimes brought hope, the days were still long.

During the first winter, when the distressing sensation of being tied up and smothered had passed, they sank torpidly into the comfort of their cocoon. Sitting in the warmth radiating from the fireplace, warmed still more by the hot soup or buckwheat porridge they had eaten, each of them with a shawl over her shoulders and another one on her lap, they sometimes worked without thinking too much about their misfortune. But when spring came it seemed to them that they would never be able to sit still all day. Waiting for Sunday was so painful that they often felt like crying out in despair.

One day when the smell of cabbage—which sickened them and was one of the Lemareurs' favorite foods—invaded the room, they put down their work, stood up with apparent calm and began screaming together at the top of their lungs. The series of emotions—astonishment, incredulity, consternation—they saw in their jailers' eyes finally made them stop screaming and burst out laughing. They didn't try to explain how they had been exasperated by the thought that only a few feet away, on the other side of the window, the air was filled with the delicate fragrance of apple blossoms.

For a long time the Lemareurs' bewildered expression made them laugh whenever they remembered it, and although neither of them had a watch, it seemed to them that their Sunday walks had become a little longer.

Depending on the weather, those walks were taken either in the beautiful town park or in the arcade of the Place du Palais. One rainy, chilly Sunday when they were passing by a shop that sold apple fritters, Monsieur Lemareur stopped and bought one for each of the girls, as well as for himself and his wife. Judging from her look of surprise and disapproval, he hadn't consulted her beforehand. Michanteau noted it and thought, *I'm afraid our troubles are about to begin.*

Michanteau had become aware that although Monsieur Lemareur had retired from the grocery business, he hadn't retired from life, and that he often sat looking at Gilonne when he was supposed to be reading his newspaper. With her natural optimism, the girl focused her attention on the bright side—the apple fritters—and tried to ignore the domestic complications that probably lay ahead.

The following Sunday, Monsieur Lemareur again stopped to buy apple fritters. His wife refused to take one. He took one for himself but let it grow cold between the two plane-tree leaves that served as its wrapping. When they had returned home and his wife was unlocking the door of the house, he slipped the fritter into Gilonne's hands, which she had been holding under her warm shawl.

The girls overheard no arguments between the couple, but from then on Madame Lemareur got up even earlier, prepared all the day's meals in advance, and no longer left the worktable to let her husband take her place. She was always placid, never disagreeable or overly demanding; she was simply there all the time.

One summer day when the window was open and birds could be heard warbling in the garden across the street, Michanteau launched into a song she had learned at the Royal Manufactory:

> *Ta grand-mère m'a dit que t'étais bien faite.*
> *Voudrais-tu me montrer tes beaux seins, Nanette?*
> *Ah! mon ami Thomas, ta demande est indiscrète.*
> *Ah! mon ami Thomas, tu ne les verras pas.**

Gilonne took up the refrain and, miraculously, so did Marie Lemareur! The three of them loudly and gaily sang the remaining verses, which, after Nanette's breasts, spoke of her arms, legs, and eyes. The girls saw Monsieur Lemareur's astounded face appear in the doorway, they saw his wife look at him with

*Your grandmother told me you were well made.
Would you show me your beautiful breasts, Nanette?
Ah, my friend Thomas, your request is indiscreet!
Ah, my friend Thomas, you won't see them!

a mocking smile; then he withdrew, offended, and they became friends with Marie.

The retired grocer went on keeping his accounts, and they wondered if he noted the cost of the apple fritters they ate every Sunday. It was now Marie who bought them, without ever taking one for herself; the fact was that she didn't like them.

Winter returned, along with their drowsy resignation. But then Conte-Nouvelles gave Gilonne and Michanteau a piece of news that revived their spirits: Mathieu was back. He had been away at war, as everyone thought, but he had finished his time and was discharged after the victory at Cassel. He was going to take up his staff again with pleasure and would be at the poorhouse on Sunday, waiting to see Gilonne.

She took Michanteau with her. Mathieu made a strong impression on Michanteau.

From then on, everything seemed easier and time passed more quickly. Two lappets, two tippets, a dress flounce, and a collar were almost finished. Marie Lemareur realized that the girls' diligence had never faltered. The end of the contract was approaching in an atmosphere of trust. The Lemareurs, it was true, would have merchandise worth nearly seven thousand livres, but that was only normal. Gilonne and Michanteau felt that their real wealth was not in the little bags of money that would delightfully weigh down their pockets but rather in what they had proved to themselves: that they could successfully do difficult lacemaking, *alone*. Alençon belonged to them!

The Lemareurs had decided to go to Caen and repeat what they had done in Alençon: hire lacemakers to work from patterns that they would buy in Paris. They now knew that selling lace could be a profitable business. They had been advised to go into it by one of their cousins in Paris, a carpenter by trade who had warned them that lacemakers were frivolous creatures and that they would have to keep a close watch on theirs if they didn't want to go bankrupt.

They apologized to Gilonne and Michanteau for having kept so close a watch on them. If they had known how perfect they were in their work, they would have left them much more on their own. Marie wept when they parted. So did her husband.

"Now that we've made those two trust us," Michanteau said to Gilonne, "they'll get themselves fleeced in Caen."

Gilonne didn't think so. Although Marie had become more human, she was as shrewd as ever and would quickly see any danger that might arise, no matter what Michanteau thought. Michanteau had a rather simplistic view of life. It was part of her charm.

They forgot about the Lemareurs as soon as they took their first free steps in Alençon.

It was Thursday, the weekly market day. They decided to go surprise Mama Bordier and her turkeys. They would spend a few days in Montsort, just long enough to work out their plans. Or maybe they would go straight to Mistress Verlot and ask her to hire them to work in the kitchen—the dreaded cook had left!— so they could earn a little more money while they rested their smarting eyes. Rich with their two hundred livres, they were determined not to spend any of it frivolously and eager to add to their nest egg as soon as possible. Gilonne knew by heart the prices of the best quality foreign thread that had to be used to make the finest lace, and they would have to rent a room with a window giving enough light to do good work.

"Can't we at least buy ourselves a dress and a pair of wooden shoes?" asked Michanteau. "The shoes I have now are too tight: They rub my feet so much I'm afraid they'll catch fire! And my dress is so short, and my petticoat has so many holes in it, that it won't be long before people can see my pretty little ass!"

In spite of Madame La Perrière's lessons, Michanteau hadn't improved her language or her manners, as she now showed by laughing loudly and pointing to the nobleman and the two strange musician-servants who came to sing in the marketplace every Thursday. "Music and dancing, that's what we need first of all," she said. "Then we'll have some apple fritters and, whether you're willing or not, a pitcher of cider."

She felt excitement rising inside her. She danced, sang with the musicians, and made everyone around her share her gaiety. It was impossible for Candelario and Zoltan not to notice the brunette who had become so animated and the blond who remained so calm. Gilonne listened to one of the songs the nobleman had composed himself, as everyone in Alençon knew. It told about the happy end of the Flanders campaign and the victories at Cassel and Cambrai, where enemy flags had been gathered like flowers and put together in a big bouquet to be presented to His Majesty.

The girls stood at the front of the crowd, eating apples and listening with their faces turned toward the singers like sunflowers toward the sun.

"Do you see what I see?" Candelario said to Zoltan.

"I do."

"Do you think that . . ."

"Yes."

The years had not made Zoltan more talkative. But his eyes were as sharp as ever. He had spotted Gilonne right away and was moved by the sight of her dimpled chin: it was exactly like her mother's. The shock of seeing Julie's daughter made him admit to himself for the first time how much he had loved the little lacemaker. She had never had the slightest idea of his feelings.

"What shall we do?" Candelario asked him between songs.

"Keep an eye on her."

They had learned of Julie's death and knew she had left a baby daughter, but they knew nothing about the child. Her sudden appearance—they had no doubt she was indeed the daughter of Julie and the chevalier because her resemblance to both of them was striking—brought back their plans and romantic dreams from the past. Candelario forgot his rheumatism and felt rejuvenated. Ah, those good old days when Julie was so hungry she could have eaten a whole chicken all by herself! Mistress Verlot's capons were so much better in that long-ago time of their youth! That beautiful young lady must be at least fifteen. And who was the girl with her?

The chevalier's daughter had just disappeared! No, they saw her running, over there. . . . Running and running . . . What was she running toward like that? Would she ever stop?

Three

So Uncle Mathieu knew. He had always known, and he had said nothing. Gilonne wondered if she should be angry with him for that, but what had happened to her was so recent and disturbing, and her heart was still beating so fast, that she couldn't decide. It was a story like the ones she used to read to Madame La Perrière in the evening, and she was its heroine!

Her thoughts were suddenly distracted by the sight she had had in front of her ever since leaving Alençon, but hadn't really seen until now: Michanteau riding behind Candelario on his horse and having a hard time holding onto his thick waist with her little arms. He was so fat, and had on so many clothes! And he was so comical too! If Uncle Mathieu hadn't assured her that Candelario was telling the truth, she never would have believed a word of what the ridiculous man had said to her. And if Uncle Mathieu hadn't told her she could trust him, she might have been a little afraid of the other one, who was taking her through the forest on his white horse while she easily kept her arms around his thin torso.

So fourteen years before, these two servants of Chevalier de Ferrières had gone all over town looking for her, to take her to her family as they were doing now!

She wondered if she would ever get used to giving the name

of father to that handsome and strange nobleman she had so often seen singing in the marketplace on Thursdays. Everything about this wonderful adventure delighted her, except having to meet Louis-Guillaume de Ferrières de Pervenchères. Her memory of him—sitting up straight, even stiffly, on his black horse and staring into the distance as he sang—didn't make her feel like hurrying toward him with her arms outstretched.

The two servants hadn't talked to her about their master, but about his mother, Lady Bertrade. It was actually to that crippled old lady that they had said they were taking her. Maybe she would never even see the singing chevalier. Or maybe not until later. This thought reassured her. Besides, she wasn't going to stay in Pervenchères very long. The Hungarian, who spoke little, had said in an effort to persuade her, "Just come and see Lady Bertrade so she can meet her granddaughter before she dies, and then you can go straight back to Alençon." She had agreed only to that. Michanteau had, of course, been greatly excited, and the idea of not going with Gilonne would never have crossed her mind. "I'm not surprised to know your father is a nobleman," she had said. "You're going to live in a castle, and that's exactly what you need." Then, after more nonsense in that same vein, she had said, "You couldn't get along without me. You're too sensitive and you think too much. Whenever something good comes along, you should take it before it can get away. Now something *very* good is coming straight toward you, and you're as indifferent as a dead fish!" Michanteau tended to see indifference in anyone who didn't shout and hop up and down at the drop of a hat.

Didn't she realize, thought Gilonne, that the noble lord who was her father had made no effort to become acquainted with his child? The servants claimed he didn't know about her birth. How had her mother died? There was too much she didn't know about her past. She would have to talk about it again with Uncle Mathieu, and find out everything. Afterward, she would see. But her real family was Grandmother Thomine and Uncle Mathieu. And Mama Bordier, and Grandmother Thomine's friends in the poorhouse. And also Madame La Perrière. And even Mistress Lescure and Gérasime. Everyone who had cared about her. She suddenly felt like turning back without seeing these people who had so unexpectedly popped into her life, like the pigeons that the magician in the gallery of the Place du Palais pulled out of a seemingly empty bag.

But wasn't she glad she no longer had to wonder who her father might be? She had to admit she felt a strange joy that swelled her heart almost to the point of being painful. The chevalier was said to be an eccentric, but also a proud warrior and a gentleman of distinguished ancestry. And what about Grand-Coeur? On that point, she agreed with Michanteau: an estate with such a name had to be hospitable. Her courage began returning. Candelario and Zoltan had told her that their master now spent much more time at the Moor's Inn than on his estate, occasionally staying there for as much as two weeks at a time. They would come to meet him at the marketplace, as they had done today, then leave him to his spinet and the silent, effective service of a discreet hostess, the kind he liked, they said. There was still the old lady. But old ladies didn't frighten Gilonne.

Eating a little buckwheat roll that Candelario had given her, Michanteau seemed to find life beautiful. She was probably saying all sorts of things to that man she hardly knew. Gilonne should have told her to be discreet. Everything had happened so quickly. She and Uncle Mathieu had found Michanteau in the marketplace, listening to the two servants with a look of amazement.

"Oh, if you only knew!" she had exclaimed as soon as she saw them. "If you only knew what's happened to us!"

Mathieu, who was a little shy—the war apparently hadn't changed him—had looked at the excited dark-haired girl and seemed to be at a loss for words. Then he had gradually regained his composure. But Gilonne couldn't tell if he was relieved or upset that the mystery of her birth had finally been revealed.

Night was falling when they reached the estate. The house was bathed in the last red glow of the setting sun. Michanteau had lapsed into silence. Candelario and Zoltan took the girls into a huge barn. The plan the two men had adopted, with Mathieu's agreement, was to explain the situation to Pompinne, introduce Gilonne to her, and wait to see what she would decide. When Pompinne was first mentioned, the girls had been surprised to learn that Mathieu knew her. He told them that one day he had gone to the estate with the intention of telling the Ferrières about Gilonne, but that things hadn't worked out as he hoped and he had preferred to leave without saying anything. Then, as he was nearing the village of Pervenchères, the recruiting sergeants had seized him.

The hay in the barn smelled good, and the girls lay down on it, exhausted from their ride.

They were also hungry. They heard cows nearby and hoped that someone would think to give them a bowl of milk. Looking around the barn, they found a basket of apples. They ate a few of them, without talking. Even Michanteau seemed anxious.

Finally they both fell asleep. Soon afterward, a tall, powerfully built woman, followed by Candelario and Zoltan, burst into the barn with a lantern in her hand and said loudly, "Where is she?"

Gilonne sat up. Her hat had fallen into the hay while she slept, and her long blond hair streamed down over her shoulders. Pompinne stared at her in silence for a few moments, then abruptly began weeping.

No one knew what to do.

Finally Pompinne got a grip on herself and wiped her eyes with a corner of her apron. When she spoke, the girls were startled by the strength of her voice.

Candelario and Zoltan, those lying, thieving, blackhearted scoundrels, had known for fourteen years—*fourteen years!*—that the chevalier had a daughter, and they had kept quiet about it until now! What could God have been thinking of when He put such half-wits on earth? There were fine young men like her son Julian falling on the king's battlefields while these two worthless creatures stole food from good people and never breathed a word about something that would have given such happiness to . . . Poor Lady Bertrade was so sick and needed good news so much! If there was any justice in this world . . .

Pompinne had to stop, out of breath.

Candelario tried to explain. It was precisely because they were thinking of Lady Bertrade, and because they had so often heard Pompinne say how much she regretted the lack of an heir at Grand-Coeur, that they had decided today . . .

"Today!" exclaimed Pompinne. "You should have brought her here fourteen years ago! It may be too late now! I'm not sure poor Lady Bertrade will understand who she is."

Gilonne was surprised that the tall, thin Zoltan and the short, round Candelario had shown so little reaction as they listened to Pompinne. She attributed their silence to the respect they must feel for the old servant.

Pompinne calmed down as quickly as she had flared up. She had to go, she said, and prepare her mistress for the news.

She turned away, took a few steps, then came back and stood in front of Gilonne with her lantern still in her hand.

"Young lady, I've missed the pleasure of making your first dress for you and introducing you to the people who owe obedience to my master, but I'm going to make up for lost time. Tomorrow—Who's that?"

Seized with sudden, uncharacteristic discretion, Michanteau had stayed in the background and done nothing to attract the attention of the woman who seemed so powerful here.

"This is Michanteau," said Gilonne, putting her arm around her shoulder. "She's the sister I've chosen for myself."

"Then we can't have one without the other?"

"That's right," answered Gilonne, smiling.

She liked this enormous woman. A slap from one of her broad, rough hands would obviously be no laughing matter, but she gave the soothing impression of being warmhearted in spite of her gruff manner.

It was agreed that Gilonne would be taken to Lady Bertrade the next day. Pompinne would prepare her mistress when she took up her bowl of buckwheat porridge. Lady Bertrade hadn't come down to have supper in the kitchen that evening; it had been one of those times when she closed the curtains of her bed and refused either to speak or to eat. Pompinne would insist that she eat some porridge, and she would then tell her about Gilonne.

Since Pompinne still talked about leaving but hadn't done it, Gilonne asked timidly, "Are you sure that . . . that I really belong here? How do you know . . ."

Pompinne's laugh was as colossal as her body. It rose all the way to the rafters of the barn.

"I'm not a fool who swallows a toad because someone tells her it's as good as a butter cake! I know the Ferrières so well that I could recognize one of them in a crowd of a thousand people. They're the only ones who have eyes and hair like yours. I've cut that hair on the heads of young and old members of your family, and I've seen those eyes laughing and crying! No one could fool me about who is or isn't a Ferrières, even at night by candlelight." And, as though she were pressing a seal into wax, Pompinne added forcefully, "That birthmark on your left wrist: Your father has one just like it, and so did *his* father, Chevalier Héribert."

With these decisive words, she majestically walked away.

Candelario felt as if he were in a theater, sitting in the front row, and he was on the verge of applauding. Zoltan smiled and continued carving a piece of wood into the shape of a spoon.

"I'd be glad to have that woman for an aunt or a cousin," said Michanteau. "She goes straight to my heart . . . But I'm starving! Isn't there a kitchen in this castle?"

Candelario explained that it had been decided to keep Gilonne out of the house for the time being because Lady Bertrade, a little eccentric, was quite capable of saying, "I won't come down for supper this evening," and then coming down anyway. But he would bring the young ladies something to eat. In honor of their arrival, maybe a piece of Pompinne's magnificent spiced apple preserves would be taken out of its hiding place.

Gilonne and Michanteau were blissfully asleep in the hay, after having eaten their fill. "Tomorrow we'll probably have beds," Michanteau had said. "This is our treatment *before* your official recognition. Afterward, things will be different." They had huddled against each other because the darkness of the barn frightened them a little once they had blown out their candle.

Michanteau was the first to wake up. She opened one eye, then the other, and then she opened them both wider. A tall woman, holding a lantern and wearing a black greatcoat, with a red wool hat over her white hair, towered above her. She had evidently been watching them sleep. Michanteau's alarm subsided when she noticed the trembling of the hand that held the lantern, and the tears flowing in the creases of the face. This was surely Gilonne's new grandmother.

Gilonne was still asleep. The imposing lady put a finger to her lips to signal that she was not to be awakened. She and Michanteau therefore looked at each other in silence. Lady Bertrade's complexion was as red as her hat. Bloodletting evidently wasn't practiced enough in this region. Michanteau would have to talk about it with Pompinne. An owl hooted but didn't wake Gilonne. Lady Bertrade turned her eyes back to the sleeping girl. Michanteau did the same, telling herself it would be hard to see a prettier sight than Gilonne lying there in the hay with her hair spread out around her head. A few more moments went by; then, in spite of her efforts to restrain herself, the old lady coughed and Gilonne abruptly sat up with a frightened expression.

There was nothing in common between the brawny Lady Bertrade and the frail, blind Thomine, but when their granddaughter saw Lady Bertrade looking at her with the eyes of a good-natured bird of prey, she felt the same tender pity she felt for Thomine. What must life in this place be like, to have transformed a noble lady into a monstrous creature? She would have liked to wipe away the tears still flowing down the wide face, and hold the hand that kept moving up to the red hat as though to put it back in place, when in fact it had stayed exactly where it was.

Who would finally speak?

It was Lady Bertrade: "You mustn't stay here. Sir Reginald is as curious as a village busybody. He'll come to have a look at you before long, and you'll be afraid if you see him. Come, let's go into the house."

Gilonne and Michanteau stood up with wisps of hay clinging to their clothes and hair. Stumbling now and then, they followed the old lady. In the chilly darkness, they crossed the big courtyard that separated the outbuildings from the house.

"I don't know who Sir Reginald is," Michanteau whispered to Gilonne, "but I do know I wasn't as scared in the barn as I am here!"

In the kitchen, Pompinne had put bowls on the table and was reviving the fire.

When Lady Bertrade had sat down, Pompinne led the girls to the far end of the room and said to Gilonne, "She's furious with Candelario and Zoltan. She accuses them of deliberately hiding you from her all these years. They've gone off to sleep, but they know what's waiting for them at dawn. I've made a fire for the two of you in one of the rooms upstairs. You'll find only one blanket on the bed, and we haven't had any sheets for a long time. We're not rich here, but sleeping between luxurious sheets doesn't make your dreams any better, does it?"

She seemed in a cheerful mood as she looked at her mistress with an affectionate smile and said, "She's all warm inside now, from happiness, and it will make her mind better. There's nothing really wrong with her mind, it just gets a little foggy sometimes. Because of her accident, of course, and also because her falconer left. She loved him as much as her son. I'll have to tell you about that ungrateful boy, but later. You can read her favorite books to her, the way he did, and that will make her miss him less. And you must have some stories you can tell her. She loves stories so much! You have to make her laugh. She likes to laugh like a child. She'll show you her forest. Her birds and trees—that's what she regards as her wealth. My buckwheat porridge is the best you'll ever find, and I'll make it for you as often as you like. Candelario and Zoltan—they're really not completely useless—will play their music for you and make you feel as if you were in heaven. You'll see, you'll see. . . . And the chevalier will soon be back with another batch of beautiful new songs. Believe me, girls, it's still possible to be happy at Grand-Coeur!''

What could they answer? That they had no intention of staying there, that Alençon was waiting for them, and also the lacemaking shop they wanted to create? A modest little shop, of course, but it would be all theirs. That they were rich with two hundred livres and didn't need anyone to help them get off to a good start in life? They said nothing.

"We'll have to give them horses," Lady Bertrade called out from the other side of the kitchen.

"How does she expect you to have horses," Pompine said quietly to Gilonne and Michanteau, "when the stables are as bare as the back of my hand? She thinks we're still as rich as in the old days, poor woman." She raised her voice: "Yes, madame, we'll give them horses as soon as it's daylight."

"Selva-Oscura for my granddaughter. He's the handsomest one. Clopu for her friend: he's her size." The old lady laughed. "Yes, he's as small as she is!"

Pompinne sighed.

"He *was* small," she said in an undertone. "He died ten years ago!"

"I want more porridge. And wine!"

"Wine!" echoed Pompinne. "How am I supposed to—Yes, madame."

At dawn they still hadn't even thought of going to bed. A young farmhand came in and sat down at one end of the table. Soon afterward Zoltan and Candelario arrived.

"You two are up early," said Pompinne. "You certainly must have been curious! Well, as you can see, things are going well. Madame is taking an interest in life again. It's God's will."

Lady Bertrade had been quivering convulsively since the two men came in. She pushed back her bowl.

"Pompinne, my crutch!"

She stood up and moved nimbly in spite of her infirmity and her weight. Her eyes had suddenly become hard. With a sweep-

ing motion of her arm, she knocked off the bowls that Pompinne
had just put down in front of Zoltan and Candelario. They shat-
tered on the stone floor, and the porridge in them formed two
big puddles.

"Out, both of you! Into the courtyard!"

The musicians stood up with surprising docility, almost smiling. Lady Bertrade took down a whip hanging beside the fireplace in the common room.

When they were outside, she pointed to the wall of the stable
and pushed the two men toward it. Michanteau stood watching
from the doorway. Gilonne stayed in her chair and heard the
whip crack. Fourteen times for each man.

"One for each year you spent away from her," Pompinne
said with satisfaction. "I was wondering how many she'd give
them. How does she know you're fourteen? Her mind isn't as
bad as some people think. It's just a little foggy sometimes. I've
already told you that. But soon the fog will clear away for good,
and she'll be the same as before. I have to admit those two aren't
completely to blame for not finding you sooner, but she's been
wanting to give them a good beating for a long time!"

"When are we leaving?" asked Michanteau.

Lying in the hay and biting on a wisp of it, Gilonne didn't
answer.

"It's pretty out here in the country," Michanteau went on,
"but in the middle of winter . . . Are you listening to me?"

"I'm listening, but I'm not leaving."

"That's what I thought! And what do you want to do here, in
this ruin?"

"Maybe I want to help rebuild it."

"Whether they're rich or poor, aristocrats are always the
same: They make other people serve them. Your grandmother
will turn you into a serf."

"You know that's not true."

"Yes, I know it's not true, and that's what bothers me. I can't
deny she's a good woman. She loves you—I could almost say
she loves *us*—and I don't see anything to stop you from doing
something for her."

"*He* may stop her."

"He? Who's that?"

"The chevalier. He'll be coming back soon. Without him,
we'd be happy here."

"What have you got against him?"

"I don't know yet. I just have a feeling that things will go wrong when he gets here."

"I don't see why. He's handsome, he's still young, and he sings. As time goes by, he'll stay handsome, he'll be a little less young, and he'll go on singing. What's there to complain about? Besides, when he's not away fighting in a war, he spends most of his time at Mistress Verlot's inn, so we won't see him very often."

"I've been thinking about what we could do here."

"So have I, and I'll bet you my next helping of spiced apple preserves that we've had the same idea. I saw you questioning shepherdesses and old women in Pervenchères, but I have to tell you they'd be bad lacemakers and you'd never be able to start a decent shop here. I've never seen people as dirty, crude, and surly as they are."

"They're the poorest of the poor. But we can do something with them."

"And we'd be using our own money, wouldn't we? In Alençon, we wouldn't risk losing it all. Here, we would. And where would we get designs and patterns?"

"Maybe from that artist who liked us at the Royal Manufactory."

"You mean he liked *you.* . . . But I don't think we should buy from him. We'd be better off with a Protestant artist who'd lower his prices because he's had almost no work since all those Protestant lacemaking shops closed down. A lot of things have happened while the Lemareurs were keeping us prisoners."

"If we buy from that artist, we won't be taking advantage of him."

"You're willing to spend as much as it takes to train women who are almost animals, and you don't want to buy cheap patterns because you'd be taking advantage of the artist! Our two hundred livres aren't going to last very long!"

"If we stay here, we won't have to pay any rent."

"Yes, I've thought about that too. I've thought about everything!"

"And what have you decided?"

"I've decided," Michanteau said with a sigh, "that we'll do whatever you want."

"We'll talk about it again, after the chevalier comes."

* * *

He arrived two weeks later, with Zoltan and Candelario, who had gone to rejoin him in Alençon that morning.

Pompinne had made no special preparations for his return. The menu would be the same. All she did was to put a pitcher of fresh water in his room.

After a discussion with Pompinne, the two musician-servants agreed not to tell the chevalier who Gilonne was. They would wait and see what happened. Candelario said that, with his usual absentmindedness, the chevalier might take a month or two to notice the girls' presence. But then he saw the anxiety in Gilonne's face and stopped his joking.

When the chevalier took his place at the table opposite Lady Bertrade, Pompinne said to him, "Your mother, sir, has invited these young ladies to stay here awhile. They read to her, keep her company, and mend her clothes."

The look he gave them was dulled by indifference, but he politely nodded toward them, greeting them and expressing his approval at the same time.

Contrary to her habit, Lady Bertrade talked a great deal. This seemed to surprise her son, but he made no comment on it.

With the buckwheat porridge there was a vegetable stew, then came baked apples, a delicacy the old lady seemed to adore. She said that long ago, when she was at home in Mortagne, they used to add a spoonful of honey to each apple, which made them even more delicious. Red honey the bees had made from white buckwheat flowers. She spoke of big fields of snowy buckwheat being "plundered" by bees, as Montaigne said. The chevalier looked at her in surprise and opened his mouth, evidently to say something, but put a spoonful of baked apple into it instead.

Lady Bertrade kept looking at the girls and appeared to be talking only to them. Did they know that bees became attached to the people who took care of them? In her childhood—she remembered this very clearly—white cloths were put on the hives each time there was a wedding, and black ones whenever there was a death. The bees liked to share the joys and sorrows of their adopted family.

"I *told* you her fog would soon clear away," Pompinne murmured to Candelario, who was smiling happily.

Gilonne watched the chevalier fill and light his pipe. When he had finished that absorbing task, he stood up from the table and walked away.

"Well, are we staying here or not?" Michanteau whispered to Gilonne.

Gilonne didn't answer and, seeing her sad expression, Michanteau said nothing more.

There was silence in the big room. Then, with her eyes still on the door her son had closed behind him, Lady Bertrade muttered, "The look of a dreamy, haughty stag . . ." Or at least that was what the others thought they had understood her to say. When she began discoursing on the Swedish army in a low voice, as though talking to herself, they decided that the fog that had briefly disappeared had now returned.

Michanteau had gone into the village of Pervenchères to find out how many people there were who might be capable of making lace. And also to visit the parish priest. "If the priest is against us," she had said, "we'll never get started. Some priests call lace a 'frivolity that encourages corruption.' If this one doesn't want his parishioners to make lace, we may as well forget about our plans."

Gilonne had gone to the barn to write to Uncle Mathieu about what she and Michanteau intended to do. Zoltan would deliver her letter next Thursday. She like Zoltan. He was usually taciturn, but one day he had talked to her about her mother. She had been a hardworking little lacemaker, he said, and a very sweet girl. He gave the impression that he was talking about a child, and this was what moved Gilonne most deeply as she listened to him. She would have liked him to go on telling her everything he knew about her mother, but he had left abruptly, in the middle of a sentence. He was an odd, interesting man. She was sure that he and Candelario were very fond of Lady Bertrade, which explained why they were willing to put up with anything from her and her servant Pompinne. The two women's scolding and bullying simply bounced off their tough hide. They must have laughed, later, at the whipping Lady Bertrade had given them.

Grand-Coeur disconcerted Gilonne; it wasn't at all as she would have imagined it. But she had already become attached to everyone there, except for the strange chevalier. She sighed and suddenly decided to stop constantly watching and hoping for a look from him. It was futile, because he never really looked at anyone. His eyes seemed empty. She had enough affection in her life, without having to beg for any from him. Jérémie had once said to her, "You should always be the one who loves less. It puts you at an advantage." It was a mediocre thought. At the time, though, she had listened to it respectfully, without understanding it. She now knew that Jérémie didn't believe a word of it—he was dying of love for the family from whom he had been separated—and that he made foolish pronouncements only to impress the admiring little girl she had been. It was time for her to adopt Michanteau's rule: Live for the moment, savor it, and tell yourself that tomorrow will be even better.

It was warm in the barn. Gilonne lay down in the straw scattered over the floor. Its smell reminded her of the attic in Mistress Lescure's house. She stretched. This was what mattered: being able to move about as much as she liked, running whenever she felt like it, being free, in short, to do with her body as she wished. She shuddered at the memory of the terrible immobility she had endured in the Lescure period of her life. She stood up and began hopping, then jumping, laughing at her childishness but taking such pleasure in it that she continued for quite a long while.

Suddenly she stopped, thinking she had heard laughter from somewhere high overhead, among the rafters of the barn. Had she only imagined it? Feeling embarrassed, as if someone had really seen her frolicking that way, she smoothed her hair and skirt and stood still, listening. She heard another laugh, seemingly from farther away. Someone was there, she was certain of it. She wasn't afraid, but she shivered. Should she inspect the barn over there, in those dark corners? Maybe she would find Candelario and be reassured. Then she heard another sound. A snore? Yes, it must be Candelario; he was famous for the little naps he took here and there.

Relieved, she began looking for the sleeper. In vain: there was no one but her in that barn! When she heard another snore she ran outside, panic-stricken, and nearly collided with the chevalier, who had just arrived.

He greeted her with the sharp little laugh she disliked. "I'll bet Sir Reginald has been up to his tricks again!"

She remembered what Lady Bertrade had said the night they first met: "You mustn't stay here. Sir Reginald is as curious as a village busybody. He'll come to have a look at you before long, and you'll be afraid if you see him."

"Sir Reginald?"

"The ghost at Grand-Coeur. Or, more precisely, one of the ghosts."

"Are there many of them?"

"We have two ghosts here, one of them a consequence of the other. The relation between them is quite natural, within the supernatural context. Shall I tell you about them?"

She timidly nodded.

He told her the story. It began with his ancestor, Palamède de Ferrières, and an embroidered silk scarf. Because of evil spells repeatedly cast on her, Lady Yolaine, Palamède's wife, was unable to finish the scarf that he intended to take with him when he went off to war. Each time the poor woman set to work, her thread became tangled and her needles broke. Palamède had to go into battle with the scarf, still bloodstained, that his father had been wearing when a Turk cut off his head. It was inevitable that, wearing such an accursed object, Palamède would also die in combat. He did. Lady Yolaine died of sorrow. Her ghost still came back to Grand-Coeur at night, loudly weeping and lamenting as she looked for her needles and thread.

Then there was Sir Reginald Lingham, to whom the King of England gave the fief of Ferrières during the occupation of Normandy.

Being a light sleeper, Sir Reginald was annoyed by Lady Yolaine's noisy lamentations. To be able to sleep in peace, he took refuge in the barn. It burned down one night when he was blissfully snoring. He perished in the flames.

"The English left," said the chevalier, "but we kept Sir Reginald. Lady Yolaine still laments and Sir Reginald still snores in the barn. You evidently heard him just now. But don't worry, he doesn't mean any harm. He likes to know the various people who stay here, that's all."

Chevalier Louis-Guillaume de Ferrières courteously tipped his hat, bowed to Gilonne, and walked away. Then he stopped and came back. She waited a little anxiously to hear what he was going to say.

"There are portraits of Lady Yolaine and Palamède de Ferrières in my mother's room. You may have seen them there. We don't have a portrait of Sir Reginald. We had one, but we sold it. Maybe he has a certain resentment against us. . . ."

Michanteau found Gilonne in a pensive mood, but she was bursting with news and had little concern for her friend's state

of mind. She had seen the parish priest, who proved to be a
fanatic. He was in despair over the poverty in his parish but was
on his guard against anything that might relieve it by means of
depravity—and, to him, lace was depravity! He was torn between fear of the devil's works and an ardent desire to feed his
flock. Michanteau had some persuasive arguments that, she
hoped, would make life easier for him, but she wanted Gilonne
to help her present them. First, however, she needed to know if
they were staying at Grand-Coeur.

"I'm going to ask if we'll be allowed to stay," said Gilonne.

She did so the next day, when the chevalier was coming out
of his library with his viol in his hand. She was so afraid of
forgetting the words she had prepared in advance that she spoke
much faster than usual. When she asked him if she could stay
at Grand-Coeur, he answered that her presence, and that of the
hopping little blackbird who was her friend, had a beneficial
effect on his mother. When she asked if she could set up a
lacemaking shop there, he raised one eyebrow in surprise, then
said it was always agreeable to see a lady working on such trifles
and she was free to spend her time making lace collars and hats,
if that was what interested her. She left him after a grateful
curtsy, with the unpleasant impression that he had judged her to
be a frivolous girl who thought of nothing but clothes. And she
wondered, irritated, how her mother had been able to get along
with such a man. She decided that from then on she would pay
no more attention to him than to the two ghosts at Grand-Coeur
and, laughing, told herself that in a way he was the third one.

In the evenings while she, Michanteau, Lady Bertrade, and
Pompinne sat in front of the fire in the big kitchen, they heard
the chevalier playing beautiful music. Sometimes Gilonne made
her way through the house in the dark and stood outside his
door, listening. She was his daughter! And, in the marvelous
world to which music transported her, she felt a kind of plea-
surable apprehension.

Her relations with Lady Bertrade, though a bit bizarre, were
nevertheless affectionate. The old lady often called her "my
child" and sometimes asked her, usually at unexpected moments, to kiss her not just on one cheek, but on both. Now and
then she told Gilonne about her life. Her stories were a little
chaotic, but not lacking in charm, and with a certain logic of
their own. Sometimes she opened her chests and gave Gilonne
one or another of the motley assortment of clothes and objects

Janine Montupet

they contained. These things were often shabby and dirty, but Gilonne valued them as proofs of affection and put them away in another chest.

She and Michanteau had a room next to Lady Bertrade's, furnished with a canopied and curtained bed, an armchair, and a table. On the walls were lingering traces of the tapestries that had once hung there but had been taken down and sold. It was Candelario, acting under orders, who handled such transactions. He claimed they overwhelmed him with sadness, but Pompinne said he enjoyed being craftier than the merchants to whom he took the contents of Grand-Coeur, bit by bit.

Pompinne was happy to see her mistress happy, and relieved at no longer having to keep a constant watch on her.

As soon as the chevalier had gone back to Alençon, Pompinne took Gilonne and Michanteau on a tour of the house. They might have been saddened at seeing all those big rooms emptied of their furniture, but instead they were full of hope and plans. They were going to restore the house to its former glory. Did Pompinne know what they were capable of, and how much money they could earn with their skilled hands? They told her all about their apprenticeship, their savings, and the lacemaking shop they intended to open.

Pompinne wasn't skeptical. She believed in lace, was aware that it could be even more valuable than the precious stones in the reliquaries of churches, and knew of many castles in the region where noble ladies used needle and thread to repair leaking roofs and rebuild crumbling walls. As far as she was concerned, the sooner they set to work, the better.

She neutralized Father Lecoudre, the Pervenchères parish priest, by badgering him until he hardly knew where he was. "When everybody in your parish has starved to death," she said to him, "you can pray God to help you, but it will be too late. He'll have taken back the chance He's giving you now. If you don't have sense enough to take it this time, there won't be a next time, and all your parishioners will be brokenhearted to find they have such a foolish priest."

When the good man saw how happy his parishioners were at the thought of having work that would save them, he wept for joy and decided to change his opinion of lace, at least temporarily. He announced from the pulpit that the lacemaking shop of Lady Bertrade de Ferrières would soon be opening. Gilonne and Michanteau chose to follow his lead and name the shop after the old lady, not only because it would be on her estate but also in the hope of making her take more interest in it and spend less time hunting wolves.

"When I see her take her musket and gallop away on her horse," said Pompinne, "I'm always afraid I may never see her again."

Zoltan offered to go with her, but she refused to let him. It was a private matter between her and the wolves, she said. She had to be lifted onto her horse, and everyone at Grand-Coeur wondered anxiously what would happen if she had a fall and couldn't get to her feet.

She killed three wolves that winter. Their bodies were found at the places where she said she had left them. All three were enormous. In the evenings after her victories she trembled from head to toe, and only Gilonne, sitting beside her bed and stroking her forehead or her hands, was able to calm her. The old lady would describe her combat in abrupt snatches of narrative; then she would doze off for a moment, awake with a start, and begin talking about the battle again, and it would be dawn before she really gave in to sleep. If, during one of those nights, other wolves were heard howling not far from the house, Gilonne had to call for help to keep the old woman from getting up and going off to hunt again.

And it was during those nights, while Gilonne's cool hands soothed her grandmother's burning forehead, that they both realized the depth of their feelings for each other. "Promise me you'll never leave me," Lady Bertrade said several times, and Gilonne always promised.

When she had slaked her thirst for vengeance by killing one of her enemies, Lady Bertrade became calmer and seemed normal for some time. In the kitchen at mealtimes, before the high flames of the fireplace, she talked with her son while the others at the table kept a respectful silence. One evening when she spoke of the excellence of the Swedish army, the chevalier became a bit irritated.

"You're behind the times!" he said. "The Swedish army is no longer the best in Europe—ours is! We have the biggest, most powerful, and best supplied army, and it's always ready at least a month before any of the others. A hundred and twenty thousand thoroughly disciplined men. You're talking about a time"— his absentminded gaze turned to Gilonne as he finished his sentence—"a time before this young lady of ours was born."

This young lady of *ours*! Gilonne blushed and looked at her father. But he had already lowered his eyes to his buckwheat porridge.

Mathieu came to help set up the shop, and Pompinne recognized him. When her suspicious surprise had passed, she wept over the disaster that had struck him just after he left Grand-Coeur, when the recruiting sergeants had pounced on him like birds of prey on a rabbit. Luckily he had come back and was still as gallant as ever, she said, giving him a friendly shove with her elbow. Lady Bertrade, however, seemed not to remember him at all.

A problem arose. Where would the workshop be located? Having it in the manor house was out of the question. The chevalier demanded silence while he was composing, and the comings and goings of so many people, even if they were perfectly discreet, would irritate him greatly. The barn also had to be ruled out: Sir Reginald's periodic manifestations would upset the lacemakers and drive them away. The stable was available, or at least the part of it that hadn't been used since most of the animals were sold. But Gilonne was opposed to it. She already saw it sheltering the horses they would soon buy with their profits from the sale of lace. She didn't say so, however, instead, she said that the light in the stable wasn't good enough for lace-making. They decided on a dilapidated building formerly used to lodge the stewards of the estate, at the far end of the park. It would need extensive repairs but its distance from the manor house, and the fact that it was directly accessible to people from the village, would justify the expense.

Mathieu went to Alençon and came back with the two girls' little fortune. Building materials were brought in. On Sunday, Father Lecoudre asked for a mason, a carpenter, and a roofer to work on the project. Pompinne had to choose from among ten times more volunteers than were needed. A month later the work was all done.

Gilonne intended to go to Alençon also, to buy thread, needles, boot warmers, candles, and glass light bowls, but when Lady Bertrade heard about it, she began trembling and let big tears run down her cheeks without making any attempt to dry them. So it was decided that Michanteau would be the one to go to Alençon, accompanied by Candelario.

The chevalier hadn't taken the slightest notice of the work

being done at the far end of the park, or the excitement of everyone else at Grand-Coeur. He was completely absorbed in composing a new song dedicated to the glory of the French navy.
When he took the time to look distractedly around him, he probably saw galleys, ships of the line, frigates, fire ships, store ships,
and galliots. During a meal one day he said that the *Royal-Louis*
was a ship with a hundred and eighteen cannons, in the same tone
as if he had been remarking that the last snow had just melted
and the first primroses would soon appear in the meadows.

It seemed that everyone in the village wanted to make lace.
The number of women and children who applied for work in the
shop was much greater than the upper limit Gilonne had set. A
selection would have to be made.

Michanteau and Candelario made their trip to Alençon and
brought back two kegs of excellent thread made in Flanders and
bleached in Holland as well as other supplies, all bought at
bargain prices from Protestants fleeing the country. In taking
advantage of their distress, she told herself, she was also pro-
viding work for the starving populations of Pervenchères.

On the other hand—and later this "on the other hand" was
proudly trumpeted abroad—she was generous to Madame Maillon, Mistress Lescure's Protestant neighbor. Madame Maillon
was a midwife, but the latest royal edict concerning Protestants
had deprived her of the right to practice her profession. Seeing
her despair, Michanteau paid her handsomely for her remedies
against lice, which she and Gilonne would need as soon as their
shop opened. Since Madame Maillon didn't intend to go into
exile, they could let her do some lacemaking for them. She had
decided to go back to needlework to keep herself alive.

After leaving Madame Maillon, Michanteau and Candelario
happened to meet Gérasime in the street. He asked them to give
his best regards to the ladies in the poorhouse, talked about the
war in Holland even though it had long since ended, and told
them he was still boiling all the food that came into his kitchen.

Next they went to the poorhouse and handed out sweets.
Things were going well there. Under the influence of a new
Courapied, who was in turn under the influence of a Jesuit who
strongly advocated physical exercise, Marie had begun taking a
short walk along the Sarthe every day and was benefiting from
it greatly. The others still hadn't recovered from their surprise.
This Courapied, they said, would go far.

On the way back from the poorhouse, Michanteau and Candelario encountered Thiphaine. They both recognized her. Yes, Candelario knew her too. Who didn't know her? Mysterious and evidently in poor health, Thiphaine took them to a secluded spot to show them four beautiful lace patterns she wanted to sell. Michanteau bought them for only ten livres without asking where they came from. She thought she could see traces of seals on them, probably those of the Royal Manufactory, but she couldn't be sure, and there was no use feeling guilty over something that was only a possibility. She had better ways of spending her time.

April came. In Châlons, the dauphin and the Princess of Bavaria had been married. Everyone, including the king, agreed that she was very ugly, and so needles in Alençon workshops were heated by strenuous efforts to turn out flattering clothes for the future Queen of France. But there was little interest in this at Grand-Coeur. The two big pear trees—thought to be about four hundred years old—that flanked the entrance of the new lacemaking shop were in full bloom. Since they were the oldest living things in the park, it seemed a good omen that they had blossomed early to celebrate the opening of the shop.

On the morning of the great day, Lady Bertrade prepared to preside over the inauguration. Father Lecoudre came to bless the shop and the people who would work in it. Everything was ready. The pear tree had even summoned several hundred bees to add buzzing music to the ceremony. The chevalier was spending the week at the Moor's Inn, which made things easier for everyone else. But when Pompinne went to bring Lady Bertrade to her chair in the new workroom, she couldn't find her. When it was discovered that her horse, Picus IV, wasn't in the stable, the only conclusion to be drawn was that they had left together. A wolf had called them. But how had she gotten onto her horse by herself?

She came back that evening, apparently unharmed by her outing, and reported that the body of a young wolf would be found at the foot of the big ash that she called Yggdrasill, after the wondrous tree in Norse legend; then she said she had lost her red hat and wanted someone to look for it. It had probably caught on a branch while she was riding.

The wolf was where she had said it would be, but the red hat couldn't be found. Everyone was relieved to know it had finally disappeared. They all felt it hadn't been good for the head it had covered so long and that things would go better without it.

"What inauguration?" Lady Bertrade asked when she was told that she had chosen a bad time to go hunting.

It now seemed clear that Marie the Traveler should be called in without delay. Pompinne explained to Gilonne that a traveler, in this sense of the word, was a woman whose occupation consisted in substituting herself for sick people and going to invoke the saint who specialized in their illness. In Pervenchères there was a very good traveler named Marie. She was born on a Good Friday, which made her all the more effective. Not every village was lucky enough to have a traveler blessed by God in that way. The only problem would be to determine exactly what Lady Bertrade was suffering from. Pain caused by her rheumatism and the stump of her amputated leg? Yes, that much was sure, and the traveler would have to be sent to Nonvilliers to pray to Saint Gourgon. But was the trouble in her head caused by brain fever, tired nerves, or fear of wolves?

When Marie the Traveler was consulted, she said it would be safer to pray to the three saints specializing in those three ailments. Saint Lié at Montigny, Saint Barbara at Marolles, and Saint Anthony at Combres. She knew those places well. She would make the pilgrimages quickly and compassionately, she said, and bring back a cure.

She came to Grand-Coeur early one morning to get the food to which she was entitled for her pilgrimage. Having been welcomed respectfully, encouraged, and accompanied for a short distance, she promised that when she returned she would give her journey its proper conclusion by saying a final prayer in Lady Bertrade's house. She would have been awaited impatiently if the first day of work in the new shop hadn't turned everyone's mind away from her pilgrimage.

Before dawn the workers climbed the hill to Grand-Coeur in single file, carrying their food baskets. Their way was lighted by three women with torches, one each at the head, middle, and end of the procession. Father Lecoudre had said he would ring the church bell at four o'clock, and they had set off as soon as they heard it. Still tormented by uncertainties, he had asked that the children be given a whole day off each week, besides Sunday, so he could go on teaching them reading, writing, and the catechism. Gilonne had consented to this with relief: It solved the problem of the apprentices' education.

There were fifteen girls and two boys between the ages of five and twelve who had been shepherdesses and shepherds until that morning. About the same number of women, from sixteen to fifty. An old man, still alert and able-bodied, also came. He had made *bisette* long ago and remembered how to do it. He would be employed to make it again, and also to bring in wood and keep the fire going in the big fireplace. It wouldn't matter if he dirtied his *bisette*, because it could be washed without damage.

The villagers were astounded when they saw, under one of the pear trees, two basins of water, soap, white cloths, and the two young mistress-lacemakers standing nearby to make sure they all washed their hands, forearms, and faces before going in to sit down at the big table. When the washing had been done, Pompinne inspected the adults' hair because Gilonne thought that doing it herself might arouse resentment in women two or three times her age. Michanteau examined the younger heads.

In spite of Pompinne's friendly persuasion, no woman whose bonnet sheltered a little colony of lice was willing to have them removed. Lice and nits gave strength and health, they said, and they would rather leave them than give them up. Two women went home anyway, feeling that nothing good could come of working for people who didn't know that lice were the vigor of the body. Three others left during the morning, but in their case it was because they hadn't realized they wouldn't be allowed time off to go home to milk the cows and make porridge for their families.

Losses were even heavier the next day: The church bell set only about twenty people in motion. As far as Gilonne was concerned, this was all to the good because it meant that the selection was being made without any decision on her part.

To some extent, all the workers were dismayed by the sixteen to eighteen hours they had to spend in the shop. They had hoped they would be given work they could do at home, whenever there was nothing else that urgently needed to be done.

On the second evening, as they watched their workers and apprentices light their lanterns and start back toward the village, Gilonne and Michanteau each stood under a pear tree, exhausted and disillusioned. The trees were still in bloom, and still as beautiful as on the day of the inauguration, but their splendor no longer touched the girls' heavy hearts. Would they

ever be able to make anything of their little troupe, so poorly
prepared for sustained, exacting, meticulous work? Yet the
women had to be given reasonable wages, and the children's
poverty-stricken parents couldn't be asked to pay anything for
their apprenticeship. A good part of the money that Gilonne and
Michanteau had received from the Lemareurs had already been
spent; would what was left be enough to cover expenses until
the shop produced salable lace? In spite of their claims, most of
the peasant women had no useful experience. They all knew
how to make *bisette*, *gueuse*, and *mignonette*, kinds of lace that
had very little value, but only three had ever made Alençon lace.
Gilonne and Michanteau would have to start almost from nothing and wait several months before seeing the first results, which
might or might not be encouraging.

And in addition to her other worries, Gilonne felt sorry for
the youngest apprentices. She was especially pained by one of
them, a frightened, bewildered little creature, barely five years
old, whose tiny hands trembled when she tried to learn how to
thread a needle or prick holes in parchment. On the first day she
had seemed to be the best-behaved girl, the one most willing to
sit still and, when it was time to leave, the one least in a hurry
to stand up. Then Gilonne had approached her and seen the little
puddle under her. The child had tried to hide it by not moving.
She didn't cry; she simply bowed her head and wouldn't look
up.

"Her name is Bichon," Pompinne later told Gilonne, "and
her mother is Mathilde, a whore who beats her until she's half
dead. She's not very cheerful, poor little thing. She sleeps in a
stable and she's almost an animal. She'll never be a good worker.
If you take my advice, you won't even try to teach her. You'd be
wasting your time and money."

At supper one evening Gilonne wore a pink drugget dress, a
pleated white batiste apron, and a light headdress made of lace
taken from one of the dresses Lady Bertrade had worn before
she was married. She should have been proud and happy at
having risen to this new social position, but she was full of
doubts and misgivings. Michanteau was always telling her that
she thought too much.

Michanteau, dressed in blue, was elated. "I know it's going
to be hard and we'll have to work like slaves, but we'll do it,

that's all," she said gaily as she helped Pompinne to set the table.

Gilonne envied her attitude. With a sigh, she pulled herself away from her thoughts and began listening to the chevalier. Since he wasn't talking about ships, he must have finished his song in praise of the French navy. He was now talking about the Vikings, another of his favorite subjects. He told how Rollo, King of the Sea, the first Duke of Normandy, had one day, during a walk in the forest, hung his gold bracelets on a tree branch to see how long they would stay there before someone took them. When they had been exposed to the wind, sun, rain, and snow for three years, he took them back. They had remained untouched in all that time because everyone knew that thieves were quickly hanged, along with anyone who had helped them.

Was it only by chance that at this point the chevalier's eyes turned to Michanteau? Gilonne wondered anxiously if her friend had been a little light-fingered at Grand-Coeur. But Michanteau was listening without showing any sign of uneasiness. Her eyes sparkled when she heard the chevalier's conclusion. "And so this pirate captain, a superb thief himself, became famous as a great administrator of justice."

A story with an ending like that was sure to please Michanteau! Gilonne smiled in spite of herself.

When the chevalier had fallen silent, Lady Bertrade asked if they knew that a wolf whose foot was caught in a trap would bite it off to free himself, then wait for his brothers to end his suffering by killing and eating him. She said this with a little half-smile that showed the satisfaction of a victim who had finally been avenged.

What was Marie the Traveler doing all this time? Was she praying enough at the feet of the healing saints? Pompinne and the girls wondered but were afraid to discuss the subject in front of the chevalier because they strongly suspected he wouldn't have approved of the pilgrimage.

Luckily he and his two servants left the next day so they wouldn't be there when Marie came back, as she was expected to do the following night.

When Lady Bertrade said she was tired and went to bed early, the others were glad she wouldn't see Marie the Traveler. They would tell the old woman nothing about what had been done to cure her. Pompinne stayed downstairs a while then, after asking to be awakened whenever Marie arrived, even if it was the middle of the night, she went up to the little room she slept in, next to her mistress's bedroom. It was traditional to feed the pilgrim at the end of her journey, to restore the strength she had lost from traveling such a great distance and saying so many prayers.

Gilonne and Michanteau went on sitting by the fire. They had some parchments to prepare for the next day and they were going to wash their hair, as they did every week because they were afraid of the lice that lived under some of their workers' bonnets. They had gone to the well several times before dark, and the big pot hanging from the hook in the fireplace now contained the hot water they needed.

They had finished washing their hair and were drying it in front of the fire when there was a knock on the door. At last! Now they were going to find out if Marie the Traveler's pilgrimage had gone well and if they could expect the fog to be permanently cleared from Lady Bertrade's mind.

It was Michanteau who opened the door. Though she had hardly ever been afraid of anything, she screamed in terror. Gilonne would have screamed too, if she hadn't put her hand over her mouth.

There were two men standing in front of them, one as terrifying as the other. The nearest one, who partly hid the one behind him, was immense. He had black eyes below his black fur hat. His clothes were also black. So was the fur with which they were trimmed, and hanging from his neck by a silk cord was a muff made of the same fur. Black, too, were the high boots that sheathed his legs, which he had spread slightly to plant himself there with cool self-assurance. The diamond buttons on his vest glittered like his eyes. Gilonne and Michanteau felt themselves irresistibly drawn to those eyes. . . . And the man dressed all in black, looking as if he might have come straight from hell, said to them, "Do you always open the door so quickly to strangers, ladies? It's very risky!"

There was warmth in his voice, and gaiety.

"Do you knock on doors without hoping to have them opened?" Gilonne asked, feeling as if she were in a dream.

"I was expecting a long discussion. I had my arguments all ready."

"You can still give them to us."

But she was scarcely listening. She had just been plunged into a whirlwind of fear by the other man, who had come fully into view when the first one took a step forward. He had a nightmarish face, with eyes that glowed like burning embers and didn't look directly at her, but seemed to be fixed on something above her head. And those slashed ears, that bead hanging from his nose, that tuft of coal-black hair on top of his skull! He wore a leather tunic with short sleeves that revealed a pair of muscular arms. How many knives hung from his belt? How many necklaces were around his neck? Gilonne closed her eyes, then opened them again. It was all true: he was still there!

"Haven't you ever seen a Huron before?" asked the man in black.

Somehow she gathered the strength to answer. "Of course I have. I see them every day, since they're as common here as dandelions in the fields."

"You're as witty as you are beautiful! Grand-Coeur must have been visited by a magician while I was away: I'd be willing to bet that you suddenly came into being when a magic wand touched a soft, fragrant, creamy-white apple blossom."

While he was away? Who was this dark intruder, with his bizarre companion?

"I'm sorry if my Indian has frightened you," he went on. "Allow me to introduce him to you. There's something reassuring about the rituals of common courtesy. You won't see his knives and his tomahawk so much when you know who he is. His name is Poisson d'Or in French. You can also call him Fulbert, his baptismal name, because he's a Christian. His patron saint is the Fulbert who was Bishop of Chartres in the eleventh century. Maybe it would interest you to know what he's doing here; he seems to interest most people. He saved my life when I was about to be killed by an Iroquois. The Iroquois are also Indians, but enemies of the Hurons and the French. Although Fulbert's pride wouldn't allow him to accept a reward, it had no objection to his keeping me company when I returned to France, and so I was able to give him what he wanted: a chance to go to the Cathedral of Chartres and see if the offering made to the Virgin by his mother, a Huron princess, was in a good place. The offering consisted of a belt decorated with beads. Fulbert was happy to see it prominently displayed and greatly admired by visitors. He'll enjoy talking about it with Father Bouvart, our missionary, when he goes back. While we were at Chartres I showed him the statue of his patron saint. He put his hand on Bishop Fulbert's nose, then touched his own and seemed pleased by their resemblance. Details of that kind can be important in converting heathens to Christianity. I must remember to tell Father Bouvart that Saint Fulbert had a Huron nose.''

By then Michanteau had recovered her voice and her presence of mind enough to ask, ''Why didn't we hear your horses coming toward the house?''

''That's a good question, mademoiselle. Fulbert and I are much more cautious than you are. I left here fifteen years ago, so I didn't know who was living at Grand-Coeur. I hoped it was still owned by the same family, but since I wasn't sure, we left our horses in a safe place not far away.''

He had been pacing the kitchen floor as he spoke. He took his hands out of his fur muff and held them in front of the fire, then he looked at the copper pots and pans hanging on the wall. The firelight revealed the Ferrières coat of arms engraved in them. He sniffed the good smell of the room.

''Was the buckwheat porridge as good as usual tonight?'' he asked. ''Were you lucky enough to get spiced apple preserves to go with it?''

Who *was* he?

He laughed, stepped over to the big table, and continued, ''This is where I used to sit, between the lanky, melancholy Zoltan and the plump, lusty Candelario. . . . Does Pompinne still hate them as much as she used to hate the three of us?''

He picked up one of the pieces of parchment that had been left on the table. He had long, shapely hands, with a diamond ring on one and a ruby ring on the other. He looked at the lace that had been begun on the parchment and said, ''He was a genius, the man who had the idea of dividing up the work of making Alençon lace and having different lacemakers, and even whole villages, specialize in different parts of it.''

''It wasn't a man,'' said Gilonne, ''it was a woman.''

''A woman? How do you know?''

He asked these questions brusquely, almost violently.

''I worked with her.''

''Where is she? Can I go and see her?''

''She died more than two years ago. Her name was Madame La Perrière.''

''I've used her idea of raising quality and increasing output by having workers specialize in a single operation. I've applied it to making things other than lace.''

''Not long before she died, she said she was sure that sooner or later the same principle would be applied to other kinds of work.''

"Tell me about it. What else did she say?''

He was attentive. It seemed that all at once nothing mattered in that kitchen except the late Madame La Perrière and her brilliant ideas.

"That's all, just that the idea would spread,'' Gilonne said. "She would have been happy to hear you.''

Why was she talking to this stranger so openly? His appearance was still as disquieting as ever, and his companion . . . .

His companion, Fulbert the Huron, stood stiffly with his arms folded, staring into space, not moving from the spot where he seemed to have rooted beside the big chest he had brought.

"He's waiting,'' said the man in black. "The Indians regard patience as a primary virtue. Besides, he's full of curiosity and he's enjoying himself more than he seems to be. When he's back home he'll say that you have moon-colored hair and eyes that are both green and blue, like the lakes of his country on certain sunny days. He's wondering, or has wondered, or will wonder, if he should give you his red necklace, the one that wards off bad dreams, because he senses fear and anxiety in you, and thinks you may be troubled by nightmares when you sleep tonight. If he offers it to you, you must accept it as naturally as he gives it. Don't worry; he has another one. He wouldn't have gone on such a long journey without extra amulets, and—''

He hadn't heard Lady Bertrade come down from her room. She was now standing at the foot of the stone staircase, with one hand holding her crutch and the other on Pompinne's shoulder. His face suddenly became serious and showed deep emotion. He stepped toward her. When he was in front of her, he took off his hat, put one knee on the floor, and kissed the hem of her dress.

"Ogier,'' she said softly. Her voice was a caress. She let go of Pompinne's shoulder and put her hand on his thick, black, curly hair. "Ogier . . .''

"Count Ogier de Beaumesnil, your vassal, Noble Lady.''

Pompinne was as stiff and motionless as the Huron. But she wasn't staring into space: She was looking incredulously at Ogier de Beaumesnil, who in his childhood and adolescence had been a falconer at Grand-Coeur.

It was just at this dramatic moment that Marie the Traveler arrived. Hearing her knock, Pompinne started, hurried to the door, and opened it. Marie came in, looking small and frail in her big, dark cloak, with her basket in one hand and her torch in the other.

She had never before experienced such a startling end to one of her pilgrimages. (She was later to describe it again and again, for the rest of her life, and it became a family legend.) Her thin face seemed to become still thinner, and her mouth opened slightly. She turned her clear, childlike eyes to everyone in turn. She was beyond surprise, beyond fear. Without really knowing what she was doing, she sat down on the low chair that Pompinne pushed in front of the fire for her.

A little later, Lady Bertrade looked at her and asked, with hardly a trace of surprise in her voice, "Who's that?" But no one answered. Marie the Traveler had been forgotten. And Lady Bertrade had been cured. To be convinced of it, one had only to see her there, looking ten years younger, with her white hair ruffled by the joyous wind of her enormous laughter.

The only doctor who had been able to drive away the fog in her mind was there before her, dressed in black velvet and fur. His dark sable muff was now keeping her hands warm, and her foot was hidden by the furs that had been taken from the chest and laid on the floor: fox, beaver, ermine, otter, marten. Some had already been made into coats, capes collars, hats, and muffs; the others were waiting for Lady Bertrade to decide what they wanted to become. A big beaver hat, decorated with pure white ostrich feathers, crowned the whole display.

Pompinne was wearing a muskrat cape with a hood beneath which her long, inquisitive nose seemed to be warily trying to sniff out the truth of what had happened. Had she really heard "Count de Beaumesnil" or only imagined it? If it was true, then the king had ennobled that . . . that . . . No, now that he was a nobleman, she didn't dare to call him what she had in the old days. She would have given anything to hear what he and Lady Bertrade were saying to each other, with their heads close together, so she vented her exasperation on Gilonne and Michanteau, reproaching them for standing there like lumps instead of going to get cider. With a sigh, she took her spiced apple preserves from the hiding place she believed to be a well-kept secret, though actually it was known to everyone, even the little farmhand.

When Ogier heard Pompinne tell Gilonne and Michanteau to

bring cider, he asked instead for a glass of milk, which was, he said, what he usually drank at this time of night.

"Is the milk still kept in a jug in the cellar? I'll go and get it. I haven't forgotten the way—I used to go there often."

"No, stay here," said Pompinne. "I know how things are supposed to be done. I'll go myself . . . sir."

This last word seemed to have difficulty getting out of her mouth, but it was still audible.

For the time being, Marie the Traveler had had her fill of observing the nobility. She turned to the Indian. Three times she looked him over from head to foot; then, silently sliding her chair in quick little advances with pauses in between, she moved closer to him. She was about to reach out her hand toward the strange knife that hung from his belt in a sheath of beaded leather when Count de Beaumesnil stepped rapidly in front of her. *That man sees everything!* thought Gilonne.

"That knife, my good woman, is used for cutting off the scalps of people the Indians consider to be too curious."

Not at all frightened, armored with the prayers she had said for others and all her disinterested pilgrimages, flanked by her protecting and healing saints, certain of her perfect invulnerability, the little old lady said in a voice as faded as the blue of her eyes. "Imagine that, sir! Just imagine!"

And she heaved a big sigh. She had to accommodate herself to the strangeness of the world.

Feeling joy bubbling up inside her, Gilonne burst into fresh, clear, delightful laughter that went on and on, flowing like a stream of pearls. Ogier was dazzled. His eyes caught fire from the sparks in hers and he laughed too. And Michanteau, and Lady Bertrade, and even Pompinne.

Only the Huron remained implacable. And Marie the Traveler went on looking.

Later, sitting beside Lady Bertrade with his glass of milk in his hand, Ogier discreetly gestured toward Gilonne and asked in a low voice "Who is she?"

"She's my granddaughter. And the other girl is the nice little thieving magpie who follows her everywhere."

Gilonne and Michanteau had come back after going away for a time to braid their hair. They were making lace by the light of the fire and the candles that had been placed all over the big kitchen and could hear fragments of the conversation between

Lady Bertrade and Ogier. Gilonne felt him looking at her, and it made her work awkwardly.

He was talking about the French colony on the Saint Lawrence where he had lived for several years. The Hurons were good allies; the Iroquois were ferocious enemies. The American Indians had already been contaminated by the vices of Europe.

Exasperated at not being able to hear anything, Pompinne went over to sit beside Lady Bertrade. She had turned back her hood, but she was still wearing her fur cape.

Lady Bertrade stroked the sable muff on her lap.

"Do you remember, Noble Lady," said Ogier, "that when I left Grand-Coeur I thought I knew everything about sables? The fact is that I knew nothing about them. There weren't any in New France; I had to go to Russia to find some."

When Lady Bertrade asked him if there were wolves in Canada, Gilonne, Michanteau, and Pompinne looked at her with some anxiety. But she was calm and her hands weren't trembling. After listening with interest to what Ogier had to say about the wolves of Canada, she said she was sorry she couldn't go so far away to hunt them. Then she laughed and added that she was getting too old to hunt wolves, even here, and that she would soon have to give it up anyway. Probably to take her mind off herself, Ogier told her about the way his Huron hunted. She would be amazed to see him, he said, standing still for hours in the piercing wind of a Canadian winter, transformed into a block of ice, waiting for his prey without letting a single muscle of his body make the slightest movement.

At this point he heard Marie the Traveler's little voice exclaim, "Imagine that! Just imagine!"

After thinking it over, the Huron had evidently decided that Gilonne had regained her calm and no longer needed a necklace of red beads to ward off bad dreams. And so, having put down his empty bowl after drinking the milk she had brought him, he took off the blue necklace that hung down over his chest and put it around her neck, deftly, without even touching her lace headdress.

Although Ogier seemed totally absorbed in his conversation with Lady Bertrade, he really did see and hear everything. "That necklace is a symbol of peace and hope," he told Gilonne. "In return for it, wish him clear skies and gentle waters for his voyage home, and plenty of deer, beavers, and hope when he gets there. Those same wishes will be helpful to me too, because we're both leaving for Dieppe at dawn, and from there we'll go to Quebec.''

Was the dream going to end so quickly, as suddenly as it had begun? It was strange, thought Gilonne, but at first, when she had seen him as a formidable intruder, she had felt more at ease with him than she did now.

"If the fur trading I've undertaken can be finished as soon as I want," he said, "and if God and the Great Spirit are kind to me, I'll be back sometime between the 'Moon of Arriving Eagles' and the 'Moon of Flowers,' as my Indian friends say. In other words, between February and May of next year.''

Gilonne calculated that eight months to a year would go by before he returned.

He was so tall that she had to tilt her head back at a sharp angle to look up at him. He discovered that her marvelous face combined purity and passion, and with a pang in his heart he told himself that whenever she chose to make use of it, the fascinating splendor of her eyes would put the world at her feet.

Suddenly realizing that he seemed to intimidate her, he laughed and asked her if the old parish priest still wore one sock.

She answered that he did, but on the other foot now, because it had become sore and the first one was healed. her bright smile, in which amusement was mingled with affection for Father Lecoudre, plunged Ogier into a rapture he might have taken for intoxication if he hadn't been sure he had drunk only milk.

When he and Fulbert were mounting their horses, he took one last look at the windows of Grand-Coeur. Then the Huron spoke his first words of the evening: "She is the flower whose seed was sown for you by the Wind Spirit.''

Ogier felt no need to ask him to explain. Saying nothing in reply, he spurred his horse and headed for the roads to Dieppe.

The Indians said virgins were mysterious flowers that hid in solitary places. But none of the spirits on the banks of the Saint Lawrence had told Ogier that at Grand-Coeur, in the land of his ancestors, he would find the most beautiful young woman he had ever seen.

As soon as the door had closed behind the intruders, Pompinne again took possession of her kitchen and asserted her authority. It was time to reestablish order. A wind of madness had been blowing at Grand-Coeur, strong enough to warp everyone's understanding. She quickly took off the fur cape that now seemed to be burning her back, put it away, and came back to face the others in the kitchen. Marie the Traveler was her first concern.

"Poor Marie!" she said. "You must be hungry enough to eat your shoes!"

The pilgrim acknowledged that she was indeed a bit hungry. She was given bread, cheese, fruit, and cider.

"I wish I had a better meal to give you," Pompinne said with a sigh, "but God has put us to the test. He can't give us everything. Through His saints and in answer to your prayers, He's cured Lady Bertrade. There's no use constantly asking to have your basket overflowing; it's never worked for anyone. It's God's will that tonight we've had the great happiness you've brought us, and also a great to-do with Indians and . . ."

No one could understand the end of her sentence.

"Who knows what else we'll see!" said Marie the Traveler, breaking her bread. She showed no sign of fatigue and seemed to be prepared—comfortably installed at the table—for the second act of the lively play being performed at Grand-Coeur that night. Seeing Pompinne turn to Lady Bertrade, she shifted her chair a little, to have a good view of whatever was about to happen next.

"What are we supposed to do with all these animal skins?" said Pompinne. "They'll at least be a treat for the moths! I think the best thing would be to put them in a chest and forget about them. We don't have to start dressing up as if we were at a royal court just because an outsider and his savage dropped all that fur on my kitchen floor! You seem to be your old self again, Noble Lady. If you take my advice, you'll go and get some sleep now. Tomorrow, when the sun is up, we'll see about getting some nice lacemaking work for you, to give you something pleasant to do."

Lady Bertrade's roar was perhaps heard by Fulbert the keen-eared Huron on the road to Dieppe. She then announced that she heard wolves in the forest and wanted to go off and hunt them immediately.

Pompinne turned to Marie the Traveler and gave her a suspicious look.

The pilgrim put down the pitcher of cider from which she had just poured her third glassful and motioned Pompinne to come closer. She then explained in an undertone that not everything had happened according to the rules. She had left just as she was supposed to: early in the morning, on foot, without having eaten. She had prayed at the start of her journey, and along the way, and in front of the statues of all the appropriate saints. But because those visitors had come at just the wrong time, she hadn't been able to end her journey properly by saying a prayer as soon as she came into Lady Bertrade's house. Her failure to do that must have undone what her pilgrimage had accomplished.

Not only had they had to listen to one visitor's senseless stories and put up with the other's evil looks, Pompinne said in her best "I told you so" tone, but now the whole pilgrimage had to be done over! Armed with that irrefutable argument, she prepared to destroy the prestige of Count Ogier de Beaumesnil in the two girls' eyes. She had known him when he was nothing but a ragged little boy without a sou to his name! He couldn't put anything over on *her*! She knew what he was made of.

But the girls were no longer there. They had taken Lady Bertrade to her room and were putting her to bed. When she had spoken to them, they thought they saw a look of complicity in her eyes. They wanted her to confirm and explain it.

"I'm sure, madame," Michanteau attacked, "that you hate making lace."

Lady Bertrade's loud laughter shook the bed and rose to the beams overhead, where the decorated motto of the Ferrières could still be read despite the ravages of dampness and cracks in the wood. The garlands of faded flowers that framed the words "The heart can do anything" were tickled by the old lady's mirth.

"I should have known that thieving magpies also steal secrets! And what about you, Gilonne? Did you suspect my secret too?"

"Well, I sometimes had a few little doubts," replied Gilonne, laughing.

"I'm glad you've finally found me out, because I was getting tired of my daily wolf hunts, even though they were quite innocent. But don't you dare, either one of you, say a word about this to Pompinne! It's not her fault, poor woman, but she's always trying to get me to do needlework, and I'm just not made for it. Lace—that's a word that terrifies me. There's always been conflict between me and a threaded needle. Ever since our ruin, Pompinne has seen our salvation only in lacemaking, and I've had to find mine in eccentricity. Yes, I know that some of my neighbors have saved their estates with their lacemaking, but I have no talent for that sort of thing. You can't count on me to turn needlepoint into roof tiles or building stones. God knows I regret it, but He also knows that He put a musket in my cradle, not a packet of needles.

"I'll go on hunting my wolves, but in moderation, just enough to make Pompinne leave me in peace. Ah, I'm glad you two know I'm not demented. See to it that Pompinne doesn't have Marie the Traveler make her pilgrimage again. I wouldn't want such obliging saints to be annoyed because of my trickery. You never know what an annoyed saint might do! And it seems silly to have inept people, like that fool Marie, act as intermediaries between the saints and us. And now, tell me what you think of my handsome Ogier de Beaumesnil."

Michanteau said that at first sight, dressed in black like that, he seemed to be the devil, and that if he were, every woman on earth would want to go to hell. Gilonne said she would like to know more about him.

Lady Bertrade leaned back against her pillows, demanded a spot of apple brandy, and began talking about Ogier. He had become what he promised to be when, after his father's death, he had joined his uncle and cousins in New France. The uncle and cousins had soon died, killed by the Iroquois, and they had left him a good legacy, which he seemed to have multiplied many times over in the past fifteen years. He had always had a taste for flawless work and well-calculated profits. He was one of the first of a new breed of men: the merchant lords. The idea of joining these two words was enough to make the French nobility howl in protest, but sooner or later it would have to be accepted, since the king himself was already bringing the words together by ennobling men engaged in commerce. That evening, Ogier had reminded Lady Bertrade of an eagle watching for its prey. She gathered that he had come to buy up lacemaking shops owned by Protestants who were fleeing the country. Did Gilonne and Michanteau know what was going on in Alençon? It was said that each day brought a new edict diminishing the Protestants' right to work. In that case, concluded Lady Bertrade, Ogier would soon be king of the town. He was said to be already on excellent terms with the Duchess of Alençon. The day before, he had dined at her palace.

"With his Indian?" asked Gilonne.

"Of course. The duchess, a very pious woman, was delighted

to learn that he's a Catholic Indian. She immediately wrote to the king to tell him how glad she was to see an example of what our missionaries have done in New France, and also to ask him to grant a favor to Count de Beaumesnil: an escort, or something like that, for the ship he's preparing to use.''

''He told you all that?''

''Not explicitly, but I was able to read his thoughts. When he told me three words, I heard ten.''

''Why did he bring you that big, beautiful hat?''

''Because *he* never liked my red wool hat either.''

How good it was to laugh with the real Lady Bertrade, and prolong the dream of that evening!

Gilonne wondered if there were dreams from which one never awakened.

She was sitting at the big table in the lacemaking shop, and after assigning work to the others she was now doing her own: an ornamental collar for a man's coat. But she was working with Ogier de Beaumesnil.

She had found all the books in the chevalier's library that dealt with America, and had begun reading them by candlelight, as Ogier had done. The same books, the ones he had read and put away so often.

And when she drank milk in the morning, she thought of what Lady Bertrade had told her. As a child, Ogier had seldom been allowed to have milk. Gilonne recalled his hand, adorned with a ring bearing a precious stone, lifting a bowl of milk to his lips on the evening of his arrival at Grand-Coeur, and she thanked God for the fitting compensations He sometimes gave.

She was keenly aware of living intensely since the coming of Ogier and the Huron. It seemed to her that for a long time, while she was working at making lace, a prisoner in body and mind, she must also have been sewing her heart and soul into a tightly closed little bag that had kept them new and untarnished for a handsome man in black. She now took such joy in being alive, in roaming through the forest and fields, in loving Lady Bertrade, Michanteau, Pompinne, and the workers in the shop, in knowing she was young, beautiful, and open to life, that she wanted to share her happiness with everyone, with all those not lucky enough to be living in the midst of enchantment, in a dream that was real life.

Bichon—who, like Lady Bertrade, seemed to be at war with

needles and thread—was the first to receive her share of happiness. With generous portions of good hot buckwheat porridge and plenty of affection, her dark-haired little head, always bowed before, gradually began to turn upward. Her frightened and mistrustful brown eyes finally brightened one day.

Gilonne discovered that the child had a passionate interest in the design of lace. She found her one evening, when the others had left, looking at patterns spread out on the table and retracing with her little finger the winding ribbons decorated with flowers and intertwined with leaves and branches. Taken by surprise in her contemplation, she looked up at Gilonne with dazzled eyes and asked how all that was done.

Gilonne was so touched that she immediately decided to have Bichon taught lace designing if she showed any talent for it. There was no lack of unemployed Protestant painters in Alençon, because Protestant lacemaking shops were still closing down. Since the Catholic shops were unable or unwilling to employ them, it would be easy to find one who, in exchange for a place to sleep, a daily ration of porridge, and a few sous now and then, would agree to make lace patterns and teach Bichon. She knew she could count on Michanteau and Candelario to turn up an artist for her.

The one they brought looked like a beggar, wearing a frayed dark cape, a felt hat that could have been used as a sieve, and an ancient pair of short boots with so many holes that all his toes showed through. But he had a likable face that reminded Gilonne a little of Gérasime's, probably because they both had a goatee and a turned-up mustache from the time of King Louis XIII.

Michanteau, Zoltan, and Candelario had found him in front of the poorhouse—to which he was being refused admittance because there was no more room—when they came to bring news of Gilonne to the old women, along with a good-sized piece of spiced apple preserves that might not really have been a gift from Pompinne. The old man was explaining to the gatekeeper that in exchange for a little space where he could sleep, even without a mattress, and a piece of bread dipped into the common soup pot, he would cover the walls of the poorhouse with paintings on any theme—ancient, religious, or modern— that the director of the establishment might choose. But the gatekeeper wasn't listening to him. Michanteau and Candelario did listen to him, and offered him buckwheat porridge and a straw mattress, but in the country.

He accepted their offer with lofty dignity. His eyes shone when he learned that Grand-Coeur had many bare walls. Speaking as if he were engaging them, rather than being engaged by them, he said that he wanted no money, only a supply of paint. He gave the address of a shop whose Protestant owner was selling everything before going to Antwerp. They went there and, for the price of a few loaves of bread, Candelario bought the pigments, oils, and brushes that the artist pointed out to him with imperious gestures. Worried in spite of her natural optimism, Michanteau wondered if Peter Theophilius Fritsch—that was the artist's name—would be easy to get along with. Candelario reassured her by saying that Pompinne had an effective training method for anyone who showed recalcitrance, and that there was no case of rebellion, however determined, that she couldn't overcome.

Zoltan was inwardly amused at the thought of how that mismatched pair of rogues, the little lacemaker and the fat Venetian, would react when the Protestant exodus had ended and they again had to pay a fair price for what they bought. He took Peter Fritsch behind him on his horse. The artist was as taciturn as the musician. Their common mount heard only their brief exchange of names during the eight-league journey to Pervenchères.

Peter was more loquacious at dinner. Having been introduced to Lady Bertrade, he spoke Italian with her, explaining that he had lived in Rome when Nicolas Poussin was also living there, and had been his pupil. He mentioned his prestigious teacher with unaffected dignity. Candelario had asked him to avoid, if possible, revealing that he was a Protestant, so as not to add tension to the atmosphere of Grand-Coeur. Totally absorbed in his art, he seemed to care so little about his religion that Gilonne wondered why he hadn't renounced it to make life simpler for himself. Michanteau suggested that he probably hadn't thought of it, which was lucky for all of them: If he had gone to knock on the door of the Community of New Catholics, they would have taken him, and kept him. The Duchess of Alençon had just opened that establishment for receiving recent converts, or Protestants who wanted to renounce their religion, and obtain spiritual and material assistance.

Gilonne introduced Bichon to Peter Fritsch and left them

together in the cold, bare common room, furnished only with Lady Bertrade's antique armchair and a long table at which fifty people could be seated. That evening she found them still there. He was sitting in front of a superb design for a lace pattern that he was about to finish, and Bichon was frenziedly crushing pigment in a mortar. She was now working on blue, and there were streaks of it on her happy face.

She and Peter had become the best friends in the world and didn't want to leave each other. When she cried at the thought of going back to the village to sleep, Gilonne decided to let her stay; there were plenty of odd corners in the house where a straw mattress could be put down. Peter had been quartered in Sir Reginald's barn, with fair warning of what to expect. He had agreed without batting an eye to be the Englishman's guest. Bichon was given the little storeroom under the kitchen stairs.

Pompinne accepted the two new mouths to feed, but grumbled that they would reduce the amount everyone else got to eat. The frugal fare of Grand-Coeur nevertheless, remained adequate for everyone. Milk, bread, buckwheat porridge, a few vegetables and apples, with meat only on Sunday—no one asked for more. And when Mama Bordier had Mathieu bring two big turkeys, Pompinne complained that they made things too complicated for her. Candelario even offered to turn the spit, but she didn't like to have him in her kitchen, so she sent him back to his flutes and viols.

Hidden behind a grim outer shell, the real Pompinne loved her master's songs and the life and bustling activity at Grand-Coeur. In the time of Chevalier Héribert, the house had always been full of traveling friends stopping over: old battle companions he had invited to come and hunt, and fair ladies staying briefly to breathe the pure air of the hilltop manor before going on to take the waters at Bagnoles-de-l'Orne. And Lady Bertrade used to say that if her husband hadn't at least met the parish priest on his way home, he would avoid dining alone with her by inviting his favorite horse. In those days, meals were served in the great common room, which still had all its tapestries and silver and pewter dishes. The kitchen was as full of people as the capons roasted in it were full of truffles, and Pompinne wasn't then the maid of all work that she was now. Ah, where were those good old days?

Unexpectedly, on the evening of the feast of the Bordier turkeys, the chevalier returned to his estate and Lady Bertrade introduced him to Peter Fritsch. He greeted the painter with his usual lack of attention, but courteously, and told Pompinne to honor his guest by serving wine. Pompinne listened to this order without comment, then forgot it as easily as the chevalier and his mother forgot that there was no wine in the cellar, and serenely put her pitchers of apple and pear cider on the table.

Conversation gradually developed between the two men. The chevalier suddenly became loquacious, the painter became eloquent, and the others, listening in silence, were amazed to see that the master of Grand-Coeur at last had his mind completely on what he was saying. Peter, being a faithful disciple of Nicolas Poussin and a great admirer of Jean Racine, compared the works of the two classic artists. There was then an exchange of ideas so brilliant on both sides that it sparkled and blazed as brightly as the fire that illuminated the room. The two talkers and their listeners would have liked to stay there indefinitely, in that big, fragrant kitchen, pampering their stomachs with roast turkey and their minds with art. For each in his own way, it was a time of delight. Candelario saw his old Orchard of Friendship blossoming in a spurt of growth that filled him with happiness. Zoltan was grave and contemplative. Gilonne felt she was catching a glimpse of what it could mean to live in such a family. It suddenly seemed to her that everything was beautiful, possible, accessible. When her eyes happened to meet the chevalier's, so similar to hers in shape and color, it seemed to her that for the first time she saw a glow of affection in them.

As the conversation turned to Rome, the two men began speaking Italian. Lady Bertrade joined in with pleasure because she liked to remember that she had once learned the language. Candelario saw the trees of his Orchard of Friendship growing and multiplying in the sunlight that warmed his heart. Gilonne felt that she had receded into the background. When the chevalier stood up from the table he said, without looking at her but with his head turned in her general direction, that it might be beneficial to spend less time making useless baubles and learn foreign languages instead. Nettled at being regarded as frivolous, but not wanting to admit that she *had* to make those "useless baubles," she said nothing and decided she would ask Candelario, Peter, and Lady Bertrade to teach her Italian, and German. . . . And why not English, which Ogier de Beaumesnil spoke?

Peter didn't eat much turkey or drink much cider. He was a

temperate man. But that supper was delectable to him. Between the goat's-milk cheese and the apple preserves, the chevalier gave him permission, and even asked him with great courtesy, to paint pictures on any wall of Grand-Coeur that might appeal to him. What subjects? Those that spoke to his heart, of course; one must never try to influence an artist. The chevalier laughed, and his laughter seemed less harsh than usual.

While she waited to learn how to design lace, Bichon went on developing her skills in crushing pigments, sharpening charcoal pencils, clarifying oils, and cleaning brushes. It had been discovered that she was eight years old, and not five, as her smallness and fragility had seemed to indicate. Her wholesome diet at Grand-Coeur had already made her look healthier, and she was so fascinated by her occupation, and worked at it so intently, that her cheeks were sometimes as red as apples.

Her mother, a loud, disheveled woman, came one day to demand the money owed to her for her daughter's work. Irritated by this intrusion, which interrupted his painting, Peter curtly asked Michanteau to pay the creature and see to it that he and Bichon were left in peace. Michanteau led the enraged woman away and told her bluntly that she could take her daughter back if she wanted to, but that she wouldn't have a single sou. Bichon was being fed, lodged, and taught a trade, which was a great deal for what she did, and nothing more would be given. The woman left, swearing and gesticulating, just as the chevalier was arriving. She railed against him as he passed, but he showed no sign of hearing her and may not even have seen her.

The painter and his helper were forgotten for more than a month. They were seen at meals, but the others were so overwhelmed with work that they paid little attention to anything else.

One Sunday afternoon when she was allowing herself to rest for a time, Gilonne went into the great common room and stared in amazement. The back wall, the one that had once been covered with tapestries, had come to life again. On it she saw the chevalier, Zoltan, and Candelario at the Battle of Saint Gotthard, smiting the Turks. The painted figures were so magnificent in their warlike passion that she was entranced. Proud of having crushed the pigments of which those men and horses were made, Bichon pointed out the details that filled her with wonder and said, "My new master is just like God, isn't he?"

Before long they were all wondering how they had been able to get along without Peter. He was everyone's diversion. Not only did the chevalier, when he was there, enjoy conversing with him at supper but Zoltan and Candelario liked talking with him about their respective countries, with which he was acquainted. It seemed that the old traveler had been everywhere, taking his paints and his poverty with him. When asked if he had ever found a lucrative position for himself, he answered, "Oh, no— there are so many painters walking on country roads and city streets!" And he added that his illustrious teacher, Nicolas Poussin, had worn out his boots and his health before he finally achieved celebrity, genius though he was. He was never sad, he said; he was able to paint, and that kept him contented.

Whenever she could, Gilonne liked to sit down in front of a window in the common room and talk with him while she worked. He would sometimes stop painting and look at her in silence. One day he told her he would like to paint her portrait as he saw her at that moment, with her serious face leaning over two diligent hands that were like pink and white birds. She looked up at him with a smile, and he said he had changed his mind: He would show her looking up at a big lace flounce that two cherubs were unrolling in front of her. Elsewhere in the picture there would be trophies of war, symbols of the French monarchy, American Indians, and handsome fur merchants surrounded by eagles and beavers, and the Indian blue bead necklace that represented hope.

She had mentioned America to him, hoping he had been there. He hadn't. She had then told him what she knew about it: the Huron she had seen, the books she had read, the handsome count dressed in black velvet. She and Peter now spoke Italian together. She liked the language and dreamed of the day when she would dare to speak it a little in front of the chevalier. She was also studying Latin. To do that, she had to take an hour away from her sleep every day. The old painter slept little and had offered to give her lessons from three to four o'clock in the morning, before the workers arrived. Michanteau, who always heard her get up, said she must be out of her mind to give up an hour in a warm bed for something as dull as a Latin lesson. Gilonne said, "Sh! Go back to sleep," and hurried off to her declensions with a happy heart. When she was studying before dawn, or reading in the library on Sunday, it seemed to her that she was shortening the long way from Pervenchères to Canada.

But in the evening, lulled by listening to Candelario read aloud, or sometimes to a Hungarian folktale told by Zoltan, or a ghost story told by Pompinne, she quickly fell asleep. In addition to the time she spent studying or reading, she worked at her lacemaking sixteen or seventeen hours a day.

As for Pompinne, she put into practice Mama Bordier's rule: "A minute saved here and another one put to good use there, and before the year is over you'll have a yard of lace." Finding that she was better at making bobbin lace than needlepoint, she had taken it up again, using a pretty pattern Peter had drawn for her. She was still sorry she couldn't make Lady Bertrade work, but she no longer pursued her with needle and thread, urging her to "at least try it awhile." Though she couldn't help thinking that an extra pair of hands would have been very useful to her, she kept the thought to herself and merely sighed.

Bichon was growing taller and beginning to draw. Zoltan, who liked to work with wood, had made her a smooth board on which she could sketch with pieces of charcoal. For the time being it was impossible to supply her with paper and pencils because they were very costly and had to be bought in Alençon. But Gilonne had promised to see about getting some for her if the *leveuse* paid a good price for the lace that would soon be for sale. Meanwhile, Bichon had to pick a flower or a leaf each morning and unremittingly try to reproduce it until her teacher said, "That's enough for today. Now you can relax by crushing some carmine for me."

One day he made her spend seven hours drawing the same stone again and again. That evening, when Lady Bertrade, who liked the child, asked what she had done between sunup and sundown, Peter answered for her, saying that she had handled enough stones to pave the road from Grand-Coeur to Perven- chères. Pompinne, who hadn't been following the conversation very closely, grumbled, "If that crazy old fool keeps treating the poor child like that, he'll kill her!"

But she was never really angry with him. She was greatly impressed by the life-sized mural he had painted. "You can't call *him* lazy!" she said. "When he works, he works! Considering what he's paid, he might have made a tiny little picture of the chevalier, but no, he made a big one, so big he had to stand on a ladder to paint his head and the sky above it, and at his age it makes you nervous to see him do things like that! No, really, he's not lazy!"

Her only complaint against him was that he had painted Candelario and Zoltan into the battle—though she admitted that a nobleman had to have an escort.

It was hot that summer in Pervenchères. But it was always cool in the big room where Peter worked. Now that he was covering its walls with paintings, Pompinne had put straw in one corner so he could sleep there without having to go out in the chilly night air to get to the barn. She had mended his cape, which, she said, was as thin as a dragonfly's wings, since it must be the same age as its owner. What *was* his age? Maybe he himself didn't know. He joked about it with the chevalier one evening at supper, saying that unfortunately the only thing he had in common with Titian was having lived to be very old, and that perhaps he too would have to be saved from becoming totally decrepit by dying of the plague not long before his hundredth birthday.

Candelario claimed that this was only affectation and that the old man was still sprightly, as could be seen from the brisk way he walked when he took Bichon on one of their periodic outings to "teach her to look at nature." He added that the painter's perfect sobriety, worthy of the famous Venetian hygienist Cornaro—who had eaten nothing but half an egg a day and thus lived the long, serene life that was the deserved reward of the abstinent—was one reason for his vigorous old age. He said this as he was savoring a soft, warm buckwheat roll he had brought from Alençon.

Peter never painted on Sunday, even when he had a strong craving for it. He said that from his strict Protestant upbringing he had kept the habit of remaining inactive on Sunday in spite of himself. He passed the time by reading or talking with Gilonne when she came to see him. She would sit down in front of a window with her lace, having obtained Father Lecoudre's permission to work on the many religious holidays until the *leveuse* came, because it was urgent to have something to sell.

They appreciated these long conversations interrupted by silences. During each silence they went their separate ways, then a little later they met at an intersection of thoughts from which they set off again together.

He liked her way of listening and then asking either the question he was expecting or an unexpected one that often delighted him. He felt that her heart was as beautiful as her face and wondered if he would ever succeed in reproducing her astonishing eyes; they were the color of a Norman sky on a sunny day, suddenly set ablaze by those dazzling little green flames.

If only he weren't so old, he would set to work the next day on the painting he had in mind: a glorification of springtime in Normandy. He dreamed of radiant white apple blossoms streaked with pink, and a beautiful, secretive young woman half hidden by its iridescent illumination, the creaminess of her skin blending into that of the petals. The Norman spring was unmatched anywhere else in the world. He had always wanted to approach it someday, brush in hand, but he had been saving it for the time when he could say to himself, ''Now I think I can try to capture that bewildering profusion of beauty.'' Now? It was very late, and yet, since he had finally found the young woman he could mingle with that prodigious blossoming . . .

One day he decided to begin the painting. If he didn't live long enough to finish it, he hoped that he, Peter Fritsch, old and ugly, would be displayed in death before his unfinished painting of the exuberance of youth and love in a Norman spring, just as the body of the handsome young Italian painter Raphael had been displayed before his unfinished painting of the Transfiguration. It would be a beautiful ending for a dreary life of toil. It would be his reward. As soon as he finished the portrait of Lady Bertrade killing a wolf—he liked the horse rearing wildly, terrified of the wolf—yes, as soon as he had immortalized her in her big white-plumed hat facing her enemy, he would begin his last painting.

He talked to Gilonne about it one Sunday and told her how perfectly her brightness and grace would fit into his composition. He was startled and puzzled when he saw her burst out sobbing. What had he said or done to upset her? She began talking about the ''Moon of Arriving Eagles,'' the Hurons, and furs. He listened patiently, trying to think of how he could comfort her. He thought he knew that young women had to cry, and also to laugh and dance, and that such things were normal expressions of their moods. He had believed that Gilonne had a strong spirit beneath her fragile appearance; he had admired her for working hard while remaining calm, beautiful, and smiling; and now she was collapsing because she had sent her heart to the bank of the Saint Lawrence!

She calmed down, said nothing more about the handsome fur

merchant and his Indian, but took up the subject of the chevalier's indifference.

Candelario and Zoltan had told Peter about the situation. He
had seen enough of the chevalier to know that he wasn't very
demonstrative, and was probably even less so with a daughter
who, perhaps, brought back painful memories. But when she
said, "He doesn't love me and I know he'll never love me,"
and began crying again, he wasn't sure she was talking about
her father. She was torn between two disappointments, he
thought, and must be mingling her sufferings from them both.
Though he had never had any daughters, he imagined that all
young women were like Gilonne: quite capable, consciously or
not, of lamenting over a small sorrow that hid a greater one.
But which of the two was the greater? He sighed; it would be
better to change the subject.

He had long been wanting to talk with her about her work,
having seen the ardor she put into it. So, as soon as she had
regained her composure, he ventured a comparison between
their respective artistic expressions. They were both artisans.
God had favored them with creative hands. They ought to be
grateful to Him every day for that. And did she know what the
royal painters said about lace, for which they made such beautiful patterns? They said that making it was an art that required
not only talent and long experience but also, to be perfect, a bit
of genius. Did she think she would gradually approach perfection and perhaps someday touch it with the tip of her needle?
Wasn't that prospect enough to bring back her smile? She gave
him a dazzling one, and he too said to himself that she could
have any man at her feet whenever she chose. Was that fur hunter
blind?

Madame Goulard, the *leveuse*, lived in Mamers. At the end
of the summer Gilonne and Michanteau asked a sheep shearer
on his way there to tell her to come to Grand-Coeur. They knew
she would arrive unannounced, to make sure no one in the region knew she was going to be there. On one of her trips two
robbers had stolen her basket full of lace, her money, and her
watch. Since then, she never traveled without being accompanied by her husband, and no one knew the dates of her journeys
or the routes she would follow.

One morning in October the Goulards were seen coming up
the hill toward Grand-Coeur. Their horses stepped in the piles

of autumn leaves that had fallen from the beeches along the road, and Michanteau remarked that it was surely a good sign to see them moving so much gold.

They weren't peasants, but they weren't quite bourgeois either. Though they were simply dressed, the quality of the cloth from which their clothes were made showed that they were well-to-do people. Over her green wool dress Madame Goulard wore a white apron as immaculate as her headdress, and she had bravely defied the royal edicts by having the hem of her skirt embroidered, which was forbidden to commoners.

The couple gave an impression of order, discernment, and self-satisfaction. They had come from far away, they said, and the roads were bad, but they had been told that they wouldn't be making the trip for nothing and that excellent lace was made here. They hoped they hadn't been deceived. Pompinne said irascibly that at Grand-Coeur nobody had ever deceived anybody, but her tone became almost agreeable when she offered them a meal.

In the workshop the lacemakers, knowing the *leveuse* had come, added these words to their morning prayer: "And please, dear Lord, make this stingy woman be less stingy than the others." But the old man who made *bisette* and took care of the fire said that his wood hadn't wanted to burn and that he had seen a black hen on his way to the shop, which meant they were in for a bad day. Then all eyes turned to Mathurine Guilloret, known as the Toucher.

"Will you go and see what you can do?"

Mathurine was renowned in the region for having succeeded, among other wonders, in making a crafty, miserly old peasant more generous to her family simply by surreptitiously drawing crosses on his back with her finger and saying appropriate prayers at the same time. She was now asked to go to the kitchen, where these two skinflints were probably sitting, and improve them with her "touch."

She stood up, deeply impressed with the importance of her mission, and asked, "What will the two young ladies say?"

"They'll thank you! What else did you expect?"

When Pompinne saw Mathurine coming, she realized what she intended to do and made it easier for her by handing her a pitcher of cider and asking her to help serve the visitors. It was first-rate cider, and Mathurine pointed this out to the Goulards. With relaxed friendliness, she put one hand on the wife's shoulder while she filled her glass, then she did the same with the husband. Pompinne mentally noted that if things went well, Mathurine would deserve to be given a bottle of brandy.

Gilonne had prepared her lace. Six months of intense work, at the rate of seventeen hours a day for each woman in the shop and sometimes nineteen or twenty for Gilonne and Michanteau, had produced two collars and a lappet. Displayed on a piece of red damask taken from the old curtains of Grand-Coeur's ceremonial chamber, those thousands of hours of toil made a good impression. It wasn't what Madame La Perrière would have called lace of great value, but its quality was perfectly respectable. Would it be to Madame Goulard's taste? Everyone knew that a merchant was more likely to buy something she would like to wear herself, so Gilonne and Michanteau waited anxiously to see Madame Goulard's first reaction. It was bad.

"I hope you didn't make me come all this way for these three little pieces!"

Her tone became more heated as she talked. Did they know how far she had traveled, and what dangers she had faced on the way? It was shameful to make good Christians risk their lives for such a small profit! They should have told the sheep shearer who delivered the message that the workshop had been in operation only a short time, rather than having him talk as if they had lace by the cartload.

Michanteau interrupted to ask what she would pay for the lace. It was all they had, and she would have to be satisfied with it.

What would she pay for it? Madame Goulard shrugged, and her husband's face took on a stern expression. One thing was sure: The lace wasn't worth the trouble of coming there.

"But what will you pay for it?" Michanteau insisted.

The Goulards seemed to consult each other with their eyes and the wife answered, "We can give you two hundred livres."

"For all three pieces?"

"Yes. I couldn't sell that lace to my customer who has a shop in the Faubourg Saint-Honoré in Paris. My husband will have to sell it at a fair, and you can't make much profit there. If you had some really fine lace, we'd pay you a good price for it."

Two hundred livres for all three pieces! They are worth much more than that! With such a small sum they wouldn't be able to keep going for the year it would take to make some high-quality lace and finish training the most gifted women in the shop. With a heavy heart, Gilonne went to get the lace collars Madame La Perrière had left them.

Michanteau followed her out of the room and said, "Let me handle it. I'll get more money than you could. Whether the chevalier likes it or not, you're one of his breed, and you've never been very good with money."

She laughed, but Gilonne knew it was painful for her, too, to give up their legacy from Madame La Perrière.

Madame Goulard's eyes shone when she examined the two collars. "I knew you had something in reserve!" she exclaimed. "But this is aristocratic lace you're showing me, lace for ladies at the court of Versailles, and you know as well as I do that such high and mighty customers pay only when they feel like it—and they don't feel like it very often!"

Pale with repressed anger, Michanteau asked in a deliberately gentle tone, "Would you please tell me *exactly* what kind of merchandise you want?"

Not at all disconcerted, Madame Goulard answered with self-assurance, "What we like is good, well-made lace that's pleasing to the eye, the kind that can be sold to rich bourgeois, foreigners, and big merchants. Those are the only people who pay well and promptly. The lace you've shown me is either too good or not good enough."

"Now we know what to show you next time," Michanteau said blandly. "We'll put this lace away, then have a farewell drink with you. I'm sorry we made you come so far for nothing."

The two buyers became more conciliatory. There was no use rushing to make up their minds. They could work out something that would be satisfactory to all of them.

Gilonne's anger brought back the pink that had been missing from her cheeks for some time. She picked up one of Madame La Perrière's collars, carefully put it back into its box, and said calmly, "We'll sell you only one of these collars. As you know very well, you'll have no trouble selling it in Paris, along with the three pieces from our shop. I want four hundred livres for those three pieces, and five hundred for the fourth."

Madame Goulard cried out in indignation—or, as Michanteau put it later in describing the scene to the lacemakers, she yelled as if she had been stabbed in the backside with Pompinne's sharpest knife.

"No! Never!" said Monsieur Goulard. "There's no use even talking about prices like that!"

But they did talk about them, for two hours. The discussion was exhausting. It was the Goulards who won. They took all four pieces for seven hundred livres, instead of the nine hundred Gilonne had asked, which was already ridiculously low. Their main argument was that nowadays one could go to Alençon and buy as much lace as one wanted from Protestants who were closing their shops and selling off their stock at low prices. And Gilonne and Michanteau knew it was true.

It was late afternoon when the transaction was finished. Not wanting to leave at the end of the day, the Goulards asked if they could sleep in the barn. Since Peter was no longer using it, Gilonne agreed, and hoped Sir Reginald would be up to his old tricks.

The phantom Englishman surpassed her hopes. In the morning, the Goulards seemed sleepy and complained of having had a bad night. Who was that visitor who had come to sleep beside them, and kept snoring and groaning so loudly?

"Visitor? What visitor?" asked Pompinne.

"We had one, no doubt about that!" said Monsieur Goulard. "My wife always says I snore loud enough to wake the dead, but that man can outsnore me any day in the week!"

Pompinne assured them that no one else had slept in the barn. And hadn't they locked the door from the inside?

"Yes, now that you mention it, we did," said Madame Goulard, suddenly remembering that they had taken all precautions to protect their purchases.

With an angelic expression, Michanteau suggested that maybe Sir Reginald . . . The Goulards asked who Sir Reginald was. She told them about him, with falsely reassuring circumspection.

Neither of them cut a very glorious figure when they left Grand-Coeur.

"At least their trip will be spoiled by the thought of what may happen to them because they've displeased the protective ghosts of Grand-Coeur," said Michanteau, "but I also hope they'll think our lace is cursed, and sell it without making the big profit they're expecting."

The others all said they shared that hope. And Lady Bertrade remarked that Sir Reginald had always shown he could be counted on to do the right thing at the right time.

Gilonne never revealed that she had seen Michanteau get up in the middle of the night, leave their room, and stay away a long time.

But after they had spent a few minutes gloating over the way the Goulards had gotten a little of what was coming to them, they realized that the future was dark. The small Protestant lace-making shops in and around Alençon would go on selling off their stocks at low prices, and it would be hard for Gilonne and Michanteau to sell what their own shop produced.

When Mathieu stopped at Grand-Coeur on his way back from a trip to Germany, he had an idea that seemed good to them. Why not offer to work directly for a large Alençon lace manu-facturer? The owners of the small shops that were closing took most of their lacemakers with them when they left the country, and as a result the two or three large Protestant enterprises that remained were short of workers. Mathieu knew that the Morel d'Arthus, for example, were trying to hire women to do outlin-ing and make *remplis*. If anyone agreed it was a good idea, he would talk to Monsieur Mortimer or Monsieur Hélye. He was sure they would accept the offer.

Gilonne, Michanteau, and Pompinne decided that this was the plan that could save them.

Mathieu stayed at Grand-Coeur for several days. The cheva-lier—who wasn't on a battlefield, for the good reason that there were none that interested him at this time—was in his room at the Moor's Inn, working on his history of the Normans' ances-tors, his beloved Vikings. It was known that he found more quiet there, as well as more comfort and better food, than he did at Grand-Coeur. Everyone wondered, however, what enjoyment he could get from good food when he never even saw what was on his plate, or from a soft bed when he was unable to say whether he had slept between sheets or on straw. Candelario believed that his master's mind didn't appreciate these refine-ments, but that his stomach and his carcass, living their own lives, enjoyed the advantages provided by Mistress Verlot.

The two musician-servants were at Grand-Coeur. They had helped with the buckwheat harvest, and under Pompinne's or-ders they now did much of the work the little farmhand couldn't do by himself. For a long time there had been no adult farmhand on the estate. Candelario sighed, but Zoltan worked with a plea-sure that sometimes made him sing. In his spare time he still whittled and made smooth wooden surfaces that Peter could use

for the sketches he planned to make in preparation for his painting of springtime in Normandy.

With the chevalier absent, the table conversation, presided
over by Lady Bertrade, was lighthearted and agreeable. Freed
from her red wool hat at last, her beautiful white hair, which
Gilonne often washed for her, stood out from her broad face
brightened by mocking yet affectionate eyes. Her shoulders were
covered by a tippet made from one of her countless furs. She
liked Mathieu and periodically asked him to talk about his travels. Even now that her mind had been "unfogged," she was
still interested in weapons. The conversation would eventually
turn to Europe as seen from what she called "Mathieu's roads,"
that is, from the viewpoint of lacemaking and the lace trade in
each of the countries he visited. Pompinne was more amazed to
hear that people in some of those countries didn't drink cider
than she was to learn that in Schleswig it was mostly old men
who made lace, that long beards were in fashion there, and that
a male lacemaker always enclosed his beard in a little bag to
keep it from catching on his bobbins. Or that in Denmark the
dead were so richly attired they wore more lace than the living.
In Sweden it was old soldiers, those who had added to the glory
of their King Gustavus Adolphus, the Lion of the North, who
made the most lace, and it was considered elegant in that country to have coffee-colored lace collars and flounces, which meant
that they were never washed. In Holland there was such a passion for beautiful lace that people put it on their door knockers
to announce a birth and went so far as to put ruffs around the
handles of warming pans!

They sometimes discussed whether the lace made by men was
firmer and of better quality, and whether thread was really well
bleached only in the Haarlem Lake region of Holland. And as
soon as there was any mention of whiteness, Peter came back
to the subject of his springtime. He had finished a score of
beautiful lace patterns and was now being allowed to do as he
pleased. Having painted Lady Bertrade as a huntress on the wall
of the great common room, he dreamed of his apple blossoms
and waited for them to appear, like a young father-to-be waiting
for the birth of his first child. The others tried to calm him by
telling him that winter was just getting started and he had plenty
of time to get ready. He would nod his head and shrug his
shoulders slightly because no one, he believed, understood the
difficulty, the near-impossibility, of reproducing all those differ-

ent whites, enemies and brothers at the same time, an orgy of subtle shades of white, along with light pinks and light blues. A dream and a nightmare.

At Lady Bertrade's request, Mathieu also gave news of the poorhouse. Since Marie was now more active and slept much less, she was no longer willing to give Conte-Nouvelles two sous a day for her prayers. They had compromised: one sou a day. Chopine had slipped away and gone to the men's section, where she was given apple brandy. After coming back with her mind in a rather disorderly state, she had insulted Coeur-de-Coing and lashed out at Marie, telling her that she was the biggest fool in the poorhouse and that others were glad to relieve her of her money. Thomine was doing well and, as always, was more concerned with others than with herself. She was even worried about Coeur-de-Coing because the Duchess of Alençon didn't like her and wanted to replace her with a nun. As for Mama Bordier, she was getting old, felt lonely, and had given a little nook in her house to the old public writer because she wanted to have someone handy to argue with. She could adjust to getting around less, but not to talking less.

In Alençon, said Mathieu, people were worried. Some Catholics felt that the king was tightening the noose around the necks of the Protestants, and there were cowards among them who insulted Protestants, especially women, in the street. It was shameful to hear them. But the Protestant women didn't take abuse meekly: They retorted defiantly and sometimes used their fingernails, without fearing the police or the danger of being deported to America. Many children were being torn away from their families. It was heartbreaking to see them being taken to convents, monasteries, or homes for new Catholics, in carts from which their little heads emerged and their cries could be heard like those of the chickens being taken to market in baskets.

It was said that the Duchess of Alençon, a very pious woman, hated Protestants. She had acquired a perfect maid who dressed her hair so attractively that she confessed to committing the sin of vanity by looking at herself in all the mirrors of her palace, more than was permissible, and she declared that an artist of that quality was worth going to the other side of the world to find. But when she discovered that her marvelous maid was a Protestant and had no intention of changing her religion, she immediately had her thrown out of the palace.

What else was being said? That Mistress Verlot had enlarged

her inn by buying the draper's house next to it. She now had three rooms where a guest could sleep alone in a bed without having to share it with noisy, foul-smelling travelers. It was also said that she was going to open a second dining room so that persons of quality wouldn't have to be disturbed by the presence of commoners. Mistress Lescure had nearly been in serious trouble. She had sold a collar made of fine *point de France* to the notary on the Rue des Tisons in Montsort. When he wore it, it made a red mark on his neck. At first it was thought that the thread was of bad quality, but this proved not to be true. Then it was thought that either the women who made the lace had cast a spell on it, or one had been cast on her, making her contaminate everything she touched. The notary had his collar washed in holy water, and the swelling and redness of his neck improved. Mistress Lescure was now sending Gérasime for news of him every morning, saying that the daily trips to and from Montsort were good for him. But if the redness and swelling came back, it would be very bad for the reputation of her shop.

One stormy evening when they were listening to Mathieu, there was a knock on the door. Zoltan, who was the only one looking at Gilonne just then, saw her turn pale, then blush, and he was struck by the eagerness with which she watched to see who would come in.

It was a peddler who asked to be allowed to sleep in the barn. He was given a bowl of buckwheat porridge and a glass of cider. He had come from the south of the kingdom to buy lace. Michanteau offered to sell him the *bisette* and *mignonette* made by the old man and the children. He reported the news that Fouquet, the former superintendent of finance, had just died in the Pignerol fortress. If he had really robbed the king, it was only justice, but if he hadn't, then it was something the king would have to settle with God someday. At least that was what people in the peddler's province thought, and they also thought the dragonnades were too cruel. People here didn't know what dragonnades were? Well, they would soon find out, because the king had ordered them to be carried out all over France. They were a new way of persecuting Protestants: dragoons were lodged in the houses of heretics to hasten their conversion, and after only a few days some Protestants begged for mercy and renounced their religion so they wouldn't have to see their wives and children tortured any longer.

Mathieu said he had heard of such practices in central Europe, he didn't remember exactly where. In Bohemia, said Zoltan, they had been playing that little game a long time, and it was a pity. Pompinne muttered sleepily that it served the heretics right, and if they didn't like it, all they had to do was change their devilish ways. Luckily Peter was absorbed in thoughts of his apple blossoms and showed no reaction. But Mathieu, who had earned the disapproval of many people in Alençon because he worked for the Morel d'Arthus, defended the Protestants. They were as good as anyone else, and sometimes better. After all, it was the Morel d'Arthus who had given the twenty livres for Gilonne's years of apprenticeship.

Lady Bertrade started. People had given money for Gilonne? They would have to be repaid without delay.

"Pompinne, send gold to that family tomorrow."

"Yes, mistress, I'll take care of it."

Pompinne treated the debt as she did requests for wine or horses: She promptly forgot it.

"Do you remember Hélye Morel d'Arthur?" Mathieu asked Gilonne. "You used to call him the handsome prince of lace. He sometimes asks me about you, and wants to know if you're as pretty as you showed promise of becoming. I suggested that he come and judge for himself if he wanted to see your shop and consider making a business arrangement with you."

"So now you're going to have us working for Protestants, Mathieu?" said Pompinne. "I don't like that."

They had a party for Mathieu on the night before his departure, with roasted chestnuts, hot spiced cider, and ghost stories. Lady Bertrade went to bed early, saying that the two ghosts of the Ferrières family were enough for her.

They all warmed their hands on their bowls of hot cider before drinking it, and Mathieu said he wasn't going to tell a ghost story, but a true one that was much more frightening. The others settled back to listen. It was the latest news from Alençon, and he had heard it three times in three different places. It had first been reported by a highly respected missionary from Chartres, a cousin of Mistress Verlot, and it concerned a young Norman nobleman, said to be from Perche, who had gone off to try his hand at the fur trade in the French colonies in America. He succeeded so well that he came back to Normandy with his pockets full of gold and bought lacemaking shops being sold by Protestants about to go into exile. He put directors, supervisors,

and mistress-lacemakers in charge of his shops and went back
to New France to buy more furs. Before leaving, he said he
would be back within six months, eight at the most. He never
returned. Everyone was wondering what had become of him,
and the missionary had just told the story. Wanting to buy even
more beaver skins than the friendly Indian tribes could sell him,
the young nobleman went into hostile territory, where he was
attacked and killed. The Indians scalped him, drank his blood,
and cooked his body in the big pot of boiling water they always
kept ready on the fire for that purpose. And they also cut out his
heart and put it into his mouth before . . .

When Mathieu picked up Gilonne, who had fainted and quietly slid off her chair to the floor, Pompinne sternly told him he
should have known better than to tell such a story to a sensitive
girl and that he was one more fool on earth.

Lady Bertrade, having come downstairs for a cup of herb tea,
stood unnoticed in the doorway and murmured, "Ogier . . .
Ogier . . ."

The winter was long, harsh, and dreary. Gilonne's friends
became aware that her smile had made up for many lacks and
that without it their buckwheat porridge didn't taste as good. In
the workshop the lacemakers sang little, or even not at all, if
she didn't give the signal by choosing either a song or a soloist.

She had had a high fever after the evening of roasted chestnuts
and hot cider, so her lack of appetite and gaiety were attributed
to a lingering convalescence.

She was overwhelmed with sorrow at any kind of bad news:
When the alarm bell announced a fire, for example, or when the
little farmhand told her he had found a neighbor's dog dead on
the road. But she consented to pose for Peter. For hours at a
time, during which she never put down the lace she was making,
he was able to lighten her grief without seeming to try. They
didn't talk about Ogier or his horrible death, but he told her
about his grim childhood in a Bavaria ravaged and pillaged by
French soldiers. He was born of a rape by one of those brutes
during a night of slaughter and cruelty. But far from detesting
him, his mother had adored him, and he would have had a happy
childhood if they hadn't been desperately poor, so poor that they
sometimes ate grass. Hearing all this, Gilonne would weep
without reserve, ostensibly for the sufferings of Bavaria.

Peter didn't know that in the evening she joined Lady Bertrade and they talked about Ogier and sighed together over the great cruelty of this world. It was now her turn to be comforting. After a time she would force herself to change the subject. Still unable to take any time off from her work, she would go on with her lacemaking while she sat on the old lady's bed and told her about the day at Grand-Coeur. Bichon had drawn the first Christmas rose that pushed up through the snow. Surprised that her spiced apple preserves were being consumed at a greater rate than before, Pompinne had wrapped a hair around the latch of her cupboard door; she was now sure someone had been stealing her preserves, but she didn't know who it was. Zoltan was carving a wooden doll for Bichon, who didn't know about it and would have a happy surprise. Candelario was sleeping more and more. To be left in peace, he slept in Sir Reginald's barn, and the two of them probably performed some fine snoring duets! The lacemakers had finished a superb flounce. If Monsieur Morel d'Arthus came someday, it could be shown to him with pride. But one of the women was sick with a fever and a bad cough; could she be given some of the honey left from last season? She kept asking for an advance on her pay so she could have Marie the Traveler go to the village of Fretigny and pray for her to Saint Andrew, who cured coughs. Gilonne and Michanteau were willing to give her the few sous, but wouldn't it be better to spend them on medicine? They were also worried about poor Father Lecoudre. He was almost unable to walk, even though he now wore two good wool socks, one on each foot.

Lady Bertrade would finally fall asleep and Gilonne would stay with her far into the night, making lace by candlelight. She sometimes thought that if Ogier had died in September, as he was said to have done, it had been in what the Hurons called the "Moon of Falling Leaves." In autumn, to have a souvenir of him that no one else would understand, she would gather fallen leaves: copper-colored ones from the rowan trees, golden ones from the poplars, and the most beautiful of all, those of the beeches. She would fill a little box with them, and it would be her way of offering flowers to Ogier's memory.

On a bright, bracingly cold Sunday, Michanteau saw a man riding up the slope toward Grand-Coeur. When he dismounted from his horse, he appeared to her as a long, narrow expanse of dark brown velvet lightened by an immaculately white collar and cuffs. Under his beaver hat, decorated only with a ribbon, he wore no wig, but with his lustrous, curly hair he had no need of one. She liked the straightforward way he looked at her. She thought she saw a little melancholy in his eyes but preferred melancholy to boredom, which seemed to her the worst misfortune that could befall a pair of eyes. Only those of certain idle, self-important noblemen were afflicted with that defect, however, and this man was a bourgeois, not a nobleman. A rich bourgeois. Everything about him gave the impression of discreet wealth, and Michanteau was sensitive to such impressions.

Knowing he must be Hélye Morel d'Arthus, the lace manufacturer whose visit was expected, she decided to take him straight to the most beautiful sight Grand-Coeur had to offer: Gilonne making lace as she posed for Peter in a pink silk dress, with her hair held in place by a crown of Christmas roses little Bichon had woven for her that morning. Since he was an artist, according to Mathieu, he might as well be shown immediately that people here knew what art was.

Gilonne had just used up the thread in her needle. Before threading it again, she rested her eyes by turning to the window beside which she was sitting. There was frost on the panes. She looked at it without really seeing.

That was when Hélye Morel d'Arthus arrived. She sensed a new presence in the doorway but didn't look in that direction. Since learning of Ogier de Beaumesnil's death, she had often told herself that she could never again bear to see a stranger suddenly come into a room. But she knew very well that doors would go on opening and that she could keep only her heart closed.

She abruptly realized that the frost on the windowpanes was like lace. Maybe that strange but attractive filigree could be used as the inspiration for a pattern. She decided to talk to Peter about it. Then, having no excuse for staying where she was, she forced herself to stand up and walk toward the man who had just arrived.

The fact that he was as tall as Ogier and dressed in dark velvet almost made her regard him as a usurper. Though he lacked Ogier's seductive charm, she had to recognize that he had a kind of relaxed dignity and a look of distinction. Then an odd superimposition of images took place. The man courteously bowing to her was replaced by the prince of lace holding out his hand to a five-year-old girl who trustingly took it and let him lead her away to confront the shadows of a big house and visit two wickerwork ladies wearing dresses of *point de France*. The little girl no longer existed, but the prince of lace was apparently still the same. Did he remember too?

It turned out that Hélye Morel d'Arthus and Peter knew each other! Gilonne heard the lace manufacturer reproach the painter for not having come to see him in a long time. Peter said he had felt like spending some time in the country, and had then met these young ladies who were kind enough to put up with his bad disposition. He was living here happily and preparing to do a painting on the theme of springtime in Normandy.

Michanteau saw the visitor look at Gilonne's portrait. Studying his behavior, it occurred to her that since he obviously wanted to look at Gilonne, it was convenient for him to have both the portrait and its original before his eyes: Without the slightest impropriety, he could praise the portrait and closely examine its resemblance to the original.

He enjoyed that pleasure tactfully, without embarrassingly direct remarks. He contemplated discreetly and marveled without reserve. Though his delight was clear to everyone, it was free of flattery and unwelcome attentions. Michanteau wondered if this was the conduct of a Protestant or that of a gentleman. She admitted to herself that she didn't have much experience with either. One thing she was sure of—and even little Bichon would have noticed it—was the fascination that Gilonne held for Monsieur Morel d'Arthus, whose eyes kept turning back to her.

When Gilonne raised her hand to take off the crown of Christmas roses that held her hair, he exclaimed, "No!" and then immediately bowed to her and apologized, saying that he would like the painting and the original to be identical a little longer.

Lady Bertrade, who had just come back from a hunt, found this bourgeois courteous and pleasant. She invited him to have supper at Grand-Coeur and stay overnight, to avoid returning to Alençon in darkness. Peter praised the great paintings owned by the Morel d'Arthus family. Obliged to talk about them, Hélye did so with reserve and discretion.

He had to be taken to see the workshop while there was still daylight, and Gilonne went to put on her cloak and wooden shoes before going outside. As soon as she had walked out of the room, he looked at the portrait once again. It seemed to him that she had left her beauty and her presence there in front of him. Feeling that strange impression, he realized how deeply he had been moved by the sight of her. He tried to attribute it to his charming memory of her as a child, but while the little girl had been exquisite, the young woman had an almost supernatural beauty that didn't need the support of memory to be overpowering.

The white film that covered the ground crunched beneath their feet and reflected the pink glow of the setting sun. Under Gilonne's dark hood, nothing could be seen except the tip of her little nose, also pink. Hélye had such a strong desire to see her whole face again that he used the first pretext that came into his mind to make her stop and look at him.

She gave him the explanations he had asked for. That dark, frozen mass over there was the Perseigne forest, where Lady Bertrade hunted wolves, and farther on . . . He scarcely heard her. He had discovered that there was something Botticellian in the shape of her superb eyes. Sublime perfection in the curve of her eyelids. And those green stars! It seemed to him that he had waited all his life for God to cast green stars into the eyes of a woman who was meant for him. He felt great love, and even greater fear, rising inside him in stormy gusts that were beyond his control. He began walking again, uncertain and joyful, feeling that he was on his way to meet a destiny for which light and darkness were still contending.

She walked beside him, calm and serene, happy to be breathing the cold, bracing air, absorbed in the pleasure of walking. Walking, she said to herself, would always be her luxury, her desire, her reward. In heaven, if God called her there someday, she would do nothing but walk and run to make up for having spent so much time sitting during her earthly life. But if she told this rich prince of lace about it, he wouldn't understand. She glanced at him beside her. Tall and slender, he seemed to her perfectly at ease as he walked with long, regular steps, and he probably made his way through life with that same ease. He had surely never been concerned with what it was like to endure sixteen or seventeen hours of constraint on a chair or bench.

She watched two crows hopping on the frosty ground, but in her eyes there still remained something of her brief look at Hélye Morel d'Arthus, something that she described to herself as the quintessence of distinction. ("Quintessence" was a word she had just learned from Peter; he had made her copy it twenty times, as she did all the new additions to her vocabulary.) Then she realized that he had the habit of sometimes smiling at the end of a sentence. A faint smile that punctuated his conversation and seemed to close one subject before he passed on to another. It was like a little blank space between topics.

He found the workshop perfect. Gilonne was surprised because she knew it wasn't perfect. He asked to see the press used for printing designs. She admitted she didn't have one, and had to have that work done in Alençon. Suddenly she was panic-stricken at the thought that what she was proposing would be worthless to this big manufacturer and that he was going to tell her so, courteously but firmly. She saw him go over to a window, stand looking through it for a few seconds, then turn back to her. The time had come: now he was about to tell her that he appreciated her offer, but . . .

"I'll never forget the evening when you so sweetly tried to warm my heart. But do you know the cold sadness I was feeling then? Marshal de Turenne had just converted to Catholicism. The last of our powerful men had sided with the king. To cheer me up, you told me the secret of the roses. Do you remember?"

Yes, she did. She smiled, a little embarrassed. What had come over her that evening, in that beautiful house, to make her tell such stories?

He wondered if he wasn't now contemplating every man's dream: innocence and purity combined with the greatest outer beauty imaginable. Then somewhere in his mind a horrible cry rang out: "Heretic!" That was what he must be to her. How could he have forgotten, even for a second, the dark future that lay in store for French Protestants? Though he ordinarily prided himself on being logical, practical, and sensible, for the last hour he had been engrossed in a dream that had no chance of ever coming true. He looked in despair at Gilonne's perfect, inaccessible beauty and saw her give him a gentle, rather distant look in return. Distant, and also quivering. Was she afraid? Did he frighten her? He told himself that he would never see anything beautiful or perfect in the world without thinking of her. From now on he was going to be unhappy.

He told her he would be glad to keep her fifteen women and six children busy. He needed such workers. But maybe it would be better not to tell them for whom they were going to make lace.

Seeing him become a little cool and aloof, she was convinced that the lack of a press for printing designs was a serious flaw in her workshop. She was sorry she hadn't let Michanteau and Candelario buy one from their endless supply of Protestants going into exile. Maybe Michanteau was right to say that Gilonne didn't see things on a big enough scale, and that in lace manufacturing the people who succeeded were the ones with the most ambition. She decided to get money for a press by selling the other lace collar left to them by Madame La Perrière. Suddenly happy with that vigorous decision, she smiled at Hélye. He was powerfully stirred and became acquainted with a pain he had never known before: an unbearable burning in his heart.

The chevalier, Candelario, and Zoltan arrived unexpectedly just as Gilonne and Hélye Morel d'Arthus were coming back from the workshop. Almost unconsciously, Gilonne contrasted Hélye's impeccable elegance with the unorthodox and somewhat slovenly appearances of Louis-Guillaume de Ferrières and his two musician-servants. There was an exchange of greetings, and a short time later they were all seated around the big table in front of the fire.

The fleeting impression that Hélye had had when he saw the chevalier in the twilight now became a striking certainty: Gilonne looked exactly like him. For a few moments he was in a state of extreme astonishment. He remembered Mathieu Perdriel's rather embarrassed answer when he had asked him why his niece had gone to Pervenchères to establish a lacemaking shop. Mathieu had quickly said something about her having a position as companion to an old lady in addition to supervising the lacemakers.

For the second time since coming to Grand-Coeur, Hélye had a pretext for filling his eyes with Gilonne's beauty, this time to compare her features not with those reproduced by Peter but with those of the man who was obviously her father. It couldn't be otherwise: Chevalier de Ferrières was the father of the marvelous, the incomparable Gilonne. His immediate reaction to that discovery was self-centered. Would it change anything for him? Would she be more or even less accessible to him?

One morning when it was raining torrents, which made her rheumatism hurt more than usual, Lady Bertrade had Pompinne dress her, and when she was ready she announced that the time had come to act.

"When will he realize that she's his daughter?" she said. "When will he *make up his mind* to realize it?"

"How should I know?" asked Pompinne.

"Well, I'll tell him. He'll be leaving soon. For where? God Himself probably doesn't know. I'm going to him now."

"He's working. He won't talk to you. And even if you tell him, what makes you think he'll remember it?"

Lady Bertrade went to the chevalier's study and opened the door without knocking. He looked up, then stood up and courteously asked her to be seated.

"What can I do for you, madame?"

"Try to listen to me, my son."

"I'm listening."

"Do you know what everyone in France is talking about now?"

"I assume you've come here to tell me, since you know how little I keep up with the news."

"The king is legitimizing all his bastards."

"Now *there*'s a burning issue! All the princes and princesses must be howling with despair! What's being said about it at court?"

"What's being said about it at court doesn't matter to me, my son. What matters to me is whether or not the king's action . . . inspires you."

"Inspires me to write a new song?"

Lady Bertrade turned pale, though she knew it was anxiety that had put that falsely lighthearted reply into her son's mouth, anxiety about complications that would trouble the calm waters of his life and disrupt his work.

"You know what I mean. What are you going to do?"

"Nothing. There's no throne at stake here. There will be practically nothing to inherit. All I had to give was the right to live here, and I gave it."

"*I* gave it."

"Very well then, we'll say that you gave it. The fact remains that she has it."

"Don't you think a family name would be more useful?"

"No. Not for a girl."

"Then you've already gone as far as you intend to go?"

"I have."

"I hope you won't regret this later. . . ."

"When that later comes, I'll be able to cope with it."

Lady Bertrade left and closed the door behind her with a slowness that told of her restrained anger.

In the courtyard she saw Candelario yawning as he tried to warm his frozen hands. She had him help her into the saddle and rode off to hunt, hoping she would meet a strong, ferocious wolf that she could kill after a fierce struggle.

It had been agreed that Mathieu would pick up some lace patterns and materials from the Morel d'Arthus establishment and take them to Grand-Cœur. Making lace from them would provide a steady, assured, and very substantial income that was beyond anything Gilonne had ever hoped for. She attributed the generous offer to the labor shortage among Protestant lace manufacturers. It was certain that more and more Protestant lacemakers were leaving Alençon to go into exile and that Catholics were reluctant to take their places.

But it was not part of the agreement that Hélye Morel d'Arthus would bring the patterns and materials himself.

He arrived early one morning, which evidently meant that he had traveled part of the night. There was no morning mist and the sun shone brightly on his gray velvet coat, turning it to silver armor.

"He's a fine-looking man," said Michanteau. "But with all the servants trotting around in his palace, I wonder why he runs his errands himself. He must like to get some fresh air. And Grand-Coeur, perched on its hill, has very healthy air!"

This time Gilonne wasn't wearing her pink silk dress and her hair wasn't held in place by a crown of Christmas roses. She now wore a gray fustian and a white linen dressing jacket, apron, and hat. Hélye found her exquisite; to him, she looked like a princess disguised as a maid. He had joined her in Sir Reginald's barn, where Michanteau had told him he would find her. It was here that the keg of Flemish thread bleached in Holland was kept, and Gilonne was taking from it the amount needed for a day's work in the shop. It was important for the linen thread to be kept in an unheated place where no wood or coalsmoke could impair its perfect whiteness. And Gilonne was wearing white cotton gloves, as Mistress Lescure had taught her, in order to handle the precious material without soiling it in any way.

Hélye was at first surprised by this precaution; then he appreciated it. Gilonne told him she had served her apprenticeship with a woman who, she now realized, was obsessed with cleanliness, but that on the whole it had been excellent training. She described how hard it had been for her to make the workers in her shop wash their hands. He told her about the bonuses he paid in his own shop when a finished piece of lace was perfectly white. She asked him how it could be perfectly white when it had been handled by so many women. Then, before he could answer, she laughed and said she understood: The bonuses gave each woman an incentive to make sure the others were always clean, because it was in their common interest. He liked the way she had reasoned quickly and accurately, with a charmingly serious expression followed by the knowing nod of a specialist who appreciated an innovation in her field. He had a glimpse of a shared life in which each would understand and help the other in working toward a common goal.

As she continued measuring her thread, she talked about Madame La Perrière, who used to say that each hour, and even each moment, ought to be lived for the purpose of improvement. She added that she too had invented something, and would tell him about it someday, when it was ready. Hearing her speak of a future that included him made him so happy that he turned a little pale.

That was the moment Sir Reginald chose to make his presence known with a loud snore. Looking up from the keg and seeing Hélye's surprised expression, Gilonne leaned toward him and told him in an undertone, with her lips brushing against his ear, that it was one of the two Ferrières ghosts, a courteous ghost of whom there was no need to be afraid. Hélye wasn't at all afraid. He hardly listened to her words, but the light touch of her lips on his ear filled him with tumultuous feelings.

"He's very curious," she went on. "He's interested in everything that happens in the Ferrières family."

Hélye collected his wits enough to ask her, without really knowing very well what he was saying, how the ghost could take an interest in anything while he was asleep. After a cascade of young, vivacious laughter, she said that Sir Reginald wasn't asleep and saw everything that was now happening in the barn, and that his snore was simply a way of saying, "I'm here."

"Is he always here when you measure your thread?"

"Almost always. I think he likes me."

He thought they were both being a little mad, and he loved sharing the madness with her.

"What did you say his name was?"

"Sir Reginald."

"Greetings to you, Sir Reginald."

"I think you've pleased him. It seems that being easily offended is his main fault."

He helped her to close the keg, and she told him the story of the two ghosts at Grand-Coeur. Lady Yolaine appeared less often, especially in winter; she seemed to dislike cold weather. But on warm summer nights she was sometimes heard moaning or dropping her thimble and scissors.

At the cost of a great effort, Hélye declined Lady Bertrade's invitation to supper. He felt it would be better not to impose his presence this time. He wanted to be able to come back the following month, bringing more patterns and materials. Gilonne had decided to have the village of Pervenchères specialize in making *remplis*, which her women were beginning to do well, and there would often be work to bring.

When he left, Zoltan and Candelario went with him. They were going to Alençon to get some pages of music that had been copied for their master by an old public writer who lived in one of the towers of the Sagory Gate. Candelario explained that it was the new song the chevalier had written. Payment for the work of copying it consisted of a dozen eggs from Pompinne's henhouse, and this accounted for the great care with which Candelario treated the little basket he had attached to his plump neck. He mentioned that he had had to overfeed the hens to make them lay eggs at that time of year, and that he was satisfied with the results.

When they reached the Perseigne forest they slowed their horses to a walk. Candelario continued talking, delivering a monologue on the inhabitants of Grand-Coeur, and in the course of it he spoke of Gilonne. As he expected, he saw that he had interested Hélye, even though he asked no questions. Before they left the forest, Hélye knew Gilonne's story.

"My friend Zoltan and I wonder if we were right to do what we felt was our duty at the time," Candelario concluded. "It may be that we misjudged how everyone would react, and that we sowed sorrow where we thought we were bringing joy. We think our master's daughter isn't happy. It must be less sad to have no father at all than to have one who won't recognize you as his child.''

As they were riding through town, Hélye made no effort to guide his horse. He was absorbed in thinking about a decision he had just made. He would marry Gilonne Perdriel, if she would have him. Maybe a young woman with a painful past and an uncertain future would be willing to marry a Protestant.

When he abandoned his horse to one of his servants in the courtyard of his house, he was smiling. And when another servant told him that his father wanted to see him in his office, his eyes kept their look of happiness.

During their supper in the big kitchen in the basement, the servants of the Morel d'Arthus house, all Protestants, agreed that this evening the news must be less bad than usual. Their young master, always so reserved, seemed pleased. Maybe the terrible dragonnades they had been dreading wouldn't reach Normandy. Zacharie, Hélye's valet, promised the others he would question his master that night when he helped him to undress. For good measure, Judith, the housekeeper, who kept the household of the widower father and the bachelor son under firm control, decided that since it was a cold night she would bring them each a glass of hot wine before they went to bed, and question them about the situation herself.

Hélye had put on his long indoor cloak, made of dark velvet lined with marten fur, and he had drunk his hot wine, but Zacharie and Judith had learned only that nothing was going worse, for the moment. Hélye had told them not to go in a group to Sunday worship in the Lancrel district. They must bear in mind that if more than two of them were seen together they could be accused of gathering to pray in the town, which they were forbidden to do. Since Hélye still seemed in high spirits, however, they were convinced that something good was about to happen. Maybe it was what they had been dreaming of: the return of their pastor, who had been exiled again after one of his sermons.

Sitting alone in front of a crackling fire, Hélye looked distractedly at Sisyphus and his rock and Atlas and his world, the two monumental oak sculptures, more than six feet high, that held up the enormous mantelpiece in his bedroom.

He thought back over what he and Gilonne had said to each other on their way back from the workshop at Grand-Coeur. He had told her that because a royal edict made it unlawful for any guild to give a mastership to more than one member of a single family, his two brothers had gone into exile. One of them was living in Holland, where he had founded a firm that dealt in sewing notions, lace, and other textiles. The other was a banker in Geneva.

"Why haven't you left too?" she had asked him. "Couldn't you have a lacemaking shop in another country?"

"This is where I belong. I like to make Alençon lace, and it can really be made only in its own town. It would lose something of itself if it were made anywhere else. Its . . . subtle spirit, I suppose. . . . Yes, it can really be made only in Alençon."

If he had left the country, as his father urged him to do, he would never have seen Gilonne again! He suddenly decided to have Peter make him a miniature copy of her portrait, which he could always have with him.

He knelt and said his prayers, asking God to bless his plans. As he was about to put out his candles, he stopped to look at the only painting in his bedroom, facing his bed: a beautiful work by Philippe de Champaigne showing the Morel d'Arthus children in the garden of the Château du Verrier, on their estate in Perche, not far from Mamers. His brother Mortimer was handsome and proud in a pose that Hélye said he still adopted often: standing with one hand on the back of a chair and the other on his hip. All firstborn sons in the family were given that name in memory of a distant English ancestor, a goldsmith, who had come to France with the invading army. Mortimer was ten at that time, and Hélye, to his left, was eight. Wearing doublet and cloaks of reddish-brown silk, they were looking at five-year-old Samuel, in a white damask robe and a lace cap, who was later to become a very serious Swiss banker. The three of them were all past thirty now. . . . Cornélie, who had just turned four was wearing a blue silk dress, blue ribbons, and a lovely apron made of Alençon lace. Several copies of the apron had to be made because Banvole, the greyhound, who also appeared in the painting, kept tearing it during the posing sessions. Samson and Josias, the adorable twins, were eighteen months old and didn't have much longer to live.

Would he tell Gilonne it would be unwise to have children? The royal edicts were becoming more and more cruel. If God gave them children, the king would take them away. Unless . . . Unless Cornélie, the little Cornélie in blue who was now a beautiful Dutch matron, would keep them until things became better in France. With the tender, maternal fullness of her curves, Cornélie was the very image of a mother. Babies were happy in the warmth of her lap. She had already had five of them. Or was it six? She would be glad to take in some nephews and nieces; she would make a little more jam and a few more of her big, heavy pies, and pamper the newcomers with her smiling affection.

But maybe he and Gilonne wouldn't have to send their children away. Maybe within a year or so the king would stop his persecution and life would become normal again. He was now making his last attempts to obtain a spectacular total conversion. But as soon as he saw it was impossible and realized that if he continued his efforts he would outrage all of Europe, impair his alliances with Protestant countries, and endanger the diplomatic support to which he attached so much importance, the persecution would come to an end.

Hélye tried to forget what had saddened him so much: the determined policy of harassment and persecution that had begun twenty years earlier and, even though it appeared to slacken now and then, was still moving inexorably forward. He tried to forget how disquieting the king's personal attitude was becoming as he grew more and more religious with age and under the influence of his confessor, Father La Chaise. He tried to forget that the king obviously wanted to be the man who would wipe out heresy in France and offer the pope the French Protestants' heads on a silver platter. He tried to forget everything except Gilonne's beautiful face.

Driving all other thoughts from his mind, he concentrated on how he would get Gilonne's consent to marry him. Just before falling asleep, he decided to return to Grand-Coeur the next day and propose to her. He had settled the fate of his future children, but he didn't yet know if they would have a mother!

As he was approaching Grand-Coeur he saw an odd little girl standing on the ice of a frozen pond, drawing on it with a pointed stick. She was so engrossed in her drawing, and so unmindful of everything around her, that when the ice broke she calmly sank into the water without uttering a sound. Hélye shouted to her, "Don't be afraid, I'm coming!" He ran to the pond, whose water came only to his thighs, and pulled out the shivering child. He took off his coat, wrapped her in it, put her in front of him on his horse, and galloped toward the house.

He was surprised to hear himself laughing. He hadn't felt this lighthearted since childhood. He laughed at the thought of what a fine suitor he was, with his clothes wet and dirty and stagnant water leaking from his boots—just the way a man ought to be when he came to ask a young lady to marry him! He had only a precarious future to offer her, and now he looked as if disaster had already struck! He leaned over the chilled little creature responsible for his pitiful appearance.

"What's your name?"

"Bichon, sir."

"You live here?"

"Yes, sir."

"What do you do here?"

"I'm learning drawing from Monsieur Fritsch. Gilonne said I could do it. She likes me."

"And do you like her too?"

"Oh, yes!" Bichon said enthusiastically.

When they went into the house, Hélye was astonished to hear Pompinne reprimand Bichon for having fallen into the water *again*.

"Next time you'll get a whipping!" she said; then she turned to Hélye. "It's the fourth time in two days, sir! She comes back with enough water in her clothes to flood my kitchen and put out my fire. One of these days she'll catch her death of cold!"

"Has there always been someone there to save her?"

"No. She manages to save herself without any help. She hops like a frog until she's out of the pond. Here, sir, drink this hot cider before *you* catch your death of cold because of that little . . . Bichon! When are you going to stop scratching things on the ice? Ah, it was a fine idea to teach her to draw, sir! Even on the walls of the cellar she puts what she thinks are flowers, ribbons, and baskets. Bichon, you little demon, swear in front of Monsieur Morel d'Arthus that you'll never set foot on a frozen pond again! Swear it!"

"I can't. The lace I draw on the ice is too beautiful."

"Wouldn't you rather draw it on paper?" asked Hélye.

"I can't. It's too expensive. Gilonne told me that if she got a lot of money for her lace she'd buy me some paper in Alençon, but she didn't get very much for it, so she said, 'Later.' "

"If you behave yourself and stay away from ponds, I'll bring you some."

"When?"

"Very soon."

He liked the atmosphere of that kitchen and attributed all its warmth to Gilonne, who burst into the room just as he was buttoning his coat, which had finally dried. She threw herself into Pompinne's arms, weeping, without having seen Hélye. Then Michanteau and Candelario came running in as if the devil were after them.

It was Candelario who explained what had happened.

The day before, one of the lacemakers had heard about Lady Yolaine and Sir Reginald, and had told the others that Sir Reginald watched over the keg of thread. They had then understood why the thread broke so often and why *point de France* was so hard to make! They shouted in the shop that with such evil influences it was impossible to work. Lace from an estate haunted by two ghosts would never be well made or sold for a good price. Accidents and spiteful tricks would always interfere. Then that morning, by a stroke of bad luck, another lacemaker had encountered Marie the Traveler and heard all sorts of nonsense from her: a sinister man in black and a half-naked savage armed with daggers forged by the devil had prevented her from praying as she should have done when she came back from her pilgrimage for Lady Bertrade. And Lady Bertrade herself was a real witch, with power over wolves. Marie had solemnly warned the lacemaker that it wasn't good even to come near Grand-Coeur, much less work there. Father Lecoudre could always try to exorcise it, but it had so many demons that such a frail little man of God, barely able to walk, could never overcome them all.

That was the situation. Two of the women were close to having convulsions, the others were weeping or shouting, and they were all ready to go back to their village as soon as they had been paid.

Gilonne had dried her eyes. Seeing Zoltan come in, she asked him, "Are they really leaving?"

"Yes, all of them, including the old man. And he's already sent away the two little boys. They were whimpering even more than the girls."

"What can we do?" sighed Gilonne.

"For now," said Pompinne, "you can come and eat my hot soup. It will do you all good, especially Monsieur Morel d'Arthus, after the soaking he got from pulling Bichon out of the pond."

Hélye had been standing discreetly in a part of the kitchen left in shadow by the pale light of a gray day. When Gilonne saw him, she uttered an exclamation of surprise mingled with joy and relief. Hearing it made him happy.

"We're terribly upset!" she said to him. "But you'll advise us. You'll tell us what to do."

He would have given anything to be able to reassure her, but he had seen such situations before and knew there could be little hope that this one would turn out well. When all the workers in a shop were gripped by panic, it was hard to bring them back to their senses. And he regarded workshops in the country as a poor idea. Peasant women were reluctant to work away from home. That was the real problem behind all the superstition and fear: Lace had to be made between milking the cows and weeding the fields. At Saint-Denis-de-Sarthon, an experiment similar to this one had recently failed, even though the good priest who organized it had no ghosts watching his thread and hadn't been visited by savages.

"Would you be willing to talk to them?" Gilonne asked timidly.

"I'll do whatever you want. But if they find out what my religion is, things will be worse than ever."

"It's all so foolish . . ."

"Yes, there's a foolishness all around us. Even more than you think."

"What do you mean?"

"I'll explain later. I must talk with you. After lunch, if I may."

She acquiesced with one of the little nods he found so charming.

He was also charmed by that country meal eaten from coarse earthenware bowls. It was a far cry from his meals at home, which, though simple, were served with great refinement, but he was sure he would never forget it. His heart would always cherish the smile that Gilonne sometimes gave him when their eyes met, a smile that was all the more moving because her face still bore traces of her tears and distress.

As they were eating their apple preserves, Pompinne said they mustn't lose hope: Sooner or later the lacemakers would calm down and be sensible.

Then Father Lecoudre arrived, gratefully accepted the chair that the little farmhand pushed forward for him, and sighed with fatigue and worry. Hadn't he told them that nothing good could come from working for sinners? With God's help, he was going to find more wholesome work for his parishioners. He didn't really feel guilty for having let them try making lace, but his conscience felt better now that the experiment was over. If the young ladies would pay those people what they owed them, they would go back to their fields and stables and it would be better that way. No, thanks, he wasn't hungry and didn't want anything to eat. But he would be happy to take a bowlful of buckwheat porridge for his little sexton of all work, who always had his mouth open, waiting for food to fall into it. What a cruel misfortune it was not to be able to feed all of God's children!

At this point Hélye said that since so many people were going hungry, it might be good to go on trying to make it possible for some of them to earn money by making lace.

The priest sighed again and said that lacemaking had ended for good in Pervenchères. "You don't know everything," he went on. "Two cows died this week. Everyone wondered what could have caused such a disaster, then someone pointed out that the dead cows belonged to women who come here every morning with their children. According to the villagers, there's a curse on the workshop and that's what made the cows die."

"But do *you* believe that, Father Lecoudre?"

"I believe what I see. I've seen two dead cows on farms that I've blessed, belonging to women who work in the shop here, which I've also blessed. That means there are things involved that are beyond my control. And the villagers know it."

"You should come and exorcise Grand-Coeur," said Candelario.

"I couldn't drive away ghosts that have been here for three or four hundred years. Think of the strong habits they've developed in all that time! I'm not going to dislodge them from either Grand-Coeur or the villagers' minds. That's how things are and we have to accept them."

"Father Lecoudre," said Candelario, "can you tell me honestly that you're not a little glad of what's happened?"

"My son, you're a good Catholic, so I can admit to you that I don't like to have my parishioners making lace to encourage sinful luxury."

"But the Church allows it!" said Gilonne.

"The *Jesuits* allow it. And they allow everything—balls, coquettishness, and only they know what else—to maintain their position and make a religion as fragile as lace, if I can put it that way, for the lords and ladies at court. Don't talk to me about that or you'll stir up my pain again. Pompinne, give me a glass of water. Water, nothing else!''

"Someday they'll find you dead of hunger on your skimpy mattress," said Pompinne, "and the rats won't have anything to gnaw from your bones. I'll give you some porridge for Sébastien, but only if you eat a little of it yourself."

"Then give me a spoonful of it, you pigheaded woman! I've already eaten—you're making me commit the sin of gluttony by eating lunch twice!"

"You know very well that the first time you had only thin turnip soup, as usual! Now that I think of it, I don't understand why you're willing to burn the little wood to cook it."

"I'm not. Don't you know I wouldn't waste wood to make soup for a useless wretch like me? Once a week I put water and turnips into my kettle and take it to the men who make wooden shoes in the forest. They cook my soup over the same fire as theirs. My kettleful lasts from one Monday to the next."

"Poor Sébastien!"

Gilonne leaned toward Hélye and said in an undertone, "Sébastien, the sexton, poaches on the land of Grand-Coeur because he's starving. Lady Bertrade knows it but says nothing. And Father Lecoudre has never understood why his kettle of soup sometimes smells of rabbit, hare, or partridge. Sébastien knows where the soup is cooked and he goes there when he can to drop something more substantial into it."

They smiled at each other, but she became serious again when Father Lecoudre insisted that the workers be paid and leave for good immediately.

"What if they were given work to do at home?" asked Hélye. "Isn't that what they've wanted from the start?"

He moved closer to the priest and waited for an answer.

"Monsieur Morel d'Arthus—yes, I know who you are—if those women knew that you're the one who's been giving them work, they'd leave even faster. All they need—please excuse me for saying this—is to find out that there's a heretic here! I'm talking in their way, not my own, because I know better than you think I know what you've tried to do to end our religious tribulations, and what you're still trying to do. But there too, sir, the Jesuits do harm, too much harm. Don't you agree that if the fire were stirred less, it wouldn't burn so high? I condemn your way of serving God, my son, but I don't believe that people who have gone astray can be brought back to the right path by killing them.''

"It's a little more complicated than that, Father Lecoudre. But I believe in a tolerant future. I don't know when it will come, but I believe in it. With God's help, it will come someday.''

"It goes without saying that you and I, sitting here in this kitchen, aren't going to solve all the problems of the kingdom. I only wanted to tell you that although I'm not one of those who dream of burning you at the stake, I have to recognize that you're not the one who can put things right here. I regret it for my parishioners' sake, believe me, because they're in dire straits. Those who have lost their only cow are desolate.''

"If I'm not the one who can put things right in the workshop here,'' said Hélye, "I can at least help your desolate peasants a little.'' He handed his purse to the priest. "Please give them this, and tell them whatever you like about where it came from. I believe that the cows died of a disease, not from the power of ghosts, and that more will die as the disease spreads. There's enough money in that purse to pay for several of them. I'm still worried, however, about what's going to happen next. The conviction that Grand-Coeur is a source of evil influences must be destroyed to avoid the harmful reactions it may produce if it goads your peasants into a fury. But you can't tell them that the money came from me, because they wouldn't want cows bought with such 'cursed' money.''

"When simple minds have seized on an idea,'' said Father Lecoudre, "it's hard to make them let go of it. I'm going to pray God to help me and send me a sign telling me how to proceed.''

He got to his feet laboriously. When he had steadied himself with his cane, he raised his eyes to Hélye, who was much taller than he, and asked with that look of a crafty peasant that all his years in the priesthood had never made him lose, "Why are you doing all this, sir?''

"What a question from you, Father Lecoudre! But don't worry: I'm not trying to wipe away an evil deed by doing a good one. It's just that charity is part of my religion, as it is of yours. I hope you don't doubt that.''

"I only wanted to say that I know you give a great deal to your own people, and that you're under no obligation to do the same for 'papists,' as you call us. . . . Thank you, sir. God help us, your people and mine!''

"When will He stop allowing us to say 'your people and mine'?"

"When He judges that we've all suffered enough to deserve our salvation. I hope to heaven that you'll be enlightened some-day. I can't believe that a man with a heart as good as yours will remain in darkness and error. I'd like to tell you something that may help you. When I go to see my friends at Port-Royal—it's no secret that I have Jansenist friends—the Great Arnault,* a former Protestant who has become a Catholic, often says to me that if we don't clear the path from both directions, each group doing its share of the work, we'll never come together."

"Using your image, Father Lecoudre, I'll say that clearing a path takes tools. You have them. We have only our hands—and some of them are always being cut off!"

Hélye suddenly seemed not to want to talk anymore. Gilonne thought he might have been irritated by the old priest's simplistic words. She saw that he was making an effort to continue the conversation even though he must consider it useless. Without realizing its full scope, she caught a glimpse of the conflict in his soul. She really looked at him for the first time, a tall, hand-some, distinguished, and elegant man whose hand, pressed against the mantelpiece, was quivering a little with impatience. She had an impulse to ask him, like the priest, why he was doing all this. Why had he helped them in their work? He could have found lacemakers somewhere else, and certainly closer to Alençon. Why had he offered to give cows to peasants who had lost theirs? She could think of only one answer: He had a kind heart. It occurred to her that what he was doing should have been done by the chevalier, but she quickly put that thought out of her mind because it was painful to her.

When Gilonne came back after paying the lacemakers, Hélye saw that she had been crying again, probably on the way from the workshop to the kitchen. But she gave him a brave smile when he reminded her that he wanted to talk with her and asked if he could do it while they took a walk. She nodded and they left.

He knew she was dejected, but she walked beside him with a kind of gaiety in her step that surprised him. He looked at her

*Antoine Arnault, known as the Great Arnault, was a Jansenist theologian who strongly opposed the Jesuits.

little wooden shoes barely touching the ground. Like a child, he thought, she wasn't affected by her sorrow enough to make her walk heavily. She seemed as light as a snowflake. He was almost afraid she might suddenly fly away and leave him all alone on that frozen, inhospitable ground, alone in life, alone with his countless worries as he faced the dark future the king was preparing for French Protestants. He had to admit that he was chained to her forever, that she had the power to make him live or die. If she said yes, he would be saved; if she said no, he would be indifferent to everything, he would almost cease to exist—which was another way of being saved.

He put his hand on her arm. She stopped and turned to him. "Will you be my wife?" he asked.

He saw intense surprise in her eyes. Her silky cheeks went from pale pink to cherry red. She put her hand to her face, as though to quell a sudden flare of heat, or perhaps to make sure she wasn't dreaming.

"Don't say anything now," he continued, having had no answer from her. "Wait. First I must explain what I'm offering you. It would be shameful for me not to tell you the kind of life you can expect if you marry me."

They began walking again, and he described the Protestants' situation. She listened attentively and seemed to have regained her calm, but her heart was pounding so strongly, that it was sometimes hard for her to hear him. Even so, she understood quite well that the Protestants were about to lose all their remaining freedoms if they didn't convert to Catholicism.

The picture he was painting of the life awaiting them was so black that he exclaimed, "And that's what I'm daring to propose that you share with me! Please forget what I asked you. I must have been mad. My only excuse is that my total attachment to you blinded me for a moment. Yes, please forget what I asked you. I wasn't myself. . . ."

Later, many of Gilonne's nights were haunted by the memory of that moment when a contemptible thought came into her mind, after rising from some dark corner of her soul: *Before I answer this proposal, I must talk with the man who's supposedly my father, to find out if I'm really his daughter or not.* A kind, generous, upright man had asked her to marry him, proving that he did her the honor of respecting her enough to give her his name even though she was born a bastard, and she thought only of using his proposal as a pretext for demanding a frank discussion with the chevalier! She was horrified to realize that her soul was so ignoble. Was it possible that such duplicity couldn't be seen in her face? She turned so pale that Hélye reached out to her, thinking she was about to fall.

She got a grip on herself, succeeded in driving away that other self, and found the strength to reply, "I don't think I'm worthy of the honor you've done me. I'm sure I have none of the good qualities you must have believed I had when you judged me fit to be your wife. What you've told me about your religion, and the situation in which it places you, wouldn't have made me decide against accepting your proposal if . . . if my heart could dictate my answer. . . . But I don't know what to tell you. Will you give me a little time to put my thoughts in order?"

Now it was Hélye who was pale and silent. What he had done was wrong. He should never have tried to draw this child—she must be at least fifteen years younger than he—into all the dangers that threatened him. What new royal edicts would tighten the noose around his neck tomorrow, or in a week?

They walked for a time without saying anything. It seemed to him that her step was less light, less joyous, and that his own was heavy with all the sorrows of the world. They reached the deserted workshop, went into it, and unthinkingly sat down at one end of the big table, facing each other.

Gilonne was the first to speak again.

"Your faith is what means most to you, isn't it?"

"It was . . . before I knew you."

"No, don't talk that way. That's not what I was trying to make you say. I only wanted to know if you'd ever give up your religion."

"Are you asking me to do that to prove my love?"

"Oh, no! Nothing could have been farther from my mind!"

She discovered that she was awkward in expressing herself on such a subject, decided that Hélye must find her stupid, and concluded that he was sure to give up the idea of marrying her. Relieved, she was able to go on talking.

"To help me know my own feelings better, I'd like to know a little more about you. But let me make it very clear to you that I don't want you to do anything against your faith because of your attachment to me. And I . . . I wouldn't do anything against mine, either."

"But considering what we are—you a Catholic, I a Protestant—and assuming that you loved me, would you marry me?"

"I've had two wonderful friends who belonged to your religion. One of them brightened my childhood, the other made me realize that lacemaking is a fine art. They were both noble and openhearted. Their memory would help me, if I needed any help, to know that Protestants aren't 'devil worshipers,' as so many fools call you. Yes, I think I'd marry you . . . if I loved you."

"And you don't love me?"

"I . . . I asked you to give me a little time. . . ."

She looked around to avoid meeting his eyes. The workshop on which she had based her future was there, lifeless. The skeleton of her hopes. The cold ashes in the fireplace reminded her of the obliging, cheerful old peasant who had enlivened the shop with his comical remarks, and had always predicted what kind of day it was going to be on the basis of how easy or hard it was for him to kindle the fire in the morning. And it was the memory of that hardworking little old man's kindly smile that made her suddenly feel as if her heart were breaking. Hélye saw such suffering in her eyes that he was overwhelmed by the conviction that he had deeply troubled her young life. *I'll never forgive myself*, he thought.

The parchment patterns lay on the table, just as the lacemakers had abandoned them when they left. She picked up one of them and seemed to examine it for a moment. He saw tears fall on it.

"Please forget what I asked you," he murmured, "and let's try to think of a way for your work to be continued, here or somewhere else. If my love for you can at least be useful in accomplishing that, take advantage of it. Tell me what you want."

She didn't answer. She didn't know what to do. She needed to confide in someone to whom she could tell everything: that she thought she had given her heart one night to a strange, intimidating, and wonderful visitor, but that God and the Indians had taken him away from her; that she had tried to prove to herself that she could run a lacemaking shop successfully, and had failed miserably; that she felt only gratitude and friendship for a charitable, selfless man who did her the honor of wanting her for his wife; that she was unhappy; and that meanwhile the man to whom she should have told all this, the man whose affection would have done her so much good, was somewhere else—on a road, at an inn, or singing in a public square. Was

she stupid, ugly, of no interest at all, to make her father not want
her as his daughter? Yet this great lace manufacturer, one of the
most powerful men in Alençon, found her worthy to be his wife!

She sighed, then took a deep breath of the air in the workshop;
it smelled of cold ashes and also a little of snuff, which the oldest
lacemakers had persisted in taking despite her prohibition against
it. It would be better to turn down Hélye's proposal without
waiting any longer. She didn't want to marry yet; she was only
fifteen. Yes, that was a good excuse that wouldn't hurt his feelings.

"Monsieur Morel d'Arthus, I'm deeply grateful to you . . ."
He looked at her. His eyes said such beautiful and touching
things that she could only add, "And I'd like to take a few days
to think before I give you my answer."

That was how words could play tricks on you, as Mama Bordier and Jérémie used to say. You were about to say some of
them, then all at once others took their place. She smiled in
spite of herself. So be it! She would wait a while to say no. Was
it cruel to do it that way?

She hadn't refused! Hélye was caught up in a whirlwind of
joy that made him want to describe in even more frightful detail
the harsh days that would lie in store for them if they married.
If she said yes, she would have to say yes to everything, or there
would be no marriage. *I'm mad. I'm going to lose her!* he
thought, but he talked anyway, like a man talking to his judges
when the fire that was going to burn him at the stake had already
been lighted.

He told her that tomorrow there might no longer be any Protestant ministers to marry them, and that if their children weren't
baptized as Catholics they would be taken away from them.
Their property might be seized, and they would then have to
travel on foot, completely destitute, to a more hospitable country—if they left while it was still possible, because going into
exile would probably soon be forbidden. He told her that in
Poitou the daughter of one of his servants had died of the brutal
treatment the king's dragoons had inflicted on her because she
refused to give up her religion. He told her other things, many
of them horrible. She listened to them without comment, surprised that she hadn't heard any of them before. He said that
although a large number of Protestants lived in Normandy—two
thousand in Alençon, out of a total population of eight thousand—it was safer than other parts of France. At the time of the

Saint Bartholomew's Day Massacre, Alençon had been protected by the intendant, who had defended it intelligently and bravely. Maybe it would be the same again this time, God willing.

"What about the Edict of Nantes*?" she asked.

"We call it 'the grave' because all our freedoms are buried in it. In all fairness, what do you think of a 'most Christian king,' since that's how ours is called, who lets Christians be martyred in his kingdom? Has he forgotten that we belong to his kingdom too? I accept the principle that a monarch holds his subjects' lives and property in his hands, but he has no right to be master of their feelings. Only God has that right."

"The king believed that the Catholic religion is the only true one and that it's his duty to make Protestants practice it for the salvation of their souls."

"He goes beyond his rights! He's a tyrant of souls! My sovereign can judge anything, except my inner feelings."

"The king is the supreme master."

"After God! And God leads me where He sees fit."

"Doesn't the king derive his power from God?"

"He also derives it from the pope, and is only his deputy. And the pope wants to wipe out what he calls heresy. The king swore to suppress it when he took the throne. I don't have to tell you that there are no more public functions for us. There are no more Protestant bailiffs or notaries—or even grocers!"

"You're still able to be a lace manufacturer."

---

*The Edict of Nantes (April-May 1598) gave Protestants freedom of conscience and civil equality. Their political organization was recognized (assemblies, deputies at court, 151 strongholds, etc.) Their freedom of worship was limited, however, particularly in Paris and nearly all episcopal cities. They took up arms again after the death of Henry IV, were finally defeated, and, by the terms of the Peace of Alais (June 1629), lost their strongholds and the right to hold assemblies. From 1660 to 1685 Louis XIV took back, one by one, the freedoms still allowed by the Edict of Nantes. On October 15, 1685, he revoked it and replaced it with the Edict of Fontainebleau, which denied legal existence to Protestantism in all parts of the kingdom except Alsace.

Alençon was one of the first French towns where Protestant doctrines were implanted under the influence of Marguerite of Angoulême and Alençon, and France was then one of the few states (with Poland, Bohemia, and Brandenburg) that allowed coexistence of the two religions.

"Only barely, and not for much longer. And if Colbert abandons us it will all be over for us."

"Do you think he will abandon you?"

"He knows the commercial strength of the Protestants but he's becoming old and tired. It's hard to struggle constantly. Louvois is younger; his ferocity and craftiness make him a formidable enemy. Father La Chaise, the king's confessor, is also very powerful. They're both calmly waiting to rush in for the kill."

"Aren't you exaggerating a little?"

He saw that he would have to tell her still more about things that seemed so far away from her. The situation was as follows, he said: France was the only Christian country where the two religions were juridically allowed to coexist, but in fact Catholicism was the only one really accepted; Protestantism was barely tolerated, and was *legally* persecuted. Protestants were "rebellious slaves" and their churches were "temples of Satan."

"Only a few threads still connect us to even a semblance of freedom, and the king may not yet be quite ready to cut them. Maybe he's holding back to avoid angering the Protestant countries too much, or maybe he doesn't have enough faith to carry his hunt for heresy all the way through to the end. At any rate, a time will probably come when he thinks he's about to face God and be called to account for his scandalous life, for all his mistresses, bastards, and vices. He'll then realize that brandishing his scepter will be useless in heaven. If he thinks he can win God's favor by crushing us, he's mistaken. He'll only give each of us a martyr's crown."

Hélye had been pacing the floor as he spoke. Now he stopped in front of Gilonne, put his hand on her shoulder, and said with a bitter laugh, "Do you know that my workers can't belong to the linen-maids' guild? Because Saint Louis created and blessed that guild, no Protestants are allowed in it!" He looked at the walls, ceiling, and fireplace of the room, surely without seeing them, but he seemed to be reading the sorrows of the Protestants in them. "Do you know why the king has never placed an order with me, the biggest lace manufacturer in Alençon? Because he feels that his mistresses' soft, white, precious skin would be sullied if it came in contact with lace made by sacrilegious Protestant hands!"

Gilonne had an impulse to put her own hand on his. How unhappy he was! She would have liked to try to soothe the desperate anger that agitated him, but she was afraid her gesture would be interpreted as an invitation to regard her as already engaged to him.

She fastened her cloak and stood up. They left. Night had fallen. Neither of them spoke.

They found Bichon drawing with a stick in the ashes of the kitchen fireplace. Michanteau studied them curiously but furtively.

Peter was glad that Monsieur Morel d'Arthus was going to stay overnight. He wanted to show him the portrait of Gilonne that he had just finished. In this one, she was depicted in a second pose. His idea was to present her in three different attitudes, surrounded by his Norman spring. During supper he explained the symbolism of her different appearances under the apple trees, but no one really listened.

Gilonne was thinking of everything Hélye had said, and examining him with interest. He was no longer only the prince of lace, he was now also a representative of a persecuted sector of the population, maybe even its leader. He seemed to her well fitted for leadership. She realized that during all those years she had spent in closed rooms, bending over the lace she was making, the town had led a life unknown to her.

Hélye saw the surprised, inquisitive attention with which she was looking at him. He interpreted it to mean, "Why has this strange, hotheaded, rebellious man come here to bother us with his obsessions?" He concluded that he must have failed to talk to her as he should have. He seldom conversed with very young women. The last one with whom he had exchanged a few words was a little Swiss cousin who had come with her father, a thread merchant, to visit them one day. He had asked her, out of politeness, without the slightest interest, how she spent her days.

"I pray, cousin."

"Then what do you do?"

"I spin cotton, to make muslin."

"And what else?"

"I spin thread for linen cloth as fine as any made in Holland or Pisa."

"Is that all?"

"Oh, no! I also spin thread as thin and beautiful as Mechlin thread."

"And after that?"

"After that I pray, cousin."

Later, his father had suggested that maybe the girl, sole heiress to his rich Swiss cousin, might someday . . .

"No, please!" Hélye had exclaimed. "If I married her, she'd find some way to spin me too!"

He wondered why he was thinking about that little fool when the incomparable Gilonne was there before his eyes. He realized that he still didn't know how he stood with her, but he was more determined than ever to marry her. Who was the solemn idiot who had said true love needed to ripen slowly?

Pompinne had just lit her fire. The little farmhand had gone to get water from the well, and Gilonne was coming back from her Latin lesson with Peter. The kitchen smelled of smoke because the wood was damp and burned badly.

In honor of Monsieur Morel d'Arthus, who would soon come down from his room, milk had been brought from the cellar. Whenever Pompinne consented to serve milk instead of keeping it to make cheese, Gilonne thought of Ogier de Beaumesnil. She had also thought of him the night before while she lay awake telling herself, uselessly, that if *he* had asked her to marry him . . . Well, he hadn't asked her, and he never would, and it was time to stop dreaming.

Michanteau had said more or less the same thing, and she had added, "Remember what I told you when you first came to Mistress Lescure's house: You can't cry and moan all the time. And what have you got against that handsome, *rich* lace manufacturer?"

"You never think about anything but money!"

"It takes a lot of it to keep yourself alive—and support the people who live off you. Do you realize that we've not only lost the workshop but also gained a little girl who's half simpleminded and an old painter who's not capable of finding his porridge by himself?"

"Bichon isn't simpleminded at all. She's intelligent, in fact. And talented."

"Before she knows how to draw lace patterns, you and I will be in heaven! In the meantime, what are we going to do with our artists tomorrow?"

"We can go on staying here a while longer."

"Without earning our living, I don't think so. Yesterday I examined the roof of Grand-Coeur. Within three months it will start falling down, tile by tile at first, then beam by beam. Their motto, 'The heart can do anything,' doesn't seem to do anything against the ferocity of time.''

Pompinne gave everyone a bowl of hot milk. A rooster began crowing just as Hélye walked into the warm, hospitable kitchen. When Zoltan, who was whittling as usual, saw the look that Hélye gave Gilonne as soon as he came in, he pushed his knife too hard and the little piece of wood jumped out of his hand. He wished no harm to the Protestants and even respected their faith, but he didn't like this one, rich and distinguished though he was, to pay too much attention to a Catholic girl who wasn't for him. He stood up and bowed politely to him; personal opinion had nothing to do with civility. He wondered if Candelario had seen anything that he hadn't, and decided to question him later. There were times when speaking was really necessary, however much the effort might cost him.

The little farmhand who had gone to bring water returned with the news that the lacemakers were coming. Since he was a little dim-witted, Pompinne thumped him in the ribs and called him a fool. He insisted he was right: He had seen a torch moving toward him on the road. Michanteau went out to look.

"They *are* coming!" she exclaimed happily. "There they are!" She came back into the kitchen. "They must have thought it over and realized that, ghosts or no ghosts, we're the only ones here who can give them work and pay them money to buy food. Quick, Gilonne, decide what our attitude should be. Shall we talk to them warmly or coldly? Shall we say, 'Thank you for coming back' or 'You've made us lose a whole day of work, and now you have to make up for it'? Decide!''

Gilonne gave Hélye a questioning look.

She hadn't yet put on her hat or pinned up the thick, shimmering braid that hung down her back, *like a golden stem, with her pretty head as its flower,* thought Hélye. Absorbed in contemplating her, he said nothing in reply to her look, so she asked him, "What do you think we should do?''

"Wait.''

"For what?''

"To see.''

"To see what?''

He walked to the door without answering. Then he stopped, turned around, and said to Gilonne and Michanteau, "Don't go out yet. Let me go and see.'' He motioned to Zoltan and Candelario, and the three of them left.

Did he want to see for himself how the lacemakers would behave, Gilonne wondered, before he decided what attitude should be taken toward them? Knowing he was with her, helping her, made her feel relieved. It must be reassuring, she thought, to have a man like that always beside you, ready to take over a large share of the everyday worries and difficulties.

He came back half an hour later, locked the door behind him, looked around for something, and seemed to have found it when he took Lady Bertrade's whip from where it hung on the wall. Then he left again, after telling those in the kitchen not to open the door for anyone. What had come over him? Was he going to whip the lacemakers?

They heard strange noises from outside: hoarse shouts, a pounding on the ground.

"Have they come to pillage the workshop?" murmured Gilonne. "Have they come for revenge?"

Dawn was breaking and, in spite of the mist, it was finally possible to see.

The lacemakers were probably still asleep, or drawing water from the well, or lighting their fires, because it wasn't they who had come, but a score of appallingly dirty and foul-smelling beggars covered with vermin.

Where had they come from? And who had brought them here?

Where they had come from was never known, but they had been brought by Mathilde the harlot, Bichon's mother, who saw them on the road and decided to use them as a means of getting even with the people at Grand-Coeur. She had said to them, "Let's go to the castle. There's food for you there, and a place to sleep." She had held the torch to show them the way, and now she was laughing wildly, dancing and singing. They were also laughing, and loudly demanding food and wine, for the love of God's poor. She had led them to the workshop, but since it had been locked, they all sat down under the leafless pear trees. Those majestic trees had surely never before seen such a squalid gathering.

When Pompinne, Gilonne, and Michanteau arrived, Mathilde was dancing with her bosom bare and her skirts tucked up in spite of the cold. And the beggars were all laughing and shouting for joy. It was a horrible sight. But not to Pompinne. When Candelario and Zoltan began trying to make the beggars stand up and leave, she stopped them. She talked to the beggars and told them they were going to eat and drink. Only after that would they leave. They shouted for joy even more loudly.

What had come over Pompinne, who was ordinarily so stingy.

"Have you lost your minds?" she said to Candelario and Zoltan. "Don't you know the risk we'd be taking if we tried to send away these people protected by God without first calming them down with hot porridge and cider?" After they had eaten and drunk their fill, they would be loaded into the hay cart and the little farmhand would take them several leagues away, where others could feed them. "And since we have musicians," she added, laughing, "Candelario and Zoltan will go with them part of the way and play for them."

The sun was up and the mist had cleared when the reeking, cackling horde was packed into the cart. Hélye had handed out a few sous, which had prompted Michanteau to say to Gilonne, "It's expensive for Monsieur Morel d'Arthus to come here! First cows, then alms . . . He must really like being at Grand-Coeur, to put up with these expenses! From now on, if anyone tells me that Protestants are rich misers, I'll say . . . What will I say?" She laughed and looked at Gilonne. "I'll say I know only one Protestant, but he's head over heels in love, so you can't use him as an example for judging Protestantism. Now, what answer are you going to give him?"

"First I'll ask my . . . I'll ask Chevalier de Ferrières what he thinks of the proposal."

"By God's splendor, as the saying goes, I have ideas but you have inspirations! Yes, go and talk to him, and maybe you'll solve all our problems at once!"

Neither Peter nor Bichon had known about the beggars' invasion of the gardens. Mathilde had stayed at Grand-Coeur, hiding behind a bush. She showed herself when the cart was out of sight. With a hard, fierce look in her eyes, she walked toward Gilonne, Michanteau, Pompinne, and Hélye, who was preparing his horse for departure.

"I want my daughter!" If she didn't get her, she said, she would go to the police. Actually, she had brought her horde of beggars only to intimidate the people at Grand-Coeur. Seeing that she had failed, she shrieked that she knew very well what had been done to her little girl with those good-for-nothing men staying there, and that old man who kept her in a cage.

Hélye nearly used the riding crop he was holding, but he restrained himself and asked, "How much?"

Mathilde's face lighted up briefly, long enough to show she was going to give in. Without even discussing the price of the child, Hélye tossed some coins on the ground in front of her mother, who immediately picked them up and hurried away.

"She'll be back for more money," said Michanteau. "If I'd been the one who paid her, I'd have asked for some kind of guarantee."

Later, when Hélye was gone and she and Gilonne were once more bent over their lace, Michanteau said thoughtfully, "There's a man who opens his purse as easily as we open our mouths. Think it over, my girl, think it over. You won't find men like that on every street corner in Alençon. You'd better not let him get away. . . . All right, just pretend I didn't say anything."

Gilonne wondered how she should dress for her visit to the chevalier: as a lacemaker, with a white apron and hat, or as a young lady of quality, in a silk dress, with matching ribbons in her hair. What kind of bastard daughter would that gentleman prefer to have, assuming he had ever thought about it? Would he even deign to look at her? She decided to dress as a lace-maker.

Until now, she had gone to the library only at night. She liked to imagine she saw Ogier reading there, perched at the top of his ladder. When she went into the big room that morning, after knocking on the door and hearing a curt "Come in," what she saw was the chevalier looking at her with both surprise and annoyance, such great annoyance that she felt a chill run up her spine.

"Would you have the time and kindness, sir, to talk with me for a few moments?"

Did he have the time, if not the kindness? He seemed to be questioning the mute battalions of books around him. Was he waiting for an answer from them, since he was taking so long to speak? He finally stood up and, still without a word, pointed to the stool that was the only seat in the room except for the armchair behind his table. They sat down together.

The silence continued, a silence that made her feel as if she were choking. Unthinkingly, she put her hand over her heart, where in her childhood she had carried the little piece of cloth stained with the blood of Jesus, and quickly drew it back as if she had burned it.

"Monsieur Morel d'Arthus, the lace manufacturer in Alençon," she succeeded in saying, "has done me the honor of asking me to marry him. Before . . . before giving him my answer, I'd like to know what you think, sir."

A raising of eyebrows. Great, intense astonishment. And still silence.

When would he speak. Probably never. She continued, perhaps with the help of Ogier, whom she glanced at up there on his ladder. "I must tell you, sir, that Hélye Morel d'Arthus is a Protestant. I know that the idea of a Protestant marrying into a Catholic family is . . . well, it may be intolerable to . . . to certain people, so I wanted to ask you what . . . what you think of Monsieur Morel d'Arthus."

Another silence. Inordinately long. Then: "Am I supposed to know him?"

The chevalier's voice was weary, overwhelmed by a vast weight of boredom and indifference.

"He spent an evening here! He had supper at your table!"

"Ah, yes . . . Now, what was it you wanted me to tell you?"

"What you think of Monsieur Morel d'Arthus, the lace manufacturer. If you don't mind telling me."

"He seemed tall to me. He's very tall, isn't he?"

"Yes, he's tall."

"He shouldn't be. He's a commoner, isn't he?"

"He is."

"One day when Monsieur Racine and I were together during a respite in the war, we studied His Majesty's French soldiers and discovered that only noblemen, who are well fed and have their limbs stretched by physical exercise, are tall. With a few exceptions: The sons of butchers and bakers, who never suffer from hunger, tend to be somewhat tall. But no one else. Therefore this lace manufacturer shouldn't be tall."

A ray of sunlight polished the spines of the books on the shelves and threw handfuls of sparks onto the gold letters of their titles.

Silence, to which that library was accustomed, had resumed its place. Gilonne broke it abruptly.

"You have nothing else to tell me?"

"What do you want me to tell you?"

"Whether you advise me to marry him, and if my . . . my family would be angry to have a Protestant become one of them."

"Then ask your family! For my part, I don't consider that I have any right to influence you. No, I see no reason why I should!"

She wondered if taking a blow like that had ever made a heart burst. Since she had to look somewhere, she raised her eyes to Ogier on his ladder. Then her face suddenly turned red and she said in a clear, loud voice, "You're tall, as a nobleman should be, according to you. But you're tall only on the outside. Inside you're a very small man. Goody-by, sir."

Later, it was hard for her to remember the end of that day. In despair, feeling as if her heart had been trampled, she walked straight ahead, without knowing where she was going. She probably went to Pervenchères and back. She remembered only stopping to take a pebble out of her shoe and saying to herself, "And besides everything else, he took me for a fool. Does he think I don't know who Jean Racine is, and what he writes, and that he cares only about the heart and the soul, and that people's emotions interest him much more than their height?"

When she got back to Grand-Coeur, she stopped for a moment in front of the stone escutcheon bearing the Ferrières coat of arms and the family motto "The heart can do anything." She felt that for the first time in her life she really understood what irony was, and that this was the best example of it she had ever encountered.

She saw Candelario and Zoltan about to get on their horses and asked them where they were going.

"The chevalier has suddenly decided we're going to Alençon immediately."

"Can you deliver a message there for me?"

They could. She asked them to wait a moment and came back with a piece of paper folded, sealed, and addressed to Monsieur Hélye Morel d'Arthus. It contained only the word "Yes" and her signature, Gilonne Perdriel.

She hurried into the house, intending to go to Lady Bertrade, but stopped when she remembered that she had gone hunting. With or without fog in her mind, Lady Bertrade would always go hunting. And anyway, Gilonne decided, there was no use making her sad. All she could do would be to sigh as she always did when someone talked to her about her son, or murmur, "Proud and haughty as a big stag. . . ." So Gilonne went to Peter instead.

She told him about her conversation with the chevalier and asked, "That was unjust, wasn't it?"

"Justice, my child, would be a simple matter if people were simple. I'm not the one who first said that, but it's true anyway. And it's even truer that the chevalier is a very complicated man!"

"He's mainly cruel, with a cruelty that comes from indifference."

"Cruelty and indifference are necessary conditions of all life. An innocent creature that never harmed anyone couldn't live."

"But I don't harm anyone, and I'm alive!"

"You're surely harming someone, without knowing it."

Irritated, she left him. He was aging rapidly. Or maybe his painting of springtime in Normandy had taken up all the room in his mind, turning it into a basket overflowing with apple blossoms.

That night, in the darkness of her room and the warmth of her bed, as she looked through the leafless branches waving outside the window and tried to see a faint glimmer of light in the black, stormy sky, she asked Michanteau for her opinion.

"If you don't marry that rich, handsome man," Michanteau replied, "you'll be the queen of fools. He must have barrels of money. . . . All right, we'll change what's in those barrels. We'll fill them with thread. Let's say he has all the thread we need—which comes to the same thing! I'm sure you can wrap any man around your little finger, but time is getting short. After what you said to your father, we'll probably have to leave."

"I don't have a father. And we can stay here a few more days. And I've already said yes to Monsieur Morel d'Arthus."

"You should have told me that from the start!"

The next day, Hélye rode to Grand-Coeur at a gallop.

When Gilonne heard him arrive, she put down the lace she was working on and ran out to meet him. The emotion that drove her toward him was chilled by the grave look in his eyes.

He dismounted and said, "The king has just forbidden marriages between Protestants and Catholics."

And even if Gilonne had had any thought of converting in order to marry him, she would have to give it up because Catholics were no longer allowed to become Protestants.

"What are we going to do?" she asked.

"I've come to tell you about the last possibility that's still open to us. Shall we take a walk while we discuss it?"

The possibility was a wedding in the chapel of the Dutch or the Swiss embassy in Paris, with a marriage contract signed in the presence of a foreign notary. France would probably never recognize such a marriage; but later, when the war of religion was over, they could be married again, this time in a way that *would* be recognized by France. Would she accept that solution?

She accepted it.

There was still a big difficulty that had to be resolved. No one here must know about their marriage, because they could be severely punished for it if it was discovered. They would have to keep it secret, which meant that officially they would have to live apart from each other. Would she accept that too?

She did, but wondered how it would be possible.

No need to worry; he had thought of everything. As far as the people of Alençon were concerned, she would become the mistress-lacemaker of the Morel d'Arthus establishment. That was still feasible: There was no edict explicitly stating that a Catholic couldn't manage a workshop belonging to a Protestant. So she would be his employee, and there was nothing to prevent her from living in the little wooden house at the far end of the park of the mansion. Since another mistress-lacemaker had lived in it ten years earlier, no one would be surprised to learn that Gilonne had moved into it with Michanteau, who would also be hired. It would be best to go to Paris as quickly as possible, before other complications arose.

They couldn't make the trip in his carriage: Traveling in it together would attract too much attention and might create problems. An overzealous policeman might ask questions and come to believe that a Protestant was eloping with a Catholic girl. Incidents of that kind had already been fomented by some of the king's representatives in the pay of Monsieur de Louvois, with the result that innocent Protestant travelers had been arrested and sent to prison. They would take a public coach, without seeming to be traveling together. Would Michanteau be willing to come with them? If she and Gilonne were questioned, they would say that they were going to visit lace merchants in Paris to try to get orders from them.

So as not to embarrass Gilonne, it was to Michanteau that Hélye gave a purse swollen with money. He asked her to see to it that his future wife lacked nothing during the journey, and not to hesitate to tell him if the sum he had given her proved to be

too small. Michanteau was also to pay her own expenses from
that money.

It was decided that the two young women would come to
Alençon in three days and that on the day after their arrival they
and Hélye would take the stagecoach to Paris.

Leaning back against her pillows with a glass of apple brandy
warming in her strong hands, Lady Bertrade had been listening
for some time. She had interrupted Gilonne only to say, ''Ah,
so it's that bourgeois you want to marry? Well, I must say he's
a handsome man.'' Then when she heard ''Monsieur Morel
d'Arthus went to Uncle Mathieu to ask permission to marry me,
since he doesn't know that . . . ,'' she had said, ''Yes, that's
true, he couldn't have done otherwise.''

Lady Bertrade admitted that she knew more about the ways
of the ancient Romans than she did about Protestantism. Living
in the isolation of her country home, she hadn't kept abreast of
the current religious conflicts. But she seemed to remember
hearing that Protestants didn't like the Virgin Mary. She decided
that her wedding present to Gilonne would be her most beautiful
possession: the marble statue of the Virgin, by Bernini, that her
father had brought her from a trip to Italy. She didn't want Gilonne to behave as she herself had done, always giving in to her
husband. Gilonne must say at the start, ''I worship the Virgin
Mary, and this statue of her is one of the most beautiful in the
world. It will stay in our bedroom.''

''Do you promise to tell him that?''

''Yes.''

''Good. And you'll be doing me a favor too. I've been wanting to get that statue out of here before Candelario could take it
off to Alençon, whistling with pleasure, to turn it into money.
You'll also take the furs Ogier gave me. In memory of him and
of me. I'll explain to him, since I'll go to heaven before you do,
that you had to look out for yourself while you waited to be with
him again. He'll understand. I'll also tell him that because of
your strange father, proud and haughty as a stag but mainly the
king of fools, you couldn't stay here. Do you want me to tell
him you'll never love anyone but him? Don't cry, my child, go
and be happy making beautiful lace with that proud bourgeois
who knows all about it, and put your mind at ease. And promise
me you won't feel sorry for me and imagine you're abandoning
me in my ruins. Bear in mind that I've been very unhappy lately,

worrying about your future and scolding myself for selfishly keeping you here. Your lace manufacturer is breaking a bond that we wouldn't have had the courage to break ourselves. But I wouldn't want you to leave here saddened by my son's attitude. He's not afraid of cannons on a battlefield but he's afraid of family responsibilities, and I think his greatest fear is of anything that might interfere with his freedom. I always say he's like a proud and haughty stag, but to be fair I should add that I myself am only a solitary wolf. It was an unlucky day for you when you came to Grand-Coeur.''

"Don't say that, Grandmother. It's not true.''

"Now I'm the one who's crying. . . . It's the first time you ever called me that . . . Do you know what I wish, Gilonne? I wish I'd known your mother. To have a child like you, she must have been a really exquisite young woman. I don't hold it against Him, but the Lord often botches things even worse than I do when I try to make lace. Let's hope He does better in heaven, but I especially hope He knew what He was doing when He put that bourgeois on your path, and that He gave him the qualities he'll need to make you happy.

"In a little while you'll help me to get up and we'll pray together one last time in front of my Virgin before you pack her up and take her away. But you'll come back, and bring your children with you. . . . Don't blush like that! You know your husband will give you children, don't you? Come to think of it, since you grew up without a mother, maybe I'll have to explain. . . . No? Good. I'll just say that if you're lucky it will be wonderful, and if you're not . . . it won't be. It's like lace: It can be the most sublime thing on earth, but it can also completely fail to come off. Do you know what I mean, more or less?''

"Yes, I do!''

"Well, at least I've made you laugh a little. But, beautiful as you are, you don't have to worry that it may fail to come off, even with a Protestant husband, because even animals . . . I'm sure I've never told you about the time I came across a wolf and his mate when they . . . Enough of this! I said we were going to pray together, and we'd better do it now!''

Lady Bertrade was the only one, besides Michanteau and the chevalier, who knew that Gilonne was going to contract a marriage forbidden by the king. Even Pompinne mustn't know it, much less the other servants. It was decided that a disagreement between father and daughter would be given as the reason for the young women's departure.

Pompinne wept and said she didn't understand how the chevalier could compose such beautiful songs if he didn't like to have children. And she was furious with Marie the Traveler, who had been sent on a long pilgrimage but hadn't earned her pay, because the chevalier still didn't see things any more clearly now than he did before.

"You'll be happier working in Alençon," she told Gilonne. "Not that I like Protestants, but you'll make good money working for this one because he's very openhanded."

Gilonne and Michanteau agreed to give half the contents of Hélye's purse to Pompinne, for the most urgent expenses at Grand-Coeur.

Candelario and Zoltan arrived just in time to help them into the cart that would take them to Alençon. Mathieu would bring it back later.

The two musician-servants didn't like the thought of their master's daughter going to work for a Protestant. They decided to watch over her, discreetly.

Peter and Bichon would stay at Grand-Coeur until spring came and was immortalized on a wall of the house. Then they would go to Alençon and work for Hélye, designing lace.

As she drove the cart, Gilonne added up everything they owed to Hélye's generosity.

"I don't know what we would have done without him!" said Michanteau, who had been mulling over the same thoughts. "He's a kind of angel sent to us by God. What's the difference if he's a Protestant angel or a Catholic angel? Do you know what I think? I think God Himself must not care whether angels or people are Protestant or Catholic."

"Unfortunately, the king *does* care!"

Since no prominent person entitled to priority had come to the stagecoach office with a letter from the Intendant of Alençon or the duchess's palace, as often happened, the driver chose Gilonne and Michanteau as the first two passengers to board the coach. A stately bourgeoise at least twice their age, with an impressive number of ribbons and bows all over her, grumbled that it would have been more courteous to let her get in before those girls. But the two men who, with Hélye, brought the num-

ber of passengers to six, seemed to approve of having beauty
pass before age.

It was such a cold day that Gilonne was buried under a big,
dark, hooded cape, but it was still impossible not to notice her
natural grace. A young gentleman, keenly regretting that he was
going only as far as Dreux, tried to decide how he would describe such perfection and was rather pleased with himself when
he thought of "luxuriant beauty combined with voluptuous dignity."

In spite of their foot warmers, Gilonne and Michanteau were
chilled to the bone. Huddled in her furs, from which some of
her bows emerged like multicolored flowers, the beribboned
lady sat as close to Hélye as she could. She knew who he was
from having often admired, and sometimes bought, the lace
produced in his establishment, and she was glad to be traveling
with him. She opened a silver flask she had been keeping in her
muff to protect it from the cold, poured some of the hot chocolate it contained into a goblet, drank it, and offered the rest to
Hélye. "It's delicious," she said, "and it's still hot."

He thanked her for her offer and said he had no doubt that the
chocolate was indeed exquisite, but suggested that she give it to
the two young ladies seated opposite them. With her expression
much less warm than her chocolate, she had no choice but to
hand the goblet first to one, then to the other. She saw that the
men in the carriage were enraptured as they watched Gilonne
push back her hood, hold out a lithe, slender hand, and put her
soft, full lips on the rim of the goblet. The beribboned lady
wasn't thickheaded: She knew when it was possible to compete
and when it wasn't. She put the stopper back in her flask, moved
away from Hélye a little, and decided to take a nap. Sleep would
refresh her complexion. Men really were fools. So much the
worse for them!

Gilonne watched her snuggle deeper into her furs and, having
known since Ogier's visit what beavers were like, she decided
that she looked like one of those plump little animals decorated
with green, yellow, and pink bows. Amusement sparkled in her
eyes, and when she looked at Hélye she saw that he too was
amused. There was something delectable about the complicity,
those secrets, even the jolting of the stagecoach.

She observed the two other men: an elegant, nonchalant blond
nobleman who wore a sword, and a timid young bourgeois who
had already become rotund. Sitting beside them made Hélye

look even better; his tall, well-built body, his distinction, and his frank, open face were enhanced by the comparison. But maybe he needed no comparison to be seen for what he was: "a fine-looking man," as Lady Bertrade had called him. He was dressed in brown velvet, as he had been the first time Gilonne saw him with Uncle Mathieu.

There was a restful feeling of security in telling herself she was going to marry someone who wasn't a stranger and was appreciated by everyone. This brought her back to thinking about her marriage, which she had forgotten a little since becoming absorbed in the novelty of traveling in a stagecoach. And traveling to Paris! She had made up her mind so quickly. . . . What would that life of concealment and pretense be like? Michanteau seemed to feel it would have a pleasantly exotic quality, but to Gilonne it was simply unfortunate, and she pitied Hélye for having to endure such suffering. Seeing him so dignified and serene, however, she recognized that he didn't appear to have been too greatly affected by it. What did he really think? She discreetly examined him again. As always, his austere clothes were unadorned by the slightest bit of lace. She remembered Madame La Perrière, dressed in either gray or brown, winter and summer; like Hélye, she had worn no frills except her large white collars and cuffs, impeccably neat and smooth. Madame La Perrière's clothes had reflected her honest, straightforward nature. The same must be true, thought Gilonne, of this man who was about to become her husband. She had a brief glimmer of hope.

Hélye kept his eyes on her with a steadiness that was beginning to trouble her. She dozed off for a time, and when she awoke she saw him still watching her attentively. She suddenly realized that he had a strange look in his eyes, a look full of tenderness that sometimes gave way to a kind of hardness. She couldn't explain that hardness but it was painful to her, like a burn.

The morning mist was finally rising, and they were all enveloped in the light veil cast over the countryside by the pale winter sun. Warm and snug in the wool cocoon of her big cape, Gilonne savored this moment of well-being; it was a treat for her body, which had grown so accustomed to the harsh discipline of daily toil. Her bliss was all the greater because she had laid her worries aside. She had made her decision: She would leave everything to Hélye. He now thought and acted for her.

She would give herself a reprieve for six days, and wouldn't take up the burden of her cares again until she came back from her adventure. Yes, it *was* an adventure, this trip to Paris for a secret wedding, so she would live it adventurously! She smiled under her hood, which she had pulled down over her face because the sun was shining in her eyes. Then she stretched out her legs and put her feet under the bench opposite her. She would never have enough of being able to stretch her arms and legs as much as she wanted.

They stopped at the hamlet of Rémalard to exchange their six tired horses for rested ones and take on two more passengers, two men of good appearance who politely introduced themselves to the other occupants of the coach. Actually, one of them did all the talking, and did it so rapidly that it took careful listening to understand everything he said. Though she missed a few words, Gilonne gathered that Monsieur Melchior de Pompignan was a learned man in search of "all curious and extraordinary things, natural or supernatural, that happen to have happened in the world." She wondered what he could have found in an out-of-the-way place like Rémalard. He was accompanied by his servant, a Dutch painter named Justus Stoffels, whose function was to draw "all curious and extraordinary things, natural or supernatural" that were worth the cost of paper and pencil. The master's body and face were round as an apple, and he had laughing blue eyes. The servant was sickly looking, and Gilonne decided it would probably be a long time before she could see his eyes because he kept them lowered, whereas Peter always said that a painter should never stop learning to look at what was around him—even death, when it came for him.

Melchior de Pompignan finally began to break through the reserve of his fellow passengers, who had left at three in the morning and were only now starting to collect their wits. The men introduced themselves; the women, as was customary, prudently remained nameless.

The blond, elegant young nobleman was from the vicinity of Le Mans, where he had a family estate that went back several centuries. The likable bourgeois, whose coat had difficulty staying buttoned over his paunch, was a baker on his way to Paris. His sister was going to be married there, to another baker. Hélye merely said that he lived in Alençon.

The cheerful Pompignan had been visiting a friend who had

a curious and extraordinary distinction: There were four ancient
Roman gold coins in his stomach. He had swallowed them one
winter evening, just at nightfall, when he was traveling to Rouen
and the stagecoach was attacked by bandits. Being an enthusiastic collector, he had been determined not to let those barbarians melt down his prized coins. Since then, he had tried several
treatments to get them back, without success. He had promised
to let Pompignan know as soon as they saw the light of day
again, so that he could have his servant draw a picture of them
and label it: "Born in 550 B.C. and imprisoned in a human
body from 1677 to 1680."

Pompignan went on talking, but Hélye was no longer listening. He had succeeded in striking up a conversation with the
painter, who proved to be a Protestant. Gilonne wondered if she
would be living only among Protestants from now on and decided that, if so, she could adjust to it. Madame La Perrière and
Jérémie had been the kind of friends who seemed to have been
sent by heaven, and it was now clear to her that she was going
to have a husband like them. She listened to Hélye describing
the portrait of his mother painted by Rembrant Van Rijn, saw
Justus Stoffel's gray eyes light up, and said to herself that this
poor man, who reminded her of Peter and seemed used to being
ignored, was now having a few moments of pleasure, thanks to
Hélye. Once again she saw her future husband's kindness and
felt proud of having been chosen by him. She decided she would
do everything she could to make him happy. She would be a
perfect mistress-lacemaker and manage his workshops with great
devotion. And she would do her best to love him and help him
if life became as difficult for him as he was afraid it would. But
she hoped he had been overly pessimistic because of his determination to be honest with her.

They reached the inn where they were to stay overnight. When
Gilonne had sat down at the table, Hélye took the chair on her
right and Michanteau the one on her left. They talked with each
other as if they were just becoming acquainted and amused
themselves by asking the questions usually asked in that situation. They enjoyed pretending to be strangers, and because of
that subterfuge they had the pleasure of learning a little more
about each other.

The two young women and the beribboned lady would all
sleep in the same bedroom. Hélye could have shared a beautiful
room on the second floor with Melchior de Pompignan, but

instead he chose an attic room where he and Justus Stoffels
would have straw mattresses. Pompignan, he whispered to Gilonne, probably dreamed of curious and extraordinary things
and talked about them in his sleep.

They all stretched out their aching bodies for a few hours and
then gathered again long before dawn, having been awakened
by a thunderous shout from the innkeeper: "It's time, travelers,
it's time!" The beribboned lady had snored, but that hadn't
bothered Gilonne and Michanteau. They had fallen asleep as
soon as their heads touched the oat-chaff pillows, which had a
good summery smell because fragrant dried flowers had been
mixed with the chaff.

The second day, colder than the first, was warmed by the
passengers' high spirits. The beribboned lady listened to Pompignan with flattering attention. Having conceived the hope of
making him see her generous curves, if not as curious, at least
as extraordinarily inviting, she encouraged him to keep going
through his stock of stories. The blond nobleman added his
encouragments to hers because he looked forward to making
his friends laugh in the castle where he was going to spend a
few days, and the baker did the same because he felt he would
have a certain success at his sister's wedding celebration when
he told about the prodigious things Pompignan claimed to have
seen.

They stopped for the night at Dreux. Supper in the inn was
quiet. Pompignan was evidently tired. Gilonne, however, was
in a joyous mood that owed a great deal to the Suresnes wine
that was served abundantly with the meal. Hélye smiled as he
looked at her.

They reached Versailles the next day. Gilonne and Michanteau stared in amazement at the park, the château, the orangery,
and the enormous iron fence that separated the king's palace
from a vast open space. Just think of living in a place like this!
But Hélye seemed indifferent and said nothing in response to
their admiring exclamations. Gilonne fell silent and leaned back
against the seat. The beribboned lady claimed she had once
witnessed the king's dinner. Michanteau, who was beginning to
suffer from having said hardly anything since waking up, asked
her if His Majesty had given her a cup of hot chocolate.

At the Paris gate they had to wait a long time while a finicky
official made customs examinations before they were finally able

to set off across the city. What a multitude of vehicles and riders! It was terrifying to have them rushing past, only a hair-breadth away. And the gathering darkness made it hard for Gilonne and Michanteau to see the splendors they had been dreaming of since leaving Alençon. At the coach house on the Rue Bétizy, Hélye rented a carriage to take them to their hotel and enable them to do their shopping the next day. In spite of the darkness, the beribboned lady saw what she called "the abduction."

"Those people didn't waste any time!" she said with a certain vulgarity that confirmed Melchior de Pompignan's opinion of her as a common woman of no interest to him. He walked away without a word.

The Hôtel de l'Isle de France, on the Rue Guénégaud, not far from the Dutch embassy, was not one of the biggest hotels in Paris; its beds were not covered with silk, and its dishes were not silver, as in a few famous inns, but it was quiet, with a clientele consisting mostly of Protestants and respectable bourgeois Catholics. There, Hélye had thought, Gilonne wouldn't be exposed to the unwelcome attentions of audacious travelers. He took a room for "his two nieces" and one for himself.

He gave them the name and address of a renowned dressmaker from whom they could buy the clothes they needed: Madame Bonnemain, at the sign of the hand and flowers, on the Rue des Fossés-Saint-Germain-l'Auxerrois. They couldn't miss the shop, he said, because the signs on that street were big and hung from supports that sometimes jutted out to the middle of the road. But he advised them to look down occasionally as they walked along, because if they kept looking up at the signs they might stumble into one of the holes in the street or step in a pile of filth.

They would have time to make themselves beautiful before meeting him at eleven o'clock the following night at the Dutch embassy. They wouldn't see him again until then because he had a great deal to do. He said he hoped everything would go well for them and that they would enjoy their outing, and he told them not to hesitate to ask the driver to show them as many beautiful things as possible. Then he wished them good night. Gilonne, who seemed very pale, gave him a trembling little smile that made him feel a pang in his heart. He would so much have preferred to stay with her, instead of abandoning her in that city and that hotel! He assured her once more that she had nothing to fear, and that tomorrow, in daylight, Paris would be glittering with countless wonders. He had no way of knowing what she was feeling. Paris didn't frighten her in the least, but she had just overheard part of a conversation between two travelers who had recently been in Canada and were talking about the Iroquois, the Hurons, and the banks of the Saint Lawrence. *Oh dear*, thought Michanteau, who had also heard them. *The last thing we need is for somebody to get Gilonne all upset!*

When she and Gilonne were finally alone, Michanteau turned to her friend with the expression of someone thinking, *Now we're going to have it out!* and said, "Listen to me. You're living in two dreams at once. In one of them, you're still pining away for a dark, handsome stranger who's dead, if not buried, a man you saw only once and might never have seen again, even if he'd come back to France. In the other, you're still hoping for a show of affection from a father who's never going to show any feeling at all for you. If you go on like this, you'll wake up someday and realize you've been chasing after shadows, but by then you may have lost the man who's offering you something solid to build your life on. Forget about your Ogier up there in heaven, where he's probably busy selling harps and trumpets to the angels. Forget about your musician-father's noble indifference. Let this prodigious fact sink into your mind: we're in Paris!"

"When you find out what it's like to be in love . . ."

"It's time I told you that you're not the only one who knows what it's like. I'm in love too, Gilonne. The man I love isn't a rich fur trader or lace manufacturer, but he's still kind and charming. No, I won't tell you who he is, because I don't think he's even close to noticing that I exist. But things are all settled in my heart, and they'll stay that way."

"You're dreaming too!"

"Yes, but I do it without hurting my chances, or anyone else's, of succeeding in life. I calmly dream of a love that will make me blissfully happy, but I know it may not happen anytime soon."

"I don't believe in calm dreams of love."

"You'll always be too emotional." Michanteau sighed. Her own dream was stinging her heart, and she wasn't far from understanding Gilonne. Her tone softened. "But I want you to know I often like your absences of reason, to talk like the lady with all the ribbons. When I'm tired from having my feet on the ground too long, I like you to help me fly. But not too high! When we were in Mistress Lescure's house you used to lie awake at night worrying that someone might kill the dog that brought food to the leper's ghost. Not long ago you took in Bichon as if we had bags of gold to hand out to all the beggars in the kingdom. And maybe tomorrow you'll say no to the man who's about to save us. I wouldn't put it past you.

"Sometimes I wonder if you haven't forgotten who we are. Living in a castle, even one that's about to fall down, may have made us lose sight of the fact that we're lacemakers. Yes, I know, we've been lucky enough to have good priests who taught us the little they knew, and we hobnob with people who know how to carry on an intelligent conversation, which makes us able to seem not too stupid when we talk. But that's all. Forget the shadow that's darkening your heart. Tomorrow you're marrying a man plenty of other women would be glad to marry. Even if you don't love him yet, you ought to have a fresh complexion for the wedding, so let's go to sleep."

The cries of the city drew them to their window at dawn. Gérasime would have been able to shovel for hours here! It had rained and the passersby were floundering in mud. At this early hour, there were many more water carriers, chimney sweeps, milk sellers, and servants than people of quality but they were *Parisians*! So, too, were even the dogs and cats.

The shop signs were swinging in a rather strong wind. Now and then some of them collided, making a noise like cymbals that drowned out the shouts from the street. Gilonne and Michanteau enjoyed the sights and sounds for a time; then they got ready to go out and see if the other streets were like this one. As she was arranging her hair, Gilonne repeated something she had said several times before: that she didn't like the idea of shopping with the money of a man who wasn't yet her husband. Michanteau again gave her the reply she had developed for that familiar refrain: "We're not doing it for ourselves, we're doing it for him, so he won't have to be ashamed of the way we look."

The driver was waiting for them, warmed by a morning brandy and smiling cheerily because Hélye had treated him with his usual generosity. They went to the Rue des Fossés-Saint-Germain-l'Auxerrois, seriously dirtied their shoes and the bottoms of their capes when they got out of the carriage and walked, but were soon standing in front of Madame Bonnemain's shop, looking up at her sign. It was a beautiful sign, showing a lace flounce and a hand holding violets, gillyflowers, lilies, and roses, so freshly painted that the flowers looked as if they had been picked that morning. Gilonne remarked on the contrast between the mud in the street and the brightly painted signs above it. Michanteau answered that she would just as soon do without the mud and lose the contrast, but she noted her friend's buoyant tone with satisfaction.

Gilonne wished Hélye would put a sign in front of his lace-making establishment in Alençon, but he had told her he didn't need one and had no desire to hear a piece of sheet metal creaking all night long. For the shop she had dreamed of opening before she went to Pervenchères she had planned to have a sign with a picture of an exquisite piece of lace on a red background singing in the wind night and day to remind her that the shop was hers. It hadn't happened, and there wasn't much chance that it ever would.

"My mistress isn't up yet!" a servant exclaimed when they pulled the cord of Madame Bonnemain's doorbell. "This is no time to come and wake people up! Where do you come from, girls?"

They went back to the carriage and the laughing driver. Embarrassed, they asked him to take them first to Notre-Dame, then to the shops of the Galerie du Palais. To simplify his route, he went to the Galerie du Palais first. They didn't dare to protest and, as a reward for their compliance, they had the elegant displays of luxurious merchandise all to themselves for quite a long time, because the shops had just opened.

At first they focused all their attention on the displays of lace, ignoring everything else. It seemed to them that the finest gallery in Paris was filled with nothing but lace. Great emotion tightened Gilonne's throat. Lace was the most beautiful thing in the world and she was a lacemaker! Even if she had to go on sticking her needle into the same hole day after day, even if she had to sit still for countless hours, she would never give up her trade, because it made her part of the great, sublime machine that used thousands of hands to produce those splendors.

With her hands trembling and her heart pounding, she forgot the patient work of so many years and looked intently at the lace spread out in front of her, showing no trace of the long suffering from which it had been born. She thanked God for letting her be what she was: an artisan and also an artist. Then, as she stood between the two rows of elegant shops draped in silk and velvet, she had a vision of the king's painters who had designed the patterns, the mistress-lacemakers directing the work, and the multitude of motionless heads leaning over diligent hands and pieces of lace. And the king passed by, bowed to them all with perfect courtesy and said, "Well done!"

With a big wrinkle in her forehead that proved the seriousness of what she was doing, Michanteau had walked along the gallery and evaluated the treasure it contained. The sixty or so shops exhibiting their fortunes there had something like two million livres' worth of *point de France*. It was enough to make your head spin. Michanteau kept hers under control, however, and said they would have to leave if they wanted to see Notre-Dame before visiting Madame Bonnemain.

As they were coming out of the gallery they saw a shop with a sign identifying it as Les Dentelles d'Or. Was that woman measuring Sedan lace the one who had persecuted poor Mistress Lescure? No matter; it was ancient history now, and they didn't have time to inquire.

The cathedral was undeniably beautiful. More beautiful than the one in Alençon? They weren't sure. It was bigger, of course. They entrusted their salvation to the Holy Virgin and made light for her with the flames of two candles of the whitest wax. They would even have paid for the gilded candles they saw at the foot of Mary's altar, but they assumed that luxury was reserved for people of quality and didn't believe themselves entitled to it. Candles matching the embroidery of the Virgin's veil! Who would have thought there could be such a thing? Refinements like that could probably be seen only in Paris.

Overwhelmed by the splendor of the cathedral, they plunged into prayer, then emerged from it abruptly, afraid they were going to be late.

As she was about to go through the door, Gilonne stopped and went back. Although it seemed wrong to burn a gilded candle for herself, she had decided that Count Ogier de Beaumesnil was surely entitled to make that luxurious offering. On his behalf, and for his salvation, she lit one of the candles and prayed for the peace of his soul. Glad of what she had done, she looked forward to telling Lady Bertrade about it. Her day was going better than she would have thought.

She and Michanteau ran to the stout driver, who laughed at seeing them in such a hurry and a little bewildered. A kindly,

placid man, he was glad to have this easy day's work of transporting two dazzled girls who didn't keep changing their minds
about where to go, and no outbursts of temper, and let him and
his horses make their way through the tangled Paris traffic as
they saw fit.

Madame Bonnemain was ready now, said the young, pert
servant, who was dressed like a lady of quality, at least by
Alençon standards.

"Ready" turned out to mean that Madame Bonnemain was
still at breakfast in an elegant canary-yellow silk dressing gown
with sky-blue ribbons, with hot chocolate, Gonesse rolls, and
Vanves butter in front of her. She proposed that the three of
them eat together while they discussed business. She was a
shrewd woman, and her customer's great beauty—she assumed
that Michanteau was Gilonne's maid—had prompted her to offer
a meal because she was sure it wouldn't be a wasted expense.
Gilonne and Michanteau accepted the invitation, noting that
ladies who liked chocolate also seemed to have an excessive
liking for ribbons.

Madame Bonnemain was asked to supply two dresses for a
simple wedding ceremony, something in excellent taste, but
without ostentation. And not too expensive. The dressmaker, a
still-beautiful brunette with lively and even piercing eyes, explained to the two innocents that she could sell them only dresses
already made, altered to fit them, because it was impossible to
make two dresses in one day. The price would be lower, and
there was no need to worry, because the dresses would be in
perfect condition.

First she took care of the "maid," choosing for her a dress
made of Avignon taffeta, a little thin, but in a lovely blue-mauve
color that was very becoming to Michanteau's golden complexion. The generous amount of cloth in the skirts made them puff
out markedly. A close-fitting bodice, open in front, revealed a
white muslin chemise trimmed with excellent Valenciennes lace.
A matching blue-mauve bow of ribbon, to be attached to the
hat, also went with the dress. There, it was perfect! It puffed
out where it was supposed to, and it was just the right length.
Not one stitch would have to be taken in it. Gilonne discovered
that Michanteau had a plump, attractive body that probably owed
some of its charm to Pompinne's porridge.

"Now all you have to do," Madame Bonnemain said to
Michanteau, "is to go a little way down this same street to my

friends Gaborry and Couteau, the shoemakers, at the sign of the golden shoe.''

Michanteau had the greedy look of a cat lapping up a cup of milk. She heaved heavy sighs that were a pleasure to hear. Gilonne, waiting for the dress that was being brought to her, said to herself that she owed her friend this moment of happiness.

Now two little girls, evidently apprentices, carried in a mountain of thick silk of the most sumptuous quality, from Monsieur Gautier, cloth merchant to His Majesty. Its color was such a pale pink that it sometimes appeared to be white. It was an ideal silk, a miraculous silk, to the touch as well as to the eye, looking as if it must have been spun and woven by fairies. The petticoat was placed over a kind of bustle made of stiffened cloth. The skirt was adorned with big bows of white ribbon, and so was the muslin bodice, which had a boat neckline and half-sleeves with ruffles and lace flounces.

In its simplicity, it was a dress worthy of a queen. But Gilonne wasn't enchanted by it to the point of losing her shrewdness. She went over to a window to examine the lace. It was good, honest *point de France*, made in Argentan, as was shown by the hexagonal bars. Madame Bonnemain now had no doubt about her customers' condition: they were lacemakers, but she didn't scorn ambitious young women if they could pay for what they wanted. She mentioned the price of the dress, but only after Gilonne had admired herself in the big mirror that took up the whole middle of the room. A hundred and twenty livres. Appalled, Gilonne took off the dress as if it had burned her. Wasn't there anything less expensive? Michanteau's dress cost twenty-two livres, and that was already enormous.

"I'm going to do something for you that I don't do often," said Madame Bonnemain, "because there are houses that specialize in it. I'm going to rent that dress to you for the night. You'll bring it back to me tomorrow morning. The rent will be ten livres, with a deposit of thirty."

It was exorbitant, thought Gilonne, but she had no hope of being able to get another dress in time. She accepted Madame Bonnemain's terms and left, taking the prodigious silk dress with her. Would she ever dare to tell Hélye what she had made him spend today?

When she and Michanteau stepped into the street, they found that the wind was blowing even harder. The signs were banging against one another with a deafening clatter, and hats were flying through the air. They ran to the carriage with their heads lowered. The old driver was asleep. They left their new dresses with him and went off to look for the shoemakers, Gaborry and Couteau, at the sign of the golden shoe. Shoved this way and that by gusts of wind, with their hair disheveled, they finally found the huge sign in the shape of a shoe. The wind was making it swing so violently that it seemed as if an invisible hand kept turning the shoe upside down to shake out pebbles that had fallen into it.

Because the shop was filled with customers, they weren't served immediately, and this gave them time to admire the elegant ladies crowded into the room. They finally decided on "Levant-style" red morocco shoes costing six livres.

When they left the shop, each with her first pair of luxurious shoes, it seemed to them that they had taken a giant step forward. No one in Alençon had "Levant-style" red morocco shoes. They had bought the same kind as a way of expressing their feeling that this was a great day in both their lives.

Suddenly they realized they had eaten nothing since the chocolate Madame Bonnemain had given them. They asked their driver to take them to a pastry shop. He told them they weren't far from the Lecoq sisters' shop on the Rue de l'Université, where Parisians all went to sweeten their palates, and that they would surely enjoy seeing its magnificent rooms.

Their enjoyment was short-lived. The shop was so crowded that they were barely able to get in. It was stylish to come there at that time of day and savor a tender brioche filled with delicately flavored fruit preserves, and servants fought with each other to make room for their masters. Gilonne and Michanteau were glad they were no longer wearing their new shoes, because people kept stepping on their old ones. They somehow managed to buy three brioches—one was for their driver—and hurried away, their heads full of the delectable fragrances that wafted from the shop.

The price of each brioche was exactly what a lacemaker was paid for two days of work! This realization brought a smile to their lips, but even they could not have said whether it was a smile of sadness or amusement. They then agreed that the preserves in the brioches were made of mandarin oranges, from China, the most expensive fruit in the kingdom, and flavored with costly spices. They could easily imagine themselves in one of those Eastern countries Peter had told them about, where the pasha's hundred wives spent their time lying under golden veils and ate only pistachio nuts and rose petals. And so, said Gilonne, for their twelve sous they had seen the best pastry shop in Paris, enjoyed a heavenly delicacy, and made a trip to the Orient. It was well worth the price.

She was amazed to realize that during the day she had often forgotten that she was going to be married that evening.

Four

THE SNOW HADN'T STOPPED FALLING SINCE THEY LEFT THE
Dutch embassy, toward the middle of the night, and it became
even heavier as they drove out of Paris. The sound of the iron-
rimmed wheels and the horses' hooves was so muffled that they
could easily have believed they were not on the road back to
Alençon but traveling through some mysterious land of silence
and peace.

Gilonne liked the feeling of being protected from the elements by the big stagecoach and Hélye's presence. He had put
his arm around her shoulders, and her head was now resting on
the velvet of his coat. His clothes were discreetly scented with
iris. Had little bags of it been put inside the lining of his coat?
At this thought, she smiled in the darkness. Hélye never wore
any lace, but he let his tailor scent his clothes, or maybe even
ordered him to do it. In any case, the result was pleasant. It was
good to lean against a solid chest that hid its strength beneath
scented velvet. Her husband's chest . . . She could hardly believe it. Their wedding had been so different from any she had
ever seen or imagined.

The ruddy-faced old driver had taken Gilonne and Michanteau to the Dutch embassy on the Rue de Tournon a little before
eleven o'clock, and servants had led them to the room where

Hélye was waiting for them. He was very handsome in a dark-blue coat covered with embroidery of the same color as the cloth, which was a supreme refinement because it was scarcely visible. No lace or ribbons, of course, but he wore a collar of the finest muslin.

A servant took the young ladies' cloaks. And Gilonne stood in the middle of the luxurious room, under the countless candles of the chandeliers, in the pale pink dress that, said Hélye, made her look like a marvelous flower straight out of a fairy tale. Seeing her blushing beneath his ardent gaze and too nervous to speak, he created a diversion by opening a red leather jewel case, taking out a necklace of big pearls whose rosy luster nearly matched her skin, and putting it around her neck. Then he gave her a rose from a vase standing on a table and told her that he wanted her to have one like it each day of their life together from now on, even if he had to go to the ends of the earth to get it.

"The necklace is for the bride," he said, "and the flower is for the little girl who told me the secret of the roses."

Grave, dignified noblemen treated Gilonne and Hélye with great consideration. It seemed that the Morel d'Arthus were well known and appreciated here. The marriage contract was signed before a Dutch notary, then the wedding ceremony was performed by a Dutch Protestant minister. Afterward, they all went to the private apartment of the ambassador's wife, where refreshments were served.

When they were back in their hotel room, Michanteau, who hadn't said more than a dozen words and scarcely dared to eat and drink, told Gilonne she wouldn't forget that ceremony if she lived to be a hundred.

"I don't know how you kept from being paralyzed by all those aristocrats," she said. "I'm not afraid of lightning, but I feel like crawling into a hole whenever I have to talk to them. You know why you're so good at curtsying, smiling, and talking the way you're supposed to with them? It's because you have noble blood. It always shows, no matter what people say. I'd have given anything to have the chevalier there, so he could see how you looked and acted, and how they all kissed your hand and bowed to you. And now I can die happy. I've seen my sister's coronation! It actually made me cry. I'd always heard about tears of joy, and now I know there really is such a thing! And to think you might not have married that man! I have to admit he intimidates me, and he usually seems very serious, but he does such nice things!''

Once again she admired the present that Hélye had given her when they went back to their carriage: a little pair of scissors with decorative engraving, fastened to a long gold chain. ''In memory of this evening,'' he had said.

It was still snowing, but the darkness inside the stagecoach was becoming a little less dense as dawn approached. Hélye withdrew his arm slowly and regretfully from Gilonne's shoulders, even though the two other passengers who had left with them—an old bourgeois couple—were still asleep. But Hélye was probably right to be cautious. Feeling him take his arm away reminded Gilonne that they would have to keep their marriage a secret, and for the first time she thought she might suffer from it. Was she already attached to him? She told herself she had mainly wanted protection. She would have it, despite the secrecy of their marriage, but that didn't satisfy her. She felt a regret that she couldn't explain and attributed her melancholy to having realized how hard it was going to be to deceive everyone in Alençon. So that she could keep the divine pink dress, Hélye had given money to one of the embassy clerks and told him to go and pay for it today, but she would never wear it again, or her pearl necklace either. Was that what was making her sad? She glanced at Hélye and saw that his face was impassive. Could she have only dreamed that he had kept his arm around her shoulders for more than an hour?

Versailles appeared through the curtain of snow, looking like a fairy palace. They changed horses.

Unfortunately, a draper from Alençon boarded the stagecoach. Gilonne had seen him before but didn't know his name; he, however, looked at her as if he knew exactly who she was. He didn't seem to appreciate Hélye's presence, but he was still courteous. He said he had just completed some business transactions at court. He had caught a glimpse of the king, who appeared to be in excellent health. Having had the good fortune to be standing in the hall when she passed on her way to visit the queen, he had also seen the dauphin's wife close up, and she was even uglier than she was said to be.

For Gilonne, the pleasure of the trip had ended. The draper was one of the people with whom she would have to keep up a pretense in Alençon. And for the moment it was urgent to mislead him somehow so that later he wouldn't see Gilonne and Michanteau working as mistress-lacemakers for the Morel d'Arthus and remember that he had seen them traveling with their employer.

Anxiously, Gilonne wondered what Hélye was going to do. Taking his cue from the draper, he too began to talk respectfully about the royal family, and then he asked about the fashion of wearing lace at court. It was at its height, said the draper. He had taken a large amount of high-quality merchandise with him, but it hadn't been enough to satisfy all those ladies. A little superciliously, he predicted that *point de France* would become increasingly popular. Hélye agreed, saying that his workshops were hardly able to fill the orders he received, and that he needed more workers. This provided him with an easy transition for saying how glad he was that he had happened to meet these two young ladies in the stagecoach, because he hoped he could persuade them to manage two of his workshops.

Gilonne and Michanteau now entered the conversation with the deference that was proper in the presence of two such eminent men. They said they were returning to Alençon after making a delivery to a Paris shop, and gave a few details. They had received many offers of employment in Paris but had rejected them because the city didn't really suit them, beautiful though it was, and they were now happy to be on their way back to Alençon. They said little about Monsieur Morel d'Arthus' offer, leaving the draper to understand that they had a number of similar offers under consideration, and that while this one was worth thinking over, they hadn't yet decided to accept it.

The draper seemed to swallow all this quite well. Then, sounding as though he were about to die of despair, he told Gilonne he was sorry he himself didn't have a lacemaking shop for which he could hire such a beautiful mistress-lacemaker. From then on, she felt as if the coach were carrying a load of gunpowder. She inwardly vowed that if she got out of this situation unscathed, if Hélye restrained himself, and if Michanteau kept her foot out of her mouth, she would make a novena when she was safely back in Alençon.

With a diplomacy that Michanteau admired, Gilonne kept the draper at a distance without offending him, and did it in such a way that Hélye wasn't angered by his attentions to her. That evening at the Dreux relay station, she went straight up to her room without eating, not having the courage to confront her adversary during the time it would take for supper in the inn. She saw that Hélye was grateful to her for her decision. Would they have a little time alone to say a few words to each other?

They had none. The draper's sharp eyes stayed on them, said Michanteau, ''like ticks on a dog's skin.'' And Hélye had to share a room with him.

The second day of the trip went by drearily for Gilonne, in an atmosphere of tension. She and Michanteau had decided to curl up in their cloaks with their hoods pulled down over their faces. They gave the strong impression that they were indisposed, sleepy, and not at all in the mood for talking. Hélye also remained silent.

Late in the afternoon of the third day, Gilonne was vastly relieved to see the ramparts of Alençon. When the coach stopped in front of the Sagory Gate, her red morocco shoes twitched impatiently. It took so long to get back into her town! Thick walls, towers, gates—what was the use of all those defenses? Who was going to attack Alençon nowadays? Finally the soldiers and customs officials finished their formalities, the driver climbed back onto his seat, and everything was closed in a din of creaking hinges and long wooden bars being dropped into place. The bells of Notre-Dame had just rung for the evening Angelus and the closing of the town.

Gilonne's happiness was suddenly dimmed by the thought that her trouble with the draper was only a foretaste of what lay ahead: From now on she would have to deceive and defend herself against a whole society. She shivered, and the obliging draper offered to go and ask the soldiers in one of the towers for some glowing embers to put in her foot warmer. He would have time to do it, he assured her, before the coach set off again. She declined his offer politely, saying it would be useless to bring fresh embers when she would be in the coach for only a few more minutes. She saw Hélye turn pale with fury and prayed that he would be able to control himself until they reached the inn where they would leave the coach.

It had been decided that Hélye would go back to his house alone. He couldn't even take Gilonne and Michanteau to Mathieu's house, where they would spend the night, because it might cause gossip. The next day they would officially present themselves at the Morel d'Arthus establishment and take over their positions as mistress-lacemakers. Gilonne would be in charge of the shop with the youngest workers, who, now that

Protestants were forbidden to have apprentices, were all at least fourteen and already knew their trade. Michanteau would be in the outlining room, where she would take patterns printed on the press in the basement and have them pricked and outlined by the thirty young men and women under her direction. Gilonne would be replacing a mistress-lacemaker who had gone to Switzerland three months earlier with her husband, a Protestant surgeon no longer allowed to practice his profession in France. Michanteau would take the place of a young man who, having refused to bow to the Blessed Sacrament as it was being taken through the town, had been arrested and sent to prison. "With my simple mind," she had remarked, "I can't understand why some Christians persecute others."

When the stagecoach had stopped at the inn, the draper kept looking at Gilonne as he gathered his baggage, and so she and Hélye couldn't put any warmth into the farewell looks they gave each other.

Hélye watched her walk away with Michanteau. The snow had stopped, but the wind was cold and gusty. They bowed their heads to protect their faces from it.

"There goes the most beautiful woman I've ever seen," the draper said to Hélye.

Hélye made no reply, but his expression was as icy as the wind.

The Rue aux Sieurs still had its harsh, sour odor, but the old tanner was no longer there. He had been replaced by his son, a perfect imitation of him. The staircase still smelled of turnip soup, and Mathieu's key was still in the hollow wooden angel.

This was the first time Michanteau had been in Mathieu's room. She expressed admiration for its neatness and cleanliness, and the secret closet for hiding lace, with a timidity that was highly unusual for her, except in Hélye's presence. This made Gilonne suspicious. Was Mathieu the man her friend loved?

"Yes, he's the one," Michanteau admitted when Gilonne questioned her. "He's handsome, brave, hardworking, obliging, and such a decent, honest man! And have you noticed that he has every single one of his beautiful teeth? They're almost as white as Monsieur Morel d'Arthus' teeth! Candelario says he looks a lot like your mother." She suddenly sobbed and said that Mathieu had never really noticed she existed. "He sees me, of course, but without seeing me! I'm your friend, and as far as he's concerned that's all I am.''

What could Gilonne answer? As far as she knew, Mathieu had had only a few passing love affairs. He talked of getting married someday, but always seemed to put it off into the in-definite future. She would have to ask Hélye what they could do to find out more about Mathieu's intentions.

Michanteau consoled herself by continuing to explore the home of the man she loved. Gilonne reflected that from now on, no matter what happened, she would want to talk it over with Hélye and ask for his advice. Was that how a woman began to love her husband?

They ate shriveled apples, drank curdled milk and went to bed, each thinking her own thoughts about love.

By the time she was ready to fall asleep, Michanteau had returned to practical reality enough to realize that they had now gone ten days without touching a needle. Would they still know how to make lace?

The mattress was filled with fresh straw, but the pillows smelled of dried flowers, mostly violets and roses. In the past, thought Gilonne, Mathieu hadn't gone in for such refinements. Was a woman taking care of his home? She fell asleep worrying about Michanteau's future, which kept her from thinking too much about her own.

In the Morel d'Arthus establishment, as in all the other lace-making shops in Alençon, work began at four o'clock in sum-mer and five in winter. Afraid of being late, Gilonne and Michanteau had arrived early. It was so cold that they preferred to walk up and down the street, rather than waiting in front of the door until it was opened. They had discussed whether or not they should wear their red morocco shoes in such weather and had finally decided that mistress-lacemakers simply couldn't wear the ugly wooden-soled shoes they had always worn before their trip to Paris. Freezing in their cloaks, they looked down at their pretty red feet briskly stepping along and hoped that the snow wouldn't ruin the leather.

They saw more than two hundred women arrive. They had emerged from that herd by working hard every day of their lives, but also because God had helped them more than most of the others. Now they had to show that they were worthy of the talent they had been given, and pass on their knowledge to others. The long thread of solidarity must never be broken.

When the door was opened, they went in with firm steps. And the soft squeaking of their beautiful red shoes, which hadn't been seriously damaged by the snow, was the most delightful sound they could imagine.

Orders had been given concerning them. Michanteau was asked to go to a first-floor room on her left. Since Gilonne wasn't going to take charge of her workshop until the next day, she was guided upstairs by a servant wearing white stockings and a dark suit with an immaculate lace collar, which seemed to be the livery of the male servants in the Morel d'Arthus house.

Hélye and his father, known as Monsieur Mortimer, were waiting in the big room with tapestries whose greenery had looked like a forest to Gilonne during her first visit when she was five. Hélye was standing in front of a window. When she came in, he turned around, hurried toward her, took her by the hand, and led her to his father.

"Father, this is my wife."

The sentence was short, but there was love in his voice. And the hand that held hers communicated strength and courage.

"Come and kiss me, my child," said the old man, "and please excuse me for not standing up. I can scarcely walk these days, and my poor health is made even worse by the tragic times in which we're living. But I'm sure your pretty face and your smile will do me more good than the bitter medicine my apothecary gives me. I want you to know that I remember you very well. It seems like only yesterday when you took it into your head to eat a foxglove flower and throw your family into a panic. But luckily I had some coffee in the house: it's good for the heart, and it saved yours. . . . I didn't know then, of course, that it had to be saved so you could give it to my son."

Gilonne was able to find the right words to answer the old gentleman. And, with the spontaneous warmth that was one of her greatest charms, she took his hand and kissed it.

By a tacit agreement, they avoided talking about religion and took up the practical problems that would have to be solved.

"If these weren't such tragic times," Monsieur Mortimer said with a bitter smile, "I'd say that your marital situation was amusing and could be the subject of an operetta. But unfortunately these are *very* tragic times."

From sorrow, fatigue, or anxiety—or, most likely, from all

of them at once—he suddenly turned even paler than he had been already. His face sagged, and for several moments he seemed unable to breathe. Evidently used to seeing these symptoms, Hélye calmly poured a few drops of a potion into a glass of water that stood on a silver tray on the desk. When his father had drunk it, he remained as pale as ever, but his face gradually became firmer.

"You ought to leave the country," said Hélye. "There's still time."

The old man shook his head.

"I've been trying to persuade my father to join my brothers in Switzerland or Holland," Hélye explained to Gilonne. "He needs peace and quiet. But he won't listen to me."

"I was born in this house, in this town, in this kingdom, and I'll die here. This is where God will come for me. There's nothing more to be said. And besides, I'm feeling better now. Sit down, my child, in that chair. Hélye, you can call them now."

Hélye picked up a little gilded bell—or was it solid gold?— from the desk and rang it. Two servants appeared so quickly that it seemed they must have been waiting just outside the door.

They bowed to Gilonne with a deference that reminded her of the way she had been treated in the Dutch embassy. One of them was a middle-aged woman, the other a boy. It was easy to see they were related. The mother had a hard, stern face that showed what her son's would be when his pink, smooth cheeks had become gray and wrinkled like hers.

"This is Judith and Zacharie. She's our housekeeper and he's in my son's service. This, my friends, is your new young mistress. You already know that you mustn't tell anyone she's married to my son. To justify her presence here, she'll be in charge of one of the workshops, and she'll live in the little house at the back of the garden. If the secret becomes known, all our lives will be in danger. I know I can count on you, so I won't ask you to swear not to say anything. But be careful about gossip. Can we trust everyone here?"

Judith said that no one would take the liberty of asking a question, or even thinking about asking one. Only she and her son would know, and they would say nothing even if they were threatened with being burned at the stake. She asked if the young woman who had just gone to work in the outlining room also knew. On hearing that she did, Judith tightened her thin lips. Monsieur Mortimer hastened to reassure her: the young woman was his daughter-in-law's childhood friend, almost her sister, and could be trusted completely.

Obviously making an effort to dare to speak in front of his mother, Zacharie said that for several days two policemen had been prowling around the house and had even come into the salesroom, claiming to be interested in buying some lace. Hélye said he knew about it and was keeping his eyes open.

"Is Madame's little house ready, Judith?" asked Monsieur Mortimer.

It was so ready that the question seemed offensive to her. She answered testily that she always carried out the orders she was given. She restrained herself from adding, "even those I don't like."

Monsieur Mortimer seemed unaffected by her attitude.

"Very well," he said, "You may go now."

Judith and Zacharie bowed and left.

"She brought up Hélye and she runs the household as she sees fit," Monsieur Mortimer told Gilonne. "She and her son would die for us, though that's something we don't expect of them. If it becomes known that we violated an edict by bringing a Catholic into our family, we alone will be held accountable. They'll only have to say they knew nothing about it, and they'll be left alone."

This conversation seemed to have drained his strength, and he asked Hélye to help him stand up.

"I don't know when we'll be able to see each other again without attracting the attention of the servants or the workers," he said to Gilonne. "Judith is an optimist: Not everyone here is as trustworthy as she thinks. I didn't want to argue with her. And she didn't choose to tell me that one of our clerks has converted to Catholicism; she must think I don't know about it. We all try to spare each other. Actually, I can sense what I don't know, or what's being hidden from me. Take that clerk—his name is Denis Fauquet—for example: I could tell he was going to convert before he did it. Our worst enemies are freshly converted Catholics who want to show their zeal by denouncing us. You'll have to be careful of that man, my child. And warn your friend about him.

"So, as I was saying, we won't see each other often. I'll regret it, because your lovely face makes me feel better. The presence of a pretty girl has always done me good. I must confess that when I was a young man my father whipped me once a week to calm my blood. Yes, it's true! Will you be afraid of me? No? Alas, I'm now a man in name only. Good-by, my child. Stay as beautiful as you are, and come to give me one of your smiles whenever it's possible.

"Ah, I was about to forget! Hélye, give me the box. Here, Gilonne, this is in memory of my wife, who would have loved you. She accepted only six pieces of jewelry from me, one for the birth of each of our children. She told me to give them to my daughters-in-law, if I lived long enough. This ring is yours. Its emerald setting suits you well: It's a deep green with intense blue glints, almost as beautiful as your eyes. Unfortunately you'll be able to wear it only in the privacy of your home. But maybe someday—a day I probably won't live to see—you'll wear it openly, in public, and that will be a sign that the king has stopped persecuting us and God has decided to put an end to our suffering."

Gilonne didn't know the value of the gift, but she was deeply moved at being treated as if she were the well-born Protestant daughter-in-law the old gentleman must have wanted. She had been right to think that the Morel d'Arthus were like Jérémie and Madame La Perrière.

Hélye slipped the ring onto her finger and kept her hand in his.

"Don't lose that ring, my child," said Monsieur Mortimer. "It's very valuable. One of my cousins is a dealer in precious stones, and he's always sold me very good ones. Are you thinking that I'm showing my true colors as a merchant? Well, it's true: I'm a merchant and I'm proud of it. Only a fool is ashamed of his occupation. Isn't that right, Hélye?"

Hélye bowed, smiling.

"Listen to me," his father went on, still speaking to Gilonne, "because there's hope in what I'm going to say. Many of us Protestants are rich. The king needs our money, and respects it. It's our sword, our weapon of self-defense. If he could disarm us, take our money once and for all, and kill us afterward, he might have done it long ago. But he can take our wealth only as we produce it, and we can produce it only in freedom. Do you see the point I'm making? We're the goose that lays the golden eggs, and that's our safeguard, the last one. It may make the king reluctant to take extreme action. We're going to suffer still more, but I don't think we'll die. Not all of us."

"Father, you're getting tired," said Hélye.

"I have only a few more words to say. But I'd enjoy talking a long time, because my new daughter-in-law knows how to listen. That's very good, Gilonne. Men have such a need to talk. . . . Here's the last thing I wanted to say. The Roman Catholic Church gives money to the king, and he needs a great deal of it. Will the Church give him even more and insist that in return he must crush what it calls heresy? Or will it stop giving and let Protestant bankers fill the royal coffers? That's the crucial question. I'm waiting for the answer. Good night, my child. Hélye, call Isaac and have him help me to my room."

A short time later, Gilonne and Hélye were alone together for the first time since their wedding.

"Come," he said, taking her hand.

They went through drawing rooms, galleries, and bedrooms. Finally, by way of a secret door at the back of a closet, they came into a little room she remembered clearly: it was the one where, long ago, he had shown her the two wickerwork ladies wearing beautiful lace dresses. The mannequins were no longer there.

"This is where I wanted to give you my first kiss," he said.

After leaving the secret room, they went to settle Gilonne into the little house at the back of the garden.

It was a wooden summer house. The Morel d'Arthus children had played in it while their nurses made lace and kept an eye on them. It had originally contained two big playrooms (one for girls, the other for boys), three bedrooms for naps, and a small dining room for afternoon snacks. Later it had been made into the home of an elderly cousin who had lost all her wealth, and still later it had been occupied by a mistress-lacemaker with no relatives in Alençon. In preparation for Gilonne's arrival, Hélye had had it completely renovated. The girls' playroom had been turned into a sumptuous bedroom with hangings of peach-colored velvet on the walls. There was little furniture, but it was beautiful: a canopied bed and two armchairs upholstered in the same cloth that formed the hangings, and a dressing table with a lace cover. On the lace was a gilded silver dressing case and a little red china vase with a rose in it.

"That's today's rose," said Hélye.

There was only one painting: the family portrait by Philippe de Champaigne.

"It's the painting I love most," he said, "so I've given it to you."

"Won't you miss it?"

"I'll come to see it often."

Did he mean he would spend his nights there? She didn't dare to ask him, but she wondered what answer she would have preferred to hear. Troubled, she began examining the painting and asked, "What kind of a child were you? You look like such a good little boy in the picture!"

"My brothers and I were three little bandits! Philippe de Champaigne deserves great credit: It must have been hard on his nerves to make us look as saintly as we do there. My brother Samuel, the one who's now a banker, was already finding ways to separate Mortimer and me from our money, and we got even with him by pricking him with a pin when the artist asked him to stay still while he painted him."

Gilonne enthusiastically praised the way the little kitchen had been arranged. It had a fireplace of the kind called German, with a raised hearth that made it possible to cook without bending over. And, wonder of wonders, there was a well in one corner of the room. Imagine drawing water without having to go outside! She was amused and delighted by these innovations.

Hélye laughed and said he had been a fool: He wouldn't have had to endure three sleepless nights while he was waiting for her answer to his proposal if he had only thought to tell her he could give her a house with all the latest conveniences.

Beneath his passionate gaze, she had the intoxicating feeling of being desired and respected at the same time. So it was possible to keep a place in her heart for a handsome adventurer without having to give up the pleasure of living with a man who loved her. Maybe things weren't as difficult as she too often believed.

Hélye went off to attend to his business, and Gilonne was beginning to put away her few belongings, which one of the clerks had brought from Mathieu's house in a cart, when Judith came in carrying a tray covered with a white cloth.

"I thought you might not have had anything to eat this morning, madame, so I've brought you some food."

If Michanteau had been there, she would have been sure to say, "She's come to have a closer look at you because she's dying of curiosity!"

But if that was true, Judith showed no sign of it. She prepared the small table that had formerly been used for the children's afternoon snacks, and stood waiting for Gilonne to sit down on the chair she had pulled out for her.

"Will you have wine or cider, madame? Monsieur has had you supplied with both."

Was she going to stay there?

She stayed, standing erect in her black dress, whose cloth was as stiff as she was. Gilonne ate her light, tasty meal in silence. Judith cleared the table and went away without having said a word that wasn't related to serving the meal. But Gilonne knew she had examined her from head to toe and watched her every move. She had also wanted to show what her behavior toward "the papist" would be: perfect service and reserved silence. And perhaps a little intimidation, too, to make it clear that she knew where the new Madame Morel d'Arthus came from: she was the niece of Mathieu the packman, who, though he was well known and appreciated by the Morel d'Arthus, was still a kind of servant.

Zacharie, who brought wood for the fireplaces, was more talkative than his mother. Away from her, he was good-humored and even cheerful. He laughed like the boy he was: he couldn't have been more than fifteen, thought Gilonne. His older brother, now in the king's army, had converted to Catholicism, and his mother had said she would never see him again. His sister was married to a merchant in Poitiers. She had met him at the Gournay fair and he had taken her away, along with the lace he had bought there. The king's dragoons had put her through some terrible times, and she had seen so much torture and killing that she sometimes seemed not to be in her right mind. Zacharie sighed and concluded that she should never have left Alençon. Here, Protestants were closely watched and punished for the slightest little misstep, but there were no dragoons. *Not yet,* thought Gilonne. She shivered and stepped closer to the big fire that in some places gave a raspberry tint to the peach-colored walls of her bedroom.

Zacharie also talked about the house and the lacemaking establishment. Since the Morel d'Arthus, father and son, wanted to live on a modest scale, there were only nine servants. The others were Eslue, the cook, who was as prickly as a hedgehog; her helpers, the twins Marie and Magdelaine, who weren't exactly overjoyed all the time; Isaac, Monsieur Mortimer's valet; Titus, the gatekeeper; Mardochée, a big footman who seemed to think he was a great lord—one day he had seen the king at Versailles, and since then he had been saying he walked like His Majesty, which made the other servants laugh, even on days when they didn't feel like it; and finally there was Jacob, the coachman, a fat man who was a little too fond of wine. Eslue had to hide it from him, and she made him kneel in the kitchen and read psalms before she would give him his food and his glass of cider. Only one glass. He did it because he was more afraid of her than of the police.

The lacemaking establishment employed two hundred and fifty workers, not counting the twenty clerks. This made it the biggest one in Alençon, Zacharie said proudly. And the press for printing patterns, installed in the basement, was the most modern one in the kingdom. The other great lace manufacturers—the Marescots, the Taunays, the Plessis d'Ocagnes—didn't yet have one like it! To bring it from Paris, sturdy Percheron horses had to be used and the shafts of the wagon had to be strengthened. Jacob would tell about that trip until the day he died. While he was on the road, he must have drunk a whole barrel of the Loire wine he liked so much. He had come into the house singing and dancing. Eslue had put his head in a bucket of water and refused to give him his glass of cider for three days. She had even made him read psalms, on his knees, while the others ate their soup. He had then scraped the bottom of the pot, looking sheepish. To Eslue's credit, it had to be said that she never complained about Jacob to the masters, and never even mentioned his drinking to them.

But Zacharie is telling me all about it, thought Gilonne. She didn't know if he was doing it as a sign of friendly complicity or as a way of showing her that he considered her to be a person of low rank.

When Michanteau joined Gilonne in the little house at the end of her day's work, she was bubbling over with happiness. Everything was so unbelievably convenient here! And so clean and orderly that Mistress Lescure would be dumbfounded if she saw it. There was a long room where the workers washed their hands: it had soap, white towels, ten washstands with tin basins, and a boy who did nothing all day but keep it supplied with clean water and towels. Another boy spent his time putting hot embers in the foot warmers. Any worker with an aching back could ask for a feather pillow! It was unheard of! The workers

sang only psalms, of course, and that wasn't very cheery, but it
wasn't too hard to listen to either. Each woman wore a big white
apron supplied by the establishment, and the inspector made her
change it when it was no longer clean enough. The Morel d'Arthus must really be rich to afford that luxury! The women were
good lacemakers, but Gilonne and Michanteau had nothing to
worry about, because they knew more than any of the others. It
was good to know that Monsieur Hélye and Monsieur Mortimer
(that was what the workers called them) would lose nothing by
having hired them. Or at least having hired them in a certain
way, added Michanteau, who was so excited by her first day that
for a time she had lost sight of her friend's situation.

For dinner they had porridge that they cooked in the convenient German fireplace. It was wheat porridge: the food stored
in the pantry included no rye or buckwheat.

"More luxury!" said Michanteau, and she then began describing the workers' kitchen. "Imagine a little room with a big
raised fireplace, like this one, and the biggest pot anyone has
ever seen. It's so big—" She stopped herself in time, just as she
was about to say "so big you could cook a man in it." She
quickly went on to tell what was served with the soup made in
that pot: a piece of bread and butter. Butter! Unbelievable! But
afterward, if you didn't wash your hands before going back to
work, you were fined. Yes, Michanteau admitted regretfully,
there were fines. Even so, she didn't mind washing her hands
to thank the Morel d'Arthus for doing so much for her.

"You'll see tomorrow," she concluded.

Then, before going up to her room on the second floor, she
let Gilonne know, in what she regarded as an elegantly discreet
way, that she wouldn't hear anything that happened in the house
until the next morning: "There's one more good thing about
this place: Nobody will bother you by bringing you *roties*."*

Gilonne had seen the most beautiful nightgowns imaginable
in the luxurious chest, padded inside with white satin and scented
with jasmine petals, that contained the toilet set made for Madame de Montespan at the Royal Manufactory. There were six
of them, made of the finest batiste and trimmed with lace as
delicate as a cobweb. Gilonne's nightgown was to Madame de
Montespan's what iron was to gold. It was a utilitarian present

---

*Slices of toast dipped in sweetened wine that, in Normandy, were brought
to newlyweds in their bed.

from Mama Bordier, made of coarse homespun linen sewn with no particular care.

When she slipped between the fine embroidered sheets in that beautiful bedroom, Gilonne felt as if she herself were coarse. She got up and brushed her hair again, making it form a cloak that partly hid her peasant nightgown.

Then she went back to bed and waited. Her day had been filled with emotions that drained her strength. She fell asleep.

She awoke in Hélye's arms. He evidently agreed with her in thinking that her nightgown was ugly, because he took it off her.

Her head had been on his shoulder when she went to sleep and it was still there when she woke up.

He was looking at her. How long had he been awake? She looked back at him and smiled. She was smiling both at her husband and at the new life beginning for her. She still hardly knew Hélye, but he had initiated her into what had to be the great mystery of that life. He caressed her shoulder and smiled at her too.

"Yes?" he said a few moments later, when her face had become serious.

"I was just . . . seeing you."

"And what do you think I look like?"

"You look like . . . " she began slowly, thinking as she spoke, and her face became even more serious. "You look like someone who wonders where he'll be tomorrow."

"Why do you say that, my darling?"

"What surprises me is that I don't know why I said it, or why I think it."

"Well, if I don't know where I'll be tomorrow, we ought to make the most of today. Do you want me to tell you one thing I love about you, among thousands of others?"

She nodded.

"I love the fact that I'm going to be with you while you grow up and your beauty develops. Yes, you're still at an age where you have some growing up to do. You'll become more fully what you are already; the most beautiful creature God ever put on earth. In spite of what you think, I know where I'll be in the future: I'll be wherever you are, looking at you and saying to myself, 'She's mine.' "

"I thought . . . I mean, I've heard . . ."

"What have you heard, my angel?"

"That you Protestants don't think very much about . . . those things."

"Is there any reason to believe that when a group of people decided they had a right to examine their religion and reform it in several ways, they also decided to give up everything beautiful and enjoyable that God created in this world?"

No, she couldn't see any reason to believe that. She decided she knew nothing at all, stretched like a kitten, and realized she was hungry. What time was it?

It was four o'clock. Hélye sighed.

"Is something wrong?" she asked.

"This time with you is about to end, and our separation is about to begin."

"But we'll be together every day, doing the work we both love so much. One of these days I'll tell you something I've been inventing. Maybe you'll be pleased with it."

He looked at her tenderly and said, "I'm going to make you lead a difficult life of pretense and secrecy, and you're braver than I am!"

"I'm not as brave as you seem to think. I'm afraid of your Judith and I'm worried about how my workers will treat me this morning. As for your qualms—Peter taught me that word; you see, I'm not trying to hide my ignorance from you!—as for your qualms about the kind of life you'll make me lead, you shouldn't have any, because it's the king who's to blame, not you. What makes him torment some of his subjects the way he does?" She paused, then said timidly, "I want to get to my workshop on time. Would you please let me get dressed."

He didn't answer. She looked at him again, and anxiety gripped her heart. Why was it that when she examined his face and saw the two little wrinkles he had at the corners of his lips, she had a premonition of disaster? Who could do anything against a man so strong, so good, so rich? No one had that power. She was only imagining things, as Michanteau would say. Michanteau was probably bursting with impatience, all ready to leave, in her room upstairs. And Gilonne was a little impatient too, at not being able to do what she wanted, without delay. She didn't dare to hurry this man who was now her husband, but she was eager to draw some water from the little well in the kitchen, wash herself, and run off to her workshop. Having heard how beautiful they were, she was dying to see the drawings and patterns she would be working from.

* * *

They already know I'm a Catholic, she thought only a few seconds after coming into the workshop. Had Judith told them? It didn't matter who had done it.

Some of the workers showed uneasiness, others suspicion, still others hatred. She had to have the strength to seem not to notice. All through the morning she tried to keep her mind only on her work. And at lunchtime, while she and all the others were on their way to the dining room, she pretended to believe it was only an accident when one of them forcefully stepped on her foot. She was heartsick when, through the tears of pain that had come into her eyes, she saw an ugly scuff mark on her pretty shoe. Forcing herself not to let anything show in her face, she took her place in line with the other women from her shop. As she was approaching the pot and holding out her bowl toward the woman who was serving, the bowl of the woman in front of her flew through the air and the hot soup spilled on Gilonne's hands. In spite of the burn, she went on holding out her bowl. When she had received her soup, she gave it to the woman who no longer had any, without looking at her or saying anything. She then walked away from the astounded worker and went to change her clothes.

When she had drawn water from the well in her kitchen, she cried for a while. Then she splashed water on her face, coated her burned hands with grease, tried to hide the scuff mark on her shoe by rubbing wax into it, and resolutely went back to her shop.

The women had finished eating and were returning to work. Gilonne took her place, at the head of the big table. When the women had settled down, she stood up. Her hands were trembling, but the main thing, she told herself, was to keep her voice steady.

"I'd like to say a few words to you. Whether you listen or not, I'll say them anyway.

"I'm here because your other mistress-lacemaker left. You know why she left, and you also know that the lack of a mistress-lacemaker in a shop means hardship for everyone. When Monsieur Hélye and his father asked me to come here, they told me how hard it was for them to find qualified women. I accepted their offer because to me, religious opinions don't matter as far as work is concerned. I go to God by my path, you go to Him by yours. I believe that your faith and mine are both good in His eyes. you're like me: You love lace and you make your living from it. So let's work together.

"I have one more thing to tell you. Not long ago I went to Paris. It's the most beautiful city in the world, everyone says so, and I went to its most beautiful place: the Galerie du Palais. That's where the finest shops are. They sell every kind of lace made in the kingdom. They have so much of it that they're packed full, believe me. It's the most wonderful sight I've ever seen in my life! If you'd been there with me, you'd have felt as if your guardian angel had suddenly taken you up to heaven, and you'd have said to yourselves, 'It's a little because of me that all this is here. I worked with some of those threads. I'm one small part of this beauty, thanks to my work and to God.' And God is the same for you as for me."

There was a long, heavy silence that no one seemed willing to break. Then, as if she were jumping into an icy river, Gilonne continued: "But maybe you're saying to yourselves, 'She's too young to know more than we do, and tell us what to do.' I started when I was five years old, like all of you. Like you, I cried in despair and screamed in pain. And like you, I survived. But if you don't think I know my trade, you can bring me your work, one at a time, and let me put my needle to it."

No one moved or spoke. Gilonne wondered what was going to happen. Then, trembling a little, she sat down and began working again.

She had intoxicated herself with words, and now she was sobering up. She had to make a great effort to stay there, making a *rempli* that she wanted to be perfect in case one of the women should decide to come and see what kind of work she did.

Not one of them came. The bell rang to announce the end of the day's work. When she gave them the signal, they all stood up and left.

She remained alone, sitting at the big table and looking at her hands, which were still red from their burn. Then she left too. She had done her best and that was all she could do. Tomorrow would be difficult. But she decided to say nothing to Hélye.

Unable to fall asleep, she sat on her bed, wearing her ugly nightgown, with a pink ribbon in her hair, and waited. There was another rose in the vase. Hélye had brought it for her, but where did he find roses in the middle of winter?

He came in rather late; his father had been ill and he had stayed with him awhile. Had everything gone well?

"Yes. Very well."

"That's not true," he said, sitting down on the foot of the bed. "I heard about it." But he didn't seem displeased. He even smiled, in fact. "You act like a little girl who needs protection, you say you're afraid of God knows what—and then you stand up to thirty-five Protestant women as tough as the leather their ancestors ate during the siege of La Rochelle!"

"So you know . . ."

"I need to know everything that happens here. I can't be everywhere at once, but my three inspectors tell me what's going on, hour by hour."

"Then why are you smiling when you know I failed miserably? None of them gave in. Not a single one!"

"You couldn't be more mistaken! You held them in the palm of your hand and then you put them in your pocket! One of my clerks told me they were so shamefaced when they left that they didn't even talk to each other."

"How do you know what they think, if they didn't say anything?"

"I know, believe me."

"Are you saying that only to solace me?"

"Of course not. And where did you learn a word like 'solace'?"

"I read in one of Lady Bertrade's books that conversation is the first art that should be taught, before singing and dancing, so I practiced it with Peter and he taught me new words. I didn't have much confidence in my talent, though, because when I talked to little Bichon she always fell asleep."

He laughed and she realized that she liked to amuse him.

"Come here and sit on my lap," he said, "so I can find out if you kiss as well as you talk."

The following days were painful for Gilonne. One lacemaker in particular, a young woman with glowing eyes, named Noémy, remained fiercely hostile. Each time she raised her head to thread a needle, she gave Gilonne a look of concentrated hatred. Waiting for that look, then feeling it burn into her, was a strange experience that made Gilonne's heart beat faster. In the hope of preventing her hands from trembling, she would sit with her back straight, push down on the floor with her feet, and brace herself against the attack. She was determined never to bow her head before Noémy's gaze. It was a long, tiring struggle for both adversaries. Finally one afternoon Noémy looked down at her work and shrugged her shoulders slightly, and Gilonne knew she had won. Her hands trembled so much that she had to stop working for a few seconds. A lacemaker came to ask her for instructions. It suddenly seemed to her that a pleasant breath of springtime air had blown through the shop. A little old woman carefully put her glasses down on the table and said, "You've told us about other kinds of lace that are made in France. Will you tell us *how* they're made?"

Gilonne explained what she knew and decided to ask Hélye, who had a collection of old lace in a big cabinet in his office, to lend her some pieces that she could show to her women. She was happy.

She always looked forward to her evenings. Sometimes Hélye was able to come and share the light supper she and Michanteau usually ate together. On those evenings the two young women worked busily in the kitchen.

Michanteau was now less intimidated by Hélye, who liked to hear her tell about the time she and Gilonne had spent in Mistress Lescure's house during their childhood. He said he had once planned to build a kind of village where young lacemakers, supervised by older ones, would live in pleasant surroundings and work shorter days. But for several years he had been forbidden by the king to have apprentices. He would take up his plan again when things were going better.

When she heard him talk about a better future, Gilonne always looked at the two slight wrinkles on either side of his mouth and worried as she had done after their first night together. Then, when she thought of his courage and determination, and the strength of those arms that sometimes pressed her against his chest until it seemed he was about to crush her, she would tell herself it was foolish to worry. Nothing could happen to a man like that.

Titus the gatekeeper had at first been so captivated by Gilonne that he was paralyzed whenever he saw her, but he was gradually becoming more self-assured in her presence and had now reached the point where he could even speak to her. One day when she had decided to go to the poorhouse at lunchtime to see her old women, he stopped her on her way out the gate to tell her about his troubles with the "deserving poor" who had been coming to the house in droves because so many Protestants had left Alençon that the churches had less money at their disposal and help for the indigent was becoming harder to find.

"I'm always on my guard," he said, "because I have to know the difference between the papist poor and our own poor. The Morel d'Arthus are known to be generous, and some of the people who come here to ask for help aren't entitled to it."

Gilonne looked at the six or seven poor wretches in front of the door and wondered how a Protestant beggar could be distinguished from a Catholic one.

"I used to question them about the Bible," said Titus, "but now they're so skinny and weak that they can't answer: They open their mouths and nothing comes out. So now I just smell them. I close my eyes and take a deep breath, and I can tell who's who from two steps away. A Protestant doesn't smell as bad as a Catholic."

He sent two people away. She followed them for a time and then, when they had turned a corner, she gave them a few sous.

That disheartening intolerance was everywhere, at all levels of society. She sighed, and when she arrived at the poorhouse she was still feeling rebellious against the authorities who not only permitted intolerance but even made it official policy.

She announced to the old women that she and Michanteau had gone to work for the Morel d'Arthus as mistress-lacemakers, but she couldn't tell any of them about her marriage, not even Thomine—there was no way to be sure she wouldn't talk about it in her sleep. She painted a rosy picture of her new life, describing the pretty little house in which it was customary for mistress-lacemakers to live, and the garden with a private entrance that could be used by visitors on Sunday.

"You don't think we'll set foot on ground owned by Protestants, do you?" Marie asked caustically. "I don't understand why the Perdriel family likes those Morel d'Arthus so much. I once asked your grandfather, Juste, what he saw in those people who belonged to Satan. He said he was glad to know they belonged to Satan, because it meant he didn't have to be afraid of going to hell. Ever since then, that answer has been stuck in my throat like a fish bone. And now you, the angel we saved— you're working for those demons! I'm sure it's Mathieu's doing. Well, you can tell him not to count on getting any of my money after I die."

"Even though they're giving you a house to live in, they're still paying you, aren't they?" asked Conte-Nouvelles.

"Yes, I'm paid fair wages."

"Let's drink to your good luck," said Chopine. "You've brought us something, haven't you?"

Gilonne had brought one of the bottles from her little cellar. She took it from under her cloak and opened it.

"What kind of wine is that? It sings and dances!"

Since her evening in the Dutch embassy, Gilonne had known what champagne was. She told them about it.

"Why did you leave Pervenchères, and the estate, and . . . everyone there?" Thomine asked quietly.

"It's impossible to run a lacemaking shop in the country. I tried, and now I know it can't be done."

"That's the only reason?"

"Yes. And I'm happier here, closer to you."

"Then you're doing all right?"

"I'm doing very well. Drink some of this wine. It will cheer you up."

"You have to tell her everything that's happening here," Marie said abruptly. "I'll take a little nap while you're doing it."

The three blind women all began talking at once. The poorhouse was going to be rebuilt. It would be bigger, prettier, less damp—a real palace.

"The Duchess of Alençon told me personally," said Conte-Nouvelles, "that we wouldn't have to suffer from our rheumatism much longer, because the poorhouse was going to be made drier and healthier. What do you think of that?"

Gilonne thought it was wonderful, but left as soon as she had said so. Her lunchtime was nearly over, and she had to hurry to get back before the bell rang to order the lacemakers to resume their work.

"Young people are always running somewhere," said Chopine. "They don't know how to slow down and enjoy themselves." *She* knew how to do it. She kept the half-full bottle for herself, since the others hadn't liked the bubbly wine very much. Gilonne must really be making a good living, to be able to afford wine like that! Chopine concluded that they were about to be rewarded at last. They had saved this child, and she would show her gratitude. Chopine decided to count the number of steps to the Morel d'Arthus house and find out if there were many holes and stones on the way.

Marie awoke from her little nap just in time to call out to Gilonne as she was going through the doorway, "Wait! I haven't told you the best part of it! Do you know where the money to rebuild the poorhouse is coming from? It's from fines paid by those devilish Protestants! Conte-Nouvelles told me they were fined again only yesterday: three thousand livres for gathering in a place where they weren't supposed to be."

As she was coming in through the gate, Gilonne saw Hélye. He frowned and gave her a questioning look. Speaking with great respect for the benefit of Titus the gatekeeper, who was straining his ears to overhear her, she said she had visited her grandmother in the poorhouse.

To her intense surprise, she saw that Hélye didn't believe her. His eyes were stern, even hard. She curtsied summarily and walked away.

Titus, who had also seen Hélye's dissatisfied expression, raised his bushy eyebrows and wondered if any woman would ever break through his master's insensitivity to feminine charms. He decided there would probably never be a mistress of the household and that, after all, it might be just as well.

That evening, Hélye listened without comment while Gilonne told him about her day. She said that two of her lacemakers were leaving Alençon to take refuge in Holland. "Two of my best ones," she added.

"Why didn't Mathieu ever tell me his mother was in the poorhouse?" Hélye asked abruptly. "She *is* in the poorhouse, isn't she?"

"Yes. He didn't tell you about it because he was afraid you'd think he was asking you to give him money so he could keep her at home. And she *wanted* to go to the poorhouse, to be with her three best friends. They'd all made Alençon lace together. My grandmother and two of the others are blind. They say that the fourth one is lucky enough to still have her eyes but never uses them. She sleeps all the time. When I was a child, I was terribly afraid I'd go blind too."

"And now?"

"I'm still a little afraid of it, but not nearly so much as before. Since then, I've realized that not all lacemakers go blind. But for those who do, it must be horrible to be always in darkness. I feel so sorry for my poor grandmother. . . ."

"Would you like to have her here, with you? She'd be better

off here than in that big, damp building that's almost in the river.''

"Her life is with her old friends. But thank you for offering to take her in. You're always so kind.''

"No, I'm not. Today I felt malicious. I must admit that I didn't believe you'd really gone to the poorhouse.''

"But why would I have told you that if it wasn't true? Sometimes I don't understand you.''

"Maybe someday you'll know what it's like to love so much it hurts. Then you'll understand.''

Besides directing her shop, Gilonne spent almost as many hours making lace as her workers did. When she had inspected their work, commented on it, and given her instructions for the day, she took up her own work. She was making a beautiful flounce, designed by Hélye, that should have given her great pleasure. Why didn't she enjoy using only her needle and thread to create those gracefully drawn motifs: stylized vases of flowers, balustrades surmounted by urns, canopied platforms? Was it because a workshop without children was dismal, especially when you knew why no little apprentices were allowed in it? Or was it the workers' attitude—they were less gay than in Catholic shops—that made the atmosphere heavier? And what about the psalms they sang? Gilonne wasn't used to them yet, and maybe they added to her melancholy. But the shop was calm now, and the workers all respected her. That was probably the reason: They respected her but didn't like her. It was hard to bear.

But she had to keep reminding herself that these thirty-five women were necessarily unhappy and worried, if not terrified. Poor Lancelotte, for example: Some time ago her head had begun shaking in a way that prevented her from working as well as she had done before. Her condition was caused by the anguish of having seen her two little brothers, aged eight and nine, taken away screaming with fear and despair. Born weak and sickly, they had survived only because of their mother's attentive care. They were now staying in the Community of New Catholics. "I'd go there and take care of them if I could,'' Lancelotte had said, weeping, "but they keep boys in one part of the building and girls in another.'' She lived with an old great-aunt, a maniacally fervent Protestant who poured a bucket of water on the head of any Catholic priest who passed beneath her window. She was known to be senile, but sooner or later the authorities would become seriously irritated with her. If Lancelotte was then discovered in her deranged aunt's house, she too would be taken away to be converted by force. "I hear my brothers crying out to me," she said. "I hear them night and day. They're calling me."

At the other end of the table from Lancelotte were the Goulard sisters, whose husbands, one a lawyer and the other a doctor, had had to flee to England so they could continue working. The sisters were still waiting to hear from them, not knowing if they had reached England safely, drowned on the way, or been caught and imprisoned. The women were so overwrought that the lace they were making now was useless, but Hélye had told Gilonne to overlook that. And he had told her to distract Lancelotte by sending her on errands to some other part of the building, or even to town, whenever it was necessary. One day when Gilonne had seen her silently shedding tears on the lace she was making, she sent her to give Hélye a folded piece of paper on which she had drawn a rose during lunchtime. That evening he had shown her that he was keeping it in a pocket "just over my heart."

Lancelotte, the Goulard sisters, Marie-Rachel, Jacquine—how many others wept and trembled with fear and anxiety? How could the shop be joyful? How could those women like her when, to them, she represented an implacable enemy? Since he had been living in that atmosphere of constant stress for some time, maybe Hélye didn't realize how unpleasant it was to work under such conditions. Mama Bordier had once said of her needlework, "It likes me to be cheerful. It knows how much better I treat it when I'm in a good mood." Gilonne would have to go and see Mama Bordier someday. But the thought of telling her she was now working with Protestants made her keep putting off that painful moment.

One morning Hélye officially sent one of his clerks to ask her to come to his office. As soon as she was there, he closed the door and took her in his arms.

"I had to see you," he said. "I had to feel you here, against my heart. There are times when I just can't bear our separations. But you don't seem to mind."

He had begun leaving her in the middle of the night so the servants wouldn't realize he was never in his bedroom. She was always asleep when he left.

"Why do you say that? I don't like our separations either."

He sighed.

"Maybe we'll miss this life someday when things are even worse."

"Are you worried?"

"No more than I was yesterday. But nothing's going well. . . . I won't come until very late tonight. We have a meeting. I won't tell you where. I want you to know as little as possible, so you won't have much to tell if you're questioned."

"But all meetings are forbidden. You'll be in great danger."

"We're very careful."

"What's the use of provoking the king? Do you and your friends really have anything so important to say to each other?"

"What's important is for the people who resist, who risk their lives, not to feel alone. I need to bring them together often."

"*You* need to?"

"You can't struggle for long if you don't feel the warmth of other people with you."

"Yes, I understand that, but why *you*?"

"Someone had to do it. Arrangements must be made for people who are going to leave the country. Guides must be found to take them across the border. We have to try to conduct our religious services first in one place, then in another."

"Couldn't you . . . Wouldn't it be enough for you to give money? Do you have to risk your life?"

He didn't answer.

They went to see Salomon Louvet, a painter who worked for the Morel d'Arthus as a lace designer.

Salomon lived in the attic of the house, at his own request. A big studio had been made for him there, with several dormer windows that, he said, opened onto the kingdom of God. He also said, "When the weather is good, I paint with my right hand from dawn to dusk. When it rains, I paint with my left hand." He had only one hand, his left one having been cut off when he was twenty, as punishment for having stolen paints and a piece of canvas he intended to use for the picture he would present to the painters' guild in Rouen as his masterpiece. The materials for a masterpiece were expensive and he was poor. He hadn't been made a master painter, and the members of the guild had threatened to slash any painting he might try to present to them. There would be no thieves in that illustrious group of artists.

Such, at least, was Salomon's account of how he had lost his left hand. Hélye said he wasn't at all sure it had really happened that way. Not all his fellow Protestants were people of outstanding virtue. But Salomon was a kind of genius, and Hélye wasn't inclined to look too closely into the winds of events that had blown him to Alençon.

Despite what he said, Salomon painted even on rainy days, and with his right hand. At Monsieur Mortimer's request, he had begun a group painting of the household servants. They were all flattered and grateful, and heaped presents on him. Eslue, the cook, often brought him a good piece of meat or pastry. Some kept their cider for him, others their white bread on holidays. Marie and Magdelaine, the sisters who worked as kitchen helpers, picked wildflowers on Sundays and brought them to him in big, stiff bouquets. Once he laughed and said to them, "You tie those flowers together as if you were making a bundle of straw! You have to think a little about what you're doing, children! And look at yourselves in that mirror on the wall. Your hair is tied as badly as the stems of your flowers. You look like chickens with their feathers ruffled by a windstorm. And you've told Eslue that you want to learn how to make lace? Would you even know which way to hold a needle? Try to think about what I'm saying. Take back your flowers, take off the bindweed you've tied them together with, separate them, and tie them together again, only this time try to arrange them in a way that will make them into something pretty. Then maybe someday you'll be able to learn how to make lace."

They looked at him in bewilderment, not remembering what he had said at the beginning of his speech, and burst into tears. He gave them the piece of cake Eslue had brought him, laughed again, and said, "Don't worry, your pretty pink faces will save you. There's sure to be a pair of apprentice pork butchers who will be attracted to them, and you'll later become plump, placid merchants. That's your destiny."

They were still bewildered but, since they saw him untie the flowers and put them in a pitcher with great care, they went on bringing him a bouquet every Sunday as long as there were wildflowers to be picked, and they always handed it to him with a smile that was a bit timorous but still trusting.

Salomon Louvet's theory on lacemaking was that skill, no matter how highly developed, was not enough. Only someone with the temperament of an artist could make masterpieces of lace.

"Take those two, for example," he said to Hélye one day, pointing to the sisters he had destined to marry pork butchers. "Even when seven years of patient effort have taught them how to handle a needle, why should you expect them to make a pretty bouquet in lace when they can't make one in a vase? Skill is one thing, taste is another."

Hélye disagreed. Magnificent lace was sometimes made by clumsy-looking creatures who seemed incapable of even tying ribbons in their hair. He had known one old hag, ugly enough to make you want to run away at the sight of her, and not at all inclined toward the arts, who was sublimely clever at joining the different pieces of a single work of lace.

Salomon admitted that there were exceptions, but kept his convictions. If apprentices could be taught to draw, look at nature, sing, understand great works of art, and read the finest pages ever written, they would then make lace fit for goddesses! Hélye told him he had missed his true calling when he went to work for a lacemaking establishment: He was made for educating Renaissance princesses who made lace in their spare time.

"They spent a good part of their time making lace," said Salomon. "And someday I'll go off to look for the masterpieces those superb women must have made."

"I have some in my collection."

"Yes, but you have them pinned up like butterflies. They're dead. I want to find them alive, in the places where they were born."

Salomon enchanted Gilonne. He was Hélye's court jester.

He gave her an enthusiastic reception when she and Hélye came to see him in his attic studio.

"Where have you been hidden, matchless beauty? I haven't seen you in such a long time! In what dark hole have you been kept?"

"You haven't seen her because you seldom come down from your lofty quarters," Hélye said calmly.

"Have you noticed that the weather has been beautiful the last few days? I've been painting!"

Salomon showed a nearly finished portrait of the two young kitchen helpers.

"What lovely little cherubs!" said Gilonne.

"No, they're little weasels. Look at them closely, see their

greedy eyes, and ask them, 'Why do you want to make lace?'
Then hear their answer: 'To make money for our dowries.' Cherubs would have answered, 'To create beauty.' ''

He was also designing a dress to be made entirely of lace, for
the Countess of Dangeau. She had asked that the main motif be
a rain of flowers. They were there, alive, in Salomon's drawing,
and it was easy to see why Hélye wasn't interested in delving
into the background of the man who had drawn them so exquisitely.

"Can we have the engraving very soon?" Hélye asked.

"No, sir. Look at the row of trefoils that forms the border at
the bottom of the skirt. The pattern for it was stolen from us
yesterday. Whoever buys it will make many copies of it, and the
countess will never wear a dress with a border that's seen everywhere! I'll have to design another one. It will take me two days
to do the drawing and the engraving."

"Why wasn't I told about the theft as soon as it happened?
It's the third one in a month."

"That's right, sir. Esaïe, who works on the press, is still
hoping it will turn out that the pattern was only mislaid. He
knows that this time you'll dismiss him. You warned him."

Gilonne knew Esaïe Granger, a poor eighteen-year-old boy
in precarious health. His mother, a fanatically religious Protestant, made him lead a life of constant privation in the belief
that it would bring him closer to God. She gave him only turnips
to eat, and it was often said that if it hadn't been for the lunches
he received at work, he would have died of hunger by now.

When Gilonne and Hélye had left the attic, she asked him,
"Do you believe it was Esaïe who, for a little money, or
food . . ."

"No. But some people would like to make me think so."

"What are you going to do? You're not going to dismiss him,
are you? If you do, no Protestant will employ him. You'd better
be on your guard against his mother too. She claims to be a
prophet, according to what I've heard."

"You already know about that?"

Hélye's voice was weary. But these incidents among the workers were only a small part of his worries. What concerned him
most was that the king still showed no sign of relenting in his
persecution of the Protestants.

To distract him a little, Gilonne told him that Michanteau kept her posted on the large and small events that happened every day at work and in town.

"Maybe she'll find my thief," he said.

"It wouldn't surprise me if she did. When it comes to nosing things out, she's as good as a bloodhound."

Before leaving him, knowing she wouldn't see him again until late that night, she urged him to be careful. Then, when he was walking away, she caught up with him and said, "Thank you for today's rose. And yesterday's. And tomorrow's."

He smiled happily. She reproached herself for not treating him affectionately often enough, then excused herself: he was nearly always so serious, and so apparently indifferent, that it was hard to remember how much displays of affection meant to him. She decided that since he wasn't going to spend the evening with her, she would spend it with his father.

Monsieur Mortimer hadn't left his bed for the last month. He said he didn't mind too much and had asked that doors be left open so he could hear the sounds of everyday activity. "I hear thread being cut and needles being pulled," he had once said to Gilonne with a brief laugh, "but—come closer, because I don't want anyone else to hear what I'm going to say: The psalms put me to sleep! It happens only because of my fatigue, but it does happen. If my inflexible father were still alive, he'd drive me out of bed with a stick and make me listen to the psalms on my knees with my eyes wide open!"

When she came into his room that evening, he was reading by the light of a six-branched candlestick that illuminated not only his book but also the works by Abraham Bosse, a great Protestant artist, hanging on the walls. There were a dozen religious pictures and scenes of Paris life. But except for the silver candlestick and the gilded frames of the engravings, the room was so simple and bare that it was almost like a monk's cell. Anyone passing in the street and looking in at the beautiful Louis XIII façade of that brick and stone mansion with its harmonious proportions would have found it hard to believe that its fortunate owner slept in such a scantily furnished room.

He put down his book, took off his glasses, and told Gilonne how glad he was to see her. She had brought a pitcher of hot spiced cider for them to drink together. When she had sat down, she asked if he would like her to read to him, so he could spare his eyes.

"Speaking of reading," he said, without answering her question, "you've never told me how many Bibles Judith put in your little house."

"Two. I suppose one is for me and the other is for my friend."

He laughed, and said it did him good. God willing, that was how he wanted to die: laughing. He spoke of how Protestants were falsely accused of always being grim-faced and gloomy. Weren't there even grimmer faces among the Jansenists and other devout Catholics?

Gilonne didn't know what to say, but she laughed with him.

As she usually did when she took off her hat after work, she had braided the gold and silver mass of her hair and wrapped it around her head. He told her it formed a queenly crown and added, "I'd like to die looking at you, my beautiful darling."

She asked him to talk about something other than death. And since she then happened to look at an engraving by Abraham Bosse showing the Galerie du Palais in Paris, with its luxurious shops, she told the old gentleman how deeply moved she had been when she discovered that temple of lace.

He listened with interest. Yes, he too had known that same emotion when he contemplated the beautiful lace that was the reward of patient work.

"Wouldn't you enjoy having some of it as trimming on your sheets or your sleeves?" she asked.

"My father was a weaver. The finest cloth he wove was never for us. I regretted that, and so I gave my children silk and lace when they were young. Of their own accord, as I myself did later, they began dressing more plainly."

"Wasn't that . . ." She hesitated to go on.

He did it for her. "Pride? And a desire not to be like those fools who put lace all over themselves, even on their boots?"

"But those fools have made you rich!"

He laughed again, and again she asked if he would like her to read to him. No, he said, he wanted to hear her thoughts, not those of someone else. She found herself talking about the people of Grand-Coeur, something she never did with Hélye. She told him about her sorrow over the chevalier's indifference to her. She realized that she now suffered from it much less than before and that it was because this delightful old gentleman was beginning to be a father to her.

As she was about to leave him, she kissed his hand. He held hers for a moment and asked, "Will you promise to be here when I 'lower my sails and come into the harbor'?"

She promised. But she also promised to come back and see him again very soon, and said it wasn't yet time to think about death because they still had many years to spend together.

She stepped toward the door, then returned to his bedside. She had a secret to tell him, a secret no one else knew yet. She leaned toward him and announced that she had recently become sure she was going to have a baby.

Seeing how strongly this news affected him, she hurried away so he could let his tears of joy flow without embarrassment.

Summer came, and with it came Peter and Bichon. Titus found them one morning at the gate, accompanied by Zoltan and Candelario.

They were taken in. Peter was given the attic rooms that Salomon hadn't occupied. Since Bichon, at her age, wasn't allowed to live in a Protestant house, Michanteau gave her the room next to hers.

The Norman springtime mural was finished now, and its splendor brightened the great common room at Grand-Coeur. Bichon told how beautiful Gilonne was in it. A nobleman who wanted to buy Grand-Coeur had looked at her a long time and asked where he could see her in person. But Pompinne, who didn't like the visitor, had said nothing.

Who wanted to buy Grand-Coeur? And was it really for sale? Gilonne would send Mathieu to find out as soon as he came back. Meanwhile, Michanteau would try to go and see Zoltan and Candelario at the market on Thursday.

It was hot in July, and since the strong smells of the town were hard for a pregnant woman to bear, Hélye wasn't greatly upset when, one Sunday morning after going to see her old women in the poorhouse, Gilonne came back supported by two women who said they had seen her suddenly fall as if she had been hit on the head. They had taken her to Monsieur Macé, the apothecary, who gave her some powdered cinchona bark in wine that made her feel better.

But after several hours in bed she didn't seem to be improving. Hélye was worried. At first he had been overjoyed at the news of her pregnancy, but then his happiness was marred by the thought that he would soon have to send her away to Holland, or to Switzerland, as she seemed to prefer. And now, knowing how many women died in childbirth, he was afraid. He kept questioning her. How did she feel? Did she want something to drink? And why was she crying? For she had violent fits of sobbing that shook her whole body.

Later, when she had stopped crying, she was pale and still, as if she had fainted again. Hélye leaned over her, surprised by her silence.

But what could she say to him? Could she tell him about the horrible and wonderful thing that had happened to her that morning? She pretended to fall asleep so she could finally be alone with the incredible experience.

She had been coming back from the poorhouse, walking briskly and feeling as light as a speck of dust in a sunbeam. She had decided, on a whim, to pass by the duchess's palace to compare its orange trees with those of the Morel d'Arthus. She smiled at the memory of walking there in the past, closely watched by the Lemareurs, and comparing herself to the orange trees in tubs that were periodically taken outside in winter for a little fresh air, then put back into the greenhouse.

She saw a handsome carriage in the courtyard of the palace. It wasn't the duchess's, which was well know in town, but another one, probably belonging to a visitor. A moment later the visitor came out and prepared to get into his carriage. By what kind of sorcery did he look so much like Ogier de Beaumesnil? Was she having a hallucination? Was she suddenly in the grip of demonic forces? No, it really *was* Ogier de Beaumesnil, alive, dressed in black. Without furs? Of course—it was July! Somehow she was brought back to earth by the realization that he was dressed for summer and not for winter, as she had seen him at Grand-Coeur. She told herself she was looking at the man who was said to have been killed by Indians in Canada. That was when she fainted. The carriage that took him away must have passed by the little group of people who gathered around her as she lay unconscious. When she came back to her senses, he was gone.

Her eyes were still closed, but she could feel Hélye looking at her intently.

Finally regaining her calm, she was able to reassure him by saying she must have fainted because of the heat. But her uneasiness returned when she remembered how much the sight of Ogier de Beaumesnil had moved her. What place did he still hold in her life? She saw her salvation in going to Geneva, as she and Hélye had decided she would do. There she would pull herself together, time would pass, she would forget, and the child whom God was giving her at such an opportune time would be the best of remedies.

She opened her eyes and saw a big bouquet of roses that seemed to have arrived by magic. She seized on them as a topic of conversation that would help her to hide her inner turmoil. "Are you finally going to tell me where those roses come from, Hélye? I never see any like them in town. And the ones that keep growing in my china vase always intrigue me, especially in winter."

He was so happy to hear her speak that he told her his secret. The flowers came from the greenhouse (in winter) and the rose garden (in summer) of the Château du Verrier, his estate a few leagues away from Alençon. Unfortunately, he couldn't take her there because the servants would be too curious about her. Was she feeling better now?

She said she was. Wisdom told her to get a grip on herself, and she had recovered enough of her strength to listen to the voice of wisdom. Ogier de Beaumesnil was back? What did it matter to Gilonne Morel d'Arthus? As a good Christian and a woman with decent human feelings, she was glad that a man thought to be dead was, by God's grace, still alive. Lady Bertrade would be happy.

When Hélye took Gilonne's hand and kissed it, she wondered with a little shudder what he would say if he knew the truth. He was even jealous of Salomon!

It wasn't until far into the night, when Hélye had left her, that she began trying to understand what she felt for Ogier, now that he had come back. It seemed to her that she had dreamed of him long ago and that her dream had left her with a kind of sweet pain from which she didn't think she would like to be completely freed. She decided it would be better not to try to analyze her memory of him, but to put it away in a corner of her heart and let it wait there.

Staggering news came from Pervenchères: Grand-Coeur had been sold, and the new owner was Count Ogier de Beaumesnil! He had paid off the mortgages, deducted the amount from the price of the estate, and paid the remainder to the chevalier, telling him that he was free to go on living at Grand-Coeur if he wished. The chevalier had preferred to move into Mistress Ver-

lot's inn with his two musician-servants. Lady Bertrade had chosen not to change any of her habits. Pompinne had acquired two
kitchen helpers. And the little farmhand was now under the
command of a big one. It was even said there might soon be a
steward. It was also said that the count was trying to restore the
estate to its original boundaries by buying back, whenever possible, parcels of land that the Ferrières had sold off, and that he
seldom went there and usually left after spending only a day or
a night.

"Have you heard whether . . . the chevalier was sad to leave
Grand-Coeur?" Gilonne asked Michanteau, who had just reported the latest news and rumors to her.

"What makes you think he's ever sad about anything? Don't
worry. He lives in a world of his own, with his songs and his
Vikings, and sadness can't reach him there."

Gilonne was reassured on that score, but there was other news
to disturb her. One morning a lacemaker disrupted the precarious tranquility of the workshop: "Do you know that the king
has forbidden Protestant artists to paint any more pictures? They
heard about it yesterday at the Plessis d'Ocagne shop, where my
sister works. She says her master just got back from Paris and
brought the news with him."

What would become of Peter and Salomon? Gilonne waited
impatiently for evening, when she could question Hélye.

A partial remedy for this new persecution was soon found.
Miniatures had been overlooked in the list of prohibitions, so
Peter and Salomon became miniaturists. Assuming that their
studios would eventually be searched, they prepared hiding
places for things they didn't want to be seen. They didn't yet
know whether or not they would be allowed to make drawings
for lace patterns. If not, they would find some way to get around
the edict.

But Gilonne was still worried.

"If the police come and look too closely," she said to Hélye,
"they'll ask why we need two men for such a small amount of
work."

Then we'll give them more work of a different kind," he
replied. "I often hear them sing. Do you know they both have
beautiful voices? We'll have them go to the shops every day,
one after another, and sing psalms. The workers will be glad to
hear them. There's still nothing to prevent a Protestant lace manufacturer from having professional singers."

He tried to seem lighthearted and did little favors for her to show that his mind was free. Knowing she had come to like a kind of anise-flavored candy, he kept her constantly supplied with it and always went to buy it himself. He sometimes rode to the Château du Verrier to have her favorite fruits picked in the orchards there.

One day when he brought her a basket of apricots, she remembered the candied apricots of the nuns in Montsort and told him how she had been strongly suspected by the police when she was at the convent. He said he was lucky to have her with him: for less than a childish story about a talking turkey, she might have been imprisoned in the basement of a convent. She laughed and played with her apricot pits as she had once played with knucklebones.

"Don't take such things lightly," he said. "There are so many dangers! You must be very careful. If you have the slightest trouble, I'll never forgive myself. No matter how painful it will be for me to see you go, I think I'm going to ask you to leave for Switzerland as soon as possible. And that reminds me: Why do you prefer Switzerland to Holland?"

"Because I adore your brother Samuel."

"You adore Samuel? What do you mean?"

"I keep looking at him in that family portrait by Philippe de Champaigne. His eyes have such a delightful expression, full of mischievous affection. After you, he's the one I like most in the painting."

Hélye seemed happy to be first in her preferences.

"He'd just emptied our pockets and he was elated over it! What do you have against Holland and Cornélie?"

"I have nothing against either of them. But look at those two small, almost invisible lines at the corners of your sister's lips. Haven't they become stern creases by now?"

"Cornélie is the kindest woman in the world!"

"The kindest Protestant woman in the world may not be overjoyed to discover that she has a papist sister-in-law who's the granddaughter and niece of packmen!"

He made no reply. They decided she would leave for Geneva early in September, after the worst of the summer heat, which, because of her condition, would be hard for her to bear in a stagecoach.

* * *

Because it had been a stormy night—crashing thunder, heavy rain, gusts of wind that bent the trees—when Ogier de Beaumesnil first came to Grand-Coeur as its new owner, Pompinne said the devil must have had a hand in all that. By "all that," she meant his transformation from a falconer into a nobleman. She couldn't get used to it. Whenever she thought about it, frowning, it seemed to her unnatural that the peasant boy who used to steal bread and bacon had become a lord who could afford to buy his master's estate, wear furs and lace, and spend money as if it were water. Who could say whether the whole affair might be related to the cases of sorcery that were going to be tried by the commission known as the Chambre Ardente, which was so often discussed in evening conversations?

One thing was sure: In His fury at seeing so many sins committed, God was hurling thunderbolts again and again to let the king know that He expected him to take stern action. An angry month of July was storming all over the kingdom; lightning flashed and rivers flooded because great lords and ladies at court had engaged in an orgy of black masses and poisonings. Maybe Count Ogier de Beaumesnil had done the same to get his title and his enormous wealth. And so Pompinne kept close and constant watch on her new master. She wasn't sure that someday, if the magic he had used for his transformations wore off, she might not suddenly see him change back into a barefoot peasant in a sleeveless tunic.

What disturbed her even more than her former enemy's social elevation was that the surprising mutual affection between him and Lady Bertrade was still as strong as it had been in the past.

Ogier had now begun spending one or two days a week at Grand-Coeur. He had a fine house in Alençon, on the Rue Saint-Blaise, but he said he liked to breathe the pure air of Pervenchères. He always came with his Huron carrying a basket of food for Lady Bertrade: pâtés of larks, thrushes, chicken livers, or tripe, and rare fruits. He and Lady Bertrade sometimes ate these delicacies in the course of an evening they spent together, when she said she felt "a little hollow in her stomach." The Huron would bring a light table to Ogier's room, with a lace cloth and silver dishes—a luxury that scandalized Pompinne and sometimes perplexed her. What if God didn't always have His mind on what He was doing? What if now and then He neglected to punish those who disdained the humble condition in which He had placed them at birth, and usurped a position among the nobility?

And that devilish man had made a room for himself that was fit for a king! Shamelessly, without respecting anything, he had turned the great common room of Grand-Coeur into a bedroom! The same great common room where for centuries the real masters of the estate had feasted! He had brought from Paris a huge bed with a canopy and curtains made of buckskin that had been decorated with beads and feathers in his savage's country. The beads shone in the dark like birds' eyes. Since they had been sewn to both sides of the leather, lying on that bed with the curtains closed must give the feeling of being watched by dozens of owls. It was a devilish bed, no doubt of it. And that strange thing had been put in the middle of Peter's paintings!

Except for Lady Bertrade's ancient armchair, which had kept its place in front of the fireplace, there was no other furniture in the room, which meant that all the family portraits could be seen without obstruction. The fact that Ogier had gained possession of his former lord's estate—surely by black magic—didn't give him the right to sleep in front of them. Why did Lady Bertrade permit such a sacrilege? Having to sell an estate was a great misfortune; allowing a lowborn upstart to snore in the presence of a noblewoman hunting wolves, a chevalier attacking Turks, and a lovely young lady picking apple blossoms was a great impropriety.

Things had been going from bad to worse since the chevalier left. Nor was he without guilt. No man of the family in the days of Chevalier Héribert de Ferrières, or of Lady Bertrade's noble parents, would have gone off like that to live with commoners in an inn. But nowadays people were liable to do *anything*.

Ogier, for example, had his Indian bed covered with fine linen sheets with lace borders as wide as those of a bishop's alb, yet he evidently never used it, because it had never been unmade. Did he sleep on the bearskins he had piled in front of the fireplace, or did he use the cot he had put in the library? Or did he ever sleep? It wasn't certain that he did, considering the number of candles he burned in the tall silver candlesticks in the library. As many as were burned in a church on Christmas Eve. That was shameful, but his insolence to the chevalier's daughter was unforgivable. He kept looking at Peter's ''study,'' as he called it, of Gilonne's face, and he lighted it with two big bronze cressets set on either side. How could Lady Bertrade let her granddaughter smile at the usurper night and day? It was another horrible sacrilege. But unfortunately there was no denying that

Lady Bertrade was closer to Ogier than to anyone else. It even seemed that she loved him more than her son.

No, God didn't seem to be watching over Grand-Coeur. And it had been that way for a long time. But there could be no doubt that someday He would turn His angry eyes to the old house and throw a bolt of lightning that would turn it into a handful of smoking ashes. Everyone knew how the Lord punished sin when He felt like it. Pompinne herself had seen fire destroy a nobleman's castle near Rémalard after it had been the scene of satanic debauchery.

Seeing her always agitated, angry, and muttering, the Huron said that contrary spirits blew on Pompinne and scattered her understanding. But of all the food in that land of the world's greatest ruler, buckwheat porridge made by that woman with a muddled brain was what displeased him least, and few meals passed without his asking for more of it. Pompinne would rather have had her hand cut off than admit she was flattered by this, and so she told Courte-Aiguille [Short-Needle], a half-blind former lacemaker whom the new steward had hired as a laundress, that it sickened her to have to sit across the table, in *her* kitchen, from that savage covered with rancid grease. Courte-Aiguille saw the Huron's skin, eyes, and beads gleaming in the dusk of her failing sight. She had a blurred image of him that she took with her to the washhouse, along with her basket of dirty linen, and to the shivers that the cold weather gave her, that image added other shivers she didn't quite know what to think of.

Pompinne wondered why a man who loved silk and lace, gold and jewels would want to go on having his meals in front of the big fireplace in the kitchen. She refused to believe he did it to please Lady Bertrade, who didn't want to change her habits, and tried to convince herself that it was because he still felt more at ease among the servants, in spite of his fortune and title.

She had to abandon that idea, however, when he gave a hunting banquet in the dining hall recently built in the new wing of the house. Choking back her rage, she grudgingly recognized that he received his guests as a great lord should: with neither too much amiability nor too little, but with what Chévalier Héribert used to call good form. And his guests, noblemen from the surrounding countryside, behaved in the same way. That evening left her feeling as if her heart had been pricked with needles.

Everything was going too well for Count Ogier de Beaumesnil. Was it God or the devil who was looking after him? And what had come over him to make him start being nice to her? Having seen her making bobbin lace, he had brought her from Flanders a beautiful lacemaker's pillow with ivory bobbins so elegantly shaped that they were works of art, as were the winders that came with them. She didn't need anyone to tell her how to answer him when he offered it to her: "You're very kind, sir, but I'm making needlepoint now, so I have no use for that trinket."

She saw the little smile he always had when someone told him something he didn't want to hear—it was one more thing about him that she couldn't stand. That stupid Courte-Aiguille, who could still see too well when it came to looking at men and was always saying, "He's the handsomest nobleman in the kingdom," would do better to forget about handsome noblemen and learn how to wash wine stains out of lace tablecloths, because wine was now so plentiful at Grand-Coeur that there was hardly any place to put it. Candelario openly pilfered it when he came to visit Lady Bertrade, but he was only stealing it from Ogier, who must have done more than his own share of stealing! Even so—and Pompinne stopped poking her fire to make a mental effort—she probably ought to tell Candelario, the next time he came to visit, that it was wrong to take other people's property, no matter who they were.

An upholsterer from Alençon had provided the stiff armchair of Lady Bertrade's ancestors with soft cushions. When she came to spend the evening with Ogier in the great common room that now served as his bedroom, he took her crutch and she sat down with a happy sigh. Her tired back then felt something like the sweet contentment that swelled her heart when Ogier came to stay awhile at Grand-Coeur.

During their evenings together they both smoked some of the rolls of dried tobacco leaves he had brought from America. He sat on the bearskins in front of the fire. There was no lighting in the room other than the dancing flames that gave life to the people painted on the walls.

Lady Bertrade always wore one of her coatdresses. They were all stained and theadbare in varying degrees, and sometimes leaves and pine needles formed strange embroidery on them. Although he had given her several ells of fine cloth, Ogier would have been saddened if she had changed her uniform. This one reminded him of his childhood and the gruff affection she had always shown for him. The memory of that affection had helped him in his progress toward the goal he had set for himself. He scarcely recalled his mother, who had died very young, but he would never forget the shrewd and tender look he had so often seen on Lady Bertrade's broad face before she closed her heavy eyelids as though to say, "Let's not have any useless sentimentality."

On those evenings, he himself always wore one of his brightly colored dressing gowns. He had a scarlet one with ruby buttons from top to bottom, which, said Lady Bertrade, made him look like a Renaissance prince. She said it matter-of-factly, as if she were commenting on the weather, nothing about her former falconer could surprise her. To her, human beings were like the trees in her forest: They kept struggling to rise into the light. The young oak, like the young human being, tried to escape from the shadows where the dwarfs stagnated. Breathing freely in the sunlight—that was the goal of life. Ogier was like the noble kings of the forest, always rising higher and higher.

One evening Lady Bertrade looked at him and was amused by what she saw: the noble oak dressed in scarlet, absorbed in contemplating the mural of blossoming apple trees. Against a pink and white background of countless petals, Gilonne danced in a short Greek tunic and sandals with silver thongs, her long hair floating in the springtime breeze. She was smiling.

"She's so beautiful!" said Lady Bertrade.

She saw a glow in Ogier's eyes. Then he closed them, and his long hands clutched the fur on which he sat. *He loves her*, she thought. She had known it ever since his return. It was a secret she had discovered from seeing him look at Gilonne's portrait.

He would talk about it someday. She wouldn't press him. She had the wisdom and patience of a good hunter. Leaving him to his thoughts, she glanced at the picture of herself wearing a beaver hat with three white feathers. She was pleased by the sprightly look Peter had given to the feathers: They were like wisps of smoke ready to leave her head and float gaily into the air. Was it his way of commenting on the whimsicality of her mind? She liked that idea. The older she became, the more she dreaded boredom and uniformity.

Ogier stood up and helped her to the table the Huron had brought in. She admired his height, his broad shoulders, his resolute face. With his straight nose, forceful eyebrows, and hard yet sensual mouth, he was a proud descendant of the strong Viking breed that had been sobered by Catholicism and nourished by Roman culture—and Norman buckwheat porridge! There was little outward sign of the storms that, she knew, sometimes raged inside him. He appeared to be a calm but ambitious man who had long since found his balance. But what dreams lived behind his smooth forehead? Were they now all centered on that wall where the firelight capriciously played over three visions of a beautiful young woman celebrating a dazzling moment of nature with all the charm of her being?

Lady Bertrade suddenly remembered with annoyance that Gilonne was married to a Protestant.

"I'd forgotten all about him!" she said aloud.

The news came to Alençon that the best guide for taking Protestants out of France and into Holland or Switzerland had been arrested and sent to the galleys. He had been questioned under torture. Everyone in the Morel d'Arthus household was afraid he might have revealed how many times Hélye had paid him to guide people who didn't have enough money to pay for themselves. Fear gripped the entire town. There was hardly a Protestant family who had not at one time or another called on this guide to help a close or distant relative, and they knew what superhuman strength it took to hold out against torture. It was announced that from now on the property of Protestants who fled the country would be seized and given to Catholic works of charity.

During this time Gilonne would have given little thought to Ogier de Beaumesnil if he hadn't been talked about almost as much as the Protestants' misfortunes. He was said to be a godsend for those who wanted to escape as quickly as possible, in spite of the great risks involved: He bought their property at high prices, and paid cash. Some said he handed out his money so freely because he wanted to add a glitter of generosity to the coronet he had acquired when he became a count. Others said he had no need to make it shinier, since it was still brand-new, but this was only the spiteful reaction of petty noblemen who had come down in the world and were living poorly, and of jealous rich bourgeois who didn't yet have a noble title to consecrate their wealth.

After Ogier had bought the lacemaking establishments whose owners were leaving the country, the only ones still in Protestant hands were those belonging to the Plessis d'Ocagne, Boisville, and Morel d'Arthus families. They appeared to be sound, but it was said that he expected them to fall, and that in the meantime he rode magnificent horses from his own stud farm, frequented the duchess's palace in Alençon and the royal court in Versailles, and inspected his warehouses in Paris.

Many other things were said about him, but not how he had survived having Indian arrows shot into him or how his head had healed after being scalped. Gilonne didn't dare to question anyone, even Michanteau. Irritated to realize that her reluctance meant she was still thinking too much about Ogier, she waited impatiently for the day when she would be able to talk about him in front of Hélye without emotion. That day would mark the end of her senseless obsession with the memory of an evening that seemed halfway between a dream and reality. She would then attach no more importance to Ogier than to any of the Morel d'Arthus' other customers. For, strangely enough, he was a customer, even though he was now a lace manufacturer himself, and he had bought many pieces of excellent lace. He had come in one morning with two of his finest greyhounds, and, after making them lie on the floor with one gesture, had summoned a salesclerk with another. In exchange for several hundred écus, a big box of lace had been delivered to his house on the Rue Saint-Blaise.

His name was also associated with the Jesuits. He often went to their school on the Rue du Marché aux Porcs. He had given money for new buildings and was evidently intent on replacing Count de Maure as the school's most generous benefactor. It was said that he wanted to hasten the creation of teaching posts for Oriental languages, not only so that the Jesuits would have a school in Alençon as big as the ones they had in Paris but also because he wanted to study some of those languages himself.

Candelario, Michanteau, and Conte-Nouvelles were the source of these reports on Ogier. Though normally stingy with words, Zoltan said that the count was a good master for Grand-Coeur and that even Sir Reginald was satisfied with him, judging from the happy snoring that had greeted Ogier when he went into the barn. Maybe it had been Sir Reginald's way of expressing his joy at seeing an old acquaintance again.

But what intrigued the people of Alençon, and kept conversation going at the suppers of the nobility as well as the bourgeoisie, was the amazing, lasting, and conspicuous infatuation

of Her Royal Highness, the Duchess of Alençon, with Count
Ogier de Beaumesnil. By what kind of sorcery had that son of
peasants, that merchant just back from the wilds of Canada, that
count whose title dated only from yesterday, been able to captivate the princess to whom everyone in Alençon knelt, from
priests to magistrates, from the intendant to the archbishop?
Curiosity was foiled by the closed gates of her palace.

Michanteau, Candelario, and the others were reduced to
making wild guesses that didn't even come close to the real story
of the friendship with which Her Highness favored the former
falconer.

Having been told of the interest he had taken in her beloved
Jesuits' school, and of the kind indulgence that the father superior of the province had shown for him in return, the duchess
invited them both to supper in her palace one evening. The
Huron, who seemed to follow Ogier everywhere, terrified her
servants and interested her guests. Standing erect in a gallery
for three hours without moving a single muscle of his body, he
was an astonishing statue that everyone came to examine.

To satisfy her curiosity and that of her little court, the duchess
asked Ogier to tell them about his travels. He did it briefly,
knowing that those who stretched out such stories too much
were seldom forgiven. When he took his departure that evening
he left regrets behind him, and not yawns. He was therefore not
surprised when the palace secretary sent him a note asking him
to write an account of what had taken him to Canada, ''in order
to satisfy Her Royal Highness's benevolent interest in that land.''

Knowing the duchess's great piety and her affection for her
royal cousin, anyone else in Ogier's place would have answered
that he had been brought to Canada by God and his desire to
serve his king. But Ogier hadn't made his way in the world by
means of platitudes. He wrote to the duchess:

*I was fifteen, your Highness, when I left for New France. My
uncle and my cousins were not expecting me there. When the
members of my family had gathered to discuss emigration,
the possibility that our Pervenchères branch might follow the
Mortagne branch had not been considered. My father had
decided that he and I would stay in France. Later we would
see who would go and join Pierre Boucher* if he asked others*

_____
*One of the first and most famous French emigrants to Canada.

from Perche to augment the population of his fief of Trois-Riviéres, on the Saint Lawrence. And suddenly I arrived without warning, announcing that I was now an orphan. My relatives were surprised and grieved, and they were taken aback still more when I told them my reasons for coming, aside from my affection for them. I had to begin by telling them—they were very ignorant—Plato's parable of the metals. The Greek philosopher said, "Citizens, you are brothers, yet God has framed you differently. Some of you have the power to command, and in the composition of these he has mingled gold, wherefore also they have the greatest honor; others he has made of silver, to be auxiliaries; others again who are to be husbandmen and craftsmen he has composed of brass and iron; and the species will generally be preserved in the children. But as all are of the same original stock, a golden parent will sometimes have a silver son, or a silver parent a golden son." I explained that although my parents should have made me of brass and iron so I could placidly work in the fields, they had, by God's will, made me of gold and silver, and that a greater destiny had called me to Canada, where I felt there was a place for the royal mixture of metals that composed me. And I concluded by saying to them, "Here I am!"

My uncle was a wise, honest, and kind man. He listened to that outpouring of adolescent self-importance and accepted it. In an effort to discern my real alloy, he asked me what, besides the prospect of long journeys and virgin lands, had attracted me to America. I replied that I was attracted mainly to commerce, on which I had definite and, I hoped, new ideas. He and my cousins let me discourse on the commercial principles of the ancient Greeks and Phoenicians. I gave a learned exposition of their respective character traits and spoke for a long time about their duplicity, presenting the Phoenicians as more devious than the Greeks. I did not conceal a certain affection for the ancient Greeks, in view of their wonderful practice of the arts and their equally wonderful civilization. They had undoubtedly been, I proclaimed in that log cabin with an icy wind howling outside, the most gifted people of all time. If I did not give my poor cousins a lecture on Greek art, it was only because I was saving it for later; that night I wanted to show that I could speak concisely, without wandering from one subject to another.

Finally I let my uncle speak.

*He said he had listened to me carefully and that I probably
had so much gold in my body that it made my words sparkle.
He told me what he thought of my Greeks and Phoenicians:
From a commercial viewpoint, it seemed to him that they were
not worth much, and after hearing me tell about their greed
and trickery he thanked God that they had never sailed to
Canada. He then told me, with affectionate good humor, that
all the men and women who had come there—all of them,
without exception—were good and honest. Canada was not
a dumping ground to which undesirable people had been sent,
but a fine French furrow in which only good seed was sown.
He hoped that, along with the mixture of precious metals inside me, I also had the good qualities of my family and my
birthplace.*

*If my uncle had been able to remain calm as he listened to
me, the same was not true of his oldest son, an excitable
young man not overburdened with subtlety, who would have
liked to state his opinion of me in forceful terms. Restrained
from doing so by his father, he had to relieve his tension by
having himself bled the next day. My two younger cousins,
less excitable and more intelligent, laughed so loudly that
their father had to caution them against waking up the neighbors.*

*Before I had recovered from the fatigue of my three-month
voyage, my relatives told me they were going on a punitive
expedition against the Iroquois. I asked to go with them and
share the dangers. My uncle pointed out to me that, in spite
of my precious gifts, I had neither the equipment nor the
training for such an expedition. As soon as they came back,
he promised, he would see about finding me work in keeping
with my metallic composition.*

*They left, singing and laughing. I never saw them again.
All four of them died in horrible circumstances.*

*Soon afterward, the leaders of the little community came
to tell me that I had inherited everything from my uncle and
cousins. I was surprised by the size of my inheritance. In
fifteen years, probably living with monastic simplicity, they
had amassed a considerable amount of money in ways that
involved no Greek or Phoenician duplicity.*

*A Jesuit appreciated my knowledge of the ancient world but
taught me to see and understand the modern, and to limit
Mercury, the god of commerce, to his proper place in it.*

Sometimes I felt regret and even remorse at the thought of my good relatives. I would then say to myself that God must have used me as a means of having them go off to meet their death lightheartedly, because a trapper had told me that during the evening he had spent with them beside their campfire they had laughed uproariously at each mention of their precious cousin's precious metals.

The duchess had two readers. Luckily for Ogier, it was not the melancholy Madame de Taunay-Rousselin who was asked to read his letter but the sprightly Marie-Ange de Motté. The former would have stumbled over every word and read each humorous line with weary contempt. The latter could still see Ogier's handsome face and hear his ironic but warm laugh. He was the kind of man she liked.

The evening began with the boredom that ordinarily hung over the palace after supper. Monsieur de Bareillon, the duchess's almoner, was dozing as usual. The ladies-in-waiting were yearning for their warm beds. The resigned expression of a dog tied to his kennel was already in many eyes when Marie-Ange decided to rouse everyone with her joyous laughter. She began reading Ogier's letter in her liveliest, most scintillating tone. The almoner was the first to smile. Then the ladies-in-waiting followed suit, and, to everyone's amazement, the duchess laughed gaily.

When Marie-Ange came to the end of the letter, Marquise du Deffant, the first lady-in-waiting, asked if it could be read again, because she hadn't paid sufficient attention (that is, she had slept through the first part of it). The duchess gladly told Marie-Ange to reread it. Monsieur de Charmoy, her secretary; Father Le Cointe, her confessor; and Monsieur de Melet, her equerry, now tried to remember this Ogier de Beaumesnil who had the supreme honor of having written a letter that entertained her. Within an hour, all forty members of her household knew there was a young nobleman—wasn't he that handsome man who always dressed in black, like a Spaniard?—lucky enough to have worked such a miracle. *His fortune is made*, thought Marie-Ange, *and he owes it to me*. She liked lace, but her meager inheritance from her mother didn't allow her to buy any. Now she saw beautiful pieces of *point de France* gently floating toward her, blown by a breath of correctly understood gratitude.

She received more than that. Ogier thanked her indirectly by sending the duchess a large quantity of fine furs from New France to illustrate his story and show what kinds of pelts could be taken there, and since Marie-Ange was the youngest and prettiest woman in the palace, she was given the soft, silky ermines. She also received directly from Ogier a big box filled with lace—the same lace he had bought from the Morel d'Arthus.

Marie-Ange de Motté was too astute to believe in anything but an alliance of interests with the count. She resolved to serve her new master without hope of more tender rewards. She wasn't old and deformed like the duchess, but she knew she wasn't a good enough match for an ambitious nobleman.

From then on, Ogier was invited to supper at the palace every Thursday, often with the Intendant of Alençon, the Archbishop of Le Mans, the Bishop of Alençon, and several eminent Jesuits and noblemen of the region, known for their deep piety. Ogier might have seemed out of place in such company if the duchess hadn't always said, at one time or another in the course of the supper, "Count, what are you going to entertain us with this evening?" But he had enough sense not to "entertain" until the dignitaries enjoying their hostess's fine wines and stuffed capons had had a chance to shine (or become convinced that they had done so) and sink into the sweet drowsiness of digestion. First he listened to them. and then he spoke. With a wide range of topics to choose from in his memory, he would seize any pretext that arose and launch into a story. Although she was very pious, the duchess liked to hear stories of magic and sorcery now and then, especially if they took place long ago and far away from her duchy. As she listened, her face took on an eager, childlike expression that was touching to see in such an ugly old woman.

The duchess was more and more pleased with her handsome merchant. She began consulting him about purchases of land and houses, or alterations she was planning to make in this or that building. The property of exiled or imprisoned Protestants was coming into her hands more and more often. Before letting her Catholic charities benefit from it, she always sent for Ogier, who, she said, never failed to give her sound advice.

Covered with the lace and furs he had given them, the members of her little court were favorably disposed toward Ogier. But they would have felt the same even without his gifts. What they liked most about him was that he entertained them. They all agreed that the palace became dreary when he had been away from Alençon too long.

A great deal of the lace he brought to the palace was for the duchess, and he brought so much that his generosity was beneficial to her town. Because of this, she showed a marked fondness for lace. But, fearing that she might be regarded as frivolous, she was careful to say and demonstrate that she wore it quite sparingly.

Ogier told her one day that she ought to be the ambassador of Alençon lace at Versailles. She promised that as soon as his workshops finished the dress-fronts they were making, she would take them to Versailles and let them be admired at court. This was the first time anyone had ever thought to talk to her about such frippery, and she was grateful to Ogier for making her forget, if only for a few moments, that she was hunchbacked.

These little palace secrets didn't reach Gilonne. She saw Ogier again only once, from a distance. The sight of him stirred strong emotion in her, but she attributed it to her pregnancy. This was during the time when she was working persistently on what she called her invention.

She told Hélye about it one evening when he seemed worried and she wanted to distract him. "Do you remember that I once told you I was working on an idea I'd had? Would you like to see the sample I've made?"

She showed him a piece of lace in which, instead of the usual ground of bars with picots, there was a net made with simpler, flatter stitches, without buttonhole stitching.

"As you can see, the meshes are only little loops of thread connected by a thread laid here, diagonally, between the motifs of the design. What do you think of it? You must have noticed that the fashion is changing and finer, softer lace is in demand. Don't you think bobbin lace is serious competition and we ought to make some changes in the way we do things? Furthermore, this new ground can be made in much less time. Will you let me have my women try it tomorrow?"

"No, not tomorrow," said Hélye. "I'm amazed by your invention. When it's put to use, it will make great changes in our patterns and our way of working. I can't tell you how much I admire you. . . . Ah, my darling, when will we finally be able to live as we have a right to do? It's . . . Listen, my angel, I don't want you to show your invention to anyone, not yet. Let's let a few weeks go by."

"But what are you afraid of?"

He looked at her tenderly. His eyes lingered at her waist. It was still so slender that no one could have guessed a new little life was beginning there.

"First I want you to go to Geneva," he said with a sigh.

"Oh, Hélye, what if someone else has the same idea and puts it into practice before I do?"

He smiled. "No one else will have such a good idea!"

"Tell me what you're afraid of. I can see you're upset."

His face became serious again. He was perhaps about to tell her what he dreaded, and how bad the latest news from Versailles was for the Protestants, when they both heard shouting from the direction of the gate near the little house at the back of the garden.

They had pulled the bell cord and were waiting.

Courapied had put their clothes in a wheelbarrow, but each of them was also carrying several bundles, probably containing things that meant so much they had been afraid to let the child take them. Slung over her shoulder, Chopine had the tin bottle that never left her. Sometimes she received liquid alms in it, "for a poor blind woman, sir." Conte-Nouvelles was holding Marie by the elbow to keep her steady on her feet. This was the first time Marie had walked across town since . . . since so long ago that no one could remember when it was. Having managed to drag her this far was an outstanding victory for little Courapied. Thomine stood calmly with both hands on her cane. She was against what was now being done, but since no one else shared her opinion, she felt she had to go with the others whether she liked it or not.

Courapied pulled the bell cord again. She was in a hurry. Coeur-de-Coing had demanded that she come back as quickly as possible. The Angelus would soon ring, and she ought to be already handing out bowls of soup at the poorhouse.

It was a warm day and the walk had been long for the old women. They were impatient.

"Maybe Protestants have doorbells that don't make any noise!" said Chopine.

"Courapied, help me sit down here, on the ground," said Marie. "I feel like I'm about to fall."

"Even on the ground she'll fall asleep, you'll see!" said Conte-Nouvelles.

"What if there's no room for us?" Thomine asked timidly.

"No room? It's like Versailles here! There's enough room for all four of your daughter's mothers, and maybe for all the other old women at the poorhouse too!"

They wore faded blue dresses, big gray aprons, and gray hats. The group they formed could be seen from a distance, and since gatherings of Protestants were forbidden a policeman came up to them and asked, "Are you Protestants?"

Though Marie had seemed to doze off, she was so stung by this question that she raised her head and even succeeded in standing up almost by herself.

"You want to know if *we're* Protestants? Just take a look and tell me if you see anything devilish about us! Come closer and . . . I know you! Aren't you Couria's son?"

He was, unfortunately for him.

"Chopine, you remember Couria, don't you? And you, Thomine? Young man, your mother gave us more trouble than God ought to allow. She was never satisfied. Always yelling that someone had taken her needle or her thread! Conte-Nouvelles, who was it who used to say that people's children don't always look like them? Well, I knew this boy was Couria's son as soon as I laid eyes on him. You all know how good I am at family resemblances. Look, Couria's son, how do you expect to do your work if you can't tell decent people from heretics?"

"You say you're not Protestants, but you'll have to prove it to me."

"Conte-Nouvelles, how can you prove you're not a Protestant to a fool who doesn't have eyes to see with?"

The Angelus rang. There was a brief truce while they all crossed themselves, then hostilities resumed.

"I don't want to hear any more talk like that," said the policeman. "I represent His Majesty and—"

"He represents His Majesty! Couria's son!"

"You'll see how fast Couria's son can get you out of here! You may not be Protestants, but you're just as bad as if you were! Go back to where you came from! Now!"

"Except for toads, you're the nastiest little animal I've ever seen, Couria's son. We won't take one step away from here, because this is where we were going."

"Then you *are* heretics! This house belongs to a Protestant. A rich one. I have orders to watch him closely."

"This little house? It's our daughter's."

"That's right, it's our daughter's."

"Whose daughter? The daughter of all four of you?"

"Yes, all four of us."

This was when the shouting began. The policeman tried to make Marie move on, and she protested loudly that she couldn't. The others assailed him, pulling on his coattails and shoulder belt and hitting him with their canes.

"You crazy old women! If you weren't blind, you'd see . . ."

Hélye arrived, followed by Gilonne and Michanteau.

"These women claim they live in your house, sir," said the policeman.

The appearance of Monsieur Morel d'Arthus, the Protestant, the devils' servant, had an immediate effect on Marie. She fell silent and stared at him in dismay. They had all talked about him often, but had never been close to him before.

"Do they really live here, sir?"

"They live with me," Gilonne said quickly, before Hélye could answer, "in this little house."

The policeman's face brightened at the sight of her. He looked at her with incredulous admiration. This was the beautiful lacemaker some of his companions had seen and told him about. Tonight he could say he had talked to her! He left regretfully once the women had gone into the garden at Monsieur Morel d'Arthus' invitation. In his mind's eye he could still see the rich lace manufacturer pushing a wheelbarrow with their clothes in it, and how the incident had made the pretty young woman's cheeks turn pink.

"Well, we're here," said Chopine, as if this fact might have escaped the others' notice.

Marie decided to explain everything, speaking only to Gilonne, without looking at Hélye.

"They tried to separate us, Gilonne. They wanted to put your grandmother above the bakehouse, where the heat would have cooked her, in a little nook just big enough for a dog to sleep in; and me next to the apothecaries' room, where the noise they make pounding their medicines all the time would have kept me from sleeping; and Chopine in a room full of snotty-nosed children; and they still hadn't decided where they were going to put poor Conte-Nouvelles, maybe outdoors in the sun and the rain, who knows? So we told them we'd been together for more than eighteen years and we weren't going to let them split us up just because they were tearing down the poorhouse so they could build it back all wrong. Even Coeur-de-Coing was on our side.

But the director said that was how it was, and we had to do as
we were told or get out. We were thinking it over when they tore
down our fireplace, our beautiful fireplace, the one that warmed
you almost as soon as you were born! We couldn't stand that,
so here we are.''

Gilonne put her arm around Thomine's thin shoulders.

Hélye smiled and said, ''There's a big room here that you can
live in, when a little work has been done to get it ready for you.
And it has a fireplace.''

Still without looking at him, and as if she were speaking to
someone else, Marie said she would take a look at it.

She saw it and described it to the others.

''The fireplace isn't as good as our old one, but it's still not
bad. We'll need mattresses and a few other things.''

''We'll send you what you need,'' said Hélye.

Then he left, still smiling. *At least this has distracted him
from all the gloomy things he had on his mind,* thought Gilonne.
But as she prepared to cope with the invasion she worried about
what Hélye would think of it when, after seeing its quaintness,
he also saw its drawbacks.

Zacharie brought four wool mattresses. Marie described
them. None of the old women had ever seen mattresses like that.
Marie also described the other things Zacharie brought. When
he had finished, she looked at him and asked, ''You're a Protestant too?''

''Yes.''

''*Everybody* must be a Protestant here! What are we getting
ourselves into?''

Gilonne decided it was time for her to make a few remarks.
She pointed out firmly that Monsieur Morel d'Arthus had taken
them in without a word of complaint, even though they had just
appeared out of the blue. He had been kind enough to give them
this big, beautiful room, and they ought to be as nice to him as
he was to them, or else . . .

''Or else what?'' said Marie. ''You're not defending the Protestants, are you?''

''If you attack them when they're helping you, yes. I work
for the Morel d'Arthus and they've given me a place to live. I
don't want you to make any trouble for them.''

''You see?'' Marie said to the others. ''You see what the devil
has done? He's changed our little Gilonne! She doesn't love us
anymore, and she loves those children of Satan!''

Michanteau advised Gilonne to go to Hélye, who was waiting in the next room, and let her try to smooth things over.

The boys' playroom, which Hélye had given to the four women, was cut off from the rest of the little house, and that was probably why he had been willing to let them stay there.

"That's an uncommon foursome," he said to Gilonne when she had rejoined him.

"It's good of you to take them in."

"I couldn't let your grandmother sleep in the street."

"Yes, but the others . . ."

"As I understand it, they're determined to stick together the rest of their lives."

"They've known each other since they were children, the way Michanteau and I have."

He suddenly seemed thoughtful, and after a long silence he said, "There are too many blind women in Alençon. If I'd been able to carry out my plan of creating a village where our workers could live in better conditions, I'm sure that fewer of them would have gone blind."

"You'll do it soon. We'll do it together. That reminds me: When do you think I can put my invention into practice? And you still haven't told me why I have to wait."

He looked at her, undecided. She meant more to him than anything else in the world, he lived only for her, and he was perhaps going to make her suffer terribly. The king was making his campaign against "heresy" even harsher. The time would come when they could no longer work there. And the time would also come when their marriage was discovered and she was judged to be as guilty as he. His nights were haunted with remorse over having dragged her, for his own happiness, into the dark hole that was opening before the Protestants. His only consolation was knowing that she would soon leave the country to give birth to their child. His heart ached at the thought of their separation, but he felt he could make up for his selfishness by that sacrifice. And once she was in Switzerland he would leave her there if things got worse in France. With the help of Samuel and his wife Rachel, she could open a lacemaking shop. That was why he didn't want her to reveal her invention now: She could use it more profitably later, in Switzerland if need be. But he wouldn't tell her that until tomorrow. He wanted one more sweet evening with her.

He didn't have it. The new tenants did their best to disturb that pleasant summer night.

Gilonne and Hélye left the window of their room open because they liked to look at the stars. It was through this window that they smelled smoke. Michanteau and Gilonne ran to the old women's room and were able to put out the flames in the fireplace before a chimney fire started. Then they had to listen to the women's grievances. Why had they been given that wheat flour for their porridge? Good porridge had to be made with buckwheat. Chopine complained that they had nothing to drink. Conte-Nouvelles expressed doubts about the wool mattresses: Straw ones were better because you could use them for scratching as well as sleeping. Even so, she would try to sleep on her wool one. Marie, however, was afraid it was going to be hard for her to sleep with all those devilish Protestants so close to her. Thomine said nothing, but her tense, worried little face was painful to see.

It seemed clear that difficult days lay ahead. And nights. In the middle of this one, Conte-Nouvelles groped her way to the kitchen door and knocked on it. Marie was in bad shape from being so close to heretics. She was choking, and acting as if she were possessed. They had given her verbena tea, which was usually good protection against the devil, but it hadn't worked this time. They needed holy water.

"There's no need for you to go to a church at this time of night," Hélye said to Michanteau when she and Gilonne told him what was wrong.

He went into the kitchen, took some water from the well, poured it into a little bottle and handed it to Michanteau.

"Let some time pass," he said. "long enough for you to go to Notre-Dame and back, then take this to—What did you say her name was?"

"Marie."

"Take it to Marie, tell her it's holy water—may God forgive us—and I'm sure she'll be cured instantly."

She was.

Gilonne and Hélye went back to bed and laughed as they tried to imagine what the old women would think of next. The comical side of the situation had finally cured Hélye's depression. He again had hope. And besides, he had his wife in his arms and didn't want to think about anything else.

* * *

The next day it was decided to make Bichon a Courapied for the old women in their new home. She would live with them—the room was very large—and go to work with Peter each day when she had finished taking care of them.

There were also complications between the two painters, who didn't share the attic of the big house without friction. Salomon recited *Les Tragiques*, by Agrippa d'Aubigné, in a booming voice as he worked, and Peter said he was going deaf from it. Like Salomon, Peter admired the famous Protestant poet who had never surrendered, not even to King Henry IV, whom he loved and revered, but, he said, hearing his great poem recited over and over again, all day long and sometimes at night, was enough to try the patience of God Himself.

When the two artists performed their assigned task of singing in the workshops, they always argued over which psalms to sing. But their bickering was a diversion for the workers, and that, said Hélye, amounted to reaching his original goal by another path. The women were becoming more and more anxious, and some were even terrified. Every day at least one of them knocked on the door of Hélye's office weeping, and apologetically asked for money to cover the cost of her journey out of the country. She would offer to repay him by giving him her family fortune: a shawl, collar, or wedding headdress made of fine lace, which she had hoped to bequeath to her oldest daughter. Hélye would refuse to take her treasured relic, give her the few livres she wanted, and wish her success in her new home. Soon he would have to resign himself to closing half his workshops.

Other women, who didn't suffer the anguish of leaving their ancestral town, their memories, and the graves of people dear to them, and then going off in fear toward the unknown, suffered in their own way. Hiding in a chest, young Lancelotte saw the arrest of her eighty-year-old great-aunt, who was taken to the Community of New Catholics and made to convert to Catholicism in a moment of confusion. But at first the old woman had screamed that she was being taken to hell, spat on the policemen, stirred up everyone in the street, and kicked so vigorously that she had to be tied up. Lancelotte said she would always hear the screams of that innocent woman being martyred. It had become necessary to stop the innocent woman's dousing of Catholic priests who passed beneath her window because she had ceased to be satisfied with merely pouring water on their heads and had begun dropping the bucket on them too.

"Little Lancelotte is becoming strange," Gilonne said to Hélye one evening. "She's started prophesying. Yesterday she threw
her work to the middle of the table, stood up, began trembling,
and told us she saw the king in hell, pricked by the devil's pitch-
fork, bleeding and repentant. She said there would be no mercy
for him, and he would spend eternity watching his blood flow.
She saw blood all over the worktable. Some of the women began
screaming. Today, more blood, this time from the shoulders of
the great papist ladies at court. Every piece of lace made by
Protestants will scratch and wound Catholic flesh, by God's will.
Lancelotte says God Himself told her to announce that. What
shall we do? I'm afraid of the effect her agitation may have on
the others. They're ready to believe anything."

"I don't see what we can do," said Hélye. "We certainly
can't send Lancelotte away. She needs the work. And she'd be
immediately taken in by the Community of New Catholics. One
of their recruiters is always prowling on our street."

Gilonne didn't tell Hélye about Lancelotte's prediction concerning him. It was foolish to attach any importance to such
ravings, of course, but Lancelotte had seemed so firmly convinced of what she was saying! According to her, the papists
were going to kill Hélye. She saw him cold and pale, with his
eyes closed. There was one cross on his forehead and another
between his joined hands. Both crosses were flaming and giving
off flashes of lightning, and would burn the soul of anyone who
looked at them.

Work in the shop was going badly. There was an order for
some big and wonderful flounces from Countess de La Roche-
foucauld-Roye. Did she know how much the workers had wept
as they plied their needles for her? She too must have wept a
great deal, since she suffered from a rupture in her family: one
branch of it had converted to Catholicism while the other remained faithful to Protestantism. There was sorrow everywhere. Even so, the workers smiled when Peter and Salomon
came into the shop gesticulating, and one said, "We're going to
sing the First Psalm," and the other said, "No, the Third!" But
when they finally came to an agreement, they enjoyed singing
so much that they forgot their quarrels.

Wanting to make life easier for the four old women, Hélye
decided to install a fireplace with a raised hearth in their room,
so they could cook their porridge and soup without having to
bend over. They emphatically rejected the plan and sent away

the mason and his helper who came to begin work on it. "What's the matter with people nowadays?" said Chopine. "They want to keep tearing down every fireplace in sight!"

The draper who had been so strongly attracted to Gilonne in the stagecoach from Paris encountered her one Thursday when she was visiting Mama Bordier in the marketplace. She tried to take refuge behind Mama Bordier and her clamorous poultry, but she couldn't escape his eager efforts to win her favor. Tenaciously he waited for the pleasure of carrying her chicken, with its head down and its feet tied together, so she wouldn't have to soil her pretty hands.

She treated him almost rudely as he walked beside her, but he seemed to take no notice, and kept telling her how hard he had tried to find her and how happy he was that he had finally succeeded. She prayed they wouldn't meet Hélye. The draper wouldn't leave until they reached her garden gate, where she was surprised to see her four old women sitting on a bench they had dragged there. Marie, awake for the time being, took a long look at the handsome gentleman wearing a lace cravat and a light summer coat made of cream-colored silk, who gracefully took off his stylish broad-brimmed straw hat and bowed to Gilonne.

"What are you all doing out here," Gilonne asked when he was gone, "instead of sitting in the garden?"

"We were prisoners long enough!" said Marie. "We don't like being behind fences. We'd rather be outside of them."

"Then you intend to be in the dust of the street every day, rather than under the big trees in the garden?"

"Under your big trees we have only birds to talk to. Here, the whole town passes by. . . . I know that handsome man who was walking with you, and I was glad to see him again. His grandmother used to be a huckster, but she managed to save up a tidy sum of money, and now the family is rich and respected. He's not married and he'd be a good husband for you. You'd be the queen of the biggest draper's establishment in Alençon. They live near the Lancrel Gate. I like that part of town."

Passersby became used to seeing the row of old women in blue dresses and gray bonnets chattering and laughing on their bench until darkness or rain drove them inside. One morning a man stopped to talk to them and addressed Marie with friendly courtesy. The three others immediately asked her what he looked like.

"He's not too bad. Somewhere in his thirties," she told them, talking about him as if he weren't there. "He's still in fairly good condition. His clothes are clean. Maybe he's a bourgeois."

"Are you a bourgeois, sir?" asked Chopine.

He said he was an innkeeper. Not here in Alençon, but in the country. He had come to town to enjoy himself a little.

"Does your wife keep the inn while you're enjoying yourself?"

"Yes. And she makes lace in her spare time."

"If she learned to make lace here, maybe we know her."

No, he was sure they didn't. She had learned lacemaking somewhere else and wasn't known in Alençon. Suddenly a little suspicious, Marie remarked that she thought she had seen him on that street before. And if he came to town to enjoy himself, it wasn't the best street for it. "You should go to the Place du Palais, young man."

He had been there. But he preferred calm places where he could think.

"You came to Alençon to think?" asked Marie. "And you made a long trip for that?" She said to Thomine in an undertone, "There's something about this man that rubs me the wrong way." Then, more loudly, "Well, good-by, sir. Maybe we'll see you again."

But he didn't leave. He stepped closer to Marie and asked, "You're not Protestants?"

"Of course not! Can't you see? Do we look like Protestants to you?"

No, they didn't, he said, but in these troubled times you couldn't be too careful. Though it was true that he sometimes came there to think, he also gave a little assistance to people who . . . were not Protestants.

"What do you mean by that?"

They were four honorable old women, he told them, and while they couldn't all see, they could hear perfectly well. And every day they sat near the house of one of the richest Protestants in Alençon. If they discovered anything useful, and if they wanted to earn a livre for each piece of information, all they had to do was wait until he came back, then tell him what they had heard.

"In that inn of yours, you must serve some odd drinks to your customers!"

"Not only are we blind, sir," Thomine said in her melodious voice, "but we're also stone-deaf. That's a pity for our purses, but it's God's will."

When the man had walked away, shrugging his shoulders, Conte-Nouvelles murmured, "If we just made up things to tell him, we'd still get a livre for each one, wouldn't we?"

"That's a bad idea," said Chopine. "You'd begin by making things up, but then, before you knew what was happening, they'd find some way to make you tell the truth."

"But what if we didn't know any truth to tell?"

"They'd make you tell it anyway."

The others assumed that Chopine must know what she was talking about, and accepted her judgment.

They had told Gérasime about their change of address. He sometimes came to see them, and they invited him to fry some fish for himself. He liked their company but declined their invitation: with time, he said, he had become used to his steady diet of boiled food and no longer yearned for more varied cooking. He did, however, talk about his troubles. What bothered him most were his trips to Montsort. His daughter still made him go there at least once a week. The notary had recovered from the swollen neck he had developed after wearing a collar made in Mistress Lescure's shop, so Gérasime no longer went to Montsort to ask about him. Instead, he went to ask to be paid. But the notary wouldn't pay. At first he had said, "Tomorrow," or "Wait until I get back the money that's owed to me." In the last few weeks, however, he had changed his tune. Now he wouldn't even open the door to Gérasime, but called from his window, "How dare you expect to be paid for a collar that was so harmful to me and made me buy medicine!" Gérasime couldn't bring himself to report this to his daughter. She had only two workers now and she worked hard all day long, even with her dim sight. Yes, she was having a miserable time of it.

"When I used to sell lace," Marie said sententiously, "I never let my customers have anything unless they paid for it on the spot."

"You never sold anything but *bisette* at two sous an ell!" said Conte-Nouvelles. "People will pay for *that* on the spot, but you know as well as I do how many noblemen buy fine lace without a sou in their pockets."

"You're saying I only sold *bisette*? That's ridiculous! I sold
the very finest Alençon lace, and . . ."

Mathieu was seldom there now to break up quarrels among
the women, as he had done in the past. He hardly ever came to
visit Gilonne. Was he bothered by her situation? Was he afraid
the Morel d'Arthus would be reluctant to see him, now that they
had no choice but to regard him as one of the family? Whatever
the reason for the rarity of his visits, Michanteau was heartsick
over it. To console herself, in the evening she came to chat with
the old women and eat from their pot of porridge. She had seen
to it that they were supplied with buckwheat flour.

July was nearing its end. It was a blue and gold summer. The
raspberry bushes in the garden gave so generously that big salad
bowls were filled with their bounty. Hélye smiled when he
watched Gilonne eat a whole bowlfull at one sitting. She ate
them one at a time, unhurriedly, but with a steadiness that
amused him. He liked to discover a gesture or a habit of hers
that he hadn't known before. She told him how she had been
permanently affected by Mistress Lescure, who had trained her
never to make any abrupt movements. She was glad to have had
that training, but it was contrary to her nature. She was always
having to make an effort to control her impatience. Lacemaking,
and life, required it of her. Maybe when she got to heaven she
could spend eternity running, fidgeting, and wriggling as much
as she wanted.

"Is it really unpleasant for you to sit still when you work?"
asked Hélye.

"Yes and no. I love making lace, but I wish . . . I wish I
could make it and run at the same time! It takes endless patience
to make lace, and I think learning that kind of patience was
harder for me than for most other girls."

Once again they talked about the school they hoped to create
someday, in which good work habits would be taught at an early
age. When would Protestants again be allowed to train apprentices?

They learned from packmen and merchants, covered with
dust from the roads they had just traveled, that dragonnades
were becoming even more frequent in Poitou and southern
France. But that was far away.

They tried to forget that since June 16 the children of Protestants from the age of seven on could convert to Catholicism

without their parents' consent. One day, when Hélye had gone to a secret meeting the night before, he told Gilonne that the Protestants had decided to have a day of fasting and would spend August 10 praying in their church.

On that day, the Morel d'Arthus house was emptied, except for Monsieur Mortimer. People left one at a time, every few minutes. Hélye was the last.

"Do you really have to go?" Gilonne asked him.

"There's nothing to be afraid of. We'll be praying, and Father de la Rue, the Jesuit who will come to watch us and report on us later, will see that there's nothing wrong with our behavior. We're still allowed to pray and fast."

But she was worried in spite of what he said.

She spent part of the day with her father-in-law, who was praying in his room, and she was unable to make him take anything but two glasses of water. When she left him, she went to her old women and found that they were about to go and stand outside the Protestant church. She couldn't restrain them. They were sure something was going to happen, and they wanted to be there when it did. She decided to go too; it would be less nerve-racking than waiting at home.

When she reached the Lancrel district, where the church was, she saw a large crowd of Catholics waiting for the Protestants to come out. She thought of turning back. She wouldn't even see Hélye. But then she thought of her old women: Maybe she could help them if they found themselves in difficulty. The people around her seemed hostile, and their shouting was becoming vociferous. They began throwing stones through the windows of the church. Now she was really afraid for her incorrigibly curious old women. They would have done better to stay home.

The crowd was becoming increasingly agitated and the stone throwing had redoubled. Not one windowpane was still unbroken. Hearing someone talk about "the assault," Gilonne learned that the departure of the Jesuit priest, sent by the intendant to act as an observer, was to be the signal, and that the crowd would then rush at the Protestants and "teach them a good lesson."

It was the opposite that happened. The Protestants burst out of the church and, with canes and riding whips, drove away the people who had expected to beat them. Standing in the doorway where she had taken shelter, Gilonne found herself in the difficult situation of having one part of her heart in each camp. She was glad that Hélye hadn't been assaulted, but she wasn't pleased by the thought that he must have pounded a few Catholic skulls. She had always dreaded that something like this would happen.

Suddenly she saw Marie sitting in the wheelbarrow that Bichon had pushed there and watching her three companions, who had charged into the fray brandishing their canes. In their unending darkness, it was possible that they had struck out at anyone who came within range, Protestant or Catholic. If so, it was a fine bit of irony.

Gilonne gathered them up and went home, planning to divert Hélye with the story of their combat.

She waited for him all evening. And all night.

He had probably come in very late and hadn't wanted to disturb her.

At dawn she hurried to the kitchen of the big house. Everyone there was in a state of consternation. No one knew what had become of Monsieur Hélye. Gilonne tried to hide her fear but, seeing how pale she was, Judith led her outside and said to her, "You must make an effort to control yourself, Madame. If Monsieur has been arrested, you must make sure no one finds out who you are, because then you'd be arrested too. Think of Monsieur Mortimer."

When Gilonne turned away from her a little, feeling a wave of nausea, Judith asked, "What month are you in, madame?"

"Two and a half."

"What did Monsieur decide?"

"I'll soon go to Geneva."

"Then I'll go with you. He would have wanted me to."

Gilonne was appalled to realize that Judith was talking about Hélye as if he would never come back.

"Tell me what you know!" she said. "What's happened to him?"

"We don't know yet. But when they decide to take one of us, we always know. . . ."

"*What* do you know? Tell me!"

"Please don't shout, madame. We must all try to save our own lives now, and at the same time try to save the others' lives."

"No, you're wrong! He can't just disappear like that! I'll go to the intendant, I'll find out what's happened, I'll explain . . ."

"No, madame, that's exactly what they're waiting for. If we go to them, they'll arrest us too."

"We have to help him! We have to see everyone who might be able to do something for him."

"I know them, madame. You don't. I'm the one who's going to act now. You must stay here and do nothing. I have my orders. I've had them a long time, since the day you came back from Paris." She sighed. "He's been constantly afraid for you. I swore you wouldn't be involved in anything. Try not to worry too much. Think of your baby."

"What shall I tell Monsieur Mortimer?"

"Nothing. He's so weak. It would kill him."

"But Hélye will come back, won't he? You know them, you've said so yourself, and he talked to you. You believe he'll come back, don't you?"

"Only God knows, madame. As soon as it's dark I'll go to see our friends and try to find out where he's been taken."

But it wasn't until early the next morning that Judith came to tap on the window of the little kitchen where Gilonne was waiting. She had refused to go to bed, in spite of Michanteau's insistence.

Judith had seen two pastors, Mehérenc de La Conseillère and Elie Benoit. She had learned that, after them, Hélye was the man the Duchess of Alençon hated most. And unfortunately her royal cousin liked and listened to her. The King's Council was going to put the three men on trial.

"But the pastors haven't been arrested, have they?"

"No. They weren't caught with weapons in their hands."

"Neither was Hélye! He didn't even have a cane! You know it's not true!"

"No, it's not true, but they claim it is. The pastors also told me that he's going to be accused of making insulting remarks about the king. That's what they always say when they have nothing else to say."

"And that's not true either! He's never said a word against the king. He respects him. He's a loyal subject. We can prove it. I'm going to see the intendant, now."

"No, you must stay here, as I've already told you. And the pastors agree with me."

"They know about me? They know I'm his wife?"

"Yes. I asked them for advice about you, madame."

"I'm not the one who matters. I'm not afraid of anything. But we have to stop them from sending him away. I'll prove he's innocent."

''What do you expect to prove, madame? That he didn't give money to everyone who asked for help in leaving the country? That he didn't give alms countless times so that the Protestant poor wouldn't have to eat in Catholic soup kitchens, where they might have been made to convert while they were digesting? That he didn't marry against the king's orders? That he didn't encourage resistance to royal pressure whenever he could? That he didn't often help in the secret burial of a Protestant who had refused the Catholic last rites? That he didn't organize meetings where Protestants decided on ways to get around the royal edicts?''

''So you think he's lost,'' murmured Gilonne.

''I didn't say that, madame. Pastor Elie Benoit can't do anything: He's in such disfavor with the authorities that he'd only make things worse for Monsieur. But Pastor La Conseillère will do as much as he can. He's not in great favor either, and he's already been exiled to Nantes for six months, but he'll talk to the intendant, who's a fair-minded man.''

Fair-minded though he was, Intendant Barillon de Morangis was unable to do anything against the duchess's implacable determination to have the three men tried and convicted.

Pastor La Conseillère was unable to give the help for which Gilonne had hoped because he was banished from Normandy and the neighboring provinces. And since she didn't succeed in having Pastor Elie Benoit exiled, the duchess concentrated her efforts against Hélye.

Gilonne waited anxiously for the verdict of the King's Council. Intendant Barillon de Morangis was transferred to Caen for not having shown enough zeal in denouncing the pastors. And still nothing was known about Hélye, not even where he had been sent.

Before leaving Normandy, Pastor La Conseillère came to tell Gilonne to stay out of sight and not try to do anything, because she couldn't help her husband and might harm herself.

''Is there really nothing I can do for him?'' she asked. ''What if I went to the king and told him about my husband's kindness, and his respect for His Majesty, and—''

''No. You wouldn't be allowed to see the king and you'd be thrown into a convent. Pray, my child. Pray with all your heart. God listens to all of us, whoever we are.''

When he had left her and was walking across the garden, she ran after him. "Tell me the truth. He's lost, isn't he?"

"I don't have much hope. But I really don't know anything."

She spent much of her time with old Monsieur Mortimer, not caring what anyone might think. He needed her. He was becoming weaker. When he asked to see his son, she said he had gone to Paris on an urgent business matter. She would take his hand in hers and they would talk about Hélye for hours. She learned more about her husband in the three days and nights she spent in Monsieur Mortimer's monastic room than she had learned in all the time she had known him. Remorse gripped her heart: She hadn't understood or loved him enough. If God allowed him to come back, she would live only for him, and would finally be the loving wife he had waited for her to be, with the smiling dignity he had always shown, even in suffering. Because he had suffered. His father knew it.

"He once said to me about you, my child, 'Someday she'll love me. I know it. And I'm waiting.' "

The last rose that Hélye had put into the china vase before he left was now a week old. Gilonne had given orders that no one was to touch it. The petals that had fallen on the lace-covered table were turning yellow. She looked at them as she lay in bed, and wept. She slept little and lightly, so Judith didn't have to knock on her door for long when she came one night to bring her horrifying news.

From a source he preferred not to name, Pastor Elie Benoit had learned who had made the accusation and what it contained. To win favor with the authorities, and also because he resented having been accused of stealing his lace patterns, one of Hélye's clerks, newly converted to Catholicism, had reported the names of six Protestants to whom he had given money for a journey into exile. A man who had acted as a guide for Protestants illegally leaving the country had recently been arrested, and his questioning under torture had done the rest. It had just been learned that Hélye had been sent to Marseille.

Marseille! The very name made the whole kingdom shudder.

"No!" screamed Gilonne. "No! Not the galleys!"

Judith took her in her arms and held her for a long time, until her sobbing died down.

"Men come back from the galleys, madame, they come back. . . . A cousin of mine spent five years in them, and then one day he was sent back to us."

Gilonne wasn't listening. She could no longer hear anything; she was aware of nothing but her despair. She would never feel anything but mingled despair and remorse.

Finally, however, Judith's voice came through to her. "I've also been told that tomorrow they'll come to close the work-shops and put them under seal. Monsieur Mortimer must be brought here, to this little house. You're a Catholic, madame; you can prove you were a tenant here, and maybe they'll let you keep this house, especially since you're taking care of four old women. We servants are in no danger for the time being. They'll try to make us convert and we'll pretend to think it over. That will gain time. But for Monsieur Mortimer there's not much time left."

Little by little, Gilonne grasped the idea that she had to go and fetch her father-in-law.

Carried by Zacharie and Salomon, he was taken into her room and put down on her bed, because that was where he would be most comfortable. He was so pale, so cold. Tears had wet his cheeks and the white collar of his nightshirt. He didn't speak and refused to eat or drink anything. He had been told nothing, but he seemed to understand what was happening.

The big house was emptied during the night. Eslue, the cook, who prided herself on having never let the kitchen fire go out in the thirty years she had been there, put it out and let her tears fall on the ashes. They all left, one after another, every quarter of an hour, as they had to do in order not to be accused of forming assemblies. Each one had a bundle of clothes and food, Eslue having divided the contents of the pantry evenly. But be-fore they left, they prayed together around the big kitchen table.

Titus was the last to go. He had difficulty locking the gate. Sobbing, he took one last despairing look at the kitchen where the Lord had given him so many good meals. Then, about to go off and disappear into the night like the others, he saw a glimmer of light coming from the cellar. He went back. Someone must have forgotten to put out a candle.

A candle was burning, but not because it had been forgotten. The two little sisters who had been Eslue's helpers had lit it to make themselves less afraid in the cellar.

"What are you doing here? I thought you'd left long ago!"

They told him, sniveling, that they didn't want to go to the papist orphanage, as Madame Judith had decided they would do. If they went there, they would be forced to lose their souls, and when a soul was lost, where could you get another one? No, they would stay here, even if they were bitten by rats.

Titus couldn't take them with him. The ill-tempered cousin who had grudgingly consented to let him stay in her house wouldn't take in two children besides. But he couldn't just go away and leave them to wander through the streets. Judith would have known what to do, but she had gone to stay with her sister, far off in the country. He decided to ask Gilonne to take care of Marie and Magdelaine. They were willing. She was one papist they had nothing against; she had twice given them anise candy.

Gilonne made room for the two sisters, even though Michanteau grumbled that their "family" kept getting bigger and bigger. How were they going to feed all these people? This concern led her to talk to Gilonne about what she should try to save in the big house.

"It will belong to you when Monsieur Mortimer dies."

Gilonne went to him and asked, "Would you like us to bring some clothes and other things from your house, before . . ."

He nodded and showed her the keys that hung from a chain around his neck.

"The portrait of my wife, my engravings," he said. "Take some lace too. And everything in the chest in my bedroom."

When, for the first time, Michanteau saw the private rooms of Hélye and his father, she whistled with admiration, then threw up her hands in despair. "We'll never be able to carry out everything!"

"We mustn't take too much anyway," said Gilonne. "If the house seems to have been emptied, we'll be suspected. And besides . . . I'm sure he'll come back."

"Even so, it's too bad we can't stop them from taking what will soon belong to you." Seeing that Gilonne didn't seem upset by the prospect of losing her inheritance, Michanteau added, "It ought to go to your child."

They took down the portrait of Hélye's mother from the wall, along with several other paintings Gilonne thought he and his father would especially want to keep. Then they carefully replaced them with some of the paintings they found in a little room with shelves that seemed to have been made to hold them.

When they had carried away many works of art, including lace, there was still enough left to avoid giving the impression that something was missing. They took their precious booty to an abandoned gardener's hut and covered it with burlap bags and rusty tools. Then, in Hélye's and Monsieur Mortimer's bedrooms, they found two strong boxes full of gold coins, which they also hid in the gardener's hut.

Now they had to get ready for visits from the police and anyone else who might be sent to investigate. They would pretend to be innocent, piously Catholic tenants who had nothing to do with their Protestant landlords. But what about Monsieur Mortimer? What if the authorities took it into their heads to look inside the little house? There was only one solution: to pass him off as an old man who had been taken in, along with the four old women, when reconstruction work was begun on the poorhouse.

The old women were astounded, and even left speechless for a few moments, by the intrusion of a Morel d'Arthus into the room they now regarded as their personal property. He was put on a mattress and covered with several blankets, but he still complained of being cold. They cautiously stepped toward him.

"What does he look like?" they asked Marie.

She whispered that he looked like what he was: a dying man.

"Don't count on us to watch over a Protestant," she said to Gilonne, who had sat down on the floor beside the old gentleman.

"I don't expect you to do that. As soon as the king's men have paid their visit, we'll put him back in my room. All I ask you to do is keep a good fire going so he'll be warm."

Conte-Nouvelles tapped on the floor with her cane, as if asking for silence, and said, "I think you'd better tell your grandmother everything. You'll have to do it yourself because I can't make myself tell what I know about you, and this is the first time such a thing has ever happened to me, believe me."

Realizing what was about to be revealed, Michanteau took Bichon and the two sisters out into the garden.

"Yes, I suppose it will be better," Gilonne said with a sigh. "Monsieur Mortimer is my father-in-law. I've been married to his son for nearly eight months. If that becomes known, I'll be in great danger of being arrested and locked up in a convent."

These words were followed by such deep silence that Monsieur Mortimer's weak breathing could be heard. Thinking that everyone must suddenly have left the room, he opened his eyes. No, those hideous gargoyles were still there. He closed his eyes and again sank down into his weakness.

"I have one more thing to tell you," said Gilonne. "I'm expecting a baby."

"Good heavens!" exclaimed Chopine. "I just hope it won't be born with horns and a tail!"

What good would it have done Gilonne to get angry? Those poor, ignorant old women were nearing the ends of their lives. She could feel only pity for them. But she knew she mustn't count too much on theirs.

She turned to Monsieur Mortimer, took his cold hand in hers, and decided to stay beside him that night.

In the other camp, the old women had decided to take time to think before saying anything about what they had just heard. They began preparing their porridge in silence. And wasn't silence the best sign of disapproval they could give? They clung to it, except that now and then one of Marie's three blind friends whispered to her, "Is he still dying?"

Michanteau examined Gilonne's haggard face.

"If you can get yourself looking human again," she said, "and act cheerful and even a little coquettish, we can bring it off."

They brought it off without too much difficulty. The policeman in love with Gilonne was very helpful. He said that she did indeed live there, with four old lunatics who took advantage of her kindness. Everyone who knew her agreed that she was a skilled lacemaker with a generous heart.

It was decided that she and the others could go on living in the little house, provided she paid rent for it to the Duchess of Alençon, who, by order of His Majesty, was the new owner of the Morel d'Arthus property. The King's Council had seized everything belonging to the family in Alençon, as well as their country houses and their shops in Paris.

It was now forbidden to enter the big house. Its contents would be sold at auction in several days.

It was time for Gilonne to think about going to Switzerland. Since it was legal for her to leave the country, she could simply take a stagecoach to Paris and another one to Geneva. But she wouldn't leave before Hélye's father had breathed his last. She wanted to be there to help him. In her sorrow, she found satisfaction in feeling useful. He refused to accept milk from anyone but her. When she succeeded in getting him to eat some fruit she felt a little less unhappy. She had gone back to her lacemaking and was now teaching it to the two sisters. The former snack room of the Morel d'Arthus children had been turned into a workshop, and the usual schedule was respected there.

Gilonne, Michanteau, and the sisters were at their work table one morning when there was a violent knock on the door. Gilonne opened it.

"Police. Are you Gilonne Perdriel?"

"You know me perfectly well."

Of course he knew her, the poor lovesick policeman. But he had been ordered to verify her identity before arresting her. The thought of going through the streets with her, which ordinarily would have overjoyed him, now filled him with despair. He had to take the loveliest creature he had ever seen and put her behind the grim walls of the Community of New Catholics. He had been told that though she was not a Protestant, she was a bad Catholic, and would have to spend a year there to "learn to do her duty." Since when had they been locking people up for not going to mass or confession often enough?

For Michanteau and the old women, there was nothing mysterious about the arrest. The police had found out about Gilonne's marriage. But from whom? Would they ever know?

Gilonne told herself that it was only fair for her to share Hélye's pain. No matter what they had decided to make her endure, it would fall far short of the horrible treatment inflicted on him.

Finally, when he had repeated it for the second time, with his blond mustache quivering, she heard the little policeman say that he wouldn't tie her hands if she promised . . .

If she promised what? She smiled at him without realizing it, and he offered to let her ride behind him on his horse. His commander had decided it would be all right for such a short distance, but if she preferred . . .

She didn't prefer anything. She said her good-byes. The old women wept. So did the little girls. Michanteau promised to close the old gentleman's eyes when he died and notify Judith for the burial.

They would all do their best, and wait. Maybe she would be back soon.

The Community of New Catholics, created at the request of the Duchess of Alençon with the king's authorization, and under the authority of the Archbishop of Sées, had the purpose of taking in Protestant men, women, and children who wanted to renounce their old faith and be instructed in their new one. Few of them went of their own free will. The head of the establishment, Mademoiselle de Farcy, didn't have an easy task, but she displayed a zeal that was greatly admired.

As far as the policeman knew, this was the first time a non-Protestant would pass beneath the cross over the entrance of the building. He was convinced that this beautiful young woman had been denounced by a rival who could see no other way to get rid of her.

"You can hold on to me if you're afraid of falling off the horse," he told her.

At the pace he was riding, she was in no danger of falling off. Would he continue to ride this slowly, letting the whole population of the town see her in the custody of a policeman?

From the animation in the streets, she knew it was market day. People coming in from the country would see her like this! But what did it matter? If they wanted to, they could even believe she was being taken to the pillory at the Place du Palais because she was guilty of theft or blasphemy. Looking straight ahead, she saw only a gray mass of people and heard only a dull roar.

The first one to recognize her was Dieudonné Desbraies, the draper. He had heard about Hélye's arrest and he now wondered why the young woman who worked for him had also been arrested. He would go to the intendant and find out. He couldn't tolerate the thought that the woman of his dreams might be mistreated for even one second. He would go to see his friends in the town hall.

The second one was Ogier de Beaumesnil. He was just leaving the duchess's palace, where he had persuaded her that for the next ball at court she should wear a dress-front his workshops had just finished. His mouth was dry from having repeated all the arguments that seemed capable of making her forget she was hunchbacked. He had convinced her that her proud, noble bearing overshadowed the deformity of her back. Magnificent lace would show to better advantage on a woman of regal demeanor than on an insignificant pretty girl. He had achieved his goal, at a cost of considerable effort, and left her with relief. When he saw Gilonne, he decided to go see the duchess again. He too knew about Hélye's arrest and also wondered why his mistress-lacemaker had been arrested. Worried, he hurried back to the palace.

The third person to recognize Gilonne was Candelario. Having recently been appointed Mistress Verlot's sauce cook, he was in the herb market, making a selection. He abandoned his tarragon, marjoram, and chives and ran to the Moor's Inn. What were they going to do to Gilonne? He had to talk with the chevalier immediately.

Mademoiselle de Farcy was middle-aged and tried to steer a middle course between gentleness and harshness in her treatment of the inmates of her establishment: She didn't want to dishearten the sincere converts, but she had to dominate the diehards.

Making the recruits "do their duty" to the faith and the king was the main concern of the Community of New Catholics. Masses, prayers, confessions, liturgical singing, rules of pious living—all this had to be either suggested or imposed, depending on individual cases, which amounted to saying that each inmate had to be treated separately. Mademoiselle de Farcy's days and nights weren't long enough for everything she had to do. She had just asked the duchess for more help and was expecting a contingent of nuns from Paris.

Gilonne Perdriel, convicted of having lived conjugally with a Protestant, was a new kind of case and would have to be treated with finesse. It wasn't known if she had voluntarily accepted this dangerous man who was now rotting in the galleys, or if he had coerced her. The second possibility, Mademoiselle de Farcy believed, was in keeping with the depravity of the Protestants' conduct:

The denunciation of Gilonne Perdriel came from a lacemaker who had been dismissed by the Morel d'Arthus establishment. But what complicated her case was the religious dossier, drawn up years earlier by the secretary of the Compagnie du Saint-Sacrement, that had been forwarded to Mademoiselle de Farcy. It claimed to offer proof of Gilonne Perdriel's heresy and told the strange, disturbing story of a little girl who had a turkey hen for a friend, talked to her, *and heard her answer*. She had therefore been in communication with the devil. The deposition, dated in 1670, was signed by a Benedictine nun in the Montsort convent whose word could not be doubted.

When Gilonne was brought to her, Mademoiselle de Farcy

was still undecided as to how to treat her. The sight of the beautiful young woman whose presence brightened the dark office as if sunlight had suddenly come streaming into it made her still more uncertain. Where had she seen that face before, and those eyes, and that hair? But it didn't matter; even if she had seen her before, it wouldn't change anything.

Since it wasn't indicated in her papers, Mademoiselle de Farcy asked Gilonne her occupation.

"I'm a mistress-lacemaker, madame."

This reminded Mademoiselle de Farcy of something. What had she been told that morning in the workshop of the Community of New Catholics? That the mistress-lacemaker had run away? Or was it that she had come down with a dangerous disease? In any case, another one was needed, and now, thank God, here she was.

Mademoiselle de Farcy postponed looking into the hows and whys of Gilonne's life and immediately sent her to take charge of the workshop, because the Community needed to produce large amounts of lace to remedy its shortage of funds. Instead of having to sleep in the crowded dormitory, the mistress-lacemaker was entitled to a little room of her own.

Needle, thread, parchment. Life seemed to continue there in the same way as before. Now there were bars on the windows, but that mattered little to Gilonne, because she felt she would always be a prisoner of her remorse and despair. And here there were no decisions to make. She could be lethargic in her unhappiness.

Only the thought of old Monsieur Mortimer sometimes made her regret her imprisonment: He was going to die without her there to hold his hand or wipe his forehead.

Unfinished pieces of lace were collected from the workers at the end of each day and handed out again the next morning. One night some valuable lace had been cut to pieces by a Protestant woman whose mind was deranged by her imprisonment, and from then on precautions had been taken to prevent such a thing from happening again.

Gilonne was given a basket full of lace by a Clarist nun to whom she paid no attention. Then she was startled to hear, "Good morning, little Gilonne."

Hélisende!

Hélisende, Sister Adelaide, Banban, the costumed ducks—it

all came back to her, as though from another world, in a rush
of precious memories.

"Oh, Hélisende, if you only knew . . ." She had tried not
to think of anything since being brought there; now she was
going to be able to cry.

When the work had been handed out, she sat down beside
Hélisende and began talking. By the time she finished her story,
it seemed to her that she had clarified her situation and things
were going better. It did her good to let Hélisende know she had
married a man she loved.

A man she loved? What had she just said? Did it mean she
really did love him?

Was it possible to visit a galley convict, to talk to him, if only
for a few minutes? As soon as her baby was born, she would go
to Marseille. During stormy weather, when he was on shore,
she would see him and tell him. Joy glowed in her eyes. Hélisende recognized the little girl she had known in the past, who
used to cry one moment and smile the next.

"Do you know how long they're going to keep me here?"
asked Gilonne.

"I heard it might be a year," said Hélisende, "but less if you
behave well."

That night Gilonne was finally able to sleep soundly.

Just as the bell for matins was rung, she felt someone shaking
her gently. Hélisende told her that an old blind woman had come
to deliver a message: "The sick gentleman is about to die and
is asking for Gilonne."

"But I can't leave!"

"Yes, you can, if I guarantee that you'll come back. Go now,
and I'll do what needs to be done with Mademoiselle de Farcy.
But come back as quickly as you can. Will you promise?"

Gilonne promised and hurried away. She caught up with
Conte-Nouvelles in the street. Monsieur Mortimer had begun
calling for her the day before. The others had kept him company,
one at a time, but it was his daughter-in-law he wanted. Then
he had fainted and they couldn't bring him back to his senses.
He was dying, no doubt about it.

Seeing Gilonne again made Monsieur Mortimer cling to life
a little longer. He even smiled at her and murmured that his
father, now waiting for him in heaven, would surely reproach
him for having wanted to be with a pretty woman until the end.
Although the effort of speaking was exhausting for him, he was

able to say a few more words, he seemed to be quoting from something, but she could make out only the end of a sentence: ". . . and the sky for a church."

Holding his hand in both of hers, she felt it become lifeless before she saw death in his face.

This man had been a father to her. She would never forget his kindness and affection. She thanked God for being merciful to him, for letting him die without knowing what had happened to his son. He had died smiling, and that, she thought, was a death reserved for the righteous.

She made the greatest sacrifice she could make for him: She put in his hands the dried petals of the last rose Hélye had given her.

Judith arrived that night and found the room full. Everyone was praying, each in her own way. She said that Monsieur Mortimer would be considered to have refused the Catholic last rites, since he hadn't asked for a priest on his deathbed. Coming after his son's conviction, this might mean that his body would be thrown into the garbage dump. He had to be buried there in the garden. Zacharie was already digging a grave under the linden tree.

"Just where we like to sit in the shade," grumbled Chopine.

Since they couldn't get a coffin without arousing curiosity, they used two blankets instead. And when it was over, Gilonne went back to the Community of New Catholics. Judith had been distressed to learn that it had become impossible for Gilonne to go to Switzerland, but Gilonne said it might still be possible after all. She now had a friend in her prison.

The women who made lace in the Community were not good workers. In spite of Gilonne's supervision, they progressed slowly. It was decided to bring in several lacemakers from the outside and have them train the others, but no Protestant lacemakers were willing to come because they all feared a trap, and the Catholics who came were treated so coldly by those involuntary converts that they didn't stay very long. Gilonne had the idea of asking Mistress Lescure to take charge of the workshop. In the past, she had always been able to gain the upper hand over even the most recalcitrant workers and apprentices, and she must still have that same forceful personality.

She came, mostly to be with Gilonne and Hélisende again but partly because she liked to rise to a challenge. She struggled to make the women take an interest in their work even though inertia and animosity were their only means of revenge against those who had forced them to renounce their faith. She was rewarded by witnessing a scene she would remember the rest of her life.

Not wanting to abandon her old father, she went on living in her house and came to the Community rather late in the morning. One day when she was about to go into the building, a remarkable procession caught her attention.

It was headed by a handsome blond nobleman who sat erect on his horse with haughty dignity. Behind him rode a buxom old lady who wore a big hat adorned with four white ostrich feathers and had a musket slung over her back and a powder horn over her chest. Finally there were two strange and strangely dressed servants. The sight of them made Mistress Lescure recognize the nobleman leading the procession: He was the one who used to sing songs to the king's glory in the marketplace on Thursdays. He had evidently given up that habit, because she hadn't seen him for quite some time.

The procession stopped in front of the door of the Community. Just then another handsome nobleman arrived, this one dressed in black. He was accompanied by his servant, the Indian of whom everyone in town was afraid, and four big dogs said to be worth their weight in gold because they were of a very rare breed.

These newcomers also stopped in front of the door. The two noblemen bowed to each other. Then the one who sang said, "Count, I'm sure we're both here for the same reason. You've occupied my land in Pervenchères. You live in my house, you probably sleep in my bed, and you're served by my servants. I don't deny that you paid generously for all that. But I ask you to let me have the pleasure of defending my daughter's honor. She wasn't included in the sale."

"You'll defend her better than anyone else could do, chevalier," Ogier de Beaumesnil replied courteously. "But if you should need help, please call on me. And as another favor to me, please take this letter. It's signed by the Duchess of Alençon and orders that Mademoiselle de Ferrières be released."

"I can't refuse you that favor, sir. Give me your letter."

The Huron took it to the chevalier; then he went back to Ogier and they both rode away.

Louis-Guillaume de Ferrières dismounted from his horse and

climbed the front steps of the building. Mistress Lescure let him pass and followed discreetly. Zoltan helped Lady Bertrade to dismount and she too prepared to go into the building, which seemed to her a kind of convent. She didn't like the look of it and wanted to get Gilonne out as quickly as possible.

The chevalier went into Mademoiselle de Farcy's office, followed by his mother, and said with a grandiloquence that might have seemed more appropriate in a song, "For more than six centuries my family has served God and the Kings of France. I myself have often extolled our sovereign's great reign in a strong and loyal voice. I devote my songs of praise to the glory of the king and the splendor of God. Give me back my daughter."

Mademoiselle de Farcy suddenly remembered where she had seen someone who looked so much like her new inmate that she felt she already knew her. There could be no doubt that she was related to this odd nobleman. But she was to stay there a year, by order of the Duchess of Alençon!

"Perhaps this will help you to see the case of Gilonne de Ferrières more clearly," said the chevalier.

He handed her the letter that Ogier de Beaumesnil had given him.

She read it and said, "You may take your daughter, chevalier, since that's the duchess's wish. I'll send someone to fetch her immediately."

"So that we won't disturb you any longer, madame, please tell her that we'll be waiting outside."

The rising sun had driven away the morning mist. The chevalier's tall, proud figure stood out against a background of blue and gold sky. That was all Gilonne saw when she stepped outside the building. She was even more surprised than she had been when Hélisende came to her and joyfully announced, "You're free!"

"This morning I've given you my name and restored your freedom," the chevalier said to her, doffing his hat. "I ask you to make good use of both in the future. It would displease me if I had to come back here and take you out of those people's clutches again. I guaranteed that from now on you would live as a good Catholic. Please don't make me regret it. Here's something that concerns you."

He handed her a roll of parchment. Just then three riders stopped in front of them: the elegant draper and two policemen.

Janine Montupet

"I've obviously come too late," said the draper, lifting his fine straw hat.

"Have *you too* come to free my daughter?" the chevalier asked in a tone that seemed to say, "I don't understand how a bourgeois like you could dare to take a hand in this."

"Yes, I have that honor. The intendant, with the agreement of Her Royal Highness, gave these gentlemen of the police an order to release—"

"My daughter? That's excellent, but useless now. Good-by, sir."

As the crestfallen draper rode away, the chevalier laughed heartily and said to Gilonne, "It seems that every man in Alençon has fallen under your spell! We'd better leave before a regiment of dragoons comes and attacks the building to rescue you."

He turned his horse away before she could even thank him. But he came back, stopped beside her, and said with an ironic smile. "In the future, it might be better if you would inform your family of your marriage plans. We could then dissuade you from them while there was still time."

He rode away again, this time so fast that he heard only an indignant "Oh!" The rest of what she said was lost to him in the clatter of his horse's hooves on the paving stones.

Candelario and Zoltan took the liberty of smiling. And Lady Bertrade said, "Kiss me, Gilonne, on this cheek for me and on the other for him, in spite of everything! I'll give him that kiss when I see him again. For once, he deserves it. Come to Grand-Coeur as soon as you can. I'll be expecting you. We miss you."

"You don't have to leave right away, do you?" said Gilonne. "Come to my house with me."

Candelario took her on his horse behind him, and they rode across Alençon.

The draper, in his fine coat of cream-colored silk, had turned a nearby corner and then stopped to see what the woman of his life would do. As he watched her leave with that strange group, he told himself he had the bad luck to be in love with the woman who attracted more attention than any other in town. She was also the hardest to classify. First he had seen her only as a dreamlike apparition, then he had learned that she was a lacemaker renowned for her talent. In the marketplace he had heard her call a poultry merchant "Mama." Soon afterward he had discovered that she had four mothers, three of them blind. This morning she had turned out to be the daughter of a nobleman from one of the most illustrious families in the region. And he had known since the day before that she had been married to a Protestant who, luckily, had now disappeared. What would he learn about her tomorrow? He sighed.

The four old women sat waiting on their bench. Quivering with joy, they sensed that there was more going on than Gilonne's return.

"Quick, tell us about it!" Chopine said to Marie.

"It's complicated. Let me understand it first and tell you about it later. You won't lose anything by waiting. The people I'm looking at aren't like anyone you've ever seen!"

It wasn't until nightfall that Gilonne remembered the parchment the chevalier had given her. It was an official declaration, signed by the chevalier in the presence of a notary, establishing her as his legitimate daughter.

With it were a few lines in his handwriting on a sheet of music paper: "Don't expect anything from my death, daughter. At best, I will leave you only eighty-six songs to the glory of our beloved king, Louis the Great, and my manuscript on the Vikings."

Why did he have to spoil his decent act? He was the most irritating man on earth.

But he was willing to be her father, at last!

Five

$\mathscr{G}$ILONNE WAS NOTIFIED THAT SHE HAD NO CLAIM TO ANY OF
the Morel d'Arthus property: her marriage was invalid by virtue
of a royal edict prohibiting marriages between Catholics and
Protestants. She was forbidden to leave Alençon without permission from the intendant, and she had to prove that she was
"doing her duty" by going to mass regularly, confessing every
week, and helping the poor of her parish by taking over the
preparation of food in the poorhouse once a month. If these
conditions were met, she would be given a certificate recogniz-
ing her as a good Catholic and clearing her of all charges.

She learned that the Morel d'Arthus furniture and art objects
would be auctioned off the following month. The house was
already being offered for sale on behalf of the duchess. Gilonne
could go on living in the little cottage in the garden until twenty-
four hours after the new owner took possession.

This situation, though trying, was nothing compared with the
painful absence of any news from Hélye.

And what was she going to do with the baby? She kept reminding herself she had promised Hélye their child would be a
Protestant. But how could she leave? How could she defy the
king's edict?

Michanteau urged her to give up her plans to leave the country, but Gilonne thought she and Mathieu could cross the border and come back without being caught. Michanteau insisted that it would be foolish to try.

Judith, however, was all in favor of Gilonne's plan. By traveling in short stages, it wouldn't be too arduous, and Mathieu would be the best possible guide. Mathieu agreed that the plan was workable, which threw Michanteau into such a rage that he finally took notice of her and saw how attractive she was, stamping her dainty foot with anger blazing in her pretty dark eyes. He laughed and offered to take her too. She was speechless for a moment, then heard herself say, "All right, if that's the way you want it, I'll go!"

But who would guard the wealth hidden in the gardener's hut? The old women and the girls? No, the fact was that Michanteau was too useful to leave. Only she could make the decisions that might need to be made, and defend the group's future.

"I'm afraid you'll have to stay," said Mathieu. "But if little excursions like that interest you, I'll make my next one with you. I'll take you to the fair at Leipzig."

Michanteau saw this as a marvelous promise going beyond a trip to Leipzig, and acknowledged that since Gilonne was determined to try her foolhardy plan, she would have to stay behind and take care of things while her friend was gone.

It was agreed that Judith and Zacharie would go with Gilonne and Mathieu. They would have to leave town before the gates were closed. Then, they would wait for darkness in the barn of an abandoned farm near Courteille. To diminish the risk of their being noticed by the soldiers at the gate, they would go through it one by one, half an hour apart, and avoid carrying enough to give anyone the idea that they intended to be gone for more than a day. Mathieu knew where to get food along the way.

Before leaving, they all prayed in their own ways.

The old women's farewell was more amusing than sad. Although they were worried about the trip, they didn't understand its real dangers. They prayed too, then Chopine said to Gilonne, "And I promise we won't walk on Monsieur Mortimer's grave. If you want me to, in fact, I'll have the girls plant some flowers on it, although I'm not sure what will grow in soil with Protestant blood in it! And besides, it's too shady under that linden tree. . . . But don't worry, we'll do what has to be done."

* * *

September cast a golden glow on the roads. There was little
rain and the nights were warm. During the day, they stopped to
rest in woods full of secrets and birdsong. There was mystery
in these solitary places, but not fear. With one keeping watch
while the other three slept, the dangers seemed diminished. At
night they always found a friendly barn, but they walked in
darkness whenever they could, because that was the only way
to avoid attracting attention.

For Mathieu, who could have made the trip in six days instead
of the eighteen it was going to take, this was a leisurely stroll.
For the others, especially the two women, it could almost have
been a pleasure too, if it hadn't been for the sorrow that weighed
on their hearts. Judith had raised Hélye from childhood, and she
was suffering as much as if it were her Zacharie who had been
sent to the galleys.

To distract Gilonne, Mathieu taught her some of the tricks
used in fighting with a staff, which had fascinated her so much
in her childhood. She made such progress that by the time they
reached Switzerland she was highly skilled in the ''dog-fooler''
and the ''bracelet.''

Discreet, and especially shy, Mathieu didn't want to meet the
Geneva branch of the Morel d'Arthus family. He left Gilonne
and the two servants at the door of the banker's big house and
headed back toward Alençon with his long, steady strides. Gilonne watched him sadly for a few moments. She was now alone
in a foreign country, with a foreign family. One thing comforted
her, however: Judith had also brought up Hélye's brother Samuel, she knew his wife Rachel, and she was sure they would
receive a friendly welcome. And Judith now liked Gilonne.

The first words they exchanged with Samuel and Rachel made
them weep tears of joy. News of Hélye had come by way of the
French and Swiss embassies. He had been sentenced to five years
in the galleys. Samuel would use his connections and he was sure
he could obtain, if not a remission of Hélye's sentence, at least an
order allowing him to serve the rest of it on land, which would be
much better for his physical condition. He had pleurisy—but there
was no reason to be alarmed. His plight was serious because of
the duchess's desire to combat Protestantism in her duchy in order
to please her royal cousin, but Samuel was hopeful.

Would she be able to go and see Hélye later? Samuel didn't
know. It was something that would have to be decided when
they had more information.

* * *

When Gilonne took little Rose on her right arm and little Benjamin on her left, she felt great joy but also a certain uneasiness. There had been no indication she was going to have twins.

Rachel and Judith took over and soon solved the problem. The hardest part was finding a second wet nurse who would get along well with the first. They knew cases of two wet nurses whose milk dried up because they got on each other's nerves. Samuel suggested looking for wet nurses who were also twins, but no one had heard of any in the canton.

Mathieu was notified by letter: "The package has arrived. You can come and get it." It had been decided that since Gilonne had to leave the twins, it would be better for her to do it as soon as possible, before she became too strongly attached to them. And she wouldn't be away for very long. As soon as she was in good standing with the police, she would be able to travel as much as she wanted. Samuel, who still had the good-natured look of the child in the portrait by Philippe de Champaigne, had told her that Rose and Benjamin were rich. They would inherit Hélye's and Mortimer's shares in the Swiss bank and the branch office in Holland. When Hélye came back, the family would try to have his conviction overturned and his property in France returned to him.

Gilonne left the twins in the care of two placid wet nurses, both in the prime of life and at the peak of their milk production, and two twelve-year-old helpers who were made to wash their faces, hair, and hands so often that they were afraid they would wear them out. Judith supervised the four of them with authority.

Rachel, a fragile young woman who was pampered by her loving husband, especially now that they were expecting their first child, was alarmed at the thought of Gilonne's having to make the long journey back to Alençon on foot. She gave her what she thought were practical clothes and accessories, but Mathieu looked at them with a dubious expression. A leather cloak? It wasn't as good as a thick wool one. Those fur-lined shoes were very heavy. And that slender cane would break as soon as Gilonne put any weight on it. Well, the weather was good, and with a little luck . . .

They left Geneva in early spring, and their luck held up. While they were on the road, the first flowers bloomed and the birds burst into song.

Gilonne reached Alençon without any blisters on her feet. Now it was time for her to set about solving the problems that had been on her mind: buying back the Morel d'Arthus house, reopening the workshops in it, and having lacemaking resumed as soon as possible. The first question she asked Mathieu when he returned to Geneva had been, "Has the house been sold?" His "No, not yet" had made her jump for joy. If she hurried, everything would still be possible.

Her old women and girls were there. And so were the two painters. Tired of wandering without a place to stay, and especially without a piece of canvas to paint, they had come back. After the elation of seeing them all again, Gilonne counted her flock. Eleven people living in the house at the back of the garden!

One evening she gathered them around her and described her plan.

They would have to create a company; that was fashionable nowadays, and it was also very practical. Her brother-in-law, the banker, had explained it to her. People gave you money, and in exchange you gave them a share in the business you were creating. Her business would be a reconstruction of the Morel d'Arthus lacemaking establishment. She had already chosen a name for it: the Norman Rose Company. She and Michanteau would put their savings into it. The other people holding shares in it would be her two children, because of their father's money hidden in the gardener's hut; Mama Bordier, who surely had some savings too; Mistress Verlot, maybe; and they would probably find others. Marie, for example: Now that she was no longer paying for her room and board at the poorhouse, she must have some extra money to invest.

It was still too early to say, of course, how much profit there would be to divide up. Samuel had said that in a beginning enterprise like theirs it was common practice for the shareholders to put their money back into the company during the first two years.

Gilonne pointed out that there would be work for everyone in the group if the plan succeeded. Then she asked them what they thought of it. They thought it was a splendid idea. Chopine suggested that they get a bottle of good wine and drink a toast to the new company.

When they thought about it, they were surprised that the Morel d'Arthus house hadn't yet been bought. It was a magnificent house, and of course it was all ready to be put to use for lace-making. The duchess must be demanding too high a price. But why was it that Count Ogier de Beaumesnil, who had been buying everything in sight and never argued over prices, hadn't bought the finest lacemaking property in Alençon? They decided to make inquiries. Peter and Salomon would ask among the sellers of painting supplies. Michanteau would go here and there, gathering as much information as she could. Chopine, Conte-Nouvelles, and Thomine would talk to people in town and try to make them talk even more.

Sitting on the floor of the old women's room, they ate a supper consisting of an enormous omelet and a pot of hot buckwheat porridge with three jars of raspberry jam poured into it. The cheeks of the three little girls were pink with happiness, the old women chewed serenely, the painters talked and talked. . . . Gilonne was finally home again.

She went to her bedroom with her heart less sad. Her babies were warm and snug in their Swiss silk, and Samuel was doing everything possible for Hélye, who, thank God, wasn't rowing beneath the whips of monsters but only coughing near Marseille. She was going to give herself a night's respite, with her mind full of her plans.

The cry that escaped from her was heard all over the house, and everyone hurried to see what had happened.

Who had been so heartless as to do *that*?

She pointed to the rose in the china vase.

No one, apparently, had known about it. And where had someone found such a beautiful, full-blown rose in Normandy in early spring?

Gilonne trembled and murmured, "He's come back. That has to be it. He's come back."

She hurried outside, ran across the garden, and stopped in front of the big house. No lights showed in its windows. The seals put on the doors by the police were intact. No one was living there.

She went back to the cottage. Marie advised her to drink a good cup of linden-blossom tea. Tomorrow she would find out where the rose had come from.

But the next day they found out nothing. Either someone in the house had brought the rose and wouldn't admit it, or else there was a mystery connected with it.

Michanteau tried to make Gilonne stop staring into space by

talking to her about their plan to revive the Morel d'Arthus establishment. She had learned that the duchess was indeed asking a very high price for the house. That was surely why it hadn't yet been bought. It was time to learn its real value by going to see a notary, then express interest in buying and ask for time to think it over—which meant time to sell the lace and art objects, except for the family portraits, hidden in the gardener's hut. It would probably be best to take them to Paris. She and Candelario would go there to bargain over prices. Although he was now a sauce cook at the Moore's Inn, it would be easy for him to get a week off.

The rose had scarcely begun to wilt when it was replaced with a fresh one.

They held a conference in front of the fireplace in the old women's room.

Marie was convinced that it was a Protestant trick, and therefore a diabolical one. Her friends agreed, but didn't say so.

"I'm sure Hélye is hiding somewhere, and this is his way of letting me know it," said Gilonne. "Maybe in his Château du Verrier . . ."

Michanteau decided to go there with Mathieu.

They came back none the wiser. The estate was under police seals. No sign of life. They had found a way into the cellars and explored them. Nothing. And in the garden there were no rosebushes in bloom.

"He once mentioned hothouses to me," said Gilonne. "Did you see them?"

"No, we didn't see anything like that. Everything is neglected and abandoned."

They decided to keep watch in the house. The unknown person who kept bringing the roses couldn't be invisible. Sooner or later they would catch him, or her.

Time passed. Twice a week the wilted flower was replaced.

News came from Switzerland. Hélye was still sick, or acting as if he were, and Samuel was making some progress. Gilonne mustn't lose hope. Her twin angels were in good health and developing wonderfully well.

So Hélye was still in Marseille. In that case, who had been coming into her room? She considered not sleeping there anymore, but controlled her fear.

Two months went by, and the roses continued to bloom in the china vase.

There were days when Gilonne forgot them because she was completely absorbed in working toward the creation of her company. They had shareholders. Soon they would be able to buy the house.

Her visit to Mistress Verlot had been rather surprising. As soon as she saw Gilonne, the old woman said without preliminaries, "You're his daughter, aren't you? I knew your mother. She was the nicest of them all."

Of them all? Who were they all? Gilonne didn't get a comprehensible answer, but in any case Mistress Verlot was interested. She had been thinking of putting some money into lacemaking for a long time. How much did they want her to invest? She offered to ask about the price of the Morel d'Arthus house, suggesting that it would "seem more serious" if she made the inquiries herself. Her offer was perhaps a little offensive, but Gilonne and Michanteau decided it had come from a sincere wish to be helpful. And the huge pile of money she represented made them feel indulgent toward her.

Mistress Bordier wasn't enthusiastic about buying the property of Protestants, but she liked the general idea of the new company. She too had some money to invest.

Michanteau and Candelario went to Paris with a large amount of lace and came back, happy and satisfied, with a large amount of money. Les Dentelles d'Or had bought part of their stock, and six other elegant shops in the Galerie du Palais had bought the rest. They could have tried to sell it at higher prices, but they would have sold less of it, and since what was needed now was the largest amount of cash in the shortest possible time, they felt they had taken the best course.

Mistress Verlot obtained an interview with the Duchess of Alençon. The great lady consented to lower the price of the Morel d'Arthus house and take payment in three installments. Gilonne, Michanteau, and the others were ecstatic. Mistress Verlot was the queen of negotiators! The queen was pleased to be so highly appreciated, but she timidly said she hadn't had much trouble getting those conditions. The duchess probably felt it was taking too long to sell the house, and wanted to get the matter settled. And maybe she was in a good mood too. The king had just given her the property of three more important Protestant merchants who had gone into exile. Her Catholic works of charity must be deluged with money.

An unexpected shareholder joined the others: Lady Bertrade.

The money she invested had come to her "in a miraculous way," she said. Her pearl necklace, which had vanished many years ago, had turned up in an old powder horn! After a thorough cleaning it had been sold for a good price, through Candelario's artful efforts, and had now been transformed into shares in the Norman Rose Company.

On June 16, 1682, on her way back from a visit to her notary on the Rue du Marché aux Porcs, Gilonne offered her face to a fine rain that soothed the heat of her cheeks.

She had talked for a long time with Monsieur Faverie, the notary, and listened attentively. What he had said to her was important. She now knew what she should do and not do. The success of the company would depend on her shrewdness and ability to organize. The old notary, who had told her three times that she was very young, had insisted on giving her instructions in his shaky handwriting:

> Never spend more than you take in. Spend less. MUCH LESS. Never forget taxes. They are numerous and heavy. (Come back to my office one of these days and have my head clerk explain them to you.) Do not think, because you have sold a lace collar for five hundred livres, and the thread for it cost only six sous, and you have paid your workers only what you are strictly obliged to pay them, that the difference is all profit. Remember that. . . .

There were two long pages like that. Did he really think she was a four-year-old child? Had he also told her she must always be able to inform a shareholder of anything, absolutely *anything* concerning the company. If she was unable to give just one piece of information, from then on there would be at least one mistrustful shareholder who would keep making a nuisance of himself by badgering her with questions: "Why buy thread in Flanders and not in France? Why buy needles from this maker and not from that one?" This was something that ought to be avoided like the plague.

She smiled. Dear old Monsieur Faverie—how little he knew her shareholders! He had seen them for only a few moments, when they came in to sign for the purchase of their shares in the Norman Rose Company. She couldn't imagine Lady Bertrade asking about the price of pins or parchment. Or Mama Bordier

handsome. But his foolhardiness would have prevented him from living very long even if he had never gone to Canada.

"You don't have to go as far as Canada to find cruelty," said Ogier. "We're calmly walking toward a display of it at this very moment. A poor young woman is going to be stripped naked in front of the whole town, and whipped until she bleeds, because she liked lace and couldn't buy any. It's true—and this is the most serious part—that she stole lace from churches, especially Notre-Dame."

They walked for a time without speaking. Then Gilonne slipped on a lump of dirt and would have fallen if Ogier hadn't been holding her arm.

"Excuse me," she said.

His face suddenly became grave, and he said with a brusqueness that startled her, "There's one thing I'll never excuse you for: marrying that gloomy, solemn Protestant!"

He had already mounted his horse and ridden away before she recovered from her surprise.

Without thinking of where she was going, she continued walking toward the church.

The whole town was there, as Ogier had said. She made her way through the crowd to join her four incorrigibly curious old women and Bichon, who had pushed Marie in the gardener's wheelbarrow. They were so fascinated by what was happening in front of the church that they didn't notice Gilonne's arrival.

Holding her torch high and looking up at the sky, the young thief asked God and the king to forgive her for her crimes. Then her clothes were pulled off and the executioner began whipping her. At each crack of the whip, followed by a scream from the victim, the old women started, and every few moments they asked Marie, "Is she bleeding yet?" Finally the executioner made Elisabeth Hobon begin walking through the streets while he continued to whip her. Blood was now streaming down her back. The square in front of the church emptied: Everyone wanted to follow her. The onlookers seemed delighted to know that there were going to be three sessions like this on three successive Thursdays before the young woman was branded on both shoulders with a fleur-de-lis.

Gilonne was arguing with Marie, who insisted on "going to see some more," and Chopine, who was thirsty and wanted to and "drink a toast" somewhere. Thomine and Conte-Nouvelles wanted to go home. She was still trying to bring them all into agreement when she saw Ogier de Beaumesnil looking at them, smiling. He approached and asked to be introduced to these members of her family with whom he didn't yet have the honor of being acquainted.

The fate of Elisabeth Hobon, the lace thief, lost much of its importance for the foursome when they heard the name of Count Ogier de Beaumesnil, the new owner of Grand-Coeur. None of the three blind women dared to ask Marie, "What does he look like?" but they were saving up a whole arsenal of questions to fire at her later.

"My father seems to have told you many things," said Gilonne, "but one thing he must not have told you, because he probably doesn't know it, is that I spent the first days of my life hidden in the poorhouse with my grandmother, Thomine Perdriel"—she nodded toward her—"and her three friends."

"Tell him our names," said Marie.

Gilonne did so, and the count bowed to each woman in turn.

In a silence charged with impatience and curiosity, they waited for him to speak again. And on the pretext of giving them what they wanted, Gilonne decided to engage him in conversation. But words again played a trick on her, as they had periodically done all her life, and a strange question came out of her mouth: "Do you have a garden with roses in it?"

"Yes," he answered with a puzzled but amused expression.

Marie, in her wheelbarrow, took it upon herself to tell him about the mystery of the roses that were put in Gilonne's room one after another, and always replaced before any of their petals fell off.

Ogier said he wasn't the one who had been bringing them. He regretted not having had the idea, but he was certain that every man in Alençon would want to bring flowers to the bedroom of the most beautiful woman he had ever seen. Even the king would have done it if he had been lucky enough to know her.

He elegantly doffed his hat, mounted Quinola, and rode away, followed by his Huron.

Marie described the count all the way home. It seemed that the three others would never know enough about him.

When she was tired of hearing that he was even handsomer than the king; that his black silk clothes, his wonderful lace collars and cuffs, and his ruby buttons, red as the thief's blood, surely came from Paris; and that he was he noblest nobleman the eye had ever seen, Gilonne told them aggressively, as if she were throwing a stone at them, that he had been a servant of her grandmother, Lady Bertrade.

They all let out a loud "Oh!" in which incredulity was mingled with indignation. Bichon stopped pushing the wheelbarrow.

Gilonne felt foolish. What had made her say that? She decided to spend the evening alone, looking over the financial records of the company. Then she suddenly remembered that the Morel d'Arthus house had belonged to her for several hours. She had the keys to it in her pocket. She told the others that she was going to look it over and make plans for setting up lacemaking operations there.

Thomine, who was able to make very accurate judgments of people's moods from the tone of their voices, sighed with relief. Gilonne wasn't angry anymore.

The foursome, having mentally buried Hélye even deeper than his father, spent the evening telling the painters and the two sisters all about the handsome count, since they had watched Elisabeth Hobon's punishment from the other side of the square and therefore hadn't met him.

Gilonne had taken a four-branched candlestick. But in spite of the bright light, she felt uneasy in the cold, dark, empty house. In the cellar she found the printing press—it must have been overlooked when the contents of the house were auctioned off—and this made her so happy that she hummed to herself as she continued her inspection. There, in the lower gallery, she would install the salesroom again. Luckily the tables, which matched the paneling of the walls and contained the lace cupboards, hadn't been auctioned off either.

They would need a few chairs, because customers liked to sit down and look for a long time at what they bought. With what painting would she replace the portrait of Madame Morel d'Arthus? She decided on the portrait of the children by Philippe de Champaigne. No one would know who they were, and they would watch the comings and goings in their house. Yes, it was still their house, and someday it would belong to Hélye's and her children, Rose and Benjamin. In that silence, and in that night of sadness but also of hope, she swore she would struggle and succeed for their sake. And she was so pleased with the idea of having the Morel d'Arthus children looking down from the wall, there in that room, that she hurried off to bring their portrait.

When she went into her room she saw Conte-Nouvelles, who, startled, dropped the rose she had been about to put into the little china vase.

"So you're the one who—"

"No, Gilonne, it's not me! I mean, I've only been doing it because he asked me to."

"Who? Tell me!"

"Stop shaking me and I'll tell you. I've always known I'd have to tell you someday."

She told her story. One afternoon when she was too hot to go with the others to visit Gérasime, she had sat down in the shade of the linden tree—no, not over the grave, beside it. She didn't see him, of course, but she heard someone pass by very close to her, evidently thinking she had fallen asleep in her chair. She stopped him by pulling on his coattail. He tried to run away. She hit him with her cane, and she must have hit him square on the head because he fell to the ground. To make sure he wouldn't run away when he came to his senses, she put her foot on his chest. Before long he woke up and said he hadn't wanted to do anything wrong. As a matter of fact, he was trying to do something good. He had been told to come and put a rose in a certain room every other day. Every day, actually, but he had said he couldn't do that because he lived too far away.

Conte-Nouvelles paused to catch her breath, then went on. "I asked him who he was doing it for. He wouldn't tell me. He just said he'd always been afraid of getting caught and not being able to go on doing what he'd been told to do. Then he asked me to help him. He'd bring me the rose in a place we'd agree on, and I'd put it in your room. And he'd give me a livre each time! A *livre*, you understand? How could I refuse? It would mean I could lend money to the company too. I laughed when I thought of its name: the Norman Rose Company!"

"What can you tell me about this man?" asked Gilonne. "Did he seem to be tall? Thin?"

"Very thin. I'd call him skinny, in fact. And tall too, probably."

"What about his voice?"

"It sounded a little cracked."

"When is he coming back?"

"Tomorrow."

"Where do you meet him?"

"Far away from here. I felt sorry for him and agreed to meet him in a place where he wouldn't have so far to go, because he keeps coughing all the time."

"He coughs?"

"He certainly does. He seems very sick, poor man. . . . But he must be very rich too, to go on giving me a livre for every rose."

"Tomorrow I'll go with you."

"You mean it's all over? I won't get any more livres? No, never mind that. I can tell you're getting angry, and I don't want to upset you. He told me you'd be happy to get the roses and I believed him. And I've never told you this before, but that stingy Marie stopped paying me to pray for her when we moved into your house. She says she doesn't need any prayers here, because she feels fine. That's not what I expected: I thought that with the Protestant air we breathe here, she'd want me to pray for her twice as much!"

No one had ever seen Conte-Nouvelles cry before. To make up for her two lost sources of income, Gilonne gave her three shares in the company.

The meetings had been taking place at the Postern Gate, the one so narrow that only people on foot could pass through it.

"Follow me from a distance," said Conte-Nouvelles, "because he'll run away if he sees you."

Gilonne saw a tall, thin man in a dark cloak, with a felt hat pulled down over his eyes. When he held out the rose, she dashed forward.

"Who . . . who are you?" she asked. She was so disappointed at not seeing Hélye that she wept.

"Gilonne!" the man exclaimed. "You've become what I knew you'd be! I always knew you'd grow up to be the most beautiful woman in the world."

"Jérémie! Oh, Jérémie!"

They both wept in each other's arms.

He felt hot to her. He had a fever.

"Jérémie, are you sick?"

He laughed hoarsely and coughed, then turned away from her to spit up blood. But she saw it.

"Where do you live, Jérémie?"

"In the Château du Verrier. He . . . your husband told me

how to find a secret room there, and that's where I've been staying.''

He coughed again.

''You're coming to my house. I'll take care of you. You'll tell me everything.''

Now there were twelve of them! And for anyone who knew Gilonne, said Peter, there was no reason to believe the number wouldn't go on rising.

Jérémie had been given a place near the fire in the old women's room, where meals were eaten because the small kitchen and the equally small snack room couldn't hold the whole group.

The old women didn't mind one more Protestant. They were enjoying themselves. They said the little house was now like the poorhouse, only better.

When Jérémie had lain down on a straw mattress, everyone was impatient to hear what he would say, but first he was given a supper of hot milk with a little apple brandy in it, and then they had to wait for him to get through three exhausting fits of coughing.

Finally he was ready to begin. Since Gilonne wanted to know everything that had happened to him since he left when she was five, he said he would have to go back a long way, so far back that some things might be hard for him to remember.

He had left Montsort in 1670. The lacemaking that was imposed on him left him deeply discouraged. He had written a book of practical mathematics for teaching children; he was rather proud of it and dreamed of having it printed. He wanted to join his parents in Switzerland, and he was in despair because Gilonne had been taken away from him by that cursed lacemaking.

He succeeded in reaching Geneva, but his parents had either left or died, he never knew which. He became the servant and secretary of a kind, scholarly man who had the bad taste to die too soon. Next he was the tutor of children who proved to be so unruly that he quickly left them. Then he was a schoolteacher and then a librarian, until he decided to go back to France to see Monsieur Pascal and talk mathematics with him. It was an unlucky decision. First of all, it turned out that the famous man was dead. And as he was leaving Charenton, where he had attended church, Jérémie was arrested with a number of other Protestants and taken away.

The charges against him were serious: He had fled Montsort after being placed in the keeping of the parish priest and forbidden to leave the country, and in his room the police found treatises on mathematics, declared them to be seditious books, and even managed to prove it to their own satisfaction.

The galleys. He rowed for five years. That was the length of his sentence and it wasn't extended, in view of his physical condition: With his constant coughing, he wasn't of much use.

He was in Marseille, waiting to leave for Paris, when a contingent of newly sentenced prisoners arrived. He spent several weeks with them while he was waiting for his release papers to be put in order. Cholera broke out, and he saw them die one after another. One of them, evidently stronger than the others, lived longer. It turned out that he was a Protestant like Jérémie, and that they were from the same part of France, almost the same town. And then, miraculously, Jérémie learned that the man was married to little Gilonne!

"We both cried," he said. "Then we began talking as if we were trying to see who knew the most about you. He did, of course. But I knew some things he didn't. He never had enough of listening to me. He would wake me up at night and ask me to talk about you. I went on doing it until the end."

"The end!" exclaimed Gilonne. "Is he . . . dead?"

"I thought you knew!"

Much later, she asked Jérémie why Hélye's relatives in Switzerland had received good news of him from the French and Swiss embassies.

"There are uninformed and misinformed embassies everywhere," he replied.

They kept him in the little house only a week. He said he had never been so happy in his life. And he told the old women so many funny stories that they adored him. The best of the food they cooked was for him. They didn't realize how serious his sickness was. Only Marie saw the blood he kept spitting up, but she said nothing. The care he needed, and her desire to give him little pleasures—stewed apples that she cooked for him, a newspaper that she went out to buy for him—helped to distract Gilonne from her sorrow. She talked about Hélye, and Jérémie comforted her.

"Why do you think he was unhappy with you?" he asked.

"Because I didn't love him enough."

"He loved you enough for both of you. A love like that can fill a man's life. Do you want me to swear he was happy? Before God, who will take me very soon, I solemnly swear that he was happy with you."

Jérémie died one morning, at the dawn of a summer day. At the hour when the roses still had in their hearts the tears they had shed for the great afflictions of the Protestants. And since he had forbidden them to call in a priest to give him the last rites, he had to be buried clandestinely, like Monsieur Mortimer, to avoid having his body thrown into the garbage dump.

Peter and Salomon dug his grave near Monsieur Mortimer's, in the shade of the linden tree.

Gilonne made a trip to Switzerland. Since she was now in good standing with the Catholic Church, she could leave France and come back whenever she pleased. She preferred to go and announce Hélye's death in person. Samuel had been expecting it.

She spent a few days with her children, surprised and delighted to see how big and healthy they were. She rewarded the wet nurses and their helpers generously, then, reassured about Rose and Benjamin Morel d'Arthus for the near future at least, she told Samuel and Rachel that she was going back to France to make their fortune. Samuel and Rachel made her promise she would come back and visit at least twice a year. She avoided saying she hoped the horrible wars of religion would end before much longer and that she would then be able to take back her children. Rachel had had a miscarriage, and the twins were now her greatest joy. Gilonne gathered that Rachel would probably be unable to have children, and she was glad that her two little angels could soften the young woman's sorrow.

Creating and printing new designs, and acquiring supplies of thread and parchment, took several months. The thread in two of the kegs arrived rotten. After a fierce struggle, Gilonne succeeded in making the seller replace it without charge. The fine linen thread required for making *point de France* was very expensive.

Gilonne decided to hire both Catholic and Protestant lacemakers. She wanted them to share the same workshops, but the painters raised the problem of singing: the Protestants would want psalms, the Catholics the *Veni Creator* or the *Stabat Mater*.

It might seem like a minor problem, but it was one that might become explosive. So Gilonne agreed to have them work in different shops and do different operations.

She was also afraid that having Protestant workers might mean she wouldn't be allowed to sell lace at court. One day when she met Ogier in town she asked him if he would mention to the duchess—who was said to be always more than willing to listen to him—that Gilonne was engaged in an experiment that would be sure to bring about some conversions. He promised.

The Norman Rose Company opened its doors to a hundred lacemakers on January 2, 1683. Ogier sent Gilonne a big bouquet of roses, with a note courteously putting her on notice that from then on they would be competitors.

The old women were delighted when they heard about those roses. Until winter, the handsome count had often passed by their bench, and had given them gifts of sweets that they told no one about. Now they were impatiently waiting for spring.

But their wait wasn't unpleasant. They weren't going back to the poorhouse. No one, from Peter to the two sisters, would have let them leave. The painters had returned to their attic and the old women blithely climbed the stairs to visit them—even Marie, who liked to be loudly cheered when she reached the top step. They listened to Salomon singing at the top of his lungs and Peter making even more noise by complaining about it.

During one of their truces, the two men had installed a bell in the attic, with a cord that went down to the ground floor. If Titus—he had come back too—wanted to signal a possible visit by the police, he pulled on the cord and the bell rang. Peter and Salomon would then quickly hide whatever forbidden work they were doing and stand in front of something they were permitted to do, either a miniature or an engraving. Once there was an alarm while the old women were in the attic, and they had a moment of intense emotion they would never forget.

They admitted having a high opinion of Peter, but if they had been pushed a little they would have avowed their preference for Salomon, even though they were certain he was a solid mass of mortal sins. They told him they had seen many thieves branded, but had never heard of one being punished by having his hand cut off, as he claimed his had been. He laughed, and they were elated: The man was an exciting mystery. But they weren't afraid of him. In this they paid posthumous tribute to Hélye: He had kept Salomon, overlooking his youthful errors and feeling he

374 *Janine Montupet*

was basically good, and they had confidence in the soundness of Hélye's judgment.

They would have given anything to be able to wander in and out of the workshops, but Gilonne wouldn't let them. They were, however, taken on a guided tour by Michanteau, who was proud to show them that kingdom, a little part of which belonged to her.

Gilonne had given her fifty of the five hundred shares in the company, and she had accepted them with the characteristic straightforwardness that made everyone like her. "I don't have any misgivings about taking them," she said, "because they'll stay in the family."

"Are you saying that Mathieu has finally . . ."

"Not yet. He'll never jump into marriage of his own accord. But I'm leading him toward it. And for once I know the road better than he does. For our honeymoon, I'll walk to the Leipzig fair with him. He doesn't really know it yet. I think I'll have a talk with him when he's finished taking the Morel d'Arthus' servants to Switzerland. After that, I don't want him to travel so much, or he'll finally be too tired. I haven't told him that either. He'll have plenty of work here. He can be a big help to us in buying materials. As soon as we can afford one, we need to buy a carriage—an old one at first—for business trips to Paris. Mathieu can also use it to go to Flanders and Holland. With two armed servants, he can deliver lace without too much danger."

Michanteau's grandiose plans were premature. The company still had very little lace to sell, and expenses had to be paid whether anything was sold or not. Gilonne respected the basic rules laid down for her by Monsieur Faverie, the notary, and spent only what was strictly necessary. But since hardly any money was coming in, she was constantly plagued by anxiety.

She had soon seen the two faces of lacemaking. There were the workers, leaning over their parchment for sixteen to eighteen hours a day. Then there were the manufacturers, who were responsible for the lives of their workers and who devoted an equal number of hours to keeping the whole operation going, with one word always in the forefront of their attention: money. The need for money was endless. Monsieur Faverie had reminded Gilonne that she had only a modest sum to take her through the first two years, when she would have to pay expenses without having anything to sell except what was left of the Morel d'Arthus lace.

She had made only one mistake, but it was a serious one. The lace that had been made in Monsieur Mortimer's time, which she had expected to sell at high prices, was hard to sell even at much lower prices. Styles were changing, and the designs of the old lace were already out of favor. She would soon be forced to have it sold at a loss in markets and fairs, because she was about to run short of money.

This realization made her go to see Monsieur Faverie. He saw only two solutions: mortgage the house, or ask her shareholders for the additional money she would need to keep the company going for another year. She said she would think it over, and left, almost frantic with worry.

She didn't want to ask her friends for more money. Raise money by mortgaging the house? It would then seem to her that the company no longer belonged to all of them. She decided to sell the pearls that Hélye had given her on their wedding night.

She didn't want to have Candelario sell them for her, and she was sure if she discussed it with Michanteau she would end up adopting the solution of mortgaging the house. Besides, for the time being Michanteau was lost in her love for Mathieu and her delusions of grandeur. Gilonne remembered that one evening when he seemed more melancholy than usual, Hélye had said to her, "The worst thing is to be alone." He hadn't been worried about money, of course, but he must often have felt isolated in his struggle against oppressive power.

Gilonne was thinking about all this when she left her office after the workers had gone home. She stopped in front of the big portrait by Philippe de Champaigne. Hélye and Samuel smiled at her in the light of the candles she had raised toward their young faces. Hélye was watching over her, from where he was now. And Samuel would be glad to give her financial help if she asked him for it. But she wouldn't ask.

She remembered one of the most painful moments of her life when she had been tied to her chair in Mistress Lescure's house. She had been seized with a panic that made her tremble from head to foot. Then she had felt her body gradually relaxing and she was able to think again. She had prayed, "Dear Jesus, take pity on me, please make this be over soon." When she could finally reason calmly and tell herself that those few hours would have to end, patience had begun spreading inside her like something refreshing she had drunk. That was what she would have to do now: act and be patient

Monsieur Rollet, the jeweler in the Place du Palais, knew her. He had once repaired her emerald ring when the stone came loose and she was afraid of losing it. He had ecstatically admired the beauty of the ring. To him, Mademoiselle de Ferrières was a person of quality.

He received her now with deference, and she showed him her pearls. He examined them in silence, weighed them in his hand, counted them, looked at them in sunlight, and finally said with a little laugh, "Did you know, mademoiselle, that there are those who would have us believe that artificial pearls, made from the scales of a fish called the bleak, can look more or less like these?"

She hadn't known, and she listened with interest. The secret of making false pearls had been discovered only recently. Monsieur Rollet didn't really believe in it. Besides, he hated any kind of imitation. But to come back to her pearl necklace, it was one of the most beautiful he had ever seen! Too beautiful for the people of Alençon. There was hardly any money on most of the country estates in the region, and no bourgeois man in town would ever pay what those hundred and four pearls were worth, to buy them as a present for his wife. If he were younger, Monsieur Rollet would go to sell them in Paris, but he was old now, and the roads were infested with robbers, as everyone knew, unfortunately.

Gilonne was becoming impatient. When someone asked her the price of a flounce, she gave it immediately.

"What are they worth, Monsieur Rollet?"

"They're fit for a queen. They must have been bought for six to seven thousand livres. You can sell them for half that price."

She sighed with relief. Three thousand livres would save her.

"Will you take them?"

"They're pearls of the finest quality, and beautifully round. Do you know where they came from?"

"My husband gave them to me."

"No, I mean: Do you know where they were born?"

He began discoursing. He spoke of vast seas, oysters, boats, divers, caravans. He went on and on. In other circumstances, Gilonne would have been amused, but now she was eager to know if she was going to get the money or not. Finally he said he knew it was foolish because he might keep them in his coffers for twenty years, but he would take them. For three thousand livres.

She was about to hurry away with her bag of money when he began talking about the emerald in her ring. Did she know how it had been taken from the bowels of the earth?

She laughed and left him, convinced that jewelers spent most of their time daydreaming. After all, they had to do something to pass the time between visits from those who sold their keepsakes and those who bought them.

She was by then in such a cheerful mood that she decided to treat herself to a little entertainment. How many days had she gone without leaving her office?

The showman who presented ducks dressed as lords and ladies was still there! Or maybe it was his son? She would have to take Bichon and the two sisters to see his performance. And what was it that had such a good smell of vanilla? The apple fritters, of course. She bought one, and while she ate it, she watched the theatrical ducks with a pleasure that came mainly from the lifting of the weight she had felt on her heart during the last two months whenever she thought of her finances. And she laughed more from contentment than at the antics of the ducks.

"When I look at your portrait, which I keep in my bedroom, I often think that you're the image of triumphant youth. And now you seem to be five years old!"

Ogier always seemed to take her by surprise. He came without being seen. Indian stealth. He must have been watching her for quite some time without her knowing it.

"Shall I dare to say that I go to sleep with you every night? Ah, it's lucky for me that you can't strike me dead with the lightning in your eyes! Maybe you'll tell me what beautiful piece of jewelry you bought from Monsieur Rollet. I like him because he loves his trade and knows it well. So many people know nothing about what makes them rich. When I was young, I railed against the ignorance of merchants who had no interest in the history of what they sold and knew only the purchase price and the sale price. . . . But I'm afraid I'm boring you."

"No, not at all."

He followed the direction of her gaze and they both saw a man looking at them intently. The tenacious draper.

"That elegant gentleman seems to interest you more than what I've been saying. I won't impose on you any longer. Goodbye."

But before leaving, he added, "I'm glad you've stopped wearing a bonnet. The hood of your cloak is wonderfully becoming to you.''

He disappeared. She shrugged her shoulders. He was too thin-skinned. On the other hand, the draper, who was now coming toward her, was too thick-skinned. Snubbing him wouldn't keep him away from her very long. He would go on watching for her in the streets, all over town, until he saw her again.

She quickly walked away, before he could come close enough to speak to her. He was heartbroken.

Six

SHE LIFTED HER SKIRTS, STEPPED OVER THE STREAM OF DIRTY water that ran down the middle of the street, and continued on her way, but she was soon stopped by a hand on her arm. For a second she thought the draper had followed her and taken the liberty of accosting her in that way, and so the eyes that met Ogier de Beaumesnil's were bright with a green flash of irritation.

"To whom are you going in such a hurry?" he asked her.

To *whom*? Did he think she was on her way to see a lover? Did she ask him if he was satisfied with the women he had recently brought from Caux, the ones he had called "the most beautiful of Norman women, full of charm and pride, with the most exquisite faces imaginable"? Were they skilled in making Alençon lace? But she wasn't sure he could judge that. She was beginning to doubt that he was a lace manufacturer at all. He was only a man who took plunder from one half of the world and sold it in the other. No one could really know lace who hadn't leaned over it for eighteen hours a day.

"Why are you glaring at me like that?" he asked. "Have I displeased you in some way? If so, tell me how I can make up for it."

What useless chatter! She didn't have time for it. Her painters

379

were expecting her to come and judge their latest work. Choosing the best patterns would take a long time. The success or failure of a piece of lace depended on the first step. She had to keep creating new and ever more pleasing designs. The people who wore lace were so demanding and hard to please! And the competition was so ruthless! She sighed.

"Is something wrong?" Ogier asked gently.

She freed herself from the hand that had been holding her arm and burning her through the light cloth of her sleeve. "I'm in a hurry. My painters are waiting for me."

"Your painters?"

They were old and ugly, as everyone in town knew, so why was he smiling like that?

"I have the painful impression," he said, "that everything I say irritates you. But I'm sure something is wrong besides that."

Something? So many things! She couldn't tell him even a fraction of them. No, he wasn't a real lace manufacturer; he couldn't even imagine what her days were like. She looked at him, having kept her eyes turned away since he took hold of her arm. How tall and powerfully built he was! And today he was dressed in gray. Had he given up black? Maybe he had done it at the request of one of the ladies in the duchess's palace. Even the pearls on his vest were gray. Monsieur Rollet had said one day how rare that color was in pearls. And that beaver hat, without a plume, adorned only with a ribbon, was simple and becoming. She was dressed in gray too, but her clothes were of linen and cotton. She smiled at this thought.

"At last!" he said. "Are you feeling better?"

Better? After all, why shouldn't she tell him about the morning she had just been through, and the afternoon that awaited her? Talking steadily, without pausing to catch her breath, she initiated Count Ogier de Beaumesnil into the life of a mistress-lacemaker.

She had to be up at four o'clock, when her workers came in, but before that she'd had to go and see her old women, who slept little, and more during the day than at night. This morning, an unpleasant surprise: Chopine had a bad sore on her foot and Marie was having fits of breathlessness. Then she had to wake up the three girls. A pity, because they were always so sleepy. And to earn an extra two sous a day, the two sisters had begun working in the evening, when they were supposed to be in bed: they pulled stoneboats from Coutances loaded with white stone that was going to be used for building a nobleman's house. The ropes lacerated their hands, and their wounds weren't healing quickly. Gilonne had found them in bad condition this morning.

Her workshops were full of injuries and ailments of all kinds. Chilblains that wouldn't heal, burns that resisted the efforts of "fire lifters."* And one of her painters was spitting up blood in spite of the sugared milk she gave him to drink four times a day. And the old lunatic who made *remplis* so perfectly kept hiding her companions' needles so the devil, whom she accused of dulling them, wouldn't find them.

As for her Protestants, what were they up to now? Twenty-five women, enough for a whole workshop, had come in that morning with all their hair cut off. They had obviously sold it, but for whom? For what? To pay for one of them, or a husband or a son, to make the trip into exile? They told Gilonne nothing. They didn't trust her as they had trusted Hélye. Someday the police would come to investigate, and then maybe she would know. . . .

But the worst part of this morning had been the inevitable "battle of verbena." By order of the Archbishop of Le Mans, she was allowed to employ Protestant women only if every day she made them drink a ladleful of verbena tea, which was supposed to drive away the devil. Even if she succeeded in making them take it into their mouths, they would somehow manage to spit out most of it. This morning they had taken direct action: they had gone to a portrait of the duchess, which the Community of New Catholics had "advised" Gilonne to display, and spat the contents of their bulging cheeks onto it. Tomorrow at the latest, the archbishop or his bishop, informed by a Catholic lacemaker, would come and thunderously denounce what the Protestants had done. She had made them bow and apologize in front of the duchess's portrait, hoping this would make their offense a little less serious, but she was still worried.

Her old women, however, weren't the least bit worried. Having come to pray with the Catholics, as they did every morning and evening, they had been there when the incident took place, and they had been overjoyed by it. Yesterday their daily invention had been to have Marie make a convincing imitation of smallpox pustules on the cheeks of the first woman to drink from the ladle of verbena tea, so that the others could all exclaim indignantly

*Sorcerers noted for their ability to heal burns.

that they would never drink after someone with smallpox. What would they think of tomorrow?

At this point in her story Gilonne laughed a little sadly, and said, "The only good part of the morning was when Titus opened a big, heavy, pot-bellied keg of Flemish thread that had been bleached in Holland. I like the bittersweet smell that comes from a keg of thread when its lid is first taken off. I've never been to the Zuider Zee, but I think it must smell like that. Sometimes it seems to me that I can hear a faint sound, like the rustling of birds flying over the thread while it soaks in the water. You must know this: Are there big birds that fly along the shore? And do they make a rustling sound with their wings?"

Ogier had a strong desire to take her in his arms and kiss her. He answered her in a rather hoarse voice, not knowing very well what he was saying.

She looked up at him, and it seemed to him that she was calmer now. In the green of her eyes there was a tender blue that gave them the marvelous color of a turquoise. He decided he would have the world's most beautiful turquoises brought to him, and give them to her. He was sure her eyes would have that shade when, someday, she belonged to him. . . .

Without realizing it, they had come to the edge of the Alençon Park. The duchess had decided to have all its trees cut down: She accused them of sheltering too many amorous assignations. Gilonne hadn't yet seen the massacre that had begun a few weeks earlier. The little river that flowed there, the Briante, no longer had a single branch to caress it, and in the distance the wood-cutters' axes could still be heard attacking the last clump of trees.

"It's so sad," said Gilonne. "The Briante won't sing anymore, and the nightingales are gone forever."

"Other trees will grow, and the birds will come back," he replied.

But the pitiful sight had brought Gilonne back to her preoccupations.

"Do your customers at court also take months, sometimes years, to pay you?" she asked. "Do they always find excellent reasons for sending back their bills? One customer said to me, 'I saw that same design in a flounce worn by a vulgar bourgeoise. Shall I send back the one you made for me, or shall I pay you only a third of its price?' And when a wedding is canceled, do you have to take back lace that was bought as a gift, knowing that in the meantime it's gone out of style and can only be sold for a low price at a fair or a market?'' Did he, like her, have a bothersome amount of lace that needed mending? Did he have insufferable customers who kept demanding repairs that took up endless time?

Yes, he had all those problems, of course, but he didn't care to tell her that his directors dealt with them.

''There's Mistress Lescure and her father!'' she suddenly exclaimed. ''Where are they going so fast?''

Just then a pink shape sped past her, heading for the far end of the denuded park.

''That's Torchette!'' she said. ''Torchette has escaped! I have to help them catch her. They'll never do it by themselves, and I'm sure they can't afford to pay the fine.''

Ogier then learned that anyone who let a pig escape into town was fined one livre.

Gilonne ran off, holding up her skirts to increase her speed. For a long time Ogier watched her little red shoes jumping over the trunks of felled trees, and once again he said to himself that he adored her.

A fine, dense rain began falling, struggling gaily against the sunlight. He saw a certain resemblance between it and Gilonne. He took off his hat, tilted his face toward the drops, and drank in those that fell on his lips.

In the course of the following week, Titus brought Gilonne a little package that ''Monsieur de Beaumesnil's savage'' had delivered.

She read the note that came with it: ''I am leaving for New France. Try not to marry another Protestant while I am gone. Or a Catholic either. A few days ago my horse Quinola stumbled over these little balls. I picked them up. Quinola wants you to have them. Please accept them.''

The ''little balls'' were her pearls. He had bought them from Monsieur Rollet. Now they had been given to her by both Hélye and Ogier. Could she accept this second gift? Would he regard her acceptance as a commitment? From what she could read between the lines, it seemed to her that she ought to send back the pearls and make him understand . . . Make him understand what? She needed time to think it over. Tomorrow she would go and ask Lady Bertrade for advice. But she had to talk to someone before then. Not to Michanteau, because she would

be sure to say, "Well, you can sell them again, if you have to."
Peter? He now had fixed ideas. And Salomon still had wild
notions. Her four old women? If she hurried to finish making
out her bills, she could join them in time for their supper.

Before leaving the house and walking to the back of the garden, she looked in on each of the workshops. She was always
glad to see her workers leaning over their lace. It was a sight
dear to her heart. It was also the most beautiful sight she knew.
If she had been a poet, she would have found words to describe
it. She would say . . . She suddenly realized that she was like
Monsieur Rollet, who, said Ogier, loved his trade. She loved
hers. Happiness swelled her heart. She could hold out for another year without too much difficulty, and she had decided to
put her lacemakers to work on the net ground she had invented.

She had almost forgotten that she was going to her old women
to talk about Ogier de Beaumesnil. It was annoying that she had
to make a decision about those pearls when she had so much
else to do. But Ogier was leaving; she would have time to think
it over while he was gone. She stopped and turned back, wanting
to try her net ground at once and wondering if her thread was
fine enough.

The pearls were in her pocket. They stayed there all day and
she never thought of them once. If her invention proved to be
satisfactory, it would change the appearance of *point de France*.
That night she had trouble sleeping.

From Dieppe, where he had gone to board a ship, Ogier sent
a special courier to Gilonne. A special courier for a short note!
He must have lost his mind! She didn't read the note immediately. It was delivered to her while she was showing her lacemakers, who shared her enthusiasm for the invention, how she
wanted grounds to be made from then on.

She worked with her mistress-lacemakers far into the night,
then opened several bottles of wine to reward them and celebrate
the invention. Pleased with the way their first efforts had turned
out, they drank a toast to the memory of Madame La Perrière.

"She'd be happy to see that we've gone forward a little more,"
said one of the women.

Gilonne went to her bedroom and was still thinking of Madame La Perrière as she undressed. Then she remembered the
pearls, and the note Ogier had sent her from Dieppe. She held
it close to her candlestick and read it: "Have you put them

around your neck, where you have that pretty little fold that is
sometimes called the necklace of Venus? How fitting that name
is, in your case! Try to think of me now and then, until the
Moon of Burned Fruit, when I will come back.''

The Moon of Burned Fruit? He hadn't bothered to translate
it—and that was just like him! He had twice mentioned his Huron calendar to her. She should have gone to the booksellers in
Alençon, or even in Paris if necessary, to find a book that would
teach her about that calendar. Ogier was the kind of man who
couldn't tolerate not having his meaning understood, or guessed,
as soon as he spoke. To be fair, she had to admit there was
something stimulating about that.

She went to her mirror and looked at her neck. Yes, there
was a little fold at its base. It was a pretty neck, round and
smooth. On the whole, Ogier was a delightful man. She went
to bed with that idea but tried not to think about him too much.
She still regarded herself as Hélye's wife. Long ago, she had
almost wanted to die because she believed Ogier had been tortured and killed. How young she had been in those days! Since
then, she had known a man's love and the pain of losing him.
But she couldn't deny that Ogier was handsome and interesting.
And generous. She would think of the best way to give the pearls
back without hurting his feelings. He would have to understand
that she was devoted to the memory of her martyred husband.
Besides, there was a good chance that he sent necklaces
and special couriers to many pretty women. She knew more
about life now. She was almost eighteen and no longer the baby
he had seen one evening at Grand-Coeur.

She got up, looked at herself in the mirror again, and brushed
her long hair once more. To be honest with herself, she had to
recognize that she was moved by Ogier's tactful attentions and
the fact that he found her beautiful.

She still wore coarse linen nightgowns. Now that she was a
lace manufacturer and the main shareholder of a company,
maybe she should buy more elegant nightgowns for herself. But
was this really the time for it? Monsieur Faverie had written that
she must spend less than she took in—much less, he had added,
underlining the words three times. Since there weren't yet any
substantial sums of money coming in, she would wait.

She went back to bed and lay thinking about her net ground.
Before falling asleep, she took pleasure in imagining how surprised Ogier would be when he learned of her creation. Would

he be angry that it hadn't been invented in one of his workshops?
He would surely begin using it immediately. There was no protection for inventors in lacemaking, and that ought to be changed.

She woke up with the thought that the Moon of Burned Fruit
had to be July or August. July seemed more likely.

For the tenth time that month, Dieudonné Desbraies—this,
she now knew, was the name of the elegant and exasperatingly
persistent draper—had come into the salesroom and asked for
her. He needed to know her opinion with regard to a lace collar
he was thinking of buying. She sighed, left her office, and went
to talk with him.

The salesroom was less crowded than the pastry shop to which
she and Michanteau had gone in Paris, but she was satisfied
with the moderately brisk pace of her business affairs that morning.

To come and choose his lace, Monsieur Desbraies had dressed
as though he were going to stroll through the galleries of the
palace in Alençon, then have supper at Mistress Verlot's inn, in
one of the two private rooms she had just decorated and made
available to her customers. Like the older Morel d'Arthus brothers in the family portrait, he wore a reddish-brown silk coat.
Gilonne looked up at the children in the painting. She liked the
knowing glances she exchanged with them while she was in the
midst of her customers and her lace. She made a slight grimace.
They understood that she was annoyed at having to waste precious time with unwelcome people. They always understood
everything.

While waiting for her, Monsieur Desbraies had been conversing with another bourgeois. "But, sir," she heard him say,
"you have to go back to ancient Rome to find such a great reign
and such unquestionable supremacy. Even at the height of her
glory, Spain never attained that supremacy. Our country rules
the world and our king is the foremost sovereign of the universe!"

The bourgeois, who had been listening to him with a sad
expression, evidently had Protestant sympathies. "France has a
bigger population than any of the other countries in Europe,"
he said. "That's helpful in gaining supremacy over them. We
have nineteen million people, almost twenty. Spain has somewhere between five and seven million."

"Numbers have nothing to do with it, sir! What we have is quality! Our king is the greatest, the most sublime, the most . . ."

Gilonne was amused to see that the handsome Monsieur Desbraies, who until then had always seemed as soft as lamb's wool, was losing his temper.

"Since you've mentioned quality, I'll point out that nowhere else in the world will you find anyone as charming and beautiful as Madame," the sad bourgeois said gallantly.

Gilonne thanked him with a nod and asked what the two men desired, intending to send them to a clerk. She never did any of the selling herself. If she did, customers would insist on dealing only with her and she would have no time for her lacemaking, which she didn't want to give up. She had come to speak to Monsieur Desbraies because she knew, from unhappy experience, that he wouldn't leave without seeing her, even if he had to wait three hours, pacing back and forth in the salesroom and wearing out its beautiful parquet floor with his sharp heels.

He wanted her to confirm his choice. He preferred this collar of *point de France.* Those two others, of Brussels and English lace, had tempted him, but he had decided to remain faithful to the lace of his town. She expressed her approval and, since she had to make a little conversation, said she had those foreign laces only because there was occasionally a demand for them, although there was nothing as beautiful as *point de France.* She offered to have the collar elegantly wrapped for him. Or would he prefer to have it delivered to his house? She was more gracious than she had intended to be, because he had bought a collar whose design would soon be out of style. He had paid two hundred livres for it and if she had kept it five or six months longer, she would have had to lower its price to half that amount.

Just then Titus brought her one of the letters from Switzerland that he always gave her as soon as they arrived, knowing how happy she was to have them. She was about to go and read it in her office when she heard a commotion from the other side of the double doors. Two clerks opened them and several people came in, led by Her Royal Highness the Duchess of Guise and Alençon. Everyone bowed low.

Gilonne stepped forward, feeling a little tremulous. Her company's fortune would be made if the duchess had decided to buy lace from her, *in person!*

A chair was brought for Her Highness. Her attendants re-

mained standing, as etiquette required. And everyone waited.
Etiquette also required that no one speak before Her Highness
did since she was of royal blood.

She spoke. At a discreet signal from her first secretary, everyone except Gilonne had backed away from her.

Ugly, badly dressed, and disagreeable, the duchess talked
about her works of charity, which were the only ones in Alençon.
The poor were, of course, God's blessed children, but they
should still be helped. To prove her humility (she didn't say this
explicitly, but strongly implied it), she had come to ask for con-
tributions herself. She was sure she would be given a good reception *here*.

Gilonne had already understood. She would now have to pay
for having been allowed to leave the Community of New Catholics before the end of her sentence. She made a quick calcu-
lation. Of the three thousand livres she had received for her pearl
necklace, she would have to consider a third of it as lost. You
couldn't give ten sous to a cousin of the King of France.

She said that nothing in the world could be dearer to her heart
than helping the poor people whom Her Royal Highness had
taken under her protection. As she convincingly told this lie,
she wondered if she had a purse fit to hold the thousand livres
she would have to part with, much to her despair. The only one
worthy of such aristocratic hands was the red velvet one with
gold embroidery in which Ogier had sent her pearls. She would
give it to the duchess and explain to Ogier when she saw him
again. He would understand.

I was naïve again, Gilonne thought when she saw that her
pretty and well-filled purse wasn't even touched by the duchess.
It was simply dropped into the coarse cloth bag that Marquise
de Deffant, her first lady-in-waiting, held out disdainfully, as if
she expected turnips to be thrown into it.

The thousand livres would be entered in Gilonne's ledger
under the heading of "miscellaneous expenses."

When the duchess and her attendants had gone, the clerks all
left for lunch. Gilonne looked up at her little friends in the
painting.

"So it goes," she said with a half-rueful, half-ironic smile.

Having decided to give her royal cousin some lace made in
her duchy, to be used as prizes in the lotteries he liked to hold
at court, the duchess diplomatically ordered equal amounts from

the Norman Rose Company and Ogier de Beaumesnil's enterprise, demanding, of course, a large discount from each.

In one of his good periods, when he was equal to the greatest,
Salomon had designed a collar, a pair of cuffs, and a fan of
delicate matching lace in excellent taste. The set was exquisitely
made on Gilonne's net ground, and Madame de Montespan took
such a fancy to it that she obtained the king's permission to keep
it, rather than putting it up as a lottery prize. When she learned
where it came from, she placed a royal order with Gilonne's
company.

Gilonne was sickened at the thought of working for the court
of the king who had caused her husband's death. But what else
could she do, since the king had the power of life or death over
her, just as the duchess had the power of life or death over the
Norman Rose Company? She had to choose: She could take
refuge in a convent, where she would have to serve only God,
or she could put up with bowing to her enemies. That was what
had flashed through her mind when she saw the duchess come
into the house of the man she had sent to the galleys. Her instinct
for self-preservation had made her pay the price of her freedom.
She had chosen then and she would make the same choice now,
in spite of herself. Hélye wouldn't hold it against her. He had
always understood everything. He knew, where he was now,
that she had to live not only for their twins in Switzerland but
also for the children who depended on her here, for her lacemakers, and for lace itself!

When she thought of Hélye, she regretted not having a portrait of him as an adult. How like him to have two painters in
his house and never to think of having his own portrait painted!
He would have liked to have a hundred pictures of her, but he
hadn't posed for a painter since the age of eight. She looked up
at that charming little boy. Would his son look like him? At that
moment, she had such a strong desire to see her children that
tears came into her eyes.

Just then another special courier from Dieppe arrived to bring
her a little package and a letter. Had Ogier boarded a ship or
not? Had the courier swum to shore? She gave him food and
drink and put the package and the letter into the pocket of her
cloak. She had decided to go to Notre-Dame to pray for Hélye
and ask him to forgive her for the concessions she had to make
to his enemies in order to survive. Afterward she would look at
what Ogier had sent her.

She prayed. Then she went to see her old women. It was a great satisfaction to have them there, and a joy to hear them talking endlessly.

This morning they were doing their talking under the linden tree. They had respected the graves, sitting around them, not on them. They said the two dead men didn't mind having them there and probably even liked listening to them, since they had both enjoyed conversation. It was a pity they couldn't settle the argument the old women were having. It had begun with a discussion of the queen's death. Poor woman, she hadn't been happy. The king had been attracted to all women except her. From there, the conversation had gone to the subject of mourning, and that was where it had turned into an argument. Chopine and Conte-Nouvelles claimed that black *point de France* was being made; Thomine and Marie maintained that no such lace had ever been made in Alençon.

"Have you heard anything about that, Gilonne? Is anyone making black lace now?"

"I've never seen any."

"You see!" Marie said to Chopine and Conte-Nouvelles. "You can't tell me that the biggest lace manufacturer in Alençon doesn't know what she's talking about!"

"I'm not the biggest. The Plessis d'Ocagnes, the Marescots, and Count de Beaumesnil are bigger than I am."

"The best way to be the biggest would be to marry Count de Beaumesnil. He's such a nice man! Ever since we saw him at the Hobon Girl's public penance, he—"

The three others silenced Chopine, who didn't seem to be entirely sober, to prevent the indiscretion she had been about to commit. But Gilonne didn't seem to have heard. Marie saw her take a letter and a little package from her cloak pocket and, consumed with curiosity, watched her read.

The letter from Ogier had been sent from an inn in Dieppe:

I have decided to write to you often. Since my letters would take too long to reach you from Canada, I am going to spend this night writing at least a dozen of them. I will leave them here and they will be sent to you regularly every week. In that way, I may escape the danger of finding you married again when I come back.

I have brought with me the portrait of you that was in my room at Grand-Coeur. (I must remember to reward the artist

*for painting it, and especially for leaving it there!) Today I
happened to meet a Jesuit friend of mine who, he says, does
not believe it is necessary for him to cut himself off from the
world in order to achieve his salvation. He came to have
dinner with me in my room, saw your portrait, and said that
he was soothed by the sweetness and beauty of your face. The
portrait does not have that effect on me. If I followed my
inclination, I would leap onto my horse, gallop back to you,
and let that ship leave without me tomorrow. But I must go
and settle my affairs in Canada. I intend to devote my life to
loving you, and for that I will need a great deal of money.
Not, of course, that I think you are mercenary. I will need
money for myself, to be free to run after you. It seems to me
that you are a woman in whom everything is always moving:
body, heart, mind. I once said to myself that a lacemaker was
a calm, sensible woman, always sitting still, who would wait
where you left her until you came back. I was wrong.*

*The emerald in the ring that I will send you with this letter
is the color of your eyes: a deep green that sometimes has
strange flashes of blue. . . .*

Those were almost the same words Monsieur Mortimer had
used when he gave her the emerald ring that had belonged to his
wife.

The ring from Ogier was in a red leather box. She didn't open
it in front of Marie, but Marie had such inquisitive eyes that they
seemed able to see through walls, and maybe she already knew
what was in the box.

The emerald ring was strikingly beautiful. Gilonne put it away
with the pearl necklace. She had read in a book on decorum that
a man should give very valuable presents only to a loose woman
or to his wife. Only the king could give any woman whatever he
pleased without having offensive conclusions drawn from it.
Ogier wasn't the king, and she was neither a loose woman nor
his wife. She thought back on his letter. Why did he have to
show her portrait to that Jesuit who was trying to win his salvation without cutting himself off from the world, and therefore
went to social gatherings and might be indiscreet? And why did
he say she was always moving, when he was the one who kept
going off until some "Moon of Flowers" or "Moon of Burned
Fruit"? It was a perfect example of unfair masculine reasoning.

If she knew where to write, she would tell him exactly what she thought of him.

Just as she was about to reread his letter, a servant came to tell her that there was trouble in the workshops.

That evening, as usual, the lacemakers had lit their candles and put their glass bowls in front of them as soon as the boy in charge of lighting had brought fire into the room. About an hour later, only the Protestants' workshops were lighted. Those of the Catholics were dark and silent. The Protestants were still working, but the Catholics had blown out their candles as a sign of rebellion.

Holding a candlestick, Gilonne peered at their determined faces. One woman stood up and said that if Protestants went on working there, the Catholics would leave. Until they had an answer to their demand for the dismissal of the Protestants, they wouldn't light their candles.

The situation was serious. Madame de Montespan had ordered a large flounce and insisted that it be delivered within a very short time. The lacemakers were taking turns working all night. If there was the slightest delay, the deadline couldn't be met. This was the first order from the king's favorite, and failing to deliver it on time would be disastrous. What could Gilonne do to get all her lacemakers working again?

By asking questions, she gradually learned what had happened. Lancelotte was the cause of it all. She was still having visions, and a group of Protestants had come to regard her as a prophet. She had recently made several predictions that came true, and this had given her an importance that was becoming harmful. If Hélye hadn't insisted on keeping her, Gilonne would have dismissed her long ago. But she liked to go on respecting Hélye's wishes whenever possible. In this case, she had been wrong. Lancelotte was dangerous. She had predicted the death of her great-aunt, who, she said, was being poisoned by the verbena tea that papist witches made her drink to drive away the demons they claimed were in all Protestants. The great-aunt had died, undoubtedly of old age, but on the date predicted by her niece. To make things worse, Lancelotte had predicted the queen's death, and the queen had just died. Now she was saying that every month she would announce the name of a papist lacemaker who was going to die. And the Catholic workers were afraid.

Lancelotte would have to leave immediately.

As soon as they learned of this decision, the Protestant lace-makers also put out their candles. They would all leave with Lancelotte if she was dismissed.

Now all the workshops were dark. Gilonne went from one to another, holding her candlestick in front of her. As she was leaving the last one, at the end of the south wing of the house, she saw the women stand up with their hands joined. This was how they stood every morning when they began their day by devoting the first few moments of it to God. Now, too, they were going to pray around their worktables. By the time she reached the other end of the gallery, she heard Catholic and Protestant prayers mingling in a kind of steady moan.

Her mind was working frantically. She wished she could talk over the situation with Michanteau, but her friend had gone off to attend the funeral of her only sister, who had died in child-birth. To help herself concentrate, Gilonne went out into the garden and began pacing back and forth. If she didn't find a solution within an hour, everything would be lost. She couldn't dismiss all the Protestants: She wouldn't have time to find sixty skilled lacemakers to replace them. And dismissing the Catho-lics would amount to suicide. She had been unnerved by those dark workshops that seemed to be watching her, and wait-ing. . . . All at once she began running to her old women.

They were sitting around a steaming pot of porridge and greeted Gilonne with happy exclamations. The two sisters made room for her between them. Then, sensing how worried she was, they fell silent.

"They've put out their candles and stopped working."

When Gilonne had finished explaining the situation, Thom-ine stood up, took her cane, and said, "Chopine and Conte-Nouvelles, come with me."

"What about me?" asked Marie.

"Not now," said Thomine. She turned to Gilonne. "Take us there."

"What are you going to do, Grandmother?"

"Take us there. I know what to do."

As they walked through the house, the three canes tapped on the floor to the rhythm of the blind women's footsteps.

"I want to go to the Protestants," said Thomine, "to the shop where Lancelotte is."

"Be careful," Gilonne warned her. "If you say one word against her, they'll turn into raging demons!"

"Chopine and Conte-Nouvelles can tell you how many times we saw candles put out before we got so we couldn't see anything."

"But you weren't dealing with religious fanatics!"

"Gilonne, an angry lacemaker is an angry lacemaker. Religion doesn't change that. Ask Chopine about the winter evening when she almost stabbed a mistress-lacemaker with a stiletto. And you, Conte-Nouvelles, do you remember when you threw your glass bowl out the window, and a poor man who was passing by got hit on the head with it?"

The three blind women stifled their laughter, joyful in their inner darkness and the outer darkness around them. They demanded that Gilonne go away and leave them alone.

When they went into the room where Lancelotte was guarded by her protectors, they loudly pounded their canes on the floor with an instinctive sense of the dramatic.

"The three of us are blind," said Thomine. "We've heard that there's a girl here who's a prophet. We can't see her, but maybe she'll tell us if someday we'll come back into the world of light."

"Don't talk; it's a trap!" said a woman. "They're papists. I know them: They live in that little house at the back of the garden. Don't talk!"

"Don't listen to her, prophet," said Thomine. "A prophet listens only to God. Yes, my friends and I are Catholics, and if you really hear God, tell us something. If you have nothing to tell us, it means you hear nothing from God."

This time all the Protestants loudly warned Lancelotte not to say anything. But she asked for silence.

"Let me listen," she said. "The Lord is speaking to me. He's saying . . . He's saying that the three blind papists are all going to die."

"When?" Thomine, Conte-Nouvelles, and Chopine all asked at once.

"Within a month."

"I need a drink to help me swallow that," said Chopine.

"God has told me! Don't blaspheme, you papist dogs!" cried Lancelotte. "Within a month! God has told me!"

"Will the prophet also tell us where the door is, so we can leave?" asked Chopine.

"You're going to die!" Lancelotte shrieked furiously. "You're going to die within a month! It's God's will!"

"Now I want you to take us to the Catholics," Thomine said to Gilonne as they rejoined her outside the Protestants' workshop.

And when they were in one of the Catholics' workshops she said, "Listen to me, all of you. My two friends and I were lacemakers for many years, and we sometimes put out our candles too. Then our beautiful lace put out our eyes. That was how God wanted it. But believe me, that Protestant prophet sees less than we do! She sees nothing, nothing at all! She was right about two deaths, but how many was she wrong about? Don't worry, God isn't blind! Lancelotte has just predicted that Chopine, Conte-Nouvelles, and I are all going to die within a month. I promise you that every morning we'll come here and pray with you. You'll see that we're still alive and walking on our own two feet. If you see us wasting away . . . well, in that case we'll talk about Lancelotte's prediction again. But we're sure it won't come true."

Chopine and Conte-Nouvelles expressed their agreement by banging their canes on the floor.

"Is there anything here we can drink a toast with?" asked Chopine. "Come to think of it, you can't see any better than I can, because it's dark in here. Even if you have a bottle, you probably can't find it."

One by one, the candles were lit again.

"Here," said one of the women. "We've got this little bit of brandy that we keep in case one of us gets so tired she can hardly sit up anymore."

"It's good enough for me," said Chopine. "I'll drink to our health—for the next month, we're going to need it!"

When Gilonne kissed her three old women, Conte-Nouvelles said a little disdainfully, "For a long time we'd been trying to think of a way to come and enjoy ourselves a little in the workshops, but since you wouldn't let us . . . Your little Thomine may not talk much, but she knows how to act when she has to."

Three boxes padded inside and out with pink satin were waiting, open, for Gilonne to put into them the superb pieces of lace that had been finished the day before. There were two complete bath sets, one for the Duchess of Quaylus and the other for Countess de Dangeau, and the flounce for Madame de Montespan's dress. She wrapped each piece in a satin leaf on which she placed a rose made of the same cloth that covered the box. She knew her customers liked this innovation.

She had just finished packing the lace when a servant announced that the Duke of Penthièvre had come to see her. He wasn't one of her customers. Not yet. But he was regarded as the foremost lace collector in the kingdom. He had lace from all periods and a wide variety of sources. For a lacemaker, being visited by him and receiving his approval was equivalent to being awarded the Croix du Saint-Esprit* by the king in person.

Gilonne made sure her crown of hair was neatly in place. She preferred to arrange her hair as she liked it, rather than according to fashion. Ogier had told her one day that it was her way of showing that she was like no one else, that she was herself, the most beautiful woman of all. He was exaggerating, as usual. What hadn't he written in those letters that came to her every week! The thought of it made her laugh, and as a result she was in a lighthearted mood when she went to receive the duke.

He was "a curious," as those who collected beautiful things—paintings, statues, books, medals, jewelry, lace—were called. And he looked the way a duke ought to look, which wasn't always the case, as Gilonne now knew. He was an impressively handsome man, but she was used to such visits and they never made her lose her head.

"I was told at Versailles," he said, "that I'd find here the pieces lacking in my collection. I wasn't told that I'd also see the most beautiful woman imaginable."

"I'm overwhelmed by your high opinion of me, sir. What can I do for you?"

"As I look at you, it's hard for me to put my thoughts in order, especially since I'm tired from my journey. . . ."

She had a servant push out a chair for him, then bring biscuits and a bottle of sweet wine.

This had been her usual procedure since several ladies from the court, on their way to Bagnoles-de-l'Orne to take the waters, had stopped in to choose some lace that would embellish their stay at the baths and might help them to overlook the unpleasant taste of the water they drank. It was now known that visitors to the Norman Rose Company were given food and drink and a comfortable chair in which they could sit at ease while excellent lace was shown to them.

*The highest royal decoration under the French monarchy.

When the duke's wine and biscuits had been put on a little table, Gilonne had two clerks bring in something Zoltan had made for her: a rectangular wooden slab covered with pink satin, which had become the company's exclusive cloth. Placed on a stand, it was used as the background for the pieces of lace being presented for inspection. She had also brought big ivory-handled magnifying glasses to help customers appreciate the regularity and delicacy of her lace. Ogier would be amazed to see all these things, she had said to herself the day before, when she received her weekly letter from Dieppe. Maybe it would make him rebuke his directors for their lack of initiative. They had only to follow her example by constantly trying to think of improvements that would please her customers.

"What I would like," said the duke, "is a piece of lace, not too large, that I could put in one of my display cases on a velvet background. I need the most beautiful lace you have, something absolutely perfect and *extraordinary*."

She had very beautiful lace, but extraordinary? Maybe not. She realized that for a collection—and what a collection!—it wouldn't be enough to . . . Suddenly she had an inspiration.

"I invented the new net ground that you see here," she said, "but only after several attempts I considered unsuccessful. Finally one piece of lace made with that ground satisfied me. It was the origin of all the others that have been made since then. Allow me to go and bring it to you, and you can judge whether or not it suits you."

It was a collar with an exquisite decorative pattern of flowers and leaves. The duke took it in his aristocratic hands with a respect that made Gilonne's eyes a little misty.

"Would I be expecting too much if I asked you to part with it? I realize how precious it must be to you."

It was precious to her because she remembered showing it to Hélye and hearing him say, "I'm amazed by your invention." But because that memory would always be in her heart, she wouldn't mind parting with the piece of lace. Perhaps it really belonged in a famous collector's display case.

"You would give me great pleasure by accepting it," she said. "It's yours."

"But it's priceless!"

"That's precisely why I'm giving it to you."

The duke took off a beautiful emerald ring and she already knew what he was going to say; by now, she was used to hearing it. "This is the color of your eyes. Green, with strange flashes of blue." He handed it to her. "But I'm still indebted to you, because this lace is incomparable. We'll see each other again, so that I can better free myself of my debt."

Either men have no imagination, she thought as she watched him walk away, *or emeralds are very common stones.* She would try to find out someday when she had the time for it.

Time, time . . . In the past, it had been money that dominated her thoughts and conversation. Now it was time.

Almost as soon as the door had closed behind the duke, it was opened for the chamberlain of the Queen of Poland.

The chamberlain was a serious, sedate man who said to her seriously and sedately, "Her Majesty the Queen of Poland wants to buy lace from you, and only from you, so here I am. But I must say you live very far away."

Far away? She lived in Alençon, the world's most important town, since it was where the world's most important lace was made. It was other places that were far away. People like this man, no matter what their rank might be, were a little foolish.

He savored his food and drink. He was very tall and thin. Everything about him seemed tired, except his lively, piercing eyes. He appreciated the delicate little brioches filled with raspberry jam and found the pear cider divine. When he had restored his strength, he began describing the strenuous life he led. Gilonne listened patiently. No one ever bought lace in a hurry. With his breath smelling of raspberries and pears, he spoke of his queen, Marie Casimir, whom the people called Marysienka. She was of French origin. He remarked in passing that he loved jam, asked about the raspberry jam he had just eaten, which seemed perfect to him, and was delighted when he learned he could take several jars of it to Warsaw. Suddenly acting as if he were pressed for time, he took from his pocket a list "written by Her Majesty's own hand." Gilonne wondered if she was expected to bow to that august sheet of paper. The list was very long.

"As soon as I leave you," he said, "I'll gallop to Vichy."

"Vichy?"

"Yes. I must bring three hundred bottles of water from there. It's written here and underlined three times."

One line per hundred bottles, thought Gilonne, but she kept her face serious.

"But to come back to the subject of lace," the chamberlain went on, "the king has also told me to buy some for him."

"For his own use?"

"No. I don't think he has any great liking for lace. He wants it for the queen's birthday. So I must have not only what's on this list but also what's needed to satisfy the King of Poland."

"We can supply you with everything you want," said Gilonne.

She had already decided to sell him the bath sets that had been made for Countess de Dangeau and the Duchess of Quaylus, and replace them with two sets from her remaining stock of Morel d'Arthus lace. The designs of the replacements were a little less modern, but she wanted to favor the Queen of Poland. She would probably give the two other ladies a lower price.

When he was completely reassured, the chamberlain resumed his eating and drinking and began talking about Vichy, which seemed to play a major part in his life.

"Their Majesties couldn't live without their Vichy water. I have to make that exhausting journey twice a year and personally escort the precious bottles of water. They're carried on three stretchers, between layers of straw, and you can't imagine how many chances there are for accidents to happen. Do you know Vichy?"

No, she didn't. Was the water there as good as it was said to be?

"What I regret, madame, is that I can't also bring back to Their Majesties the gaiety and amiability that you find everywhere in Vichy. For Vichy water to have its full effect, according to doctors, you must drink it in a contemplative frame of mind and treat it as respectfully as if it were holy water, and at the same time you must be in excellent humor. Doctors even prescribe dancing! But since the king and queen often have cares and worries, they don't drink their Vichy water in the right atmosphere. To give them the diversion of becoming acquainted with something new, I've learned the bourrée, a dance that's greatly enjoyed by ladies and gentlemen during their stay at Vichy." He suddenly turned pale. "I think I've forgotten it! I'm so tired!"

He stood up, clumsily danced a few steps, then asked, "Can you tell me if I have it right? Maybe my bourrée is like one of your local dances."

It happened that Monsieur Dieudonné Desbraies arrived while

Gilonne was taking a try at dancing the bourrée with the chamberlain of the Queen of Poland. As he waited, holding an enormous bouquet of flowers, he paced back and forth in the salesroom.

It also happened that it was now the Moon of Burned Fruit and that Count Ogier de Beaumesnil, having returned to Alençon the day before, also arrived at the Norman Rose Company.

He saw that fop waiting with his flowers, then he went into Gilonne's office and saw her dancing, at ten o'clock in the morning, with a tall, thin man elegantly dressed in royal blue taffeta.

And it further happened that Gilonne was wearing an emerald ring, but not the one Ogier had sent her.

Scowling as he had done in his childhood when he felt he wasn't making enough progress in taking his life where he wanted it to go, he said with a gentleness belied by the fury in his eyes, "I'll come back when you're not occupied with such serious matters."

Through Lady Bertrade, Gilonne had returned Ogier's gifts to him. Michanteau had been outraged when she learned of it. Gilonne must be out of her mind, she fumed, to throw away jewelry that might have saved the company in a time when it was short of money.

Gilonne didn't argue. She only regretted that in a moment of abandon she had talked about her private affairs to Michanteau, who could never understand them, any more than she could understand about milk.

"You're spoiling them," said Michanteau.

"Do you think Gérasime used to spoil us when he gave us hot milk on cold days?"

"He gave it to us only on very cold days, not *every* day, the way you're doing!"

"Remember how we used to dread that worktable, and how good a little kindness made us feel?"

"You think you're a lace manufacturer, but you're only an innkeeper. Milk for some, verbena tea for others, porridge for the old women, and lunch for everybody! Then there's cider and tobacco for the painters, and their singing in the workshops! No, I was wrong: This isn't an inn, it's only a tavern that by some miracle turns out a little lace once in a while."

There was some truth in what Michanteau said, and she had reason to be upset, because she had the most unpleasant task:

collecting payment of bills. Since few people paid without being forced to, it was work that took up a great deal of her time. It required quickness, tenacity, and guile, and she excelled at everything it involved: hurrying back and forth between Paris and Versailles by stagecoach, breaking through barricades of servants to reach the anterooms of aristocratic or bourgeois houses, capturing a front-rank position in the crowd of other creditors and shouting more loudly than anyone else to have some chance of being heard. What mattered was not so much getting close to the customer as pushing away the others, so as to be among the privileged few who would share the contents of the purse that the customer would toss to his steward, telling him to pay the most urgent debts and then fleeing from the clamoring pack of creditors.

For each Duke of Penthièvre or Countess de Dangeau, who paid immediately and in full, there were many others who demanded the finest lace, knowing they would pay for it only in part, or not at all! What was to be done? Should the company turn down orders? Or take them only from Madame Lavalette, the beautiful butcher's wife, who paid for her collars with good beef, mutton, and pork?

Gilonne and Michanteau were in despair when one day an incomparable opportunity arrived in the person of the most honest, pious, and powerful woman in the kingdom: Madame de Maintenon.

For Gilonne, suddenly finding herself facing Madame de Maintenon's steward (to draw up the contract) and her mistress of the robes (to choose the lace) was like stumbling against bags of gold on the ground and having only to bend down and pick them up. The king's new favorite didn't wear much finery, but she gave many presents and they were all of excellent quality.

It was a gray April day soaked by endless pattering showers. Michanteau and Mathieu were preparing for their wedding, and praying that the sun would be among the guests. A whirlwind of prestigious orders descended on the four largest lace manufacturers in Alençon that day, driving away the rain with gusts of promised gold. The orders were for nothing less than all the lace accessories and ornaments to go with a set of furniture for the king. The Norman Rose Company's share of this bounty was a request to make a bedspread for His Majesty's bed.

With her usual kindness, Madame de Maintenon gave the artists of Alençon full power to create their own designs in total independence of the Royal Academy of Painting. This meant that Gilonne's company would have its first chance to do something completely original for the court. She was so excited that she threw her arms around Michanteau and said, ''Your happiness has brought us good luck, and your wedding will be even better than we thought! With an order like that, we'll all have supper at Mistress Verlot's inn!''

She had her two painters, Salomon and Peter, compete with each other for the designs. She was sure she could make them work together later, when she had chosen the best of what they had both done.

Madame de Maintenon had specified the royal emblems that were to appear on the bedspread: the eagle crown, the fleur-de-lis, and American Indians, because His Majesty attached great importance to his colonies in America.

''How are we going to stylize Indians when we've never seen any?'' asked Salomon.

''You saw Ogier de Beaumesnil's Hurons when they were terrifying the whole town,'' Gilonne pointed out.

''We saw them wearing his green, blue, and gold livery, but we can't show them dressed like that.''

''Use your imagination! No, wait: Michanteau and I once saw one dressed in Indian style. Do you remember, Michanteau?''

''I remember the frightening look in his eyes, and the feather on his head, and his knife, and how he stood perfectly still. But that's all.''

''He was wearing a blue necklace,'' said Gilonne. ''Or was it red? Yes, red. I'm sure of it.''

''Ogier de Beaumesnil is sure of all the details. For such an important order, he won't refuse to help us.''

Gilonne was on her way to Ogier's house. She knew she was the one who could most easily and quickly get the information needed in order to have two Indians, complete with feathers and beads, on the royal bedspread. She was sorry her amorous draper couldn't oblige her, because it would have been less unpleasant for her to go to him than to the handsome Count de Beaumesnil, with his mocking smile. But at least it wouldn't take long.

To show that there was nothing coquettish about her visit, she had neglected to change clothes. She was wearing a simple light-blue linen dress with a little lace only on the collar and cuffs, and she had simply twisted her hair under a linen headdress held in place by two pins in the shape of bees, a gift from Hélye. Those pins, made of gold and diamonds, were so beautiful that she sometimes wore them as decorations on the front of her dress, which made some men remark that her bodice was well defined. She hoped Ogier wouldn't make her waste time listening to such foolish talk. She would try to get pictures of American Indians from him in less than ten minutes.

When she arrived at Ogier's house, a Huron she didn't know opened the gilded gate and led her through a garden to a big vestibule with a marble floor. He didn't smile and didn't even seem to see her. But now that she knew something about Huron behavior, she was sure he would talk about her in the kitchen and describe her dress, and even her bees, more poetically than the gallant fools who were always pursuing her.

Although she intended to make her visit as short as possible, she couldn't help noticing the beauty of everything around her. Perhaps because the sight of all these splendors tired her eyes, she closed them. When she opened them a moment later, the Huron was in front of her. She hadn't heard him make the slightest sound when he came back. These Indians . . . He asked her to follow him, led her through two or three drawing rooms, and left her in an immense room that opened onto a flowery garden.

Ogier came very quickly, wearing a sapphire blue dressing gown.

"I was told that I had a visitor, 'a woman with bees gathering the honey of her hair.' I immediately knew it was you, because I know those two pieces of jewelry. They're luckier than the ones I sent you. . . . No, don't be irritated. Just tell me what brings you here so early in the morning."

"So early?"

"Don't you know it's not yet six o'clock?"

No, she hadn't known! After getting up and having breakfast with her old women before dawn, she had felt as if the day were already half over. She discreetly glanced out the window. It was true: The sun had just barely risen. How could she have acted so thoughtlessly? And Ogier, of course, was standing there looking at her with that smile of his. No matter, she had to take the plunge.

"I've come to see you because yesterday I was given a royal order—"

"I know."

"It's for a bedspread."

"I know."

"Madame de Maintenon wants to have Indians on it."

"I know."

"Oh! Do you always know everything?"

"In this case, I do, because I'm the one who sent Madame de Maintenon's people to you and advised them to order the bedspread from you."

"I see. And did you also advise them to have it made with Indians on it?"

"No, but I'm delighted that Madame de Maintenon thought of it herself, because that's why you've come to see me. I already know what you want. I'm going to give you two beautiful drawings of Hurons and Iroquois. Not only beautiful, but also moving: the stains you'll see on them are the blood of the Jesuit who was killed soon after making them."

Why did he have to tell her about that? All she wanted him to do was give her the drawings and let her leave.

He laughed, took a key from an engraved silver cup, stepped toward a cabinet, and said, "You're always in a hurry, always running. Will you ever take time to live?"

Time to live? What did he mean? She already *was* living . . . for her lace.

As sunlight finally came into the room, a strange table emerged from the shadows. She stared at it with intense curiosity.

Ogier came back and said, "I see you're looking at my table of the world. It belonged to the Emperor Charlemagne. He had it made of cast gold. The whole world is engraved on it and he used to look at it to contemplate his empire. I succeeded in making an old Greek merchant part with it. He made me wait for years and wanted to give me his daughter with it, so that the thing he valued most highly would stay in his family. I was finally able to have the table without the daughter. Look here, at this green dot, this miniature emerald: it's Alençon. . . . What's the matter?"

"How did you have the wonderful idea of doing this? Now that I see it, I don't understand why I never thought of it myself! All those years of suffering, when the idea was so simple, so obvious . . . Tell me how it came to you."

"My table is the only one of its kind," he said, "and it was touched by Charlemagne himself, but you don't care about it at all. What interests you is this.'' He gently took the piece of green parchment she had been holding. "I now realize how foolish I've been. I tried to please you with pearls and heartfelt love letters, and I accomplished nothing. What I should have done was to court you as a lace manufacturer. I'll begin doing that now. Here, I'm giving you this little invention that seems to fascinate you so much: a piece of parchment dyed green. No one else knows about it in Alençon or anywhere else in the world of lacemaking. It's yours.

"I had the idea for it last night. Three samples of thread had just come to me from Flanders. I put them on my green velvet sleeve to compare them with three samples from my own thread-makers. I saw them all very distinctly, and suddenly the idea came to me: We ought to dye our parchments that color to reduce the strain on our lacemakers' eyes. That's all. Well, not quite. The color also had to be indelible. I remembered that Fulbert, my Huron prince, had necklaces dyed in colors that never rubbed off. I also remembered how he got that result. I did a few experiments. French chemists will find a way to dye our parchments just as well.''

"But what if they don't?''

"It won't matter, because in that case my gift to you will include sending to Canada for what's needed to make good dye. Does that reassure you? No? What's wrong?''

"Do you believe that if someone had thought of this sooner, my grandmother and her friends, and all the other lacemakers who have gone blind, would have kept their sight?''

"Maybe. Maybe longer, at least.''

"So I won't go blind someday,'' she said softly, "thanks to you. . . .''

"Don't think about that! Don't think even for one second that your eyes might die!''

"I don't think that now. Because of you, lacemakers won't go blind anymore. I thank you for all of them.''

"I don't care about all of them. I only care about you.''

"Then I thank you for myself.''

She stepped forward and kissed him on the cheek. A moment later, her lips had somehow moved to his.

When he finally let go of her, she murmured, "Oh, I didn't know . . .''

"You didn't know what, my darling? How a real kiss could be?"

He was smiling. She blushed and felt a little dizzy. All she could think of to say was: "I have to go. Someone's waiting for me."

"Someone's always waiting for you, my angel. And do you know how long *I've* waited?"

"But . . ."

"You owe me nothing, of course. . . . Well, no, now you do owe me something."

"I've just . . ."

"For good measure, give me a little more of your precious time. Share my breakfast with me. It's been waiting for me since you came. I haven't even had a glass of water this morning."

It was true that she had come to his house at dawn. The least she could do was to give a few more minutes of her time to the man who had invented dyed parchment for lacemakers, given her pictures of Indians, and spoken of her to Madame de Maintenon. If it hadn't been for him, would the new favorite have given an order to the Norman Rose Company? Gilonne was suddenly assailed by the idea that he might have been helping her for a long time. She had often wondered why the Morel d'Arthus house hadn't been sold sooner, and how she had been lucky enough to acquire it when she came back from Geneva. Had he had a hand in that too? And what about the printing press she had found in the cellar of the house? Had it really been forgotten there? She felt her cheeks turning red again and pressed her hands to them.

"What's the matter? Aren't you feeling well?"

"My house, the press . . . Was that you too?"

"Now that you remind me of it, I'm happy to remember that I began courting you in a more intelligent way than I realized at the time."

"Thank you," she said quietly. "For everything."

She suddenly felt insignificant in that vast house, a little lacemaker floundering in a sea of worries and anxieties. She was nothing compared with this man who was the king of the town, owned a solid gold table that had been made for Emperor Charlemagne, used precious stones for buttons. A long row of them were now glittering like stars against the blue background of his dressing gown.

"Please sit down," he said, "unfold this little lace napkin, and tell me if you prefer coffee or chocolate."

She asked for chocolate. He poured it for her. It had a deliciously pungent taste. She blushed once more at the thought that savoring a sip of that chocolate was like the beginning of the kiss he had given her. Only the beginning. Afterward, that swirling sensation . . . She didn't want to think about it.

"How do you like the chocolate?" he asked.

She finished her cup, set it down on the saucer very gently (it was such fine china), thought a while, and said, "I wonder . . ."

"What do you wonder?"

That way of looking at her! It was almost as if he were kissing her again.

"I wonder," she said resolutely, "if it's not a drink for idle noblemen and frivolous ladies, or . . ."

"Or?"

His eyes burned her like fire!

"Or for useless people, different from me. I have so much to do that I can't let the soft, creamy sweetness of chocolate drain my strength away."

"You're too conscientious," he said. Then, seeing her stand up, he asked, "You're leaving?"

"I can't stay any longer."

"Just another minute. There's a question I've been wanting to ask you for a long time." He had to say something, anything, that would make her stay. "I've always wondered if lacemakers think while they work and, if so, what they think about."

Was he making fun of her? She gently squeezed the dyed parchment in her hand, held back a smile, and said, "Yes, we lacemakers think while we work. I'll spare you fifteen years of my thoughts, but I can tell you some that have gone through my mind in the last few months. I've often thought about Versailles. I went there several times to deliver dresses for Madame de Montespan in the days when her hold on the king was beginning to weaken and she hoped that new clothes might revive his interest in her. Someone in the palace tried to swindle me by selling me the exclusive right to supply lace handkerchiefs for the king to use at night. I would have lost quite a bit of money if an obliging nobleman hadn't told me that in private the king uses only hemmed batiste handkerchiefs, and never the lace ones he uses in public. I didn't like Versailles. I thought about it for a long time while I worked. Why? Because the whiteness of our lace, the whiteness we take so much trouble to preserve, is spoiled too quickly there. And because I had the bad luck to be with Madame de Montespan one day when the king came to show her a new medal celebrating the glory of his galleys, with these words on it: 'French dominion over the Mediterranean is assured by forty galleys.' And do you know what color those galleys are? They're red, from the blood of Protestants.''

Ogier hadn't taken his eyes off her for one moment, but had he been listening to her? Would he have preferred her to talk about what she could see from her window while she worked? Did he expect her to say how often she had seen him ride by, escorting the duchess's carriage while she shared it with the vivacious Marie-Ange de Motté, whose strong liking for Count Ogier de Beaumesnil was known to everyone in town? But Marie-Ange de Motté was only an obscure little reader to the duchess, while she, Gilonne de Ferrières, had attracted the attention of the king himself!

She had been helping Madame de Maintenon try on a dress when His Majesty came in and exclaimed, "What beauty! It outshines the diamonds in the crown, even my Sancy diamond!"

At the time, she hadn't understood the disagreeable reaction of Madame de Maintenon, who said caustically, "Let's not exaggerate, sire. Pretty, yes, but not dazzlingly beautiful." Later, as she was about to leave the palace, she overheard one ironically smiling courtier say to another, "There's the marvel the king compared to his most beautiful diamond!" So the king hadn't been referring to the beauty of the lace dress, as she had thought, but to her own!

But she wouldn't tell Ogier about that. In fact, she would say nothing more to him about anything.

Nothing more? Yet she heard herself say, laughing, "It's lucky that Mistress Lescure has never seen Versailles! People there don't wash their hands as much as she thinks they do, and she'd be heartbroken to see how quickly her whitest white turns gray. And yesterday, while I was making lace, I kept thinking about a nobleman at court who finally paid me for the six collars he'd ordered, but had to sell his last farm to do it. Can you understand why anyone would act that way? Because he liked to wear lace so much, that man has nothing now, and maybe his family has nowhere to live.''

"Don't be sad."

"I'm not. Yesterday I was thinking about how senselessly some people behave, but the day before yesterday I was laughing at my old women's latest prank. They had the idea of stretching a string across the street where they spend most of their time, so that a policeman they don't like—he's the son of a spiteful woman they knew in their youth—would fall on his face when he was making his rounds at night."

Then she began telling him about Michanteau's wedding. Michanteau had been so pretty, with her long brown hair hanging down her back, held by a cord of wildflowers she had woven herself, according to custom. The wedding had taken place in the village of Courteille, where Michanteau was born. Candelario and Zoltan had insisted on being the only musicians. . . .

Why was she telling him all this? Whenever she was with him, words played their old trick of coming out of her mouth by themselves. What else was she going to say? She had to leave, quickly. She straightened her hat with an automatic gesture, then curtsied and hurried away.

As she was about to reach the door, Ogier caught up with her.

"You're forgetting your Indian drawings."

But he noticed that she hadn't forgotten the piece of dyed parchment. He smiled and let her leave, promising himself that it wouldn't be for long.

One Sunday, after Vespers, Titus was dozing in the gatehouse when a carriage came into the quiet street and stopped in front of the gate.

After some discussion and shouting, Titus went to Gilonne, who was doing some bookkeeping with her shutters closed. Two strange and noisy men with authorizations from the intendant and the archbishop were demanding that the salesroom be opened, he told her.

From the enormous carriage, two equally enormous men got out and walked into the salesroom, while the Morel d'Arthus children looked down at them from the wall. They had the self-assurance of victorious conquerors, and their red boots pounded loudly on the floor. Thunderous laughter, for which no reason was apparent, filled the big room while Titus opened the windows to let in the sunlight. With customers who had authorizations bearing the red and green wax of prestigious seals, there was no risk in selling openly on Sunday.

A little man with silent footsteps and humble bearing followed the important personages. He was the interpreter of Igor Filatiev and Sergei Nikitin, merchants from the house of the powerful Prince Vasili Golitsyn, favorite of Sophia Alekseyevna, Regent of Russia. They had been sent to Normandy to buy pear trees, falcons, and lace for the prince.

Michanteau was at home with her husband, the old women were dozing under their linden tree and had heard nothing, and the painters were off gathering herbs. They had suddenly developed a passion for medicinal plants, and Gilonne hoped that the soothing herbs would calm them to the point where there might be a reconciliation between them.

Dieudonné Desbraies, who happened to be passing by with a bouquet of roses in his hand (as he happened to do every day), took the liberty of coming in after the Russian gentlemen. Titus was glad to see him because he felt it wouldn't be good to leave Gilonne alone with these two big louts even though they had been sent by an illustrious prince. The slender, elegant draper, dressed in pale green, his neck and wrists snowy with fine *point de France*, stared in dismay at the visitors' height and width. He seemed fascinated by the enormity of their paunches, underscored by belts tightened low over their coats. He stood in the doorway of the room, rooted to the spot, with his roses pressed over his heart.

The merchants' covetous looks made Gilonne uneasy. And she wasn't amused by the way each of them occasionally took off his hat to scratch his head with both hands, or ruffled his big black beard and then smoothed it on the lustrous satin of his shirt. What had come over the intendant and the archbishop to make them send such people to her?

The interpreter's explanatory speech, delivered in a monotonous voice and punctuated by the two merchants' exuberant laughter, can be summarized as follows:

His Excellency Prince Vasili Golitsyn already had ten thousand apple trees, but he had only Hungarian pear trees and wanted some Norman ones. While he, Jacob Bacri, was talking here in Alençon, hundreds of gardeners were preparing the soil of the prince's orchards and making protective straw matting for the five thousand trees that France had sold to him. Golden cages awaited the falcons that had been bought. Only the lace still had to be acquired. It was well known that the world's best lace was made in Alençon. But if Mademoiselle de Ferrières could swear on a crucifix that her lace was the best in Alençon, she would also have to swear that it was superior to the lace possessed by His Excellency Prince Nikita Romanov, because the two merchants would run a serious risk of having their heads cut off if they went back to Moscow with lace inferior in beauty and value to that which adorned the clothes of Prince Romanov. Though Mademoiselle de Ferrières might not know it, Prince Golitsyn had two hundred and fifty clocks made in Europe, four hundred Venetian mirrors, and six dozen of the biggest china vases that ever came out of a kiln! It was therefore unthinkable that the finest lace should not find its way to his palace.

How was Gilonne to guess what Prince Romanov had? How could she know the standards by which the lace she sold these men would be judged? She felt like saying that all her lace was unworthy of the two princes in question, but she couldn't afford to miss a chance to take in money, and she mustn't displease the intendant and the archbishop, who had recommended her to these strange customers.

Titus had withdrawn, after leaving one of Gilonne's staffs within her reach. Ever since the night when three thieves had come into a workshop to steal lace and he had watched her drive them away with a very effectively handled staff, he had seen to it that such a weapon was never far from her reach.

She was about to begin opening her drawers and displaying her merchandise when one of the Russians opened his coat, took a falcon from inside the fur lining, and put it on his gloved fist. The bird shook itself.

"He caught a cold on the way, so Sergei Nikitin has been keeping him warm," the little interpreter explained. "He's a valuable bird because he's been trained to put out eyes."

Gilonne spread her lace on the table. The two merchants had stopped laughing and were even watching with interest. She told him that this was not only the finest lace but also the most durable, because its cordonnets were reinforced with horsehair, which gave them firmness and strength.

Jacob Bacri, the interpreter, translated these words for the merchants. The one holding the falcon guffawed and took from one of his pockets what seemed to Gilonne a bloody pigeon's wing. Before she could make a move to stop him, he picked up one of her most beautiful lace handkerchiefs and rubbed it on the raw flesh. Then he took off the falcon's hood and threw the handkerchief high into the air. The falcon flew up, caught it before it fell, and tore it to shreds.

"He wanted to see if you were telling the truth about the strength of your lace," said the interpreter, with disappointment and a little reproachfulness in his voice. "But don't worry, they always pay for the damage they do, always . . ." He suddenly cried out, "Be careful! That bird is trained to put out eyes! Sergei Nikitin always takes him along when he travels, because of bandits. Be careful!"

Gilonne ignored him. As soon as she recovered from her horrified surprise, she had picked up her staff and tried to hit the bird with it. But she had never attacked such an enemy before, and her most skillful blows struck only air. The two Russian merchants were laughing loudly enough to shake the paintings on the walls. She ignored them too. Above the diabolical music of the little bells tied to the falcon's feet, she heard the moans of blind women who lived in darkness while fat pigs laughed at their suffering and let their beautiful lace, for which they had given their sight, be torn to pieces. When she finally struck down the falcon, she felt as if she had just avenged her grandmother and her blind friends.

Dieudonné Desbraies had been watching her, petrified: She had a bleeding gash in her forehead, her hair was undone, and her bodice was open; she was magnificent, sublime, an angel armed by God! The falcon fell at the draper's feet, and since it didn't seem to be dead, he gave it a final blow with his big bouquet of roses.

Just then, after pushing his way through the crowd that had gathered outside the house, Ogier burst into the room, picked up Gilonne, and carried her out. His abduction was as rapid as the falcon's attack on the handkerchief had been.

Dieudonné saw the woman he loved being taken away from him and the two monstrous Russians walking toward him. It was all over: He couldn't struggle against the too handsome, too rich, and too powerful Count de Beaumesnil. But would he struggle against the savages in red boots who were advancing inexorably on him?

He stood still, offering himself as a sacrifice to barbarity. He was going to die there, on the floor of his beloved's house. Maybe she would think of him each time her pretty little feet touched that floor. . . . He drew himself erect, took off his hat, and held it in his hand. It was his way of greeting the death coming toward him. He closed his eyes. When he opened them again, the two merchants had picked up the falcon, which was only slightly wounded, and were stroking it gently and talking to it in the tone of a father comforting a sick child.

He, Dieudonné Desbraies, the most successful draper in Alençon, was also still alive. And alone. His bouquet, having failed to kill the falcon, now lay on the floor, looking to him like a memorial to the death of all his hopes. He left it there and picked up the torn lace handkerchief. He would keep it forever, in memory of that tragic day.

Without a word, Gilonne had let Ogier put her on his horse and then settle behind her on the saddle. Now they were galloping out of town.

She remembered only having heard Ogier say, "Enough!" But what had she done wrong? Didn't she have to kill that horrible bird?

A little later, she wondered if those Russian brutes had pillaged her salesroom, and was surprised to realize that she hardly cared whether they had or not. It seemed to her that nothing mattered, nothing was worth preserving except the warmth she felt from being pressed against Ogier. And also that light fragrance, perceptible only when her face touched his silk doublet. Was it the scent he ordinarily used? In any case, he used it discreetly, and she approved of it.

The hoot of an owl changed he course of her thoughts. Was it already night? How long had they been galloping like that? And where were they going? As he held the reins his arms enclosed her. She turned her head, raised her face toward his, and asked, "Where are we going?"

"Home," he answered, and kissed her eyelids.

Leaning back against his broad, warm chest, with the sweetness of his kiss still on her eyelids and deep inside her, she accepted his answer as perfectly natural.

Still later, when night had completely fallen and they were in the heart of the Perseigne forest, it seemed to her that there was such brightness in her that everything around her should have been dazzled. And when the plain suddenly appeared as they were leaving the cover of the great oaks, she said "I love him!" to that vast expanse and made herself heavier against him. He felt that abandon and held her more tightly in his arms. Sensing that she was offering herself to him at last gave him such powerful joy that pain briefly gripped his heart.

It rained during the last part of their ride, and they were wet by the time they reached Grand-Coeur. He dismounted and handed the reins to one of his Hurons. She remained alone on Quinola for a moment, a very short moment, but during their journey there had been such an intense fusion between his strength and all the marvelous new sensations rising in her that now, without him next to her, she felt deathly cold and bereft of everything.

"You're frozen," he said, taking her in his arms and carrying her toward the house.

"No, no. . . ." she replied, without realizing that she had spoken.

As always, since no one ever knew when the master of the house might arrive, there was a roaring fire in the bedroom fireplace.

He put her down on a big, strange, and magnificent bed.

She cried out in surprise when she saw Peter's mural. There were so many people in that room! She closed the bed curtains so that none of them could see her while she took off her wet clothes, tossed them on the floor, and stretched out languidly between the soft sheets. Then she discovered the countless eyes of the beaded embroidery on the curtains. She laughed happily: This bedroom was a public place!

For several seconds she was unaware of Ogier looking at her through the opening in the curtains on the other side of the bed. When she finally saw him, wearing a long dark blue dressing gown, she smiled at him. She was a little afraid, but her heart was as joyous as a lark at daybreak. His gaze was like a warm garment covering her nakedness. She closed her eyes. But her eyelids, lowered between the world she was leaving and the one into which she felt herself being hurled at such dizzying speed, were a weak barrier.

He lay down with his head on a snowy pillow, in a profusion of lace, then leaned over her. She was suddenly lifted by a wave of triumph. He was hers, this superb, powerful man, this man who now seemed to want to be rich only in what she would give him of herself. The words he murmured to her said so. She listened to the love song that set her body aflame. Then she heard nothing. It seemed to her that her heart was too small to contain all the blood rushing to it and that her body was too frail to hold all the intoxicating life welling up in her. She ceased to be only herself as she was shaken by the storm stirred up and controlled by the man to whom she now belonged. Then, through waves of wonder, she realized that she had begun taking part in the incredible adventure, rather than simply watching it happen to her. She opened her eyes and gave Ogier their mingled greens and blues.

At some time in the night, Gilonne, half asleep, thought she heard someone weeping. Had Lady Yolaine chosen that night to come back once again and look for her needles and thread? No, a well-bred ghost like Lady Yolaine wouldn't be so tactless as to come at such a time. Gilonne smiled. Ogier, who had been looking at her, saw that delightful little smile. It was the final drop of happiness that made his heart overflow. And in a surge of tender emotion, this man generally regarded as hard, demanding, and even insensitive said humbly, "Thank you, dear God, for giving her to me at last."

Beneath the caress of Ogier's hand wiping the moisture from her temples, Gilonne sighed with well-being. Later—she couldn't have said how much later, having lost the notion of time—a very pure sound broke the silence and woke her completely. A nightingale, she thought. It was like the song of the air coming in through the partly open window and the gap between the bed curtains. Ogier wasn't asleep. With his head resting on his arm, he was still looking at her. In the first glow of dawn she saw his eyes shining as brightly as the Indian beads sewn on the curtains. She stretched cautiously, wishing she could keep the fullness of that moment: the beginning of daybreak, the light of love in the eyes of the man she loved, the nightingale's song to the new day. But, without realizing it, she moaned softly.

"What's wrong, my darling?" asked Ogier.

She could now admit to herself that she had always felt a need to talk to him because he understood her better than anyone else and seemed to sense everything inside her. She huddled against him, with her face on his warm, protective bare chest. "Maybe it will seem foolish to you," she said, "but I like to tell you everything that goes through my mind and my heart. . . . When I was a child, what I dreaded most of all—because it was punished more than anything else—was breaking the thread of the

lace I was making. And now I hope so much that the thread of
our love will never break.''

"I have very effective ways of preventing breaks like that. But
the danger, it seems to me, is that you'll become passionately
interested in something and go off after it. If I were sensible, I'd
tie you—''

She interrupted him with a little cry. "No! You can do anything but that. I'll never let myself be tied down again!''

Pompinne found only one way to counteract the blows that
Ogier had struck against her ascendancy over Lady Bertrade.
After spinning and dyeing the yarn herself, she knit another red
hat for her mistress.

"You couldn't sleep with those ostriches on your head!'' she
said. "To keep your head warm in cold drafts, there's nothing
like good wool from our own sheep.''

Lady Bertrade didn't resist. She knew that Pompinne couldn't
be overcome without a long siege, and she didn't feel she had
the strength for it.

And so Rose and Benjamin Morel d'Arthus stared at her
strange strawberry-red hat, which she had decorated with jay
feathers, as they listened to her tell the terrifying story of Lord
Wolf-Eater.

The twins pressed up against each other and shivered with
delicious fear, lying on the warm feather bed of the big lady
who knew stories they had never heard before, stories that would
have frightened Aunt Rachel. She would also have been frightened by the long hunting knife with which the big lady cut an
apple tart into pieces, and she wouldn't have let them eat so
much of the tart either. But Aunt Rachel was far away. They had
spent long days in a carriage to come here. Their new Uncle
Ogier had black horses more beautiful than any of Uncle Samuel's, and dark-skinned servants who never talked, but made
them laugh with the faces they made. Yes, poor Aunt Rachel
would have been afraid if she had seen all this.

Rose suddenly began crying. The wolves in the story had
scared her, and she felt a little like throwing up.

Gilonne, who had been watching her children and Lady Bertrade for several moments, hurried forward to comfort Rose.

As usual, Lady Bertrade had traces of gunpowder on her face.
As a result, the tears of happiness that trickled down her cheeks
left streaks of a color difficult to describe.

Standing in the doorway, Ogier watched them all, looking very much like the visitor dressed in black who had arrived at Grand-Coeur one winter evening.

Gilonne knew that Rose and Benjamin would have to go back to Geneva. France wasn't a good place for Hélye's Protestant children. When she was getting them ready for their journey to Grand-Coeur, the gentle and apprehensive Rachel had decked them out in satin, ribbons, and lace, fearing they would be recognized as Protestants if they wore their usual simple, unadorned clothes. Geneva would continue to be their refuge for a long time to come. Gilonne would wait for them. With Ogier, who had promised to bring them to her as often as possible.

With Ogier . . . and in the constant exhilaration that made her lose her head a little. Sometimes she hardly knew what she was doing. What was the important thing she had been thinking about that morning? She had to remember it. It was an idea that had just occurred to her, and she had lost it when Ogier suddenly kissed her. What *was* it? It was about a new technique that had begun taking shape in her mind, something that would change the appearance of her lace. She had to think about it. She had to *be able* to think about it. . . .

But since Ogier was looking at her unsmilingly, with his eyes shining and the serious, almost hard expression that said, "You're mine," a torrent of happiness poured into her heart. She would have plenty of time to think about her lace tomorrow.

About the Author

JANINE MONTUPET is an expert on the art and history of lacemaking, lace curator for the Musée des Artes Décoratifs in Paris, and honorary Mayor of Alençon. Born in Algeria, she now divides her time between Alençon and Newport Beach, California.